Warrior Brothers

Erik Gordon Bainbridge

For Tim

Published by Marin Web Works
PO Box 197
Woodacre, California 94973

www.marinwebworks.com

First Edition

ISBN-10: 0-9777141-0-1
ISBN-13: 978-0-9777141-0-0

Library of Congress Control Number: 2005938856

Printed in the United States of America

Dedication

To the ceremonial roundhouse and the people who dance in it.

Preface

Warrior Brothers' Carlos, Sophia, and Cody Jackson are fictional characters, living in the future, but their people, northern California's Coast Miwok and Kashaya-Pomo Indians, are very real.

The traditional territory of Coast Miwoks before the arrival of the Spanish was today's Marin and southern Sonoma Counties, now bustling suburbs of San Francisco. Like so many other coastal Native California people, the Coast Miwoks were decimated by three very different waves of colonization, in the 18th century by Spaniards and in the 19th century by Mexicans and Americans. By the mid twentieth century, Coast Miwoks had lost their tribal recognition and were thought by many non-Miwoks to be extinct.

Coast Miwoks were not extinct, however, and after a struggle they regained Federal recognition in 2000 as the Federated Indians of Graton 'Rancheria, a victory that was celebrated by Coast Miwoks and their supporters on a rainy day in February 2000 in the ceremonial roundhouse at Kule Loklo in Point Reyes National Seashore.

The traditional Kashaya-Pomo territory was coastal California, north of the Russian River in the vicinity of Fort Ross. Their first contact with people from outside North America was with Russians who treated them more as trading partners than as conquests and in some cases intermarried with them.

Although they lost virtually all their territory and today have a reservation that consists of just 40 acres, the Kashaya-Pomo people's isolation saved them from the fate of so many other Native California peoples, and has allowed them to continue their language and traditions with relatively little intrusion by the outside world.

More information about the Coast Miwok and Kashaya-Pomo peoples' history, traditions, and lives today can be found at the web sites below and on the next page:

Coast Miwok tribal website: www.gratonrancheria.com

Coast Miwok history: www.gratonrancheria.com/ourpeople.htm

Kashaya-Pomo tribal website: www.kashaya.homestead.com

Kashaya-Pomo history: www.kashaya.homestead.com/history.html

Kule Loklo Volunteers: www.kuleloklo.com

Marin Museum of the American Indian: www.marinindian.com

Miwok Archeological Preserve of Marin: www.mapom.org

Pt. Reyes National Seashore: www.nps.gov/pore/history_miwok.htm

Acknowledgments

I want to thank the people who read my manuscript and gave me such helpful feedback and criticism: Rita Altshuler, Charleen Baugh, Abigail Bridge, Fran Jaekle, Cary Jones, Don Legnitto, Shawn Maloney, Dr. Frances McManemin, Dr. Sandy Parry, Diana Robinson, Jeff Silva, Gary Wasley, Karen Waters, Joy Wieczorek, and Peggy Williams. This is a better story because of them.

Most of them made such a great effort to be helpful that I hate to single any out for particular praise, but I must mention two: Dr. Sandy Parry and Don Legnitto. Sandy voluntarily undertook the gargantuan task of proofreading two versions of the manuscript. Any errors in the book are the result of editing after she finished. Don, who before reading it threatened to be a harshly honest critic, provided detailed notes and encouragement that were a tremendous help.

Francis Ford Coppola also deserves thanks. This story is much stronger and the book is better because of his zoetrope.com website. I've honed my storytelling skills there, I've learned about publishing from fellow writers there, and a zoetrope.com member (Charleen Baugh) read and critiqued my manuscript.

Finally, I owe a debt to the late Buzz Anderson, who inspired me like few others have. His death was a tragic loss to the world.

Table of Contents

Prolog

The young dancer had been on Carlos' left front shoulder ever since one day in high school when, in a burst of teen bravado, he took the design and his college savings to the best tattoo artist in San Francisco.

He based the design on a 19th century drawing of a young, male California Indian dancing in full ceremonial regalia, but deliberately gave the tattoo a much more in-your-face attitude. After getting the tattoo, he went bare-chested or wore shirts that revealed it whenever weather permitted and often when it did not. When he finally got to play basketball for the Space Academy, he reveled in the stares and good-natured ribbing it provoked.

That was two decades ago. Today, Carlos was married and a father, and the young dancer had become simply part of who he was. It was a part he now kept to himself, like the necklace he wore every day beneath his uniform. His grandmother made the necklace for him before he left Earth, using plain white beads she ground from clamshells, like those his ancestors made back in the days when a man's wealth could be measured by the clamshell beads he possessed, before Europeans came and transformed the land into California.

For Carlos, the necklace and the young dancer weren't things to be shown off, but quiet reassurances that no matter how far he traveled in the galaxy, a part of him was always home.

The Marco Polo

Carlos hurriedly changed from his regular United Space Fleet captain's uniform into his best formal dress uniform, put on the black dress shoes he always kept carefully shined and ready for these occasions, and then paused to look in the mirror. When he was sure his decorations were straight and everything was exactly as it should be, he stepped into the front room, where his ten year old son Cody was teaching Billy Jobanga to dance California Indian style.

"Dad, can Billy dance with us tonight?"

Carlos was relieved to see that Billy's black eye was all that remained from the boys' argument yesterday. "Yes, but I might not be there. This meeting could last a while."

Envy lit up Billy's eyes. "Captain Jackson, are you really going to meet the Bug?"

Carlos was always amazed how fast news could travel.

"Yes, Billy. But it's not really an insect."

"Why do people call it a bug?"

Carlos wondered that himself. Even he'd begun referring to it as the "Bug" despite knowing better. After promising to explain it to Billy later, he left for the meeting.

When he entered, everyone stood to greet him—except, to no one's surprise, the Bug.

Lieutenant Ho turned to Carlos. "Captain Jackson, this is our guest. I cannot yet pronounce our guest's name." Switching to German, she introduced Carlos to the Bug as "Unser Kapitän Carlos

Jackson" and then waited while the automatic translator produced a squeal that the Bug appeared to understand. It turned to face Carlos briefly and looked away. "We still haven't been able to learn their protocols for meetings like this," Lieutenant Ho apologized.

Carlos took his seat at the table. Lieutenant Ho and her exhausted looking staff followed suit. Addressing the Bug, Carlos said, "You are welcome as our guest on the *Marco Polo.* I will see you are provided with whatever you require."

While Lieutenant Ho repeated it in German and it was repeated in Bug, Carlos watched the Bug. It looked exactly like Lieutenant Ho had described it, an eight-foot tall cross between an ant and a spider, sitting nonchalantly on its haunches, a coolly insolent look on its face.

Lieutenant Ho had warned Carlos before the meeting that the Bugs were superb at mimicking other species' facial expressions and body language, but she didn't know how well the Bugs understood the meanings behind them. Carlos waited, wondering whether the Bug intended looking insolent. When it failed to respond or even to look at him, Carlos asked, "Are you sure German is working, Lieutenant?"

"The Bugs use an extremely precise vocabulary. It correlates better with German than any other language we've tried. We know it understands much of what we say."

"That's progress."

"Yes, but now we have a new problem."

Carlos glanced over at the Bug. It had turned to face him and was staring sullenly.

"What now?"

"When Bug is translated into German, it produces long, complex words and sentences that even native born Germans have trouble understanding."

"Can't the computer handle that?"

"Yes. That's not the problem," Lieutenant Ho replied, "the problem is that no matter what we try, translating what we say into Bug just makes us sound like low life thugs."

Carlos turned to face the Bug again. It was still staring at him. There had been no change in its facial expression.

"Captain, it thinks we stole this ship. Nothing we say seems to change its mind."

The meeting continued for hours but accomplished little. The Bug's condescension was all too common among the civilizations the *Marco Polo* crew had encountered, but its conviction that they were hooligans was a new and potentially a more serious problem. The Bugs would not hesitate to take action if they viewed the *Marco Polo* as a menace.

Carlos finally left after it became clear that his presence wasn't helping and might actually be making Lieutenant Ho's job harder. He was a military man, not a diplomat. He knew he lacked the delicate sensibilities of Lieutenant Ho and her experienced negotiating team. Carlos felt drained. It was dinnertime, so he went to the mess and ate at a table with Rudy Petrovich, the *Marco Polo*'s unofficial historian and poet.

"Do you ever wonder Captain, what changes have taken place on Earth? I mean, for them it's been a century since we left."

"Yes, I think everyone does." He reflexively reached up and touched his shirt, feeling the reassuring presence of his grandmother's necklace beneath it. Because of being in stasis for most of the journey, the *Marco Polo* crew had aged only eleven years, while the people they knew on Earth had all lived out their lives and died. Carlos' grandmother, his parents, his tribal elders, his brothers, all were gone. Even the earthen ceremonial roundhouse would be gone by now. By the time he returned, even the coastal California hills and valleys he loved so much could have changed beyond recognition.

"Captain, when we return, we'll be ancient explorers stepping out from the past. Revered, but archaic remnants of a long ago world."

Carlos admired Petrovich's way with words.

"We're not only the greatest exploration vessel ever launched from Earth," Petrovich continued, "we're Earth's first time machine."

"If the Bugs don't exterminate us," Carlos thought, but kept it to himself. He made a mental note to consult with Petrovich the next time he needed to make an inspirational speech to the crew.

He was finishing his meal when Lieutenant Ho contacted him.

"Captain, we're done for today."

"Did you make any progress?"

"None. The Bug left. It said it needs to consult with someone before continuing negotiations."

"Who?"

"It wouldn't say, Captain. We'll know more tomorrow."

* * *

The *Marco Polo* was a small, self-contained community whose nearly 1,000 members would spend over half their lives living and working together in a confined space. There were few secrets among them, so when no visitors were on board, the Captain could occasionally be seen uncharacteristically out of uniform, striding to a cargo bay barefoot and wearing only shorts, vest, and his California Indian dance regalia.

Tonight was one of those times. Going to the cargo bay, Carlos looked much like the young dancer on his shoulder, with an ornately carved stick in one hand, a bamboo dance whistle suspended from his neck, a band of flicker feathers covering his forehead, and a train of feathers hanging from his waist. When he reached the cargo bay, most people were already there, ready to start their once a month Saturday night of traditional dancing by indigenous people and their friends from across Earth.

His wife Sophia, wearing the traditional dress of her Kashaya Pomo people, kissed him warmly.

"Carlos, you look worried. The Bug?"

"Yes."

"It will turn out OK," she said reassuringly, "Relax."

Cody, dressed in dance regalia like his father's, was playing a virtual world game with Billy. In the game, which the crew had obtained by barter at the last civilization they visited, the boys played defense commanders of allied planets working together to fend off an attack by the vicious Lekadians. The boys had learned early that it was much better for their avatars to die fighting than fall into the clutches of the cruel and always treacherous Lekadians.

When the game was first brought onboard, Carlos was curious to see whether the boys would play the defenders, as the game's designers intended, or whether they would choose to play the Lekadian attackers. The Lekadians, after all, were humanoid, the only other humanoids the *Marco Polo* crew had heard of anywhere in their travels, while the defenders were life forms unlike anything seen by humans before this journey. The boys never hesitated. They played the alien life forms fighting the humanoids every time.

Born in space, Cody and Billy had grown up visiting alien civilizations. For them, Earth existed only in scenic holograms, a planet that adults spoke about longingly, but which otherwise had little meaning. Cody and Billy nearly always felt far more at ease with the aliens they visited than did the adults on the *Marco Polo*, and they had learned the inspirational ancestral legends that alien youth in every civilization were taught about heroic defenders fighting off Lekadian attacks.

To Cody and Billy, being distrusted everywhere they went simply because Lekadians looked like them was reason enough to hate Lekadians. Adults on the *Marco Polo* had a more important concern: would Lekadians treat relatively primitive fellow humanoids from the far away, unknown planet Earth any less cruelly than they treated all the other races the crew had encountered?

No one knew the answer.

Cody and Billy put the game away, and Carlos opened the evening with a prayer. After the prayer, the cargo bay came alive with people dancing each other's dances, singing each other's songs, and praying traditional prayers.

The evening was a welcome relief from the day's stresses, but couldn't erase the concern Carlos felt about the Bug and what might happen if it couldn't be convinced of their good intentions .

* * *

The next morning was unusually stressful, a series of problems that each demanded Carlos' unbroken attention. Lieutenant Ho was meeting with the Bug and had assured Carlos that she would call him immediately if he was needed. When he finally got a break in the early afternoon, Carlos took Cody and Billy to the basketball court to shoot some hoops, as they did every Sunday afternoon.

The crew had learned never to interrupt him except for the most urgent matters when he was on the basketball court with Cody. Today their game was interrupted by one of those very rare calls. It was from Lieutenant Ho. "Captain!" Ho's voice quivered with excitement. "You're not going to believe this, sir, but the Bug bartered us information about where we can find other humanoids! We're not alone out here." The news was electrifying. The Bug was probably only doing it to get riff raff out of its neighborhood, but as long as the information was legitimate, Carlos knew no one onboard would care.

Carlos immediately convened a staff meeting, where Rudy Petrovich broke the news that the crew had been waiting so long to hear. "The Lekadians are real, sir. We know where to find them."

Everyone gasped.

"The Bug gave us the coordinates of the Lekadian home world," Petrovich continued, "There are many different groups of humanoids in that sector of the galaxy." After waiting for everyone to quiet down, Petrovich continued his presentation. "The Lekadian Empire is the largest group. They're a vast empire. If the Bug's information is correct, they're highly advanced, one of the oldest civilizations in the galaxy."

"That makes us the hillbillies again," another officer shot back.

Carlos had a different concern. "We can't risk an encounter with the Lekadians until we learn more about them. What about the other humanoids?"

"There are some just a few light years from us," Petrovich replied.

"What do we know about them?"

"It's a single planetary system with two closely related humanoid groups inhabiting separate planets. The advanced ones live on the planet Tarfil and its two moons. Tarfil is a huge planet with such powerful gravity that few outsiders ever visit the planet's surface. It has a conservative society with a strict moral code and is ruled by a small group of families. The two moons are just the opposite. They contain spaceports that are hubs for freighter traffic between the Lekadian Empire and nearby star systems. Tarfil's moons are open zones, where activities that are banned as immoral on Tarfil are tolerated."

Carlos interrupted, "Decadent and corrupt societies on those moons, I assume. Probably controlled by crime syndicates?"

"Yes sir, all of that," Petrovich replied, "Prostitution, trade in smuggled goods, widespread gambling controlled by crime syndicates, abductions, many unsolved murders, corrupt law enforcement, rumors of a slave trade, it's all on Tarfil's moons."

"So why should they interest us?" asked Carlos.

"They're a lot like Earth, sir. They're not so different from us."

A few officers grumbled objections.

"What I mean is, the people on Tarfil's moons aren't likely to look down on us as backward. According to the Bugs, the only reason they are technologically advanced beyond Earth is their proximity to the Lekadian Empire. They got their technology from the Lekadians."

"Are they occupied by the Lekadians?" asked an officer.

"Tarfil's not a Lekadian colony, but there's extensive Lekadian infiltration. There are Lekadian schools for Tarfillian children, Lekadian ships are in permanent orbit, and there's a Lekadian ambassador living on Luna One. There's no way to avoid meeting Lekadians there."

"What about the other group?"

"They live on the planet Quogue. According to the Bugs, they're too primitive to be worth visiting."

"What do we know about them?" asked Carlos.

"Not much, except they were occupied by the Lekadians several generations ago, during a minor war."

"The Lekadians don't occupy the planet anymore?"

"No, Captain."

"Do we know anything else about the Quogians?"

"That's all. They're considered peaceful and intelligent. It's just that they're primitive."

"Any standing armies? Wars?"

"Nothing. Not even any signs of a warrior class, though there are some displays in Lekadian museums of armor and swords from an ancient Quogian warrior class that died out long ago."

"They have no armies, no warriors, today?" Carlos asked.

"None."

Carlos summed it up. "So we have humanoids living on Quogue…"

"They're for all practical purposes full fledged humans as far as we can tell, Captain, not just humanoid."

Carlos asked, "If they're so primitive and peaceful, how did they drive out conquerors as brutal and advanced as the Lekadians?"

No one had an answer. Everyone agreed on the need to visit the Quogians before encountering any Lekadians.

* * *

Among the information they got from the Bug was the Quogian language, in a form that was easily programmed into their translator.

Carlos had always enjoyed learning new alien languages. Now, working in his family quarters to learn this one, Carlos discovered that Cody also had a knack for learning languages, and soon, the two were working as partners in learning Quogian, with Sophia frequently taking part. For Cody, it was all a game. For Carlos and Sophia, it was the first time Cody had shown an interest in anything involving reading or writing, and it meant less opportunity for the boy to get into fights. They consequently made every effort to make learning Quogian into something the family could have fun doing together.

As the *Marco Polo* left the Bugs' system forever behind, Carlos' crew programmed the ship to make the voyage to Quogue. Unless the computer woke them early for an emergency, ten years would pass on Earth before they awoke again.

Earlier in the journey, the crew would think about the time that would pass on Earth while they were in stasis, unable to refrain from calculating how much loved ones they left behind would age while they themselves slept the unaging sleep traveling in space. By now, however, everyone they knew on Earth had died. The passage of time on Earth while they were in stasis was losing its meaning. One exception was the handful of crew who had left children on Earth. They still cared about the passage of time there, and from time to time they would calculate when a new generation of their descendants might be born, or they would marvel at the fact that so many of their descendants on Earth were now older than they were.

As usual, Carlos was the last to enter a stasis chamber, waiting until he was certain that everything was secure. He knew it was only his imagination, but he could almost feel the excitement of everyone on the ship at the prospect of meeting other humans when they next awoke from stasis. He just hoped he wasn't leading them into an elaborately planned trap.

Quogue

Ten Earth years after leaving the Bugs' system, the crew emerged from stasis a few days away from Quogue. As life onboard the ship returned to normal, they began running whatever tests they could from a distance, becoming more and more excited as they learned that everything on Quogue was as the Bug reports indicated. The atmosphere was nearly identical to Earth's, the planet's surface was covered with blue oceans and large forests, and the gravity was close to that of Earth. It all seemed too good to be true.

Drawing closer, they learned that there was little sign of industrialization on the planet. The main atmospheric pollutants were from burning wood and coal. As the planet rotated through its night side, there were no lighted areas that would indicate large urban centers.

Finally, they settled into orbit and made more detailed observations. There were towns, but they were small, the roads were narrow and probably dirt, and ships used sails. Sampling scans of much of the planet's surface indicated a few areas were there were remains of industrial machinery, but as far as they could tell, it had been destroyed and buried.

There was a considerable amount of space debris in orbit around the planet, much of it made from manufactured materials the crew had never encountered before, but which sensors indicated for the most part was completely inert. After extensive analysis, Carlos' experts assured him that the debris posed no more threat than space debris they encountered at other planets they had visited. There were a few old mines in orbit, evidently left over from a war, but they were easily identified and avoided.

The only thing that was different here was that the planet's occupants appeared to have rejected technology. From what they could tell from space, Quogians were living roughly at the technological level of eastern Mediterranean peoples around the times of Christ and Muhammad.

Carlos decided to land at a coastal village on a large harbor. It was connected by a patchwork of dirt roads with many other towns and villages and was probably a relatively significant trading hub. Usually Carlos let Lieutenant Ho and her staff make first contact, but all the evidence indicated that this would be an unusually easy first contact. He decided that this time, he would handle it himself.

Carlos had made great progress learning the Quogian language with Cody. The two of them even came out of stasis early to work on it, so Carlos shouldn't have been surprised when Cody asked to accompany his father to the planet's surface. He was adamantly against it. It was simply too dangerous for his son to be down there before they knew how Quogians would react to their visit.

Surprisingly, Sophia supported Cody. Carlos expected her to be even more strongly opposed than he was, but as she so often did, she surprised him. "I think the best way to approach them is for you and Cody to go by yourselves. No one else. Having your young son with you will signal your peaceful intentions."

Carlos immediately objected, but Sophia persisted, "No, listen to me. Just the two of you. Don't take any translating machines, no technology at all."

"I've got to have my communicator."

"OK, just keep it hidden, with the audio off. You speak their language, so does Cody. With people like these, showing you know at least some of their language will mean much more than having a slick translating device that knows everything. Don't intimidate them. Make them sympathize with you. Be as natural and down to earth as you can. No uniform. We'll make up some simple clothes for the two of you, in the Quogian style. Of course, you'll have armed guards in the shuttle, but leave them there. Don't use them unless you have to. Just go as father and son wanderers, seeking friends far from home."

If anyone else had suggested this approach, he would have simply dismissed it, but too many times in the past, Sophia's intuition had in the end been more productive than the logic, discipline, and training he relied upon. On the rare occasions when she suggested strategy, he had learned to listen.

To cement her case, she added , "Quogian men all wear tattoos. Your dancer will be perfect."

No matter how much he would in later years regret other decisions made that day, Carlos would always be grateful for Sophia's intuition, and for having the wisdom to follow her advice.

* * *

The next morning, after verifying with the medical staff that they had all received necessary treatments both to protect them against Quogian diseases and to keep Quogians from contracting Earth diseases, Carlos and Cody boarded the shuttle with two armed guards for the trip down to the planet's surface. Before they left, Sophia came to wish them good luck, embarrassing Cody by kissing him and straightening out his clothes. When she kissed Carlos, he quipped, "You can straighten out my clothes anytime you want!"

Sophia quipped back, "I'll straighten you out tonight!" Then she handed him a small pack. Opening it, he found his and Cody's clapper sticks, the traditional elderberry musical instrument of his people that he played in ceremonies, and a small player containing recordings of traditional songs. Before he could say anything, she said in a soft but authoritative voice, "They need to be with you."

Piloting the shuttle himself, a rare opportunity since becoming captain, and the first time ever with his son onboard, Carlos landed on the beach just outside the large seaside village they had selected, making the approach near enough to be noticed by villagers, but not close enough to seem a threat. Stepping out of the shuttle onto the soft sand, he took in deep breaths of fresh air that seemed so much more like Earth's than any he had breathed in a very long time. Only the sight of the strangely designed sailing ships in the harbor signaled that unless they had traveled back in time to some unknown civilization, this could not possibly be Earth.

Leaving the two armed guards sitting in the shuttle, Carlos and Cody walked slowly along the beach toward the village. Both were dressed Quogian style—baggy pants, open vest, no shirt. Cody looked like he was enjoying himself, but Carlos felt awkward out of uniform. It was the first time the young dancer on his shoulder had ever been visible while Carlos was on duty.

First contact went smoothly, far better in fact than Carlos had dared hope. From the start, it was clear that Sophia's intuition had made all the difference. One thing working in their favor was that Quogue was a strongly patriarchal society, with little role for women outside the home. The father-son relationship was valued above all others. Despite the deep distrust most of the villagers felt for anyone from space, they had an inherent sympathy for the father and son wanderers who had strayed so far from a home they might never see again. They welcomed Carlos and Cody by giving them a tour of their village, which they said was called HarborSide. The tour started at the enormous obelisk in the center of the village. The obelisk served both as monument and as a communal timepiece, the time of day being the name of the location the obelisk's shadow fell upon.

At the base of the obelisk, facing a platform, was a painting of three youthful warriors, their faces painted, wearing armor and holding swords. While villagers explained to Carlos that the platform was where village elders officiated over town meetings and where priests conducted some sacred rituals, Cody turned his attention to the painting on the obelisk, staring at it raptly. One of the villagers told him, "They are the Warrior Brothers. They were three boys in ancient times who made our ancestors powerful and prosperous. The Lekadians banned all paintings of the Warrior Brothers. Now, we are bringing them back."

The villagers began leading Carlos to the next spot on their tour of the village, but stopped when they saw Cody still at the obelisk, fascinated by the youthful warriors. One of the villagers said, "Your son can feel the power of the Warrior Brothers."

"No, my son just likes fighting."

"There's nothing wrong with fighting, if it's in a just cause. Dariel is no fighter, he hates fighting, but he's the one who brought the artist here to paint this."

"The monks selected Dariel. They thought he was a fighter," added a second villager.

"Dariel said his path was on the sea. He said the monks only selected him to paint the Warrior Brothers on the obelisk."

"Those crazy monks," scoffed a third villager, "It's all nonsense. Anyone who believes it is as crazy as the monks." The horrified looks on most of the others showed this to be a distinctly minority opinion.

"No one fools Dariel. If he believes, then it's real," responded the second villager, receiving gestures of agreement from most of the villagers around him.

Cody was staring at the painting of the three young warriors, oblivious to the debate going on around him. The first villager knelt beside him saying, "I'll wager you'd like to wear armor like that!"

"Yes."

Cody's answer unsettled some of the other villagers. A few murmured in low voices, "The boy is not Quogian" and "He can never be a Warrior Brother." Within moments, the crowd was hustling them away from the obelisk and toward the next stop on their tour, the home of the village headman.

They spent the next few hours touring religious shrines, a few homes, the blacksmith, and some weavers. Through it all, Cody tagged along impatiently, looking back frequently at the painting of the young warriors on the obelisk. Now however, as they came out of the last weaver's shop and saw the harbor spread out below them, Cody's interest shifted from the young warriors to the harbor and docks where a few boats were moored, with fishermen doing maintenance on them.

One of the villagers noticed the fascination in Cody's eyes. "I think your son wants to visit the fishing boats."

"My son was born in space. He never saw boats or fishermen before today."

"Then we will visit a fishing boat next." The villagers led Carlos and Cody from the village down to the harbor and onto a dock. "Most of the boats are out fishing now."

Cody gazed in awe at the fishermen busily mending nets and doing maintenance on the few boats that were in the harbor. One of the villagers told him, "We will introduce you to Captain Dariel. You will like him, Cody. He is the one who had the Warrior Brothers painted on the obelisk."

Another villager warned, "But don't ask Captain Dariel about it. He doesn't like to speak of it."

Finally reaching Dariel's boat, they approached the gangway and requested permission to board. Dariel assented with a grunt and then asked, "These are the space travelers everyone is talking about?"

"Yes. Captain Dariel, son of Xander, I introduce Captain Carlos, son of Jackson, and Captain Carlos' son Cody," hastily adding, "They are not Lekadian."

"Anyone can see that," Dariel shot back curtly.

Dariel was a taciturn, reserved man, with calloused hands and a face that was sun and sea weathered far beyond his years, the sort of face seen in pictures of people on Earth a century or two earlier, and of course never seen on starships. Like all Quogian men, his black hair was tied back in braids, he wore an earring, and he had a large tattoo on his chest, visible through his open vest.

Carlos felt obliged to ask a few questions, not really caring about the answers and barely hearing Dariel's terse, stiff responses. Even with his own villagers, Dariel appeared almost wooden, reminding Carlos more of the ship's wooden mast than of a man. But when his crewmen asked Dariel's advice, Carlos heard life in the captain's voice. He clearly felt more at ease with his crew than with people who spent their days on land. It was an attitude Carlos could understand. When he saw Dariel's demeanor both relax and came alive when commanding his crew, he suspected that despite the unbridgeable gulf between them, Dariel was someone, a fellow captain, he shared something with.

Cody could restrain himself no longer and blurted out a flood of questions, which Dariel tried his best to answer. These answers, Carlos noted, were far more lively than those he gave adults. Before he knew it, Cody was scampering around the ship, Dariel in tow, Carlos and a few villagers trying to keep up, as Cody asked one question after another and Dariel answered with an almost childlike enthusiasm.

Finally, Dariel turned to Carlos. "Captain Carlos, it would be my honor to have you and your son as guests on my boat at sea tonight to see the moons rise." When Carlos hesitated, Dariel continued, "It will be very beautiful. Your son will never forget it."

Reluctantly, Carlos consented, but only after Cody begged him. He couldn't remember his son ever looking so happy.

"Return to my boat at CobblerTime." Seeing the perplexed look on Carlos' face, Dariel explained, "CobblerTime is when the shadow of the obelisk falls on the cobbler's shop."

When they left Dariel's ship, villager leaders were waiting for them. The news they brought was not good.

"The elders welcome you and your son to stay. The others, however, cannot come down. That is how the Lekadians started, just a few of them. But then more came, and they took over. You and your son, however, the two of you are welcome to stay as long as you want."

A little before CobblerTime, Carlos took Cody to the shuttle to dejectedly file his report that unless villagers changed their minds, no other crewmembers would be coming down, at least not to HarborSide. Maybe some other village would be more welcoming. After completing his official report, he spoke with Sophia, promising they would return in the morning.

Carlos' two guards at first insisted on accompanying him on Dariel's boat, but were clearly uncomfortable with the idea of sailing at sea on a ship like one that the ancient Phoenicians might have used, so Carlos told them, "Go back to the *Marco Polo*. Get a good night's sleep. Come back for us in the morning"

When the sun finally set, Carlos and Cody were relaxing on the deck of Dariel's boat, out on the sea, dry land just a dark outline on the horizon, watching the stars emerge one by one, listening to the crew gossip and tell stories that men of the sea had told for generations. The night sky here was similar to the one Carlos had seen all though his childhood on clear nights in Northern California's coastal hills, but twisted around. There were stars Carlos had never seen, while others that shone on Earth couldn't be seen at all here. Carlos found something else he shared with this sea captain, a lifetime of studying the stars, as Dariel spoke the name of each of the stars in various constellations that Cody asked about, and Carlos gave the Earth names for those stars that could be seen from Earth.

Some constellations were simply distorted from how they looked on Earth. Others were completely new, formed from the tangle of distorted once familiar constellations with stars not visible from Earth. One of those unfamiliar constellations was Dariel's favorite, the Warrior Brothers. Carefully pointing out the stars that formed the boys' helmets and swords, Dariel told Cody, "The Warrior Brothers were brave boys, just like you, only a little older. They now live forever among the stars. It was their reward for first bringing the secrets of metal to man."

"Are they the ones painted on the big stone thing in town?" asked Cody.

"Yes, on the obelisk, those are the Warrior Brothers. When the Lekadians were here, they would not allow pictures of the Warrior Brothers. We could see them only in the sky. Now that the Lekadians are gone, we can have paintings of them again, like in olden times."

"They said you painted them…" Cody began to say.

Dariel interrupted him, "They told you of that, did they?"

"We were not supposed to speak of it. I apologize for my son."

"It's OK, Captain Jackson, one thing I like about boys like your son, they speak the truth. They haven't yet learned to keep our lies."

"You don't have to speak of it," said Carlos.

"You will be gone from our world tomorrow. There is no harm in speaking of it with you. Besides, it's no secret. I just don't want people making me seem more important than I am. I did not paint it myself. I found an artist from another village to paint it. The monks told him what the Warrior Brothers looked like."

"Were you a warrior?" asked Cody.

"No, many generations have passed since we had warriors. The Warrior Brothers promised they would someday return when they were needed again. They will bring back our warriors, and will bring new weapons for the warriors. Monks are traveling around the world, looking for the new Warrior Brothers."

"In town they said the monks selected you."

"Me a warrior? No. They selected me to be a monk, to spend my life traveling with them, seeking the new Warrior Brothers. It was an honor few are offered."

"Why aren't you a monk now?"

"When I was about your age, Cody, I started training to be a monk. But one day both my brothers were killed in a storm at sea. I was the only son left."

"I'd rather be a sea captain than a monk," Cody blurted out.

"What I wanted was of no concern. My family needed me. My father was growing old. There was no one else to command this boat after he died. The monks agreed that for me to become a monk would not be honorable."

"Do you still wish you could be a monk?" asked Cody.

Dariel thought for a few moments before answering. "I love the sea. There's no place I'd rather be. But the monks will someday change our world when they find the new Warrior Brothers. That would be an honor above all others. It's too late for me now. But maybe that painting will inspire someone else to become a monk and seek them out."

Carlos had tired of this discussion of monks and their mystical quest. He turned his attention to the lapping of the waves and to sounds of fish occasionally leaping from the sea. His apprehension about being on a boat had subsided completely. The gentle swaying still unnerved him whenever he tried walking, but sitting here, looking up at his own realm of the stars, the ship's swaying was almost comforting. Mesmerized by it all, he no longer heard as Dariel answered Cody's torrents of questions about warriors, life on the sea, and the quest of the monks to find the new Warrior Brothers.

As the horizon gradually brightened, even Cody and Dariel ceased talking and joined Carlos and the crew in silently watching the sky. Soon the two half moons rose in unison from a fogbank floating over the sea, almost blindingly bright, completely washing out the night sky and making every ripple in the sea between them and the moons shimmer like a jewel. The Warrior Brothers and all the other figures in their starry world vanished with the rising of the moons, but the sight was still magical. Carlos wished with all his heart that Sophia could be there to enjoy it with them.

Dariel pointed to the horizon. "Look, Cody. There. Your ship is about to rise, like a star." Carlos had no idea they had been watched so closely, or that Dariel would know precisely when the *Marco Polo* would become visible on the horizon. Seeing the surprised look on Carlos' face, Dariel said, "We are not a great space-faring people like you, but we know the stars. I've watched your ship since you arrived. Until I today I thought it was a new kind of star. I did not guess it was a ship!"

After that, they sat silently watching as the *Marco Polo* crossed where the Warrior Brothers had been just a little while before. Each was lost in his own thoughts. The only sounds were the lapping of the waves and the creaking and slapping of the rigging. Looking out over the water to where the double moons brightened distant hills and silhouetted fogbanks, Carlos knew he would always savor the memory of this moment, being lost in the beauty of it, thinking he could almost make his life here, living with Sophia and Cody in this idyllic paradise, working for Dariel as a simple fisherman. He longed to have Sophia beside him, and wondered how she would react if she heard him say something so totally out of character as to suggest living on this planet, or on any planet for that matter.

Of course, he knew it was only a moment's fantasy. As beautiful as this world was, it was no more beautiful than Earth, although the double moons were striking. Carlos knew that no matter how much he enjoyed this evening on Dariel's boat, his place would always be in the stars. He could live no other way. This was the dream that had drawn Sophia and him together when they were teenagers, defining who they were and leading inexorably to a life together in space.

Carlos was jarred out of his reverie by the buzz of his communicator. Its raucous tone seemed so out of place here on this boat. It was Sophia calling. "Something's wrong. I can feel it. Are you and Cody OK down there?"

Her intuition was usually so unerringly accurate that Carlos now found his ego almost enjoying hearing her worried for no reason.

"You don't have to worry. Everything's fine. Cody is enjoying himself. So am I. We really wish you could be here. It's beautiful."

Sophia didn't answer right away. Then she screamed, "My god, Carlos, it's up here. The trouble's up here."

Carlos shouted to Dariel to take him back to the nearest land. Within moments, Dariel was barking out commands and the crew was scurrying to raise sail.

Carlos spoke into the communicator again, "We're heading to the nearest land. Get a fix on our location. Send a shuttle down for us."

"I love you Carlos. Tell Cody I love him."

"Sophia, what's wrong?" He paused, waiting for an answer that never came. "Sophia? Sophia!"

There was only static on the communicator. Looking up toward the *Marco Polo,* he watched as it moved toward one of the moons, then lost sight of it as it passed in front of the almost blindingly bright moon. Waiting silently, Cody clutching his hand, he listened futilely for clues in the relentless static coming from his communicator. He was relieved to see the ship when it passed beyond the moon, becoming faintly visible in the sky again. But then there was a flash that was blinding even against the two moons, followed by a rain of shooting stars.

When it was over, the *Marco Polo* was no longer in the sky.

Accabo

(Seven years later)

Accabo had only rarely been outside the fortified perimeter enclosing what once was the Lekadian spaceport on Quogue. The teenager grew up hearing his grandfather tell exciting tales from his youth about boldly venturing far beyond the spaceport to retrieve machinery and technology left behind by the Lekadians during their hasty retreat. His father and uncles also had their own tales of youthful adventures, of traveling to sites of former factories and technology centers, seeking odds and ends they needed for the varied collection of equipment that had already been saved, so future generations would have hope of getting at least some of it functional again.

They told gripping tales of sneaking to the sites late at night, of tunneling deep into buried debris just to retrieve small components whose function they did not understand, knowing only that they might be needed, and of other Quogians engaging them in fights, in which people were often killed or maimed. Even Accabo's brothers, both older than he was, could remember a time when people could embark on daring adventures beyond the spaceport walls.

As the youngest in his family, Accabo had missed out on those exciting times. Today, people at the spaceport lived under frequent siege. Members of their little community were one by one drifting away to join relatives living simple, non-technological lives elsewhere. The barbarians outside gave safe passage to families leaving the spaceport to live elsewhere, provided they carried the flag of truce and pledged not to return. Anyone else took their life in their hands going outside the walls.

Although Accabo and the others in the spaceport had the same dark skin and black hair as most other Quogians, they dressed very differently. They cut their hair short, wore efficient uniforms that mimicked those of the Lekadians, and avoided the open vests, beards, earrings, and tattoos favored by Quogians outside.

Accabo loved being alone on the defensive ramparts that surrounded the spaceport during interludes between attacks, when no barbarians were in sight, and no warriors were around to give him a hard time. This was a special place for him. It was here, seven years ago, that he saw the flash in the sky of the star he had been watching for three days. Later, when he heard itinerant storytellers tell the tale of Starman, the traveler from space whose magnificent space ship exploded into a rain of stars, he knew it was Starman's great ship that he had seen.

For several years afterward, people in the spaceport hoped that Starman was a Lekadian and the vanguard of a larger Lekadian return to Quogue, but when no more ships came, people gradually lost hope. Today, most in the spaceport dismissed the tale of Starman as a false hope—all except for Accabo and his father, Locaru.

Accabo and Locaru still worshipped at the shrines of the Quogian Gods of Technology and of Space Travel. These were the newest Quogian gods, who were discovered after the Lekadians introduced technology to Quogue. Accabo prayed to the God of Space Travel daily, always being careful to leave the offerings she liked the most and always pleading with her to let him travel in space as Starman's apprentice. Starman had to come to the spaceport. Accabo could imagine no other future for himself than traveling in space with Starman.

The sight of an approaching spaceport warrior jolted Accabo out of his daydreaming. Hurriedly scrambling down the nearest stairs, he walked toward the grove of trees in the center of the spaceport, passing the corral, and warehouses of technology stored since his grandparents' time, and finally entering the grove. This was Accabo's realm, and it was the great secret that people two generations ago so carefully hid within the grove of fast growing trees: the former Lekadian launch pad, and the only ship the Lekadians left behind, the *Dembu*, an ugly, squat, rusty space freighter.

"Accabo, is that you?"

Accabo recognized Esiu's voice. All he could see of Esiu were his two feet dangling from one of the propulsion tubes.

Without waiting for Accabo to reply, Esiu lowered a crude wooden box and said, "I need more grease." Accabo grabbed the box and ladled more grease into it from a container that was left over from the Lekadian occupation, and then Esiu pulled the box back up.

Esiu was a few years older than Accabo, but was the only one left in the spaceport besides Accabo and Locaru who still really cared about the *Dembu.* Esiu didn't share Accabo's passion for learning the *Dembu's* technology, but his dogged determination to remove every trace of rust and to lubricate every moving component in the *Dembu* made him indispensable. Thanks to Esiu, the rust that still mottled the outer skin of the *Dembu* no longer immobilized moving parts. Every joint, every cable, every hinge now moved as freely as when it was new.

When they were growing up, Esiu was Accabo's nearly inseparable companion, but that changed last year, when Esiu became a father after marrying Accabo's sister. Now, the only time Accabo and Esiu saw each other was when Esiu was working on the *Dembu.* Accabo noticed that Esiu had gradually stopped talking about someday living in space, and that recently he had stopped hiding with Accabo whenever the defense horn sounded. Instead, Esiu now fought with the warriors and was proud of a small scar he received fending off a barbarian attack.

Locaru had been working on the *Dembu* all his life, dedicating himself totally to enabling his son and other young people to make a new life for themselves among Lekadians, away from the superstitions and ignorance of Quogue. Accabo had been helping his father since he was old enough to hold tools. The growing assaults by barbarians on the spaceport only increased the urgency, but father and son were fighting a race not only against time, but against reality. The ship had sat unused for several generations. No one knew why the Lekadians left it behind. The original Lekadian maintenance records had vanished, so no one knew what its repair history was or whether it contained some potentially disastrous flaw, and most importantly, no one knew how to pilot it. Accabo was trying to learn by reading incomplete Lekadian training manuals, but there could be no training flights. His first flight would be their only chance of escape.

Accabo was about to climb the ladder to join his father inside the *Dembu*, where they were close to getting the *Dembu*'s computers working again, when the dreaded defense horn sounded. Within moments, Locaru had scrambled down the ladder, and Esiu had crawled out of the propulsion tube. Both were putting on armor and picking up weapons that, like all spaceport defenders, they always kept close by. The weapons, basic bows, arrows, and spears, were a constant reminder of the single grudge that every spaceport defender held against the Lekadians. When the Lekadians withdrew, they took with them every modern weapon in the spaceport. It was bad enough that they left so many loyal Quogians behind to fend for themselves, but they left them no weapons for defense against the vast majority of Quogians who resented Lekadians and despised any Quogian who had served them.

"Coming?" Esiu asked, a hint of derision in his voice that Accabo had not detected before.

"I'll stay here and protect the *Dembu*," Accabo replied, knowing that Esiu knew it was a lie. Before Esiu became a father, he used the same feeble excuse for getting out of defense duty. Now, Esiu talked instead of the need to protect his children and eagerly answered most defense calls.

"Accabo is needed here," Locaru said firmly, then ran with Esiu through the trees to join the other warriors.

"It's probably just a false alarm," Accabo told himself after they left.

But it wasn't a false alarm. He heard shouting, then sounds of battle that were much closer than usual, followed by a rarely sounded second defense horn. Women, many carrying weapons, most with children, came running through the trees.

"Barbarians broke through the wall," one shouted.

"They're in the spaceport," another one said.

Accabo donned his armor and picked up his weapons. This time there might be no way to avoid fighting. The women ordered the children into the *Dembu* and formed a protective line around the ship, ready to die before they would let barbarians get to their children.

Accabo stood with the women, awkwardly trying to hold his weapons like he had seen real warriors holding theirs while trying to ignore the scorn dripping from the women's faces.

To his relief, the sounds of battle faded away without incident. Finally, the all-clear horn sounded, but was quickly followed by the wailing horn. This was not good. Cautiously putting down their weapons, the women herded the children out of the *Dembu* and headed to their homes, bracing themselves for bad news. The wailing horn meant only one thing: spaceport defenders had been killed.

Esiu came running from the trees. Blood was gushing from one arm.

"Your father," stammered Esiu, gasping desperately for breath.

Accabo took off running.

"Outside the main gate," Esiu managed to shout before collapsing.

Running into the meadow outside the gate, Accabo struggled to keep from vomiting. Everywhere he looked, he saw blood, severed limbs, sickening wounds, corpses of so many he knew. Hardened spaceport warriors were weeping openly. Accabo ran up to his two brothers and saw they were comforting Locaru, who was blood soaked and dying. Accabo's brothers were large, strong men, very different in appearance from the more wispy Accabo and Locaru. They usually delighted in taunting Accabo for his weakness, but now tears rolled freely down their cheeks. Accabo knelt alongside them over their father.

Locaru struggled to speak. "Accabo, go to space. When you launch *Dembu*. I want to be there. Bury me at *Dembu*. Promise. Bury me at *Dembu*."

Accabo and his brothers promised. Moments later, their father was dead.

The cemetery had been full for years, so people in the spaceport usually cremated their dead, but an exception was made for Locaru. For the first time in a long time, Accabo and his brothers worked together as a team, digging the grave and burying Locaru where he requested, next to the launch pad, just meters from the *Dembu.*

* * *

The next several days were devoted almost entirely to memorial services, cremations, and working feverishly to firm up the ramparts so barbarians could never penetrate them again. Even Accabo worked at strengthening the ramparts. The loss of so many fighters and weapons was a severe blow, and after the last of the cremations, came a new loss, a fresh exodus of spaceport residents, mostly families, parents who wanted to assure their children a future, leaving to join barbarian relatives outside, never to return. Today Esiu was joining the exodus.

Depressed at losing his father and now his only friend, Accabo wandered up to the ramparts to be alone. It was a quiet, beautiful day, with no barbarians in sight and few warriors on the ramparts. Lost in thought, Accabo looked down on the meadow where his father died, not noticing his brothers walk up to him.

"We miss him too," one brother finally said, breaking the silence.

Accabo turned to face him. "He shouldn't have been out there. We needed him inside, getting machines working."

"If we don't keep the barbarians out," said his other brother, "there will be no machinery to get working."

"If we don't get the machinery working, there's no reason to keep the barbarians out," Accabo retorted bitterly, "we might as well just become barbarians ourselves, like…"

"Like Esiu?" asked the first brother, turning around to look inside the spaceport, down at the corral where Esiu was hitching two helsteeds up to a wagon.

Accabo barely recognized his old friend. Esiu had left behind forever the carefully tailored Lekadian styled clothes that people in the spaceport wore. Now he and his family wore the crude, loose fitting clothes of barbarians and caps that disguised their short hair. He carried under his arm the rolled up flag of truce his wife had made, which he would unfurl after leaving the spaceport and hold high for safe passage into the barbarian world.

Accabo's other brother said, "Esiu was becoming a good warrior. We need more like him."

Accabo thought to himself, "Why are you letting Esiu leave if he's needed so much?" He didn't have to ask why. He knew the answer. Esiu wasn't the first to leave, nor would he be the last. Accabo's brothers might themselves be next to leave. Esiu was leaving for the same reasons everyone else was leaving. The people of the spaceport were losing their commitment to the dream that brought their grandparents together. Those with families worried that if they stayed, their children would die in a war that had been lost long before they were born. Increasingly, those who remained were, like his brothers, unmarried warriors who looked forward to battle and were more dedicated to defending the machines and equipment saved at the spaceport than to using or repairing them. It was only a matter of time before they joined those who had already fled the spaceport to take up lives in the barbarian world, maybe even joining those besieging the spaceport. They wouldn't be the first.

"We need someone to take Esiu's place on the ramparts," said one of his brothers, "You're not a child anymore, Accabo. You belong up here with us, not playing with those damned machines." He motioned toward two female warriors saying farewell to Esiu. "Even women are becoming warriors now. The barbarians mock us for it."

"The Lekadians had women warriors," Accabo began to reply.

"They also had advanced weapons we don't have," his brother retorted.

"Besides," his other brother said in a mocking tone, "if you spend more time up here in the ramparts with us, maybe you'll see Starman! Maybe you'll see more space ships in the sky!" Both brothers broke out laughing uproariously. As they headed down to say farewell to Esiu, Accabo could hear them still laughing. He couldn't hear what they were saying, but he knew that as usual, their laughter was at his expense.

Looking back down at the corral, Accabo watched as his brothers warmly embraced Esiu. Accabo tried to imagine his old friend becoming a barbarian, not just wearing barbarian clothes, but fully barbarian, with long, braided hair, tattoos, and earrings. It was difficult to imagine such a fate befalling Esiu, but Accabo knew that Esiu himself was resigned to it. Accabo even had the feeling that Esiu secretly liked the idea.

Seeing Esiu and his family getting into their wagon, Accabo realized that he had only moments to go down and say farewell. Hurrying down from the ramparts, he was waiting for them when they reached the gate. After a tearful farewell with his sister, he exchanged farewells with Esiu, who told him, "If you had children, you would understand. You are always welcome to join us."

"Me, a rancher?"

"I never thought I would be a rancher. But I need to do what's best for my family."

"My family will live in space, Esiu."

"Still waiting for Starman … grow up, Accabo, there is no Starman. That, out there, outside the spaceport, that's your future. Not space, not the spaceport. The spaceport won't be here a year from now. Admit it."

Accabo wanted to argue, but he knew that with each departing family, their little community grew weaker and closer to defeat. It was people like Esiu leaving that would lead to their defeat as much as the barbarians.

"Don't worry, I won't tell anyone about the *Dembu*." Taking up the reins, Esiu added, "You are always welcome to live with us at the ranch, Accabo. Remember that."

The gate remained opened just long enough for Esiu and his family to exit, then was closed and bolted as Esiu raised the flag of truce high on a pole and rode with his family away from the spaceport. Accabo went back up to the ramparts. Watching his old friend until he was out of sight, Accabo felt more lonely than he ever imagined he could feel.

Barbarians

Light from the setting moons flooded through the open hatch of the cramped crew cabin. After seven years at sea, the brisk predawn air was no longer an unpleasant jolt to Carlos as he crawled out of his bunk. His once wobbly legs had toughened into sea legs that stood firm even during storms that used to terrify him. Standing naked at the hatch next to his bunk, he marveled at how he had adapted to this life, away from the controlled environment of space ships and space suits in which he had spent most of his adult life, and that he now actually enjoyed the brisk air of the hours before dawn.

Dressing, he put on the same clothes that any Quogian fisherman wore at sea, a warm woolen tunic, baggy trousers, and a woolen cap that reminded him of caps that some people wore on Earth. Unlike most Quogian men, however, Carlos still wore his hair cropped very short, as he always had before coming to Quogue, and he still declined to wear an earring. He was able to avoid getting a Quogian tattoo because Quogians assumed the young dancer in his tattoo was the mark of his own god, which in a way it was.

His principal concession to Quogian style was that he had grown a beard, though in keeping with his military training he kept it trimmed much shorter than most Quogian men. For anyone other than "Starman," his close cropped hair and his refusals to adopt a traditionally Quogian male appearance would have raised serious questions about him, but "Starman" was permitted eccentricities not granted to ordinary Quogians.

The bunk opposite his was Dariel's, who like nearly all Quogian captains, slept with his crew, next to the hatch, and was always the first to leap into danger in an emergency. It was so unlike the starships Carlos had served on. He admired this about the Quogians. Whatever else there might be to criticize about this obdurate race steadfastly trying to emulate ancestors who would find alien the very unchangingness that current day Quogians imposed on their world, Quogians would not tolerate anyone putting on airs of superiority over another.

Carefully feeling his way along the bunks and through the crowded swaying hammocks, trying not to stumble over shoes and scattered clothing, he took one careful step at a time deeper into the still dark crew cabin, always prepared for the occasional wave that threatened sending him careening into sleeping crewmen. He himself had spent several years on one of these hammocks before graduating to a bunk. The memories of the many nights he was awakened by a crewman's careless stumble made him careful. Reaching Cody's hammock, Carlos waited just long enough to hear his son mutter a groggy "good morning" and then, stifling the impulse to remind Cody that first light would be in just moments, groped his way back to his own bunk. Taking care not to disturb Dariel, sleeping just across the narrow aisle, he picked up a package from under his bunk and stepped out through the hatch.

* * *

Dariel was lying awake the entire time, eyes closed, planning the tasks he would have his men do today, barely paying attention to Carlos' pre-dawn movements. After seven years, these movements were as predictable as dawn itself. It had been a struggle for Dariel to persuade Carlos to take the first mate's job, for reasons Dariel still couldn't understand, unless Carlos really thought he had a hope of someday traveling back into space and finding his way home. The reason Carlos had offered for his reluctance to take the job was his ignorance of fishing, but years of serving on Dariel's boat had taught Carlos far more than he himself probably realized. In any case, his experience at commanding men made him a natural for the job, regardless of his fishing skills.

No woman should ever board a vessel. Every Quogian knew that. It was one of the most basic rules a captain enforced, for a woman only brought misfortune to a vessel. Dariel had heard many tales of

Quogian ships that were lost at sea during the Lekadian occupation because of Lekadians forcing them to use women as crew. He had also heard hard to believe tales about Lekadian men and women dressing alike and doing the same work, incredible tales that no intelligent person would believe.

Yet Carlos said that even on his ship that traveled through space, they had a large number of women, many doing the work of men. Even his wife was onboard. And Carlos said that many ships had a woman as captain. Could Carlos' people be smart enough to send ships through the stars, yet not know something this basic, that any ship carrying a woman on board is tempting the patience of the gods?

Dariel could not understand. He did make it absolutely clear to his new first mate, however, that he was never under any circumstances to allow a woman to board this vessel.

Dariel owed something to Carlos far greater than gratitude for seven years of loyal service and hard work. Carlos had brought him a son. Until Carlos' arrival, Dariel's wife had born him only daughters. The night that Carlos' ship first appeared in the Quogian sky, Dariel had a dream of his wife giving birth to a son. It left no doubt in Dariel's mind that, after so many years of disappointment, he was finally going to have a son who could someday take over for him. As he expected, his wife was soon pregnant, and when she gave birth, it was to his first son, Xander. Dariel knew he owed it to the arrival of Carlos' ship, the new star in the heavens that vanished so suddenly, but not before blessing him with a son.

"May Alaron favor us today, Starman," Dariel heard the helmsman call out as Carlos stepped onto the deck, and he heard Carlos' automatic reply, "May we deserve his grace." Dariel admired how well Carlos had learned Quogian ways. He doubted whether he could learn half as well as Carlos if he found himself suddenly stranded in Carlos' strange world that allowed women to work onboard ships.

He heard Carlos call to the helmsman, "And may he show us the way to RedFins today."

"Trust Alaron, brother, he will not fail us, for we serve him well," the helmsman called back.

* * *

Carlos had mixed feelings about this growing ease he felt with Quogian language and customs. It gave him a feeling of gratification to know he could fit in so well with these fishermen he admired and liked so much, but it also meant that he was slipping ever so much further away from his own world in the stars. He had even grown accustomed to being called "Starman."

Despite being "Starman," the stars themselves now seemed more distant than ever. When he was a child in coastal California, he could at least dream of someday traveling in space. Even if he himself never left Earth, he knew others could. He exchanged messages over InterPlaNet with youths who routinely traveled around Earth's solar System with their parents. Their tales fired his dreams.

Now, however—what was there to say about now? Only two ships had visited Quogue in generations, the *Marco Polo* seven years ago, and Lara's just a year ago. If only he had known about Lara's arrival! It might have been an opportunity to leave with the Lekadians who landed on the beach outside HarborSide, bringing her and her son Tobin to live with relatives they had never met. The Lekadians had left immediately, leaving her and her son Tobin alone on the beach. After seven years being stranded here, Carlos would have gladly taken his chances with the Lekadians if it meant even the smallest possibility he could return to the stars.

Villagers still spoke bitterly about Lara's grandfather, Ban, brother of Dariel's grandfather Xander. Ban served the Lekadians faithfully during the occupation, doing all their bidding, forcing even his relatives to attend Lekadian schools and to reject their own language and all their parents had taught them. He fled to one of Tarfil's moons to escape his relatives' wrath when the Lekadians withdrew, and never returned.

The shuttle that brought Lara to her relatives might have been the only chance for Carlos and Cody to somehow make it back to Earth, or at least back to the stars, but they had missed the opportunity. There might be none other in their lifetimes. The Lekadian shuttle had landed only a short walk from where Carlos was sleeping, coming so close to giving him escape, but now leaving him more devoid of hope than ever.

Although Lara and Tobin both considered themselves Quogian, and were related to half the residents of HarborSide, in many ways they were more outsiders even than Carlos and Cody. Both had been born on Tarfil's Luna One and until last year, they had never been on Quogue. Lara's grandfather, Ban, was still bitterly hated for the reforms he tried to introduce into Quogian society for the Lekadians. Lara and Tobin were resented simply because they were Ban's descendants.

From what Carlos had been able to learn, Lara was a professional shuttle pilot before her marriage. Her recently deceased husband was an architect and chronic gambler who designed extravagant casinos, and hobnobbed with the high level mobsters who owned them. Tobin spent most of his youth in boarding schools on Tarfil and its moons, while Lara and her husband cavorted around the Empire. Why had Lara brought Tobin to this planet where neither of them was wanted and neither had a place? Carlos wondered about this often, but Quogian etiquette didn't permit asking, and they never spoke of it.

Adding to the mystery was the fact that Lara had lost most use of her legs in a shuttle accident. On a more modern planet, there would be greater conveniences to help her get around. On Quogue, those who weren't able bodied were expected to stay at home, out of sight, doing whatever work they could manage at home. Lara refused to conform to that expectation. She was constantly wheeling herself around the village, or on her good days, using crutches. She was allowed to become the village teacher only because no one else wanted such a low status job.

Trying to forget missing his only opportunity to get off this planet, Carlos walked around to the boat's stern. He liked the early morning, when he could be alone with the stars and the first light. He even enjoyed the now familiar sound of waves slapping against the hull, a sound that seven years ago was so new to him. The double crescent moons, once as alien to him as the waves, were now simply part of the cycle of daily existence. For weeks, the moons had been drawing closer to each other. This would be the last night they would form two distinct crescents. Tomorrow, when the moons rose, they would rise as a single crescent, signaling the beginning of a new FourDay, and the crew's return to port for the festivities.

As he did every morning at sea, Carlos went to the platform at the boat's stern, where he and Cody would sing prayer songs at dawn. The songs were mostly traditional songs that Carlos had learned from his grandparents and from Uncle Cody. Some had been sung for generations. Singing every day at dawn was his own innovation on tradition, a consequence of being at sea most of the time and working too hard during the day and evening to even think about prayer. It was also the best way he could think of to keep Cody grounded in the sacred traditions of his ancestors.

After sweeping away debris and drying off the night's wetness, he set down the music player and waited, holding his clapper stick. The clapper stick and player were all he had left from the *Marco Polo*, other than Cody. He still had his communicator, but there was nothing useful he could do with it.

His thoughts drifted back to Earth. Were California Indians still following ancient traditions? Had Northern California Indian people continued to recover from the cultural disaster of the nineteenth and twentieth centuries, or had they, like so many other indigenous people, become totally assimilated into the larger culture, leaving once treasured traditions behind and forgotten? Unless he somehow found a way to return to Earth, Carlos would never learn the answer. All he could do was keep those traditions alive here, as best he could fifty light years from Earth, and hope that he and Cody were not the last ones in the universe keeping up ancient ways.

Waiting for Cody, he felt the same apprehension he had felt so often lately, the fear that today might be the day Cody would not show up to join him at dawn to sing prayer songs. He knew his son was under pressure from his friends to be like them, to worship the Quogians' many special purpose gods, rather than following traditions that even on Earth might now be forgotten.

Carlos was glad at least that the beginning of the work day no longer meant that Cody had to serve the altar of Alaron, which was built into the bow as it was on every fishing boat. Serving Alaron was a task always assigned to the youngest and most junior member of the crew. Dariel had offered to excuse Cody from the responsibility, but Cody didn't want to be treated differently than any other apprentice. Properly maintaining Alaron's altar was viewed as a test of a young fisherman. If Alaron didn't approve of how he was served, the youngster would never survive as a fisherman on seas that belonged to the god.

A year ago, after four years of Cody maintaining Alaron's shrine, Dariel gave Lara's son Tobin the job after taking his wayward relative's son into his crew. Carlos wondered whether the Quogians in the crew appreciated the irony that after four years of a California Indian maintaining Alaron's altar, an atheist had now taken over the job, two non-believers maintaining the altar to a god the crew believed determined their success or failure, even their life or death.

Although tending Alaron's shrine was by tradition assigned to the most junior member of the crew, it was viewed among fishermen as one of the biggest responsibilities on the ship, for Alaron was quick to take offense. Every seaman had relatives and friends who had never returned home from the sea after someone in their crew had offended the god. Every fisherman's son knew at an early age that failing to properly maintain Alaron's altar would not only end any hope of ever becoming a fisherman, but of ever getting any respect in the village.

Parents told and retold their young sons tales of the boy whose neglect of his duties to Alaron led to the death of several crewmen. To spare his unhappy family any more shame, the boy left their village forever, ending up living a miserable life on the squalid fringes of a spaceport on a Tarfillian moon. No one could imagine a worse fate.

Carlos wondered whether Quogian boys ever asked their parents the question he asked himself every time he heard the story, "Just how did that kid manage to get to Tarfil without a spaceship?"

Alaron might simply be superstition, but Carlos couldn't entirely dismiss the fishermen's keen awareness that their very lives depended on the god's whims. He knew from his years in space that starship crewmembers were not really so different, if the words "Fate" or "Luck" were substituted for "Alaron". They might not have an altar to a God of Space onboard a starship, but all crewmembers were keenly aware of the slim thread of circumstance that kept them alive so impossibly far from home and rescue, and how a moment of carelessness or bad luck could in an instant break that thread, as it had for the *Marco Polo* seven years ago. In that sense, these fisherman were not so different from Carlos' own long lost crew.

Carlos was about to begin singing by himself when he heard Cody exchange greetings with the helmsman. Running onto the deck shirtless, his clapper stick wedged under his belt, Cody pulled on his woolen fisherman's tunic as he ran toward his father. Cody was of medium build, lean and muscular, but not looking unusually strong, or like the boxer he was in his free time. He was a little taller than the average Quogian, with a nose that twisted sharply to one side from being broken in a boxing match, and he was missing a front tooth. His hair was long and braided, and he wore a considerably larger ear ring than the ones most men wore, a style favored by more dominant males, and which carried with it the message "Don't mess with me, I can beat you and all your friends." Like all Quogian fisherman, he wore a wool-like hat, and like all fishermen other than his father, he bore the mark of Alaron tattooed on his chest. Cody murmured, "May Alaron favor us today."

"Alaron is not our God," Carlos shot back, realizing immediately that he sounded much harsher than he intended.

"It's just something people say."

"I know," Carlos replied softly, "may we deserve his grace."

Before beginning, Carlos gave the helmsman the usual signal that they were starting. The crew was surprisingly respectful of the ritual that Carlos and Cody followed every morning, doing their best not to interrupt or distract them. As much as he resented being trapped here, on this planet, and in this life, Carlos was grateful for being with people who welcomed him so warmly despite his ways that they found so alien, and who went so far out of their way to accommodate his spiritual traditions.

They began their morning prayer songs, playing clapper sticks and singing while the sun emerged from the horizon, accompanied by the recorded sounds of his grandparents and other far away and long dead elders singing the ancient songs. When they were done, Carlos signaled the helmsman and then they headed for the mess, where they got their morning's rations, the heavy bread, dried fish, dried fruit, and hot beverage that were the traditional breakfast of Quogian fishermen at sea. They joined Tobin and several other crewmen at a rough, cramped table, where one of the crewmen was regaling the others with a tale about Tobin's feats during the last FourDay.

"Cody! You're just in time. I was just telling them about that time Tobin saved your butt."

"Don't you have any other stories?" Cody asked, knowing nothing would stop the man from telling the story they had all heard him tell so many times before. "Besides, I could have beaten those guys."

"No way you coulda beat them," the man retorted before resuming his story, "but there's no shame. Like I said before, they were big guys, all four of them. Two of them were holding Cody. They held him real tight. The other two were pounding him pretty bad, his face and chest were all blood. Me and Tobin was both pretty drunk. Well, I was drunk. Don't matter how much Tobin drinks, it never seems to affect him much."

"We all know how much it affects you," joked another crewman, to the merriment of everyone else.

"Me and Tobin didn't think twice…"

"I'd be surprised if you thought once," laughed another crewman.

"I was there. You weren't. Cody, tell them the truth, me and Tobin saved your butt, right?"

"All I saw was that guy hit you," Cody replied, "He sent you flying. You were on the ground until I helped you get up later."

"OK, it's true, but I was there for you, right? Me and Tobin weren't afraid of those guys. They were big, too."

"Yes, it's true, you were there for me."

Feeling better, the man continued his story. "Cody's right, after the guy hit me, I stayed on the ground. He hit me real hard. He was a boxer, like Cody. I'm no boxer. But you shoulda seen Tobin. He picked the guy up, like the guy was a pillow, and just tossed him up in the air. High in the air. When he landed, by Alaron, I never heard a sound like it. I heard his bones break when he landed. He was just lying on the ground, bleeding, moaning. Then Tobin went after the other guy. Same thing. High up in the air, like he weighed nothing. And he was even bigger than the first guy. Then he came down and hit the ground. Crack went his bones! He didn't move none after that either. Then Tobin did the same thing to one of the guys holding Cody. Up in the air. Down to the ground. Crack. Moan. Those three guys were crying. Big tough guys, crying and bleeding."

Tobin broke in. "Cody was hurt bad, but he finished off the fourth guy pretty good. He just kept punching the guy until the guy was lying on the ground and begging Cody to stop."

The first crewman continued his story, "Then we walked away, all three of us, Tobin, Cody, and me…"

Cody interrupted him. "After we helped you back to your feet. That guy hit you pretty hard."

"Yeah, like I said, he was a boxer. I'm not. Anyway, the three of us just walked away, leaving them moaning and bleeding. We sure taught them a lesson. Big, tough guys, crying like little girls. They won't bother any of us again."

Carlos remembered that night. He was accustomed to seeing his son occasionally get badly bloodied in boxing matches, but in street fighting, there were few who could best him, so it was a shock when Cody came home that night beaten up so badly. Nonetheless, Carlos was proud that it took four aspiring boxers, seeking revenge for a championship fight in which Cody defeated a boxer on whom they had placed large wagers, to beat up his son. None of them would have dared taking him on by themselves.

Everyone finished breakfast quickly, anxious to get all their work done today, so they'd have the entire FourDay free. As Carlos climbed up to take his turn at the helm, he could see Tobin roughhousing with Cody as they worked to get out the nets they would be checking and mending.

The story about Tobin reminded Carlos' of Dariel's warning when Tobin first joined the crew, "The boy killed a man on Tarfil, just by punching him. Keep an eye out. Let me know if you ever think he poses a threat to the crew." Dariel wouldn't say any more about it and swore Carlos to secrecy. In the year since, neither Carlos nor Dariel had seen any sign at all that Tobin might be a danger to anyone, but every time Carlos saw the two boys playfully throwing mock punches at each other, he still felt a twinge of apprehension.

In fact, Tobin had an amazingly gentle disposition, impulsive, always cheerful. He was a tall boy, large, with just enough fat covering his muscles that someone casually seeing him for the first time would think him simply large, maybe even soft, and not suspect just how phenomenally strong he really was, the result of growing up and lifting weights in the intense gravity of Tarfil. When he arrived on Quogue, he still wore his hair short, in the Lekadian style, but was letting it grow longer. He was having a problem with it though, because his hair was curly, a rare trait on Quogue, and as it grew longer, it also grew up and out, impulsive and uncontrollable, rather like Tobin himself. It was now pushing up on the interior of his hat, giving it a more rounded, bulbous look than the hats on other fishermen, and protruding wild uncontrollable fingers of hair from under the brim, hiding much of his forehead, and dancing over his ears and neck.

Like all fishermen, Tobin generally wore a heavy tunic at sea, sometimes with a shirt over it for additional warmth. He had only recently begun wearing an earring, finally yielding to Cody's persuasion that he should try to look more like other guys, but chose to wear a small one, feeling no need to declare his dominance with a larger, more assertive earring.

Despite Tobin's gentleness and always cheerful spirits, there was no doubt in Carlos' mind that Tobin could kill any man in HarborSide with a single blow, yet he had never seen Tobin angry even once. There was always a smile on the boy's face, he had an easy laugh, and despite the deep grudge HarborSiders still held against his great-grandfather and everyone descended from him, Tobin had become enormously popular in the year since he arrived.

So what made Tobin kill somebody before coming to Quogue? That night the four guys attacked Cody was the only fight he had ever been in since coming to HarborSide. If he didn't kill even when he was in a blind rage at the sight of his best friend being savagely beaten, could it have been cold and calculated murder? Or simply self-defense, as Carlos hoped?

None of it explained why Tobin killed someone. Carlos was certain of one thing, however. Cody was all Carlos had left from his life with Sophia. He would not hesitate to kill anyone who threatened Cody's life, even charming Tobin.

Whenever Carlos realized he was thinking these thoughts, he immediately banished them from his mind. The simple fact that he could even think these things disturbed him. He liked Tobin, not only because the boy was so affable and such a hard worker, but because he had become Cody's closest friend. Cody needed a loyal friend, and from all appearances, Tobin was that friend. Carlos' years of experience as a star ship officer told him that Tobin was a good kid, and that whatever had led him to kill someone, it might never happen again.

Carlos wished desperately that he had Sophia here to guide him. She would know the answer. His one consolation was that Cody was showing signs of inheriting her power of intuition. Perhaps the simple fact of Cody being best friends with Tobin might be all the reassurance he really needed. Nonetheless, every time he saw the boys throw playful mock punches at each other, as they did just about every day, Carlos felt himself cringe and wished again that Sophia were here to offer him guidance.

Riding The Redfin

The rest of the morning passed uneventfully. The crew worked together mending nets, carefully checking sails and rigging, and scrubbing down the decks, trying to get everything done while at sea so they could spend their FourDay just having fun. Carlos was at the helm. There was a mixed feeling of joyous anticipation of the next morning's start of the FourDay festivities, but also of regret at returning without having caught a single RedFin.

RedFins were enormous fish, a favorite food that would be heavily in demand with the visitors who even now would be flooding into HarborSide for the FourDay festivities, but more importantly, they were the source of much of the oil used for lighting and cooking. They weren't as large as Earth's whales, and Carlos had no idea whether they were actually fish, but they served a similar function in society that whales had served in Earth's past. RedFins were rare and elusive. A boat could sail for weeks without its crew finding one. Dariel was known as one of the best at finding them, but he had failed to find any on this voyage. They were now returning to port without a RedFin for the first time in years, a disappointing way to start a FourDay. Every Quogian on board was wondering how they had failed Alaron.

Then it happened. A lookout high on a mast bellowed out the magic words, "RedFins ahead! RedFins ahead!" Peering carefully in that direction, Carlos could just make out the tall scarlet fins. It could only mean one thing: a school of RedFins. Immediately Carlos rang the bell, over and over, as crewmen dropped what they were doing and scrambled to their stations.

Dariel shouted, "Lower the boats!" Within moments, the two harpooning boats and the long rope rigging that served as a ladder were lowered, and crew scrambled over the side and down the rigging, taking their places in the boats. Dariel took the harpoonist position in the bow of the larger boat, and Cody took the harpoonist position in the other, with Tobin next to him.

The hunt for the RedFin had for generations been the epitome of a fisherman's life, the pitting of men in a small boat against a huge fish that could easily demolish the boat and kill the men in it. Every fishing family had tales of men who had been killed hunting the RedFin. But every fishing family also had tales of heroism and comradeship on these hunts, and every son of a fisherman dreamt his entire childhood of taking part of in these hunts when he was of an age to join his father at sea.

It was RedFin hunts that almost instantly cemented Tobin's popularity when he first joined the crew a year ago. Before Tobin, one thing was always certain about RedFin hunts: the number of harpoon boats you sent out was the maximum number of RedFins you could catch. They swam in schools, and once the harpooning had begun, it was impossible to get close enough to harpoon any of them again. Tobin changed that. He also added an element of fun that only the impulsive and strong Tobin would have even a hope of accomplishing.

Carlos stood at the helm, like everyone else looking forward to Tobin's performance after the first RedFins had been harpooned. He watched carefully as the two little boats rowed out to where the scarlet colored fins were idly circling, as always feeling a twinge of concern about Cody's safety, but also pride at the respect his son had earned from these fishermen.

Dariel and Cody threw harpoons virtually in unison. To no one's surprise, Dariel's was a nearly perfect throw. After a brief struggle by the wounded RedFin, Dariel threw a second harpoon that finished it off. Cody's first harpoon missed, but the second hit the RedFin. His boat bobbed and raced wildly as the RedFin fought the harpoon and the men hauling in the line connected to the harpoon. As the RedFin tired, Cody threw two more harpoons, finally killing it, to the cheers of his rowers.

In the old days, before Tobin joined the crew, this would have been the end of the hunt. Tobin changed all that. After towing the RedFins back to the ship, both boats rowed back out to near where the RedFins were swimming. As usual after a harpooning, the Red-Fins were no longer swimming together in slow circles, but were now swimming erratically, some of them leaping from the sea, others swimming slowly, their enormous scarlet fins twitching violently.

Slowly and cautiously Cody's boat rowed closer to the RedFin that was furthest from the others. Caution was required. Agitated RedFins were always unpredictable, and on the rare occasion that they acted in unison, not even Tobin would risk getting in their way.

The RedFin was swimming slowly but its fin was twitching wildly, always a dangerous sign. Tobin began blowing on a whistle he wore hanging from his neck. As he played a sequence of tones, the twitching of the RedFin's giant fin slowly subsided, and as it subsided, Cody cautiously signaled his men to row closer. Tobin crouched carefully in the bow, waiting for the right moment, signaling Cody to move the boat slightly closer. The men rowed a single stroke and then, on Cody's signal, lifted their oars from the water. The boat drifted towards the RedFin. No one made a sound. No one moved. Tobin crouched perfectly still, waiting for the right moment. When they were in exactly the right position, Tobin leaped from the boat, his powerful legs carrying him farther than anyone else could dream of jumping, landing squarely on the back of the RedFin. The RedFin lurched into the air, trying to buck Tobin from its back, as Tobin desperately tried to lock his legs around the one narrow portion of the RedFin, while continually blowing a sequence of tones on his whistle.

Enormous bursts of water repeatedly blocked the men's view of Tobin as he rode the fish bucking in and out of the water, blowing his whistle the entire time. Gradually, the bucking subsided. Tobin looked ecstatic, as he always did when riding these enormous beasts. As the RedFin gradually eased its struggle and settled into swimming slow circles, Tobin rode victoriously, his hands held high, completely its master, to the applause and cheering of the crew. Everyone praised the magic powers that Alaron had given Tobin's whistle.

Steering the RedFin to Dariel's boat, Tobin jumped off into the water and swam rapidly back toward Cody's boat, leaving Dariel to harpoon the RedFin. Dariel had only a moment to do the job. He had to be successful the first time. If he only wounded the now enraged RedFin, it might either demolish his boat, or attack Tobin. There would be no second chance.

Despite the harpooning skill Cody had developed, neither he nor any other man in the crew would have chanced throwing that harpoon. The risk both to the men in the harpooning boat and to Tobin would have been too great. As always, however, Dariel dispatched the RedFin with a single harpoon throw, making it look easy, and shrugging off the praise of his crew.

Everyone agreed that Alaron had favored them today. It would be a good FourDay after all.

* * *

It was nearly sunset when they reached HarborSide. The late afternoon before a FourDay was always a dramatic sight, with the harbor more filled with boats than at any other time, and the sails of yet more returning boats growing larger on the horizon. Even before they docked, they could see jugglers rehearsing on the beach, and the tents and wagons of storytellers, craftspeople, and others being erected just outside the village. The FourDay would officially begin at dawn, and last until the fourth dawn after it. No one would work except at the most necessary tasks, and many of the stringent moral constraints normally imposed on everyday behavior would be joyously ignored. Dariel's crew faced working late into the night, unloading and helping process the RedFins they had caught, but no one cared, for when they were done, they would be free for four days, four days of unbridled fun. The three RedFins they had caught would bring them much honor from the village and its visitors.

After hours of nonstop work, the muscles of everyone except Tobin were aching deeply. When Carlos found himself alone with

Tobin and Cody for the first time since Tobin's ride, he couldn't resist asking the truth about how Tobin controlled RedFins.

Tobin looked around furtively to make sure no one else could hear and then, after making Cody and Carlos promise not to tell anyone, he explained, "It's not Alaron's magic like they think. I learned about RedFins in a Lekadian school. The school was for us kids from backward planets. I skipped a lot of the classes, but I liked biology. One day the teacher told us about when they studied the RedFins."

"When the Lekadians occupied Quogue?" Carlos asked.

"Yes. Everyone here hates the Lekadians for the occupation. That's why you can't tell anyone where I learned it. All it takes is a whistle like mine. I made it myself as a class project. They had a RedFin in an aquarium. I trained it with the whistle, had it doing all kinds of tricks. The Lekadians aren't bad like everyone here says."

"I wonder how much else the Lekadians learned about this planet?"

"A lot. About Quogue, about a lot of other planets. Maybe even your Earth. If only people here would stop hating them, they could learn a lot from the Lekadians."

"You certainly learned about RedFins from them, Tobin."

"If I stayed in school, I'd know a lot more, not just about Red-Fins. They tried to teach me. I guess I'm a true Quogian even if I wasn't born here!"

Noticing another crewman coming within earshot, Tobin said loudly, "And I thank Alaron for helping me ride that RedFin," then turned to Cody and asked, "Are we still going hunting after the FourDay?"

"Of course," Cody replied.

Overhearing them, the crewman said, "May Alaron give you guys the strength! Everyone I know is just going to sleep as long as they can after the FourDay."

It was late at night when they finished processing the RedFins. Carlos decided to go home and get a good night's sleep, but there was a lot already happening in the village, with many performers rehearsing and others setting up their tents, so Cody and Tobin headed into the village.

As Carlos walked alone from the dock, he saw a movement in the sky. By the time he looked up, it was gone, but he was certain he had seen something, a light moving fast, high in the night sky, something made by advanced, intelligent beings, but it all happened so fast, he couldn't be certain. He couldn't rule out a visiting fireworks master trying out some new and secret fireworks. It had happened before. Probably it was just a shooting star, but deep down, in his heart, he couldn't shake the feeling that it was a ship.

Festival

The predawn hours before a FourDay began were always a welcome change from the quiet sameness of life in HarborSide. Unfamiliar people sleeping and cooking in wagons and tents and on the bare ground everywhere, and in the fields and forests nearby, preparing for the next four days, when few would rest or sleep, and when the usually impervious wall that separated fantasy from daily life would become porous. Here and there, performers would be rehearsing, singers, actors, story tellers, jugglers, magicians, while young men getting an early start strutted around watching, sometimes cheering, other times hooting lewd suggestions. Most HarborSiders, however, just slept, enjoying the last night of unbroken sleep they would know for the next four days. There was an air of anticipation afoot in the town, like a long darkening sky before a summer storm, but more fun, a foreview of coming days of frolic and games and loosening of the restrictive social mores that regulated daily life on Quogue.

Carlos always enjoyed having these itinerant performers around. They were a refreshing change from the unchanging routine of life here. Every village had tales of a daughter who had been abducted by some traveling troupe, or a previously responsible son who had abandoned all to run away with some actress who had beguiled him with her wiles. Ordinary Quogian women dressed conservatively, even the young single women striving never to stand out, or to exert sexual attraction on men—at least they pretended not to—but the women in these itinerant troupes dressed outlandishly, lived freely, and had no hesitation about advertising their sexuality. Single Quogian men often had wild flings with them before settling down and marrying a woman from their own village or one nearby.

Carlos took his time walking home, enjoying watching the performers, feeling a secret kinship with these itinerants who were so alien to HarborSide, and so far from their own homes. Few of them recognized Starman in the dark of the night. He enjoyed the anonymity, but at the same time indulged in some self-pity about the fact that unlike these performers, he could not go home at the end of the season, and even if he managed to someday get home, everyone he knew there would have died centuries ago. Still, he did want to go home. He wanted to complete his journey, and to let the descendants of his crew know the fate of their heroic ancestors.

When he first was marooned here seven years ago, there were no vacant houses in HarborSide, so Dariel added several rooms to a cottage behind his own house for Carlos and Cody, adding them to the many relatives, now including the Lekadia-loving Lara and Tobin, living with Dariel as an extended family. It didn't offer Carlos as much privacy as he was used to, but it was no less private than any other home in town. People here just took it for granted that they knew most of everyone else's personal lives. Nonetheless, Carlos was surprised as he approached the cottage to see that a lamp was lit in his front room. Entering, he found Lara sitting in her wheelchair.

There were rigid rules for how single men and women were supposed to meet on Quogue. The same strict rules applied to married men and women whose spouses had died, and definitely precluded them from meeting alone in the privacy of a home. The tradition of men and women being formally introduced by family members made it even harder for exiles such as Carlos and Lara to meet under approved circumstances. Carlos wondered what could be so important that Lara was so flagrantly violating Quogian moral codes.

Lara was looking up at a sketch of Sophia hanging on the wall. Hearing Carlos enter, she said, "She was beautiful."

"I'm no artist. That's the best I could do. She looked much more beautiful than that. But she wasn't just beautiful. She was intelligent, strong."

"Like Lekadian women." They both knew she didn't have to add that intelligence and strength were not respected in Quogian women, who were only supposed to serve their husbands and fathers, and to raise their children. Lara was in every way an anomaly among women on Quogue. Other women, young and old, single as well as married, dressed in baggy, plain clothes that did everything to obscure both their sexuality and their individuality, reminding Carlos of how some cultures on Earth had until recently treated women. He often wondered whether things had progressed or retrogressed on Earth in the centuries that had passed there since he left, but was beginning to resign himself to never knowing.

Lara made sincere efforts to abide by Quogian expectations of how proper women dress, hoping to make her son's life easier. However, having lived her entire life in Lekadian society, where women were assumed to be strong and intelligent, it was impossible for her to completely reduce herself to Quogian expectations. Consequently, her clothes were less baggy and a little more colorful than other women wore in HarborSide, not enough to be scandalous, but enough to tag her as a woman who was and always would be an outsider, regardless how popular her son had become.

Like her son, Lara was taller than most Quogians, though this was apparent only when she walked using her crutches. Also like Tobin, she had hair that curled and refused all efforts to subdue it, despite her best efforts to straighten it to look at least a little more Quogian. The same curly hair that people found simply amusing on Tobin was viewed on Lara as the final proof that she simply wasn't Quogian enough. For Carlos, however, it simply added to the intrigue he felt about the one interesting woman he had met on Quogue.

Looking at the picture again, Lara asked, "You still love her, don't you?"

"Yes. I miss her every day."

"I can only imagine what it's like. I loved my husband, but he caused us a lot of pain. He's dead now, but it's because of things he did that I brought Tobin here." This was the closest she had ever come to telling him why she and Tobin came to Quogue.

Carlos hoped she would say more, but she did not. Finally he broke the awkward silence. "Tobin rode another RedFin today. He's amazing."

"Yes, he is," Lara replied, "he's great with animals, fish, anything in nature. He's just not so good in school. He never could concentrate on anything very long. I guess that doesn't matter so much anymore, here on Quogue, does it?"

"No, not here. Cody too, he can never catch up on the education he's lost being here. If we ever get back to Earth, I don't know what he will do. I've done my best to teach him reading, but it's so hard here. He sees no value in reading, or mathematics."

"That's the trouble," Lara replied, "when the Quogians rejected the Lekadians, they also rejected all learning. Cody already reads and calculates better than any Quogian. Learning more won't do him any good here."

"It just hurts to see him making the same mistake I made at his age."

"You came out OK, Carlos."

"It was only thanks to my Uncle Cody. I was a real hell raiser when I was a kid. He turned me around, got me dancing in the roundhouse, singing prayer songs, respecting my family, respecting myself. It's only because of him that I went to college."

"And became a starship captain," added Lara.

"I didn't start out as captain. When Captain Escobar was killed in an attack, I was selected to replace her."

"Your uncle was right about you. So were the people who made you Captain." Lara wheeled herself to Carlos' table, where a crudely bound handwritten book sat open with a pen Carlos had made alongside it. Looking at the book, she asked, "What language is this? I've never seen anything like it."

"English. My language on Earth. I am keeping a journal, in case Earth ever sends a ship here. I got the paper from some storytellers passing through, and I bound it together myself."

"Is there any hope that your people will rescue you?"

Simply thinking about the answer was painful for Carlos. "No, no hope at all. We transmitted a report back to Earth before our ship exploded, but even at the speed of light, I'll be an old man before Earth receives it. If they send a rescue ship, it will take generations to get here. I only keep this journal in case some future traveler from Earth finds it."

They remained silent for a few moments. Finally Lara said, "That's what we have in common, you and me. We're both stuck in on a planet where we don't belong, with no way out." Before Carlos could reply she added, "I really shouldn't be here. We don't want people gossiping about us. I'm not totally crippled, if you know what I mean," she said laughing. "You're sure Tobin is OK?"

"He's fine."

"I just wanted to be sure nothing happened to him."

As she wheeled herself out of the house, Carlos puzzled over why she had come in the first place. There had been many other times when Dariel's ship had come in late at night, but she had never seemed so worried about Tobin before. Carlos sensed she felt genuine fear.

* * *

The first day of festivities featured competitions in which fishermen, ranchers, blacksmiths, and many others showed off their skills. Cody had been out all night with Tobin, returning home just in time for dawn prayers with Carlos, and after catching a little sleep, left for the first of the competitions.

Like most of the younger, single fishermen, Cody and Tobin had discarded their sea tunics for a sleeveless vest made from an animal hide, exposing their tattooed mark of Alaron, which identified them as fishermen. Other young men wore similarly exposed tattoos of the mark of the god of their trades. Carlos and Tobin wore a quiver of arrows and a bow slung over their shoulder next to it in a calculatedly cavalier manner and of course always carried their harpoons.

Competition winners would wear their medals for the entire FourDay, hanging from a leather strip. A man who managed to win several competitions would proudly wear all of them, clanging against each other on his chest as he walked, allowing all standing nearby to know simply by hearing that a champion was striding by.

By the end of the day, Tobin had two medals. Cody had three, two of them in first place, but with a second place in harpooning. Dariel had won the harpooning first place, as he did year after year. Some were now kidding him that he might soon lose his top rating to Cody, but Dariel always replied with a few monosyllables to the effect that, "Cody is good. I leave it to Alaron." Cody's best performance as usual was in archery, in which he easily outperformed everyone else.

Carlos had no expectations of winning anything, and he didn't, but he at least improved on his past performance. He just wished there were enough basketball players for a true game. When they weren't at sea, more fishermen were joining Carlos and Cody at the community hoops they had set up. Soon there would be enough for a meaningful competitive match. That day couldn't come soon enough for Carlos.

* * *

The next day was Cody's big boxing match. He had done well over the past year in matches against some tough opponents, but this time, he was matched against his most formidable competitor yet, a blacksmith from a distant town, a man with a reputation for being a dirty fighter. Carlos had tried without success to persuade Cody to turn down the match.

Tobin arrived at the boxing tent before Cody, amusing himself as usual by giving demonstrations of his strength, and collecting on bets made by onlookers that he would not be able to lift wagons or other impossibly heavy objects, always stunning those who did not know him. A few young men challenged him to meet them in the ring, but as always he refused. Except for the time he stopped the attack on Cody, he had refused every opportunity to fight, even when it meant losing face—much to Cody's annoyance.

When Cody arrived, Tobin left his admirers and accompanied him into the tent. By the time Cody stepped into the ring, a large crowd of spectators had gathered, including most of the crew from Dariel's boat. The blacksmith was much larger and looked much stronger than Cody expected. He was used to his father pleading with him not to box, but was surprised when even Tobin suggested that this fight might not be a smart idea. Looking out over the spectators, however, Cody saw fellow villagers, particularly the crew from his boat, cheering him vigorously and loudly, trying to drown out the derisive hooting from the blacksmith's out-of-town supporters. He could not let his friends and his village down.

Cody, the local favorite, was announced to the audience, to the cheers of his supporters and the jeers of the blacksmith's. Then the blacksmith was introduced, also to cheers and jeers. Looking around the audience, Cody noticed four strangers sitting alone, the only ones in the crowd neither cheering nor jeering, but he thought nothing of it, to his later regret.

Quogian boxing matches allowed no rounds or pauses of any kind, and there were no rules other than a vague, undefined prohibition against throwing "unfair" punches. The match was over when one of the fighters could not or would not get up. On rare occasions, this meant a fight to the death, but this had never happened in HarborSide, and only rarely elsewhere within memory. Referees had the power to halt a fight if a fighter was using grossly "unfair" tactics, but rarely did.

The fight looked hopeless from the start. With a questionable punch, the blacksmith knocked Cody to the ground almost immediately. Cody got right back up, but as the fight continued, he received most of the blows, unable to mount an offense against the blacksmith's anvil-like fists.

Carlos and Lara sat in the front row, watching unhappily, while Tobin stood next to the ring, shouting encouragement and advice, as Cody absorbed one blow after another, many of them unfair. Cody's fans were shouting derisively that the blacksmith should forfeit the fight, but the referees never seemed to see the questionable punches. No matter how much abuse he took, Cody fought on, ignoring his injuries.

A stubborn and resilient fighter like Cody could suffer serious injury at the hands of an opponent like the blacksmith, if his will was strong enough to get back up on his feet every time he was knocked down. Carlos watched and worried. Every time he saw his son knocked to the ground, he prayed that Cody would stay down, and not risk head or more serious facial injuries by getting up and being hit again. Each time, however, Cody staggered to his feet, only to absorb more punishment. His face was covered with so much blood that Carlos couldn't understand how Cody could even see through it.

The fight lasted far longer than anyone expected. Several times it looked like it had ended with Cody's defeat, but the bloodbath resumed once again when he staggered back to his feet from blows that even many of his friends hoped would keep him down. Each time the blacksmith struck Cody with a questionable blow, the jeering grew louder, directed at referees as well as the blacksmith, and each time Cody struggled back to his feet, the cheering grew louder and wilder.

Gradually the blacksmith appeared to tire, moving more slowly, not evading as many of Cody's punches as before, and no longer knocking him to the ground. The blacksmith nonetheless appeared equally determined to outlast his opponent, and was still inflicting some bloodying blows.

Carlos finally could take no more. He stood up, but Dariel put his hand on his shoulder to keep him from going anywhere, saying, "Let the boy finish. It will shame him if he stops now. He will forfeit the match."

Carlos, however, could think only of the brain damage and permanent facial scarring Cody could suffer. Breaking free of Dariel's strong grip, he went to Tobin, who was shouting encouragement to Cody.

"Tobin, it's gone too far. Make them stop, now." Even if it meant Cody never spoke to him again, at least his brain and face would remain intact.

Tobin turned to Carlos, but before he could say anything, the audience broke into a deafening cheer. The match had ended with the blacksmith on the ground.

Tobin and Carlos jumped into the ring. Cody was covered with blood, gasping for breath, barely able to stand, while his opponent lay on the ground, not moving. The audience surged forward to congratulate Cody, climbing over the ropes into the ring, as the blacksmith's supporters struggled to carry their hero out against the surging crowd. While Carlos and Tobin wiped away the blood and dressed Cody's wounds, well wishers were pressing in on them, some handing Cody flowers or drink, all wanting to congratulate him, a few wanting to simply touch him, perhaps hoping that some of his power would rub off on them. Cody barely had the strength to sit up, and seemed only partially conscious of either the well-wishers or father and Tobin cleaning him up.

Finally Tobin forcefully cleared the fans away, driving all but Dariel's crew out of the ring. No one dared challenge the strong youth from Tarfil, so the audience quickly cleared out of the tent, leaving Cody slouched and bleeding, still breathing laboriously.

Sitting in the ring, letting others clean his wounds while Tobin cleared the tent of spectators, Cody again noticed the same four impassive strangers, not sharing the excitement that animated all the other spectators, but peering one last time at him and Tobin before joining the crowd leaving the tent.

When Cody finally left the boxing tent with Tobin, he had two black eyes, another missing tooth, and cuts and bruises all over his face, torso, and limbs. Everywhere they went, Cody was congratulated for winning his match, often by outsiders he had never seen before. He suddenly felt starved, but was too exhausted and in too much pain to care where he ate. He just wanted to sit down and be left alone, so he passively followed Tobin to a tent that wasn't in the village proper, like most of the other food vendors, but a short walk down the beach, far from well-intentioned fans smothering him with congratulations.

In the tent, they found monks offering meals of traditional food the way it was prepared on Quogue centuries ago, long before the Lekadian occupation, and telling tales of ancient heroes and gods while their listeners ate. It didn't sound appealing to Cody, but he was too hungry and exhausted to offer any resistance. At least it was a place where there weren't well-wishers constantly besieging him.

There were other story telling troupes visiting HarborSide, but this was the only group of monks telling stories. The stories they told were from Quogue's nearly forgotten distant past, stories that would have been illegal under the Lekadians. Maybe because of the monks' out of the way location, there weren't many listeners, but the ones who were there looked enthralled by the stories they were hearing.

Cody was immediately recognized by some in the tent as the brave young fighter who had won the bloody boxing match everyone was talking about. He tried downplaying it, but they would not listen. People at the tables nearest the storytellers insisted on yielding their seats to Cody and Tobin, in honor of Cody's great victory that reminded everyone of heroic victories of heroes in the past. The monks brought them dishes of food unlike any they had seen before, prepared especially for them in honor of the fight, as it was eaten by warriors celebrating victories in battle many generations ago. While they ate, they listened to the monks telling the stories of great valor from Quogue's long ago history and legend, and heard repeatedly how the Lekadians did their best to suppress the stories by destroying their monasteries and scattering the monks, but that now, the stories were being told again for the first time in generations.

Every now and then, Cody or Tobin caught a fleeting glimpse of an old monk, who clearly tried to stay out of sight. His face was horribly mutilated, and drained of all color. His clothes covered his entire body except for his face.

"I wonder what happened to him?" Tobin asked in a whisper.

"I hope it's not the food," Cody replied, "let's get out of here."

They stood up to leave and as they did, two of the monks rushed over to them.

"Wait. Is it true that you are the Cody who is son of Starman?"

Cody thought it a stupid question, since he was the only person on the entire planet named "Cody", so of course he was the son of the famous Starman, but he forced himself to politely answer, "Yes."

"Return tonight, without fail. Both of you."

Another monk added, "We will have a special performance, for the two of you only."

The only way they could get the monks to let them leave was to promise to return after dark, even though they no intention of returning

"Remember, after dark, when everyone else has left, a special performance for the two of you, and for no one else. You must come, both of you," they heard one of the monks reminding them for what seemed the tenth or twentieth time as they finally managed to get away. Cody, now feeling his energy somewhat revived, wasn't thinking about ancient stories. The only thing on his and Tobin's minds was the exotic women dancers they had been hearing about.

As they left the monks' tent, they didn't notice four men, sitting in the back of the tent, get up and follow them out.

* * *

While Cody and Tobin were enjoying the exotic dancers, Carlos and Lara were in a story telling tent. It was Lara's idea to go there. Storytellers there were scheduled to tell the legendary story of the arrival of Starman. Carlos had heard many versions of his arrival told over the years, all of them embellished. He had no interest in hearing it again, but Lara wanted to, so he had agreed.

The tale the storytellers told about his arrival wasn't much changed from last year. It was heavily romanticized, making him appear like a hero defending his ship and his wife, when in fact he had simply abandoned them by going out on Dariel's boat that first night on Quogue. The question of whether he could have prevented the *Marco Polo*'s destruction if he had been onboard still haunted him. Lara, however, enjoyed the story, even knowing how much the facts had been enhanced. Carlos suspected there might be a little envy in her attitude. There were many HarborSiders who wished she had never come home to her grandfather's village and who had given her and Tobin a much cooler reception than they had given Carlos and Tobin.

To Carlos' relief, the story finally ended. Later, walking alongside Lara as she wheeled her chair home, Carlos noticed that she was unusually quiet. He tried to make idle conversation. "The night we got into port, I saw something in the sky. I expected the storytellers to add it to my story as an omen of sorts, but they didn't. I guess they didn't see it."

This got Lara's attention. "What did you see? Tell me. Exactly."

"Probably just a shooting star. But it could have been a ship. I was hoping it might be your Lekadian friends coming back. If it was, I was hoping they might give Cody and me a ride off this planet."

"Does Cody really want to leave? He seems pretty happy here." When Carlos remained silent, she continued, "If what you saw was a ship, it wasn't my friends. They won't be returning. What did it look like?"

"Almost like a shooting star, but it was gone before I could get a good view of it. I just had the feeling it was a ship."

"Carlos, you've got to do something for me."

"Anything."

"Watch for strangers in town."

"The town is full of strangers."

"Look for strangers who don't fit in. Please—Tobin's in danger."

Carlos couldn't believe what he was hearing. "Tobin? Why Tobin? He's popular. Everyone likes him."

"I can't tell you more. I don't want you in danger too. Just tell me right away if you see anyone suspicious."

"I'll talk with Tobin and Cody about it, Lara. I'll make sure they take precautions."

"No, don't. Tobin thinks he can take care of himself."

"He can."

"No, he can't, not against this. Just don't say anything. If Tobin knows I've told you, he'll only get angry at me."

They had reached the front door of her cottage. Taking Carlos' hand, she thanked him for his understanding and friendship. After an awkward pause, they said good night, and he left. Walking home, he wondered whether he would ever forget Sophia.

That night, trying to get at least a few hours sleep, but unable to get his mind off what Lara told him, he finally gave up on sleeping. Restless, he left the cottage and wandered aimlessly around the village, discreetly trying to study every stranger he encountered, even striking up conversations with a few. He couldn't imagine that anyone he saw or spoke with could be someone from another planet here to harm Tobin. The idea was just too preposterous.

Carlos could think of only one person to ask for advice: Dariel. He had no doubt where to find him. Walking along the dock toward the boat, stepping around and over spectators watching fireworks, many of them making love, he found Dariel on his boat, alone, watching the fireworks. After Carlos told him about Lara's strange fear about someone trying to harm Tobin during the FourDay, Dariel asked, "What do you make of it?"

Carlos replied, "I think it's Tarfillian police after him for that killing he committed before he came here."

Placing a reassuring hand on Carlos' shoulder, Dariel smiled, assuring Carlos that nothing like this was the case. "The boy was defending himself against gangsters angry at his father. That's all. If someone's after him, it's definitely not the police."

"Why is it a secret that he killed someone, if it was really self defense?" Carlos asked.

"Lara wanted him to have a clean start here. Tobin was hanging out with a bad class of kids on Tarfil. He was a hero to them because he killed a hoodlum. Lara brought him here to get away from that."

"But you were so worried about him being a killer when he first came on board."

"That was before Lara told me the full story."

" Lara's his mother," Carlos asked, "Can you trust her to tell the truth about what happened?"

Dariel looked Carlos straight in the eyes. "She's blood to me. Blood doesn't lie to blood about things like this," Dariel concluded, with finality.

Carlos had learned from experience that when Dariel used that tone, it meant end of discussion. But Carlos had also learned that Dariel was an impeccable judge of character. If Dariel accepted Lara's word, then Carlos saw no choice but to accept it also.

Sophia

"Follow me."

Sophia hadn't even seen the guard approach, but she had learned not to question. Meekness was a necessary survival skill she had learned in this camp. Saying nothing, she obediently turned and followed him.

They passed other humanoid inmates, all of them gaunt looking and shaven headed like Sophia, and all wearing overalls identical to hers. Most looked aside when they saw Sophia being escorted by the guard.

There usually were only three reasons for guards abruptly taking inmates like this one had taken Sophia. It was either for a special work detail, or for punishment from which inmates rarely returned intact, if they returned at all, or to The Room. Sophia saw they were headed for The Room.

Every woman and many men in the camp knew and dreaded The Room. It was where guards took inmates for their own private pleasures, usually sexual. Actually, there were several rooms, but they were all the same, all equally dreaded, and all referred to simply as The Room. Sophia knew what would happen in The Room. It had happened countless times before. A brutal guard would require her to perform any act he demanded. Sophia had learned to dull herself to what was happening in The Room, so she waited passively while the guard opened the door and called to another guard inside the room, "Kwe, I don't know why you wanted this old one, but here she is, have fun with her." With that, the guard shoved her inside, closed the door, and left her alone with the guard named Kwe.

Kwe was young, humanoid, but from a race Sophia had never before seen, and with an unexpectedly gentle look on his face.

"Don't worry," Kwe assured her, "sit down."

It wasn't the tone of voice guards usually used.

There was a bed and a single chair in the room. Kwe moved the chair closer to her. Sophia sat on it. Kwe sat on the bed, far enough away not to seem a threat.

Sophia guessed that this was the new guard Reyas had told her about.

"You are Reyas' friend," Kwe said gently, "she has told me how good you've been to her. She thinks of you as a mother."

Reyas was right, Sophia thought, this guard wasn't like the others.

Kwe's voice took on a more somber tone. "You may relax, I will not dishonor my fiancée by doing anything shameful to you. But please, the other guards must think I have done terrible things to you. It is expected."

Sophia understood his caution. Twice before she had seen new guards like Kwe, young men with honorable intentions who had no idea what they were getting into when they signed on for the job. Both guards had disappeared mysteriously and were never seen again after other guards learned of their kindness toward inmates.

"I understand. I will tell everyone how cruel you are."

"Thank you, Sophia, I appreciate that." They sat awkwardly for a few moments. "Reyas told me you come from far away, from a planet no one has ever heard of."

"Yes," Sophia replied, "we call it Earth. It's fifty light years away. We came on the greatest starship Earth ever made, the *Marco Polo*."

The *Marco Polo*. In a flash, Sophia's thoughts were back on that magnificent ship. Its last moments would forever be carved like stone in her mind. The years since that awful day had dulled none of the pain, nor brought her any closer to accepting the reality of her new existence. Night or day, sleeping or working, those moments would never leave her. Neither would the regrets that never ceased haunting her as she replayed in her mind the events that led up to that day. There were so many decisions, big and little, that she and others had made that resulted in the *Marco Polo* being in that place at that time. In the middle of the night, she relived every one of those decisions, desperately wishing she could find just one that would undo what was done despite knowing that the terrible present was all the future she would ever have.

Kwe interrupted her thoughts. "Reyas said you never learned what happened to your husband and son?"

"That's the worst part. I don't know. That sea captain they were with might have been part of the plot. Carlos and Cody might be slaves on some other planet."

Tears began running down Sophia's normally stoic face. Kwe handed her a tissue. "Tell me about your world, Sophia, please."

After wiping away her tears and regaining her composure, she told Kwe about Earth, and their journey on the *Marco Polo*, and that because they were in stasis during much of the journey, many generations would pass on Earth before they returned. Kwe was apparently from a primitive society on a fringe world somewhere. He had never seen a true city, and had only fleeting contact with advanced civilizations. He listened to her wide-eyed. Finally it was time for her to go.

"Kwe, I must partially remove these overalls so it looks like you have been rough with me.

"Thank you. I will honor your privacy." He turned to face the other way while Sophia opened up her overalls and removed her arm from one side.

"Thank you, Kwe."

"They expect me to do this…"

"I understand"

"I will send for you the next time it's my turn with the women. But now you must go."

Sophia opened the door and walked out, pretending to cry as she walked from The Room and pulled her overalls back on. She hadn't talked so much about Earth, or about Carlos and Cody, in a long time, and now the memories flooded back over her as she walked back to her dormitory.

She would never forget that night when Carlos and Cody were spending the night on a boat on the planet's surface with a fishing captain they had only just met. She was on the *Marco Polo*. Her work shift was over. She was relaxing in her quarters, but feeling painfully alone with Carlos and Cody both gone. She had forgotten what loneliness was. Perhaps she had never really known loneliness before.

Their cabin felt so dead without them. At first, that's all she thought she was feeling, just loneliness, the void left in the cabin by the absence of the two people she loved most. She remembered regretting that she agreed to let Cody go to the planet's surface. She could so easily lose both of them. It would be bad enough to lose either one, but both? At the time, she could imagine nothing worse.

When she felt those feelings of foreboding first creep into her soul, she thought it was simply predictable fears arising from having Carlos and Cody both on a boat with strangers somewhere at sea on a strange planet. Carlos had assured her that the boat's captain was a man who could be trusted, but he had only just met the captain. How could he be so sure?

Unable to sleep, or even to sit still, she walked to a lounge, and looked down at the planet's surface, hoping no one would talk to her. She wanted to be alone. She did not want empty reassurances from well meaning friends who had no more idea than she did whether her loved ones were safe. The planet's night side was just coming into view, glowing bright under those double moons. Somewhere down there on that enormous ocean was a boat, and on that boat were her husband and her son. She knew where the shuttle had landed, and that a sailing boat couldn't have strayed too far from there, but still could travel far enough that anyone with malicious intentions and the knowledge or luck to take away their transponders could make it very difficult to track them.

The feelings of foreboding grew. She couldn't shake them. She kept staring at the planet's surface. There were no storms, not even clouds in the sky anywhere near where Carlos was. If something was wrong down there, it wasn't caused by the weather. The foreboding was weighing more heavily upon her soul, sucking her in like quicksand, enveloping her. It was something she had never felt before.

She raced to the intercom, and asked to be put through to Carlos, immediately. When she finally heard his voice, she blurted out, "Something's wrong. I can feel it. Are you and Cody OK down there?"

Carlos tried to reassure her, "You don't have to worry. Everything's OK. Cody is enjoying himself. So am I. We really wish you could be here. It's beautiful." He sounded so happy. For a moment, she relaxed. Simply hearing the reassuring voice of the man she loved made her feel better, especially hearing him sound so much happier and more relaxed than she had heard him sound in years. She would gladly put up with being lonely for one night if being down on that sea made Carlos and Cody so happy.

But then the foreboding returned, stronger than ever, an almost palpable blackness swallowing her soul. Suddenly she knew with an awful certainty that the danger wasn't to her husband and son, but to her. She screamed, "My god, Carlos, it's up here. The trouble's up here."

She heard Carlos say, "We're heading back. Have the shuttle waiting for us," and tried to remember what to do, but found her mind fuzzy. She realized she was having trouble standing, and looked around for a chair. Then the door to the lounge burst open. Armed men barged in. One of them was raising a weapon toward the intercom. She blurted out, "I love you Carlos. Tell Cody I love him," and heard Carlos cry out, "Sophia, what's wrong?" just before the intercom was blown apart, its shards lacerating her face, barely missing her right eye.

She was groggy. It wasn't until later that she realized she'd been injured. Looking around, she found it difficult to make sense of what she was seeing. She was barely able to stand. She saw other crewmembers in the lounge collapsing, or staggering around. A few had wet cloths over their noses. A few attempted to resist. She watched numbly as one by one they crumpled under the weapons fire of the intruders. Finally unable to stand any longer, she collapsed. Lying semiconscious on the floor, she slowly realized that the intruders must have flooded the lounge with a gas of some kind. She tried putting a handkerchief over her nose, but she was too late. It was a struggle simply to remain conscious.

Unable to do anything, trying simply to comprehend what was happening, she watched as the intruders separated out the older people to the back of the lounge, while making everyone else, including Sophia, struggle to their feet and stand groggily in line. They were led by the intruders out into the corridor, with stragglers being brutally kicked or hit. All along the way, every cabin door was open, but only the very young, the old and the very few sick or incapacitated were still in them. Young children, left behind after their parents were taken, wailed loudly. In the corridor, the line of captives staggered slowly toward an unknown fate, stepping numbly over bodies of friends and colleagues who had been killed or who lay too seriously wounded to move. No one knew whether it was the dead or the living who were the fortunate ones.

Under the cold eyes of their captors, all too eager to beat into unconsciousness anyone unable or unwilling to move passively forward as ordered, the line of barely conscious crew staggered along the corridors, slowly making its way off the *Marco Polo*, and onto an adjacent smaller ship.

Even as drugged as she was, Sophia was surprised when she saw that ship, unable to understand how it could have gotten there without detection. She was near the tail end of the line of captives, and so was able to see what happened after the hatch was closed behind them, and the ship they were in pulled away. Before her eyes, that awful moment she would never forget, she saw the *Marco Polo* explode, taking with it not only all their dreams, but the many living crew who were still on board, infants, young children, a pregnant woman, the wounded, the old, all dead in a flash.

But perhaps they were the lucky ones.

Sophia and the rest of her crew were led down a corridor filled with cages, each cage containing a barely conscious humanoid, some semiconscious with a desperate look in their eyes, others simply lying on the floor, eyes closed or staring into emptiness.

It all had to be a bad dream from which she would awaken. But every time she woke up, she was back in a filthy cage. Her surviving fellow crewmembers' cages were scattered in different parts of the ship. All were fed barely enough to stay alive, and were kept in a numb, hazy submissiveness by drugs in their food. Sophia no longer had any idea how long it had been since she was captured, days, weeks, she had lost all track of the passage of time. Lights were on continuously. Once in a while new prisoners would be brought in, or dead or seriously ill prisoners would be carried out. Time came to mean only the cycles of slowly awakening to a flood of memories and regrets, then of eating and losing consciousness again.

The only consolation for Sophia was that Carlos and Cody were not onboard when they were attacked. She would not be able to bear the thought of them, especially her son, enduring a fate like this.

One day, she awoke from her drugged state to find herself no longer on the ship, but in an involuntary labor camp. Eventually she learned the camp was on an otherwise unpopulated planet in a no-man's space that was technically part of the Lekadian Empire, but was unpoliced, and regarded as too dangerous for most travelers to pass through. Many of the inmates in this camp were in fact travelers who made the fatal mistake of taking a short cut through this part of the Empire, and were captured. About two thirds of the *Marco Polo* crew ended up in the labor camp. There was no way of knowing where the others were, or how many were still alive.

During her first years in the camp, Sophia kept detailed records of the passage of time, desperate for anything that would help her keep a connection with life as it was before. One day, however, she and many other slaves were herded without warning onto an awaiting ship. Later she learned that the slavers had been alerted that Lekadian authorities had learned of the existence of the illegal camp, and were sending a battle cruiser. The panicked guards evacuated as many of the inmates as possible onto their two ships.

After takeoff, inmates heard the ships firing missiles, obliterating the camp and killing all the inmates who had not been evacuated. Long time inmates knew this was done to destroy all records and witnesses that would allow Lekadian authorities to link the guards with the camp. A few days later, the inmates on Sophia's ship were herded off the ship, into a new involuntary labor camp, where she had lived and worked ever since. She never learned the destination of the other ship, or anything about her fellow crewmembers who were on it.

In her new camp, Sophia no longer bothered to keep track of the passage of time. It seemed pointless. She didn't have the records she kept in the first camp, and although she could probably have reconstructed them, she had lost the will. Like her fellow inmates, she simply stopped thinking about time.

She had worked a variety of jobs in the camp, but always declined to work as a trustee, one of the camp's more plush jobs, and was now doing menial factory work. Many languages were spoken in the camp, representing the diversity of the origins of the inmate population there, with Lekadian being the common language that most people spoke or learned to speak. Sophia had gradually learned Lekadian, but the knowledge of the Quogian language she had gained on the *Marco Polo* made that more of a "first" language for her in the camp, making it easy to learn the closely related Tarfillian language. As a result, she mostly socialized with Tarfillians.

One of those Tarfillians was Reyas, a girl of about Cody's age who, like Tobin, had been raised on Tarfil and its larger moon, Luna One. This is all Sophia had ever been able to learn about Reyas' early life. Reyas was ostracized by most of the other inmates, who were resentful of the life of privilege the guards had formerly let her lead. She lived in the guards' private quarters, had nice clothes that had been confiscated from recently captured inmates, and had a full head of luxuriant hair, all in exchange for submitting to the guards' sexual demands, while other children in the camp, shaven headed and malnourished like their parents, suffered and often died. She was returned last year to the general slave population. Although Sophia became her friend and protector, Reyas never once spoke a single word about her prior life, either in the camp or before.

Sophia would never forget how strikingly beautiful Reyas was when she was first returned to the general camp population. Reyas was a tall girl, unusually strong physically, and on the day she was returned to being an ordinary slave, she had just a touch of fat hiding her muscles. Most striking of all, however, was her beautiful, long black curly hair.

Reyas' hair lasted barely a day. The guards shaved it off the next day, seeming to get an unusual pleasure from the girl's tearful protests. It wasn't long before eating normal inmate rations and working long hours reduced Reyas' fat to nothing, giving her the same gaunt look of all the other inmates, but not ending the resentful memory the other inmates would always have of seeing this privileged girl crying at the loss of her gorgeous hair, when everyone else had lost so much more.

Reyas was Sophia's main friend in the camp these days. There had been a time when Sophia was close to other survivors of the *Marco Polo* in this camp. During the early years of their captivity, the crew had tried to stay unified, attempting to remain in contact with each other, and those who happened to have the same three days off would spend it together, comparing notes on how everyone was doing, and discussing plans for escape.

None of these plans ever succeeded, however. The only outcome was the death of some participants. Gradually most of the rest succumbed to the despair that all but suffocated life in the camp, until only a few even identified themselves any longer as *Marco Polo* crewmembers.

Crazy Old Monk

The first night of the FourDay had turned out to be a complete bust, and the second night was turning out to be more of the same. Cody and Tobin had started out convinced that with their medals dangling noisily from their chests and Cody's now famous boxing victory, that actresses and other female performers from out of town would be swooning over them, but so far, only native born Quogian guys were getting women. Rather than seeing Cody and Tobin as heroes, too many of the women they pursued were put off by Cody's black and blue face, Tobin's funny hair, and their non-Quogian accents.

It was Tobin who remembered. "Hey, the monks. They told us to come back after dark."

"Tobin, they tell that nonsense to everyone. They won't even remember us."

"They'll remember you. How could they forget a face like yours? It's a mess."

"I earned this face."

"Come on, Cody, at least they have food. I'm starved."

Cody didn't feel like hearing any more legends about dead men no one ever heard of, but Tobin was hungry and there was nothing else to do anyway, so they returned to the monks' tent.

They found the tent now completely deserted, except for the monks sitting idly at the tables. When Cody and Tobin walked in, the monks sprang to life, offering them tea and plates piled high with foods favored by ancient warriors.

After the boys had eaten all they could, the monks cleared away the tables, and brought out pillows and rugs for them to recline on. Later, Cody remembered noticing that someone had closed the tent while they were eating. They were now alone with the monks. Lying down on the pillows, he felt drowsy, almost as though he was seeing the tent through a haze. Like his father, he didn't drink alcoholic beverages, so he was going to ask Tobin if this was how being drunk felt, but Tobin appeared to be away in his own world. Before Cody could get his attention, the old monk, the one with the horribly disfigured face, entered the tent and down on a pillow right in front of them.

After making sure the boys were comfortable, he began telling the tale of the ancient Warrior Brothers.

Cody was feeling very sleepy.

The monk began, "It was a thousand generations ago, before there was knowledge of metal, when people everywhere used only stone knives and hatchets. There was a poor chieftain whose wife had born him no sons because of a god's curse. One day, three very young orphans were found wandering alone in the chieftain's territory. No one knew where they came from, or if they even had the same parents, only that they needed a home. Even though the chieftain and his people had little, he shared what food his family had with the young strangers, making them welcome, and treating them as part of his family."

Cody felt his eyelids growing heavier.

"Years passed. The chieftain raised the boys as his own. They were becoming sons any father would be proud of. Then famine struck. The priests told the chieftain that the gods were unhappy because he was preventing the boys from achieving their destiny. They told him that sending the boys away was the only way to end the famine. His people would starve if he didn't. Heartbroken, uncertain whether to believe the priests, but also not wanting either to offend the gods or to cheat the boys of their destiny if the priests were right, he sent the boys away. Before they left, he gathered all the supplies they might need for their long journey. He gave them food, and bows and arrows, and axes, and knives, and spare axe heads and knife blades, and seeds to grow more food in their new home, and plenty of warm clothes to get them through the cold of winter."

Trying to stay awake, Cody forced his eyes open. The old monk's disfigured face was too painful to look at, so Cody stared at Tobin, unable to tell whether Tobin was asleep or just listening very intently.

The monk continued, "Before the boys left his territory, he made them commingle their blood with each other, and swear that they would be brothers always. He made them swear the most sacred oath never to part from each other, and to defend each other to the death. The boys then swore a sacred oath of their own, that they would someday return and repay the chieftain for all the generosity he had shown them. They tried to console him, but nothing could diminish the grief he was feeling, or the fear he felt at the mortal dangers that would face these three brave youths. With great sadness, he rode with them to the end of his territory, then watched helplessly as they rode into the distance, and finally out of sight, heading for their unknowable fate."

Cody for a moment was convinced he could see the chieftain weeping as the boys rode away, but snapped out of it, deciding he had momentarily fallen asleep and had dreamt it. He sat up erect, trying to stay awake.

He listened as the monk told about the boys wandering alone in the world seeking their destiny but never finding a home or a place they could remain long. "They learned to fight, for it was the only way to survive among strangers and thieves, and everywhere they went, they defended the innocent and those who were generous with strangers. They fought robbers and evildoers, and the more they fought, the stronger they grew. Finally, they were defending entire villages against fire breathing dragons and evil sorcerers, even fighting the giants who live in the clouds. Everywhere they went, they freed people from those who terrorized them, and village by village, their fame spread across the land, even to far lands where they had never set foot."

Suddenly Cody became aware that even with his eyes open, he was seeing the dragons. He could almost feel their fiery breath. He turned to ask Tobin if he saw them too, but didn't have to ask. The look in Tobin's eyes left no doubt that he did.

The monk was still telling the story, recounting the courage with which they faced dangers that included fearsome dragons and wily sorcerers. "Eventually, even the dwarves deep below the ground came to hear about the boys, and to fear them. The dwarves invited the boys into their dark, loathsome realm, offering to teach them their greatest secret. They asked in return only that the boys promise they would forever afterward leave the dwarves alone. From the dwarves, the boys learned how dig up ore and smelt it into metal, and how to make metal things of all kinds. They made helmets and breastplates from metal, and metal points for their spears and arrows, and blades for their knives, replacing the stone, leather, and bone that people had always used. When the boys finally left the realm of the dwarves, after giving their word never to bother the dwarves again, they cast aside their old stone points and blades, and jettisoned their protective breastplates made of bone and leather. Now, they used only metal. Most importantly, they knew the secrets of metal."

The monk paused to drink some tea. Cody felt like he had actually seen the dwarves, and the boys working the raw ore into metal and pounding it into whatever shapes they wanted, but was unsure exactly how he had seen them.

Continuing his tale, the monk told about the boys finally returning home to the old chieftain. "They taught his people to mine ore, and to be blacksmiths, and to work metal into plows for their farmers, into pots for their women, and into weapons for their warriors. They gave their knowledge freely to their people. This knowledge changed how people lived, and made them strong and prosperous."

"Many years later, after long and respected lives, the warrior brothers' time in this world was drawing to a close. As a reward for serving their king and their people so selflessly all their lives, the gods assembled and agreed on one of the very few things the gods had ever been able to agree on. They gave the brothers their youth back, and put them forever in the sky, among the stars, where people could see and remember them forever. The gods decreed that the boys would forever be called the Warrior Brothers, always watching over us from the stars, ready to return from the sky if someday in the future the people of Quogue needed them. The gods have decreed that even fire breathing dragons, those fearful beasts the Warrior Brothers used to fight, this time will submit to the brothers, and carry them meekly on their backs, wherever the brothers want to go."

Finished, the old monk drank the rest of his tea and reclined on his pillow, while other monks refilled his and the boys' drinking mugs. Cody was amazed at how this story teller made him feel part of the story, to feel he was there, a thousand generations ago, to feel he was one of those boys. He could see the gods giving the aged Warrior Brothers their youth back, and giving them a place in the stars. For a moment, it was almost like he was back on the *Marco Polo*, looking down on the planet's surface from the stars.

The old monk signaled Cody and Tobin to move closer to him. With his face only inches from theirs, he whispered, "We have lost our warriors. We have lost our history, we have lost everything that once made our people strong. We need our warriors back. For many years, we monks have wandered, looking for the new warriors. The Lekadians tried to stop us. They destroyed our monasteries, they took away our sacred books, and they took everything we had. They scattered us, but they could not stop us. We have kept looking, but until tonight, we found none. Tonight, we have found them. You are those warriors. We all agree on this."

The other monks all murmured assent.

The old monk continued, "If you agree, there will be a public ceremony tonight. You will become brothers, and you will be given the protection of our gods."

Tobin asked, "What if we don't agree?"

"Then nothing more will be said of this. Now leave this tent, both of you, and think about it outside with clear heads. We will be gone in the morning, no matter what you decide. Make your decision tonight."

As the boys were leaving, the monk added, "If it is your destiny to be warriors in the Old Way, you will do it, there's no way you can avoid it, you will end this night Warrior Brothers in the ancient

Quogian tradition. If it's not your destiny, I pray you will have the wisdom not to come back."

Cody asked, "Why?"

"Because if you return, we will anoint you Warrior Brothers of the Old Way in public, tonight, in the village center. If it is your destiny, you will be Warrior Brothers forever. All the storytellers will tell tales of your courage and strength. But if you choose falsely, you don't even want to think about the fate that will befall you. Now leave, clear your heads, and return only if you accept the responsibility of being Warrior Brothers of the Old Way. Have the courage to make the right decision. This isn't a game. Do not return unless you know in your heart that it is right."

Cody and Tobin left the tent, wandering along the harbor, occasionally encountering lovers or small groups of drunks, but saying nothing, letting the cool salt air clear their heads and bring them back to a world that no longer felt as familiar as it did just a few hours ago.

The world had changed but in a way neither boy could express.

Tobin was the first to speak. "Let's do it."

Cody was stunned. "They're just crazy monks. They were controlling our minds. You of all people should see that. You don't believe them, do you?"

"Of course not. It's all nonsense. I know they're completely nuts. But what harm is there in doing it?"

"Other than being knocked dead by their gods?"

Tobin laughed. "That's right, you and your father believe in this god stuff. Well, I don't. I don't believe in gods, or priests, or crazy old monks. Who knows what happened so far back in time? No one. Besides, you don't really believe there were ever dwarves or giants or fire breathing dragons, do you?"

"On Earth, they had stories just like that. Maybe…"

Tobin didn't let him finish. "Did you see them too, the fire breathing dragons?"

"Yes, and I felt the heat of their breath."

"It's all a trick, Cody, they controlled our minds the same way I control the minds of those RedFins. It's all just a mind control trick they've learned."

"Tobin, if it's all a trick, why go along with it?"

"Just think, Cody, what it will be like if we're warriors. Did you see that armor they have? That's for us! Imagine if the story tellers really do praise us as warriors tomorrow!"

He waited for Cody to think it over before continuing, "Think of the women. This village is loaded with beautiful women, actresses, from all over the region. They're only going to be here two more days, then it's all over. Then we'll go on our hunting trip and then back on the boat. No more women like these until the next FourDay. What are we now? Just fishermen. What's a fisherman to these women? I have funny hair, your face is beat up, both of us talk funny, everyone knows we don't belong here."

"You really think they'd go for us?"

"Cody, you've got to believe in yourself. That's your problem, you don't believe in yourself. That's why you have all these fights, and a face that looks like shit."

"And you do believe in yourself?"

"Of course. I studied with a martial arts master on Luna One. That's what he taught us. If you believe in yourself, really believe in yourself, then you can make others believe in you too, and you don't have to fight. You have to be strong, of course, but if you have to fight, it means you've already lost, because you're not making others believe in you."

"How are guys going to believe I can beat the crap out of them unless I actually beat the crap out of them?"

"Believe it yourself. I'll show you. Let's go back there and tell those monks that we are their warriors. We'll believe it. Totally. We'll believe it even more than they believe it."

"I thought you agreed that they're just crazy monks."

"They are. That's the whole point. If you can believe the stuff they're saying, then you can believe anything. You can even believe in yourself. Come on, what's the harm? We'll be warriors for two days, we'll have some great sex with beautiful actresses, and then we'll go back to being fishermen."

"But everyone will know what fools we made of ourselves."

"No, guys will talk for years about how we conned those monks into getting us great sex. We'll be famous. Every guy in every port will talk about us. Everyone will wonder why they didn't think of it."

"You really think we can do it?"

"A piece of cake. Think of those actors. They know they're not really the heroes they play. Every actor knows that when the performance is over, he'll just be some ordinary guy again who picks his nose. But while he's acting, he believes."

"And you think it will be the same for us?"

"I know it will! Come on. We'll be the only warriors in town! In the region! The only warriors on the planet!"

Looking up at the sky, Cody said, "The Warrior Brothers went to the stars…"

"And we came from the stars. It's perfect! You and me, we're naturals to be the Warrior Brothers. Come on. There are a bunch of actresses just waiting to spend the night with a true warrior. Two days only. We'll do it for two days, and then we're Tobin and Cody the fishermen again, with the funny hair and the beat up face, just like any actor."

Feeling there must be some reason not to do it, but not finding it, Cody reluctantly stood up and followed Tobin back toward the tent. When they were almost to the tent, Tobin stopped. "Remember, Cody, you've got to believe. Believe everything. Even if you know every bit of it is crap."

"Suppose I laugh?"

"Don't. For the next two days, you're an actor. It's only a role. You're going to love it. Just remember, no matter what they say, no matter what they do, no matter how much you feel like laughing, you will believe everything they tell us."

"I don't know, Tobin."

"It's only two days. You can do it. Just keep your mind on those actresses. Never forget them for a moment."

They entered the tent, where the monks were waiting for them and welcomed them back.

Abduction

After a few hours of intensive instruction by the monks, much praying, and finally learning how to paint the sacred warrior's mark on their faces whenever they needed the gods' protection, the monks led them to a small, low tent, hidden from view, in which a fire was burning. The boys were ordered to strip, and then entered the tent, followed by the old monk and two others. The boys sweated profusely in the heat, sweat pouring from every pore of their skin. There was no relief from the heat. The monks relentlessly added wood to the fire, ever increasing the heat inside the tent, making it almost unbearable, though the monks scarcely seemed to notice.

The old monk with the disfigured face spoke. "When you leave here, you will be purified, ready to become warriors. Tobin, your ancestors purified themselves this way for all history, until the Lekadians stole our traditions and our legends from us. We cannot teach it all to you, but the knowledge is in you, as it is in every Quogian, you just need to find it. Being a traditional Quogian warrior isn't just fighting. It's mostly spiritual. You will have to learn for yourself, but it is within you. When you purify yourself like this, you make yourself ready to receive the knowledge."

Tobin asked, "What about Cody? He's not Quogian."

"All we know is that Cody is a Quogian warrior, though his ancestors are elsewhere. Just as your connection, Tobin, is with the past, Cody's might be the future, where we are going. We do not know. It will be up to the two of you to lead the rest of us. Now, no more talking. We will pray."

Cody couldn't resist asking, "Shouldn't there be a third Warrior Brother?"

"If there should be a third, you will find him," was the only reply he got.

The three monks began singing. Finally, after listening for a while and being prompted by the monks, Cody and Tobin joined the monks in singing. The monks then led them in bowing their heads in prayer. Cody snuck a glance up from his prayer position and saw Tobin grinning at him. Looking around to be sure all the monks had their eyes closed in prayer, Cody jabbed Tobin in the ribs. When Tobin grinned even more widely, Cody looked back down at the fire, biting his cheek almost to the point of drawing blood to keep himself from breaking out laughing.

The heat in the tent and the boring prayers felt like they would never end. Eventually, after what seemed like days, they did end. The monks led them, dripping sweat, out of the tent to the water's edge. Gleefully the boys jumped in and swam away from shore. When they were out of earshot, Cody asked, "Do you believe, Tobin? Do you really believe?"

"I believe, brother, we will get some glorious sex tonight. I believe guys will be talking about us for years."

"I believe my father will kill me if he hears about this."

"What's your father going to do, punish a genuine reincarnated Warrior Brother of the Old Way?"

Laughing uproariously, they tried splashing each other into submission, then swam back to shore and returned to the waiting monks in the main tent, where they dressed. After making the boys pray again, the monks led them to the village center, where the raised platform on which village council leaders sat during public meetings had been prepared for the ceremony. As they approached the platform, Tobin was whispering wisecracks about it to Cody.

The boys had expected the village square to be empty at this time of night, but to their surprise, there was a crowd gathered to watch. Following the monks up the steps to the platform, they saw a younger monk holding the armor that they would soon wear. Pointing to the three Warrior Brothers in the sky, the old monk proclaimed to the crowd that two of the Warrior Brothers had come back from the stars to save the planet. He prayed while two other monks burned incense and herbs, and then with great somberness, the old monk put a metal breastplate first on Cody, then on Tobin. After another prayer, and after pouring some holy liquid on the helmets, he very ceremoniously placed the helmets on each of their heads. The monks then led the crowd in prayer.

After all heads were bowed, Tobin whispered to Cody, "This is for real!"

Cody wondered whether it was mind control by the monks again. He knew what Tobin was feeling, it was a power, an energy, something he had never felt before. It had to be mind control. "How did the monks do it?" he wondered to himself.

Tobin whispered, "You feel it too?"

Cody nodded his head. He knew it was just the monks somehow controlling their minds, but it just felt so real. "Is this how the RedFins feel when Tobin controls their minds?" he wondered. He could feel the strength and experience of ancient warriors flowing through his soul, even though he knew it was all a mind control trick by the monks.

"I apologize that we have no swords to give you," the monk said when he was done praying. "During the Lekadian occupation, they took away all the swords used by our ancient warriors, along with most of the armor."

Cody asked, "How can we be warriors without swords?" surprised to hear himself even asking the question.

The monk replied, "Your strength, both of you, doesn't come from swords, but from inside you. Besides, you both have your arrows and harpoons. Those will serve you just as well as swords."

Finally the moment came when they would become brothers. "Will you now take the blood oath?" the monk asked.

Feeling some trepidation, both boys replied, "Yes." Their bravado had melted. Mind control or not, it was all a lot more real than they expected. The monk painted the mark of the warrior on their faces in the traditional way, then took out a knife, cutting a gash first in

Cody's hand, then in Tobin's. This was no mind trick. The pain was real, and the blood that flowed down their arms was warm. Ignoring their startled gasps of pain, a priest held their palms together, holding their hands high, letting their blood commingle. As blood flowed into each other's veins and down their arms, the monk commanded them, "Repeat after me, I swear I will always defend my Warrior Brother and that I will always serve the people of Quogue, even at the cost of my own life."

Cody and Tobin, stunned at the pain they felt, and almost sickened at the feeling of warm blood running down their arms, repeated the oath as the monk commanded. The monk loudly proclaimed, "Henceforth, these two are no longer boys, they are men, bearing the spirits of the most ancient and revered warriors of our past. They are the Warrior Brothers, come back after a thousand generations to restore the ancient ways in Quogue!"

The priest then denounced the Lekadians for taking away their myths and memories and even the warriors' armor of the past, concluding, "These two young men will change all that. They will bring back what the Lekadians took from us, and more." Pointing to the painting on the obelisk of the original Warrior Brothers, the priest predicted, "Someday, paintings of these two warriors will also be there." The spectators broke out in wild cheering.

No one noticed four men, their faces shrouded under hoods, standing impassively in the crowd, their eyes fixed on Tobin.

Cody couldn't take his mind off an actress in the crowd whose eyes were fixed on him.

As the two boys left the platform, the monks warned them, "Do not remove the warrior's mark tonight. Leave it on until dawn. Terrible things have happened to warriors in the past who washed off the paint before dawn. Be very careful about this."

The next few hours would always be a blur in both their memories. They found themselves being regaled and hailed by people they had never met, nearly all from outside the village, being offered food and drink, strutting around the village in their armor and warrior paint, and meeting more admiring women than they ever dared hope for. They remembered dancing, and singing, and a troupe of jugglers performing in a circle around them in their honor. They also remembered talk of a spaceport somewhere on Quogue, where the last holdout of Lekadian supporters were trying to bring back the days when Lekadians ruled the planet, when Quogians were forced to attend Lekadian schools, abandon their language, and forget their ancient stories. People repeatedly toasted Cody and Tobin not only as heroes, but as the warriors who would lead the final assault that would destroy the hated spaceport.

Eventually they ended up on the beach, on blankets they obtained somewhere, each making love to a stunningly beautiful actress. Cody was with the actress who gazed at him so intently when he was on the platform, and was feeling the greatest ecstasy he had ever known. Their armor lay abandoned in the sand nearby.

Tobin got up, waded into the water, and washed the warrior's mark from his face because it was smearing off onto his actress. Cody tried reminding him of the monk's warning not to remove the warrior's mark until dawn, but somehow, lying here with this beautiful woman, it was hard to take anything the monks said seriously. Cody immediately felt silly for saying anything about it, and turned his attention back to his actress.

In future years, when they thought back to this night they would never forget, it always seemed more than a little ironic that although it all started with the desire to masquerade as warriors to get some beautiful women, one detail they would never be able to recall from that tumultuous evening was the names of those two women. They never saw them again.

Cody happened to glance up as Tobin was drying his face, the warriors' mark washed completely off. Grinning broadly, Tobin gave him the Quogian fisherman's sign that signified a bountiful catch and then lay down again. Cody turned his attention back to his actress.

Gradually, Cody became aware he was hearing sounds that were not Tobin's lovemaking. Then he heard a shrill scream from Tobin's actress. Looking up, Cody saw four shadowy figures holding Tobin tightly while injecting him with something. Cody jumped to his feet, naked, reaching reflexively for his bow, pulling an arrow from his quiver and shooting it. One of Tobin's attackers buckled over in agony as the arrow struck, then was struck by Cody's second arrow. He fell to the ground, dead. Cody barely had time to reach for a third arrow when he saw one of the attackers point an alien weapon at him. Cody leaped behind a large rock, but was too slow. Suddenly his leg felt like it was on fire, his fleshed burned deeply, leaving him stunned and writhing in pain. He could only watch helplessly as the actresses ran away in terror and the shadowy figures dragged Tobin away into the darkness. It was all over in moments, leaving Cody alone with the body of the man he had killed.

Struggling to remain conscious, Cody staggered to his feet, picked up his bow and arrows and, stumbling like a drunk, tried to follow them. Tobin's abductors were heading in the direction of the monks' tent. Suddenly it all made sense to Cody. He had no idea why the monks would be after Tobin, but clearly the monks were in on it.

By the time he reached their tent, Cody had recovered enough strength and consciousness to position an arrow in his bow and draw it taut before barging into the tent, ready to let the arrow fly for even the slightest cause. The pain in his leg was excruciating. His anguish and terrible pain blinding him to what was before him, he shouted out, "Where's Tobin? Give him to me!"

Then he saw. Tables and chairs were overturned and strewn about. Pillows were cut open. The place was a mess. The old monk was lying on the ground, with a wound similar to Cody's. The other monks kneeled over him, crying, praying, encouraging him to stay alive. One of the younger monks rose to his feet and stood defiantly in front of Cody's arrow, his breast against the arrow's point, refusing to let Cody come any farther into the tent.

"This is your fault, Cody. We refused to tell them where to find Tobin, so they did this. You should have been here to protect us. It was your responsibility as Warrior Brothers. Instead, the two of were cavorting on the beach like any low animal. You two aren't warriors. You're just no good little boys. You weren't even able to defend yourselves. What kind of warrior is that? You let them take your friend, even though you made the most sacred of oaths to always defend each other, even at the cost of your own life."

Cody turned and staggered outside, each step on his wounded leg wracking him with pain. He tried running down the beach, toward a dark cove, following the abductors' tracks. The only way he could make progress was by staying below the high tide mark, where the sand was wet and his feet didn't sink so deeply into it. Finally, exhausted, the pain nearly blinding, he rounded a cove, completely out of sight of the harbor, only to see a small space shuttle rise from its hiding place. In just moments, it was out of sight. He followed the trail of Tobin being dragged as far as where the shuttle had been. The trail stopped there. There was no sign of Tobin anywhere.

Frantic, not knowing what to do, or where to turn, Cody staggered back to where the attack occurred. Their armor still lay in the sand, as did Tobin's harpoon, bow and arrows, and the medals they both had won. Hoping that Dariel was on his boat, he staggered onto the docks, still naked, stumbling over lovers, nearly knocking several people into the water, being cursed loudly by people who assumed he was drunk, until crashing into Carlos, who was just leaving Dariel's boat. He nearly knocked his father into the water. With Carlos supporting him, he returned to the site of the attack, as fireworks lit up the sky above them. Dariel followed closely after them, after getting some first aid supplies from his boat.

Carlos was furious with Cody, angrily berating him for acting so irresponsibly. "Who knows what diseases you might have gotten into your blood from their knives? You went against everything I've every taught you about common sense, about contact with aliens, everything. I thought you had some common sense. What were you thinking?"

While Carlos continued his tirade, Dariel silently washed out Cody's wound, daubed it with an herbal compound, and wrapped it in cloth. Cody had never seen his father so furious, and except for occasional bursts of pain, barely noticed Dariel cleaning and wrapping his wound.

Still angry, Carlos picked up Tobin's belongings. "I'll take these to Lara and tell her what happened. She's going to be heartbroken. You've let both of us down, Cody. How can we ever trust you again?" Motioning to the armor, he continued, "Take that junk back where you got it. But wash that paint off your face first. All of it."

As Carlos walked away, carrying Tobin's things, Cody waded into the water with the help of Dariel, but hesitated.

"The harm's been done," Dariel said softly, "there's nothing more to be feared in washing it off now."

With Dariel helping him stand steadily, Cody washed the paint from his face. The cold, salt water felt refreshing. After all the paint was washed off, they returned to the beach, where Cody dressed.

"Sit down," said Dariel, "rest. Wait for me." He walked back to his boat A few moments later, he returned and handed Cody a crutch, saying, "You can stay on my boat if you need to be alone," and left.

Cody slowly hobbled to the monks' tent, trying to hold both sets of armor in one hand, while struggling to use the crutch with the other. The loose sand made it especially awkward. Feeling both embarrassment and dread at having to face the monks again, he reached the tent still not knowing what he would say, or whether they would even let him enter.

Cautiously opening the flap, Cody entered the tent, looking around carefully. The old monk was now looking somewhat better. His wound would not be fatal, though it would require a long recovery. He was sitting on a rug, propped against a pile of pillows, talking with the younger monks. This time, Cody was allowed to enter. One of the monks invited him to sit with them, and offered him tea. Cody handed them both sets of armor, saying he was sorry, that they weren't really warriors, and confessing, "we only did it to get sex."

The old monk put down his tea, and looked at Cody. Sounding very tired, and speaking slowly, he said, "We know why you did it. We knew from the start. You thought you were fooling us. But the truth is, you were fooling only yourselves. You are warriors, both of you, only you are not yet ready to know it."

"No, it was all a joke. I'm no warrior. I let them take him, my best friend."

"And your Warrior Brother," added the old monk. "The shame and the pain will haunt you forever."

Cody awkwardly got to his feet, using Dariel's crutch to help him stand, while saying, "I only came to return your armor."

The old monk looked up at him. "Do not leave yet. There is more to say."

The same young monk who earlier had defiantly barred Cody from entering the tent now stood in front of him again, this time barring him from leaving. Hearing the old monk repeat his command to come back, Cody turned and sat down. "I can't stay long. My father's going to be looking for me."

The old monk spoke again. "It often takes a long time, years, decades, before a man sees the truth about himself, before he can acknowledge his own strength." A monk brought Cody some more tea. The old monk continued, "Keep the armor. Someday you will see the truth. On that day, you will don the armor, and take on your destined role."

Cody felt foolish even talking to them, but nonetheless asked, "Just how will I know this?"

"Cody, we in this order can not see the future. Maybe others can, but we cannot. What we can see clearly that others can't see is the past. We can see even the distant past clearly. We can see things that were completely forgotten many generations ago, clearly, like they were right in front of us, but we cannot see even a moment into the future. I am sorry, but we cannot tell you when you will become a warrior, or even if you ever will. All I can tell you is that it's up to you."

Still feeling foolish for even taking part in this conversation, Cody asked, "So how do you know, if you can't see the future?"

"All we know is what happened to warriors many, many years ago, and what the moment was that made them know they were warriors. For people like you, Cody, the moment usually came after a long period of letting other people tell them that they were ordinary, and not true warriors. If you are like them, Cody, a day will come when you will see a truth, a truth no one else sees. Even the people you respect the most will laugh at you for the truth you will see so clearly. When that happened to men like you in distant history, what they did at that moment determined whether they became warriors."

The monk paused to rest, still exhausted from his wounds, then continued. "When that moment arrived, the true warriors stood their ground, proclaiming the truth of their vision. They took their armor from where they had hidden it, they painted their face with the mark of the warrior, and from that moment on, they were warriors."

"Suppose that moment never happens?"

"The moment always happens. The important thing is what the man does. Some men stand up, proclaim themselves a warrior, and face the world bravely. The others return the armor to us. Sometimes they say they weren't meant to be warriors. Other times they accuse us of being frauds. When that moment comes for you, you will have two choices: you will tell the world the truth of who you are, or you will sit back and for the rest of your life be whoever others want you to be. Those are the choices every man faces, not only born warriors like you. We do not know when this moment will happen for you, only that this is how it has happened for thousands of years to others just like you, and that the moment will come."

Cody asked, "What about Tobin?"

"He already knows the truth, that the two of you are warriors."

"No, he doesn't. It was all his idea. It was a joke to him."

The old monk looked solemnly at Cody. "We told you we can see the past. We can see things that happened many generations ago, but we can also see what happened just a few moments ago. The only thing we cannot see is the future. We can see why you decided to become warriors, and we can see what your friend was thinking when he was being carried away tonight."

"What was he thinking?" asked Cody.

"He was struggling to free himself from the strong grip of those three men, but he was drugged. He could not control his arms or his legs. He saw his helmet and breastplate rolling around on the sand.

He saw the remains of the red paint he had washed off his face just moments before, all smeared on the towel he had used to dry himself. He saw you bravely shooting arrows at his abductors, no matter that they were aiming far more deadly weapons at you. He saw you willing to die to free him, your brother. At that moment he knew the truth of all we said. You and he are both warriors, you are brothers, and Tobin knows it. There is no doubt in his mind."

Cody answered, "But he is a prisoner, somewhere in space. I don't know where. How can he be a warrior now? How can he even believe it?"

"He has no problem with belief. But you must give him back his armor, and you must paint the mark of the warrior on his face. You have sworn an oath to do this, and he swore it to you. He would die to save you. You cannot ignore your oath. You must rescue him. You must give him his armor back and restore the mark of the warrior to his face, even if you never again wear yours. Even if you die doing it, even if you never acknowledge that you are a warrior yourself, you must do it for Tobin. He expects it. He is waiting for you."

"But how can I?"

"That is for you to learn. There is nothing more for us to say. Take the armor with you. Give Tobin's armor to him when you rescue him, and paint the mark of the warrior on his face, even if you never wear yours. Do not wear it again until you know with all your heart that you are the warrior we believe you are."

Giving him a sack to hide the armor and paint and telling him to protect it at all costs, the monks bade Cody farewell.

Cody hated lying to his father and Dariel. He had never lied to either of them before. But the monks were right about one thing, even if they were completely demented about everything else: standing on that platform, his blood mingling with Tobin's, he had sworn an oath to always protect his friend. He had to save him, if it meant his own life. Just in case the monks were right, he had to keep the armor and warrior's paint until after he saved Tobin, even if it was all totally crazy. After he saved Tobin, they could throw all the armor away, and go back to their old lives, having fun the way they always did. In the mean time, he knew he could not risk getting rid of it, but also that he could not tell his father or Dariel.

He tried walking down the beach, to where he could hide the armor where no one would find it, but walking was too difficult, so reluctantly he returned to Dariel's boat, fearing what Dariel would say. He could not lie to Dariel, but he dreaded telling him the truth. He prayed Dariel would be asleep when he arrived at the boat.

Dariel wasn't asleep. He was sitting on the deck, watching the last and best of the fireworks, which Cody had barely noticed in his obsession with his grief and pain. As Cody walked up the gangway onto the boat, he saw Dariel look down just briefly at the sack he was carrying. Cody was still unsure whether he would lie or tell the truth to Dariel about what was in the sack. Before he could say anything, Dariel spoke.

"I trust you, Cody. You will do the right thing."

"Suppose I don't know that the right thing is?"

"When the time comes, you will know."

"Dariel…"

"Say nothing. There are good hiding places in the hold. Then come back up and enjoy the fireworks." Feeling relieved that he neither had to lie to Dariel nor admit to disobeying his father, Cody hid the sack in the hold where other crewmen would not find it, then returned to sit silently with Dariel, watching the fireworks, neither of them saying a word.

* * *

The next two days were the worst Cody had ever known. His father still angry and disappointed, Tobin abducted, and everyone seeming to know about them being anointed as warriors and swearing to defend each other to the death, he couldn't get away from reminders of how his recklessness had led to his friend's abduction. Actually, there was a lot more sympathy for him in town than he realized, but he refused to hear it. Most of all, he hated being pitied for being taken in by some demented monks.

His rock during those two days was Dariel, who neither pitied him, nor showed anger or disappointment. He simply encouraged Cody to take one step at a time, then another, not worrying about anything else, and provided him a ready and non-judging ear for his laments. Cody ignored the rest of the FourDay, hid his medals away, and spent most of his time sitting idly on the boat. When Dariel went home to be with his wife and children, Cody remained on the boat. Although most in the village had lost their pleasure in the FourDay after Tobin's abduction, there was still more enjoyment going on, mostly by outsiders, than Cody could tolerate.

By the end of the FourDay, however, he knew he had to act. It was when he and Tobin had planned going on their hunting trip, a trip they'd been looking forward to for weeks, and he knew he had to devote those days to finding a way to get off the planet to rescue Tobin. Remembering the talk he had heard about a spaceport that supposedly existed somewhere on Quogue, Cody ran to Lara's to tell her, and to insist that they had to find it in case there was a ship there they could use for getting into space.

Arriving at Lara's, he found Carlos already there, and learned that for two days, they had been working without success on ideas for getting off the planet.

"There's a spaceport…" Cody began to say.

"No one knows where it is," interrupted Carlos.

"How do you find a spaceport on a planet that has no maps?" asked Lara.

"Storytellers probably know where it is," Cody shot back.

"We already asked them," answered Lara.

Carlos added, "Some storytellers probably know where it is, but not the ones here."

Cody wouldn't give up. "We have to find it."

Carlos tried to rein in his optimism. "Even if we find the spaceport, if the Lekadians left any ships behind, it's probably because the ships didn't run."

Lara added, "And it was two generations ago. Even if the Lekadians left good ships behind, and Lekadians never leave good ships behind, they have sat for several generations. They're not going to be space worthy now."

"What good is the spaceport then?" asked Cody.

"Because there might be communications equipment there that we can use to contact the Lekadians."

"Lekadians!" Cody blurted out, anger in his voice.

"I don't trust them any more than you do," Carlos said, "but we have no choice."

Sounding exasperated, Lara said, "The two of you don't know what you're talking about. I've lived with Lekadians all my life. I have Lekadian friends. My husband and I both worked for Lekadians."

"You like what they did to this planet?" asked Cody, anger in his voice.

"Cody, you see how backward Quogue is. The Lekadians only wanted to help Quogians become educated and civilized."

"You mean make them Lekadian slaves," Cody shot back.

"Like it or not," Carlos said, "the only way to rescue Tobin is to contact Lara's Lekadian friends. Do you really want to rescue Tobin?"

Cody reluctantly nodded his head.

"Then we have to contact the Lekadians. We have no choice. But first we have to find the spaceport. This won't be easy. No one knows where it is."

The next day, Cody and Carlos went to Dariel together to tell him they were not sailing with him, but instead would go looking for the spaceport.

As so often happened, Dariel was a step ahead of them. "I have already told the rest of the crew that we're not going to sea until we learn the spaceport's location. They are right now questioning all the storytellers in town about where they might find people who know the location. Then, the crew will spread out. They will go to those places. They will find someone who knows where the spaceport is." Then he added, with his usual note of finality, "You two will stay here in HarborSide and wait for one of them to return."

"I'm not going to sit here and do nothing," Cody blurted out.

"You won't be doing nothing," Dariel said with a smile, "I have lots of work for you on my boat while it's in port."

"But..."

"When one of the crew returns and tells us where the spaceport is, that's when you will leave."

Farewell

"Can't you do anything right?"

Accabo immediately regretted his outburst. The youngsters meant well. Their eyes showed the hurt they felt at his rebuke. Unsure what to do, he took the Lekadian lubricating device himself and tried demonstrating how to lubricate joints without wasting scarce grease, but the effort only reminded him that he wasn't that much better at it than they were. His skill was with electronics and logic circuits, not grease. More than ever he missed Esiu's easy wizardry with grease. Lubricating an entire spaceship with the small amount of lubricants the Lekadians left behind was a skill Accabo never appreciated until Esiu left the spaceport.

Silently vowing to be more patient this time and hoping the youngsters hadn't noticed his own clumsiness, he handed the device back and watched as one of them nervously tried again.

The wail of the defense horn jarred all of them to attention. It was becoming almost routine. As always, the older youngsters made sure the younger ones knew where to hide, then took up their weapons and waited for Accabo to lead them to the ramparts.

Being a tutor meant that Accabo could no longer evade defense duty. If he didn't lead his eager youthful charges to the ramparts every time the defense horn sounded, he would lose all respect in their eyes, and with it, any hope of getting them to work on the *Dembu.* Without their help, the *Dembu* would never fly.

Grabbing his weapons, he led his pupils through the trees that surrounded the *Dembu* to positions just below the ramparts. They wouldn't actually fight unless barbarians penetrated the walls, but would stay in relative safety, handing water and weapons to spaceport defenders while incurring minimal risk of injury. Nonetheless, it was still closer to the fighting than Accabo wanted to be. Keeping the youngsters from seeing his terror was always a struggle.

They took their positions, and like the warriors just above them, they waited for the attack. One of the warriors called down, “Accabo, get up here.”

The last place Accabo wanted to be during an attack was in the open, on the ramparts with the warriors, but he had no choice. If he didn’t comply, he would lose the respect of his charges so, hoping they didn’t see how scared he was, he stepped up to the ramparts.

He wasn’t prepared for what he was about to see. Under the wary eyes of spaceport defenders, three barbarians slowly approached, carrying the flag of truce. The defenders stood ready for treachery, watching suspiciously as the barbarians approached.

“I don’t believe it! Look who it is,” a startled warrior shouted.

Accabo looked more closely. There was something familiar about these barbarians. Then he saw. It was Esiu, the wizard of grease turned barbarian, accompanied by his father and brother. All three had once fiercely stood defense on these walls, but it wouldn’t be the first time a former spaceport resident had approached the spaceport carrying the flag of truce to conceal treacherous intentions. The warriors on the ramparts stood ready to launch a barrage of arrows and spears as the gate was opened, the three men entered, and the gate was closed and securely bolted behind them.

With the gate secure, a few of the warriors around Accabo relaxed and went down to greet their former comrades. Accabo, however, felt only disgust at Esiu’s appearance. Esiu was once his friend. Now he was fully barbarian. Accabo had no desire to get any closer.

Returning to his youngsters, Accabo told them, “It’s only Esiu. Let’s go back to work,” and led them down the steps to return to the *Dembu*.

Seeing him leaving, Esiu cried out, “Accabo!”

Accabo kept walking. One of the youngsters said, "Accabo, Esiu's calling you."

"Keep going," Accabo replied, determined to ignore Esiu.

Esiu called more loudly, "Accabo!"

Accabo kept walking.

Finally Esiu bellowed, "Accabo! Come back here, you ass," so loudly that Accabo could no longer ignore him.

After telling the youngsters he would meet them at the *Dembu*, Accabo turned and walked back towards Esiu. The closer he came, the more intense became his disgust. Esiu now wore his hair long, tied in two short ponytails, not yet long enough to braid, but getting there. He wore rings in both ears, and his open animal hide vest revealed a large tattoo of the god of ranching. Even worse, to complete Accabo's disgust, Esiu embraced him warmly, like an old friend, making Accabo smell the vile odor of the vest, and feel the earring against his cheek.

"Accabo, old friend, you don't approve of me."

Accabo didn't reply.

"Life is good out there, Accabo."

"I'll never turn barbarian, Esiu."

"We're not barbarians. We just want our wives and children to be safe. When you are a father, you'll understand. I used to think like you. You know I did."

Accabo remembered the old Esiu, and this was not him.

"I have not come to argue. I bring news that will interest you more than anyone else."

Accabo couldn't imagine what news a barbarian could bring that would interest him.

"Accabo, Starman is coming!"

Accabo stared at Esiu in disbelief.

"You were right all along, Accabo. Starman is real. He's coming."

"Here?" Accabo stammered.

Accabo's brothers and some warriors nearby laughed loudly, as they always did at the mention of Starman.

Turning to them, Esiu said, "He's real. Accabo was right about Starman." The warriors looked skeptical. "Starman is real." Turning to face Accabo again, he continued, "Starman is coming, here, to the spaceport. He needs your help."

"You've actually met Starman, Esiu?"

"No, we only spoke with his messenger. He will bring Starman here. Starman's messengers searched all over the world for the spaceport. Finally some storytellers who knew about us brought one of them to our ranch. We promised him we would come and tell you, so you will let Starman in when he arrives."

Esiu had one more bit of news for Accabo. "Starman has a son. He is said to be around your age, Accabo."

"Starman has a son? Is he coming here?"

"Yes. His name is Cody, that's all I know."

For the rest of the day, Accabo was excited as he had never been before. Later, he joined his brothers for the feast in Esiu's honor, but he scarcely paid attention to what was being said or done, unable to keep his thoughts away from the deliriously exciting news that not only was Starman coming, but his son was coming too, someone who could work with Accabo, and understand him. After the feast, Esiu joined Accabo's brothers and the other warriors in getting drunk and partying wildly. Disgusted, Accabo returned to the *Dembu* and worked all night on the ship, finally falling asleep at a control console just before dawn.

Esiu woke him up a few hours later. "I am returning home, Accabo."

Trying to ignore how badly Esiu reeked of the fermented beverages he imbibed so heavily the night before, Accabo walked from the *Dembu* with him. As they approached the gate, where Esiu's father and brother were waiting, Accabo's brothers joined them.

Esiu said, “If things don’t work out with Starman, Accabo, remember, you are always welcome at our ranch.”

“I’ll never get the ship ready for Starman if I have to answer the defense horn all the time.”

Accabo was shocked to hear one of his brothers reply, “Ignore the defense horn. Work on the *Dembu.*”

“We do it as a favor to Esiu,” Accabo’s other brother added, “he asked us to spare you from defense duty. We do it for him. A warrior.”

Accabo looked around at his brothers and at Esiu, speechless.

“You and the youngsters who help you won’t have to answer any defense horns until Starman comes,” his brother continued, adding, “unless barbarians penetrate the walls. Then everyone has to serve defense, of course.”

“Of course,” Accabo agreed.

“After Starman leaves, you will go back to your usual defense duty,” his other brother added sternly.

After Esiu left, Accabo set to work, redoubling his efforts to check and recheck the *Dembu*, doing everything he could think of to make sure everything was working. Everyday, Accabo spent nearly every waking minute working on the old ship, encouraging the youngsters to work harder, checking every connection, testing every system, finally even test firing the engines briefly. When he thought he had done everything he could possibly do, he started over again, and checked for things he might have overlooked, or perhaps hadn’t tested adequately.

Each night, Accabo lay in bed, fantasizing the meeting with Starman and taking off into space, the trusted lieutenant of Starman and his son.

Five days passed, then ten, but Starman still did not show up. Accabo’s brothers were growing skeptical. Accabo tried his best to ignore his growing fear that Esiu was wrong, and Starman wasn’t coming, or even worse, that the barbarians had maybe even killed Starman and his son.

Nothing could have prepared Accabo for what happened next.

* * *

One evening, Accabo was working alone in the ship. The youngsters were home eating their evening meal with their families. He heard someone climbing the steps. Wondering who it might be, he walked to the hatch and to his shock saw a barbarian, long hair, tattoo, earrings, the works, with a spear slung over his shoulder and carrying a bow and quiver of arrows.

It was Cody.

Trying to remember his training, Accabo grabbed his bow, notched an arrow into it, and stepped outside. Aiming the arrow at Cody and mustering all the authority he could command, Accabo barked, "Drop your weapons!"

"I'm a friend," Cody replied.

"Drop your weapons or I'll kill you." When Cody didn't respond, Accabo added, "Now. Drop them now."

Cody let his bow and arrows fall to the ground.

"The spear too, barbarian."

"It's a harpoon."

"Drop it barbarian."

Cody dropped his harpoon.

"Now, go back down, no tricks." Accabo carefully followed Cody down, keeping his arrow pointed at Cody.

"You'd better be careful who you point that thing at," Cody taunted him, contemptuously adding, "little boy."

When Cody reached the ground, Accabo commanded, "Walk straight ahead. No tricks," and followed him, his arrow against Cody's back.

"You don't know how to use that thing, kid."

"I do too," Accabo retorted. "Don't try anything or you're dead." Savoring the thought of the hero's welcome his brothers would give him for capturing this barbarian, Accabo let his attention waver for a moment.

Catching him off guard, Cody whipped around, knocking the bow and arrow from Accabo's hands, and punching him hard in the face. Accabo buckled. In an instant he was on the ground, sprawled on his back, blood flowing from his nose, Cody on top of him, fist raised, ready to strike again.

* * *

Carlos and Lara doubted whether the *Dembu* was worth even investigating so they had gone to look at the spaceport's transmission equipment first. It took only a few minutes for them to conclude that there was no hope of sending a message from Quogue to Lara's Lekadian friend. Discouraged, they let Accabo's brothers lead them, Lara in her wheelchair, through the clearing to the old launch pad, where the first sight that greeted them was Cody pummeling Accabo.

Accabo's brothers broke out laughing.

Carlos yelled, "Cody, stop that, now!"

Reluctantly standing up, Cody muttered to Accabo, "Don't ever try that again."

Accabo, bleeding and unable to open one eye, replied with stunned disbelief, "You're Cody? You are the son of Starman?"

"Cody, get away from him," Carlos barked. Cody obeyed.

Looking up at the rust coated *Dembu*, Carlos and Lara both felt their hearts sink.

"It's hopeless," Carlos muttered under his breath to Lara.

"I know these old freighters," she whispered, "they were manufactured on one of Tarfil's moons generations ago. Horrible ships. No one uses them any more."

"That bad?" Carlos asked.

"I'm amazed to see that one still exists. Even when they were new, they were unreliable, difficult to control. Their crews hated them. Their owners usually ended up selling them for scrap."

"No wonder the Lekadians left it behind." Carlos replied. Turning to Accabo, he introduced himself, Lara, and apologetically, Cody.

Mustering whatever dignity he could manage while repeatedly using his shirt to wipe blood running from his nose, tears welling in his eyes, Accabo got to his feet and stood erect like an officer, facing Carlos, giving him a Lekadian officer's salute. Accabo had rehearsed this moment for years, over and over again, along with the words his father had taught him to say when Starman finally came. Now, standing in front of Starman himself, he finally had the opportunity to say the words he had dreamt for so long of saying. "Captain Carlos Starman, I Accabo orphaned son of Locaru, respectfully request the honor of serving my apprenticeship under you. I will be your student and most obedient servant in everything. My life is yours to do as you will." Accabo then bowed to Carlos in the traditional Lekadian way, remaining bowed, until Lara signaled to Carlos that he was expected to touch the back of the boy's head. Carlos did so, and Accabo stood up erect, looking proud and expectant, despite blood still trickling from his nose and a blackened eye that wouldn't open.

When no one said anything, Accabo announced proudly, "Welcome to the Starship *Dembu.*"

Cody snorted rudely.

Ignoring Cody, Accabo continued, "Captain Starman, I know how to read the language and the command codes of the Lekadians. I can repair machinery and computers. I have done it all my life. I have studied the records the Lekadians left and I know how to find the mines that still orbit our planet from their war. I have studied navigation. My starship is at your command."

Unsure what to say, Carlos thanked Accabo and replied that he would have to inspect the ship. Deep down, however, he felt sick at what he would find. Breaking the reality of it to this enthusiastic boy who wanted so badly to please him would not be easy. He didn't know how he would do it.

"I'm the only one who knows these old freighters," Lara said, "they're not like the slick galactic cruisers you're used to, Carlos." Carlos helped her from her wheelchair and carried her up the stairs, followed by Accabo and behind him, Cody with his weapons.

Suddenly realizing that Cody was behind him, Accabo whirled around to face him and commanded. "Leave that junk outside. On the ground."

"No one takes away my weapons. I already taught you that once."

Accabo blurted out scornfully, "You're the son of Starman? You think you're going to use a bow and arrow in space? A spear?"

Cody answered, "Don't you know anything? It's a harpoon, not a spear."

"I don't care. Leave that junk outside."

"No one takes my weapons." Cody moved defiantly closer to Accabo.

"You're not bringing this stuff on my starship."

Cody snorted, "You call this a starship? The toilets on our starship were better than this piece of junk."

Accabo shouted, "At least I have a ship!"

Carlos intervened, ordering, "Stop it, both of you! Cody, wait outside."

Sitting down resentfully on the launch pad outside the *Dembu*, Cody watched Accabo flash a snide, triumphant grin in his direction before turning to lead Carlos and Lara into the ship's interior, with Lara leaning on Carlos for support.

* * *

It took several days of working day and night to get the *Dembu* ready for space flight, but to both Carlos' and Lara's amazement, the old ship appeared to have at least a chance of making it into space. Before beginning the work, Carlos addressed Accabo's request to be his apprentice by warning him that they were only flying to Tarfil. If they could persuade Lara's childhood friend Lewelle to help them rescue Tobin, they would be taking a Lekadian starship from there. If they didn't get Lewelle's help, they didn't know what they would do next, but in either case, there wasn't any future for the *Dembu* beyond this flight.

"Accabo, if you go with us, I can't promise you will ever return home."

"I have wanted to live in space all my life. Where you go, I will go. It is what my father wanted. He worked on this ship his entire life so I could travel into space. I will do anything you ask. Just don't make me stay here." When Carlos didn't answer, Accabo continued, "Besides, I'm the only one who knows this ship. You need me."

Carlos discussed it with Accabo's brothers before making his decision, finally reluctantly agreeing to take Accabo along with them. Cody wasn't pleased about it, making his displeasure clear to Accabo at every opportunity.

They held off clearing away the trees that hid the *Dembu* as long as possible to avoid discovery by the spaceport attackers. When launch day arrived, Accabo's brothers ordered as many men as they could spare from defending the walls to cut down the trees. After some intense back breaking labor by Cody and spaceport defenders clearing away the trees while Carlos, Lara, and Accabo did last minutes tests on the *Dembu*, all the trees were cut down, the debris was cleared away, and the *Dembu* was ready for take off.

Before the launch, Accabo went one last time to visit his father's grave at the edge of the launch pad. Carlos and Lara let the boy and his brothers kneel at the grave for a while, then walked over and quietly joined them in paying final respects to Locaru, who finally would get his most fervent wish, to be present when his son traveled in the *Dembu* into space. Still annoyed, Cody waited for them inside the *Dembu*.

When Accabo was done praying, he bid his brothers farewell, and then proudly boarded the *Dembu* with Carlos and Lara.

Lekadians

The launch went flawlessly. Accabo's face was radiant as he and Lara carried out Carlos' commands and the *Dembu* responded, struggling little by little from the launch pad where it had sat for generations, up through the clouds, and finally escaping Quogue's gravitational tug. Each creak and groan of the little ship brought him closer to the dream of life in space and contact with the Lekadians that Accabo and his father had shared all their lives.

Despite the skepticism of Carlos and Lara, Accabo never doubted for a moment that his ship would launch successfully and carry them to Tarfil. Now that they had left Quogue behind, and were on the way to Tarfil, he couldn't resist gloating over their obvious relief at surviving the launch.

"You see? I told you the *Dembu* is a worthy starship!"

Cody snorted derisively. He was sitting in the rear of the cockpit with nothing to do, stoically trying to maintain disinterest in either in the ship or in the new sights ahead by focusing all his attention on the image of Quogue receding to a distant speck. He never once looked up from the image, not even to mock Accabo.

"My starship is the only way you'll rescue your friend, Cody. You can't do it without me and my ship."

As usual, Carlos put a stop to the bickering by giving another command to Accabo, and by asking Cody to monitor some instruments, neither of which really needed doing, but it usually bought some peace for at least a little while.

Despite Carlos' initial misgivings both about the *Dembu* and about bringing Accabo along, Accabo turned out to be right when about being the only one able to keep the *Dembu* running. The ship was a patchwork of brilliant but temporary solutions to engineering problems that Accabo and his father had been neither schooled nor equipped to solve. The takeoff had severely stressed many of these temporary fixes, and much of the flight was spent with Carlos and Lara finding problems, and Accabo repairing them. Without Accabo's mechanical brilliance and his intimate knowledge of the *Dembu*, Carlos knew there was no way they would have gotten very far. They would have died a slow death, floating helplessly somewhere in space on a disabled ship, without even a means of signaling for help.

Ignoring Carlos' attempts to smooth relations between them, Accabo and Cody solved the problem themselves by simply avoiding each other as much as possible. Cody found the materials on board to construct a makeshift area in a cargo bay where he could practice archery and throwing his harpoon. He spent most of his time there, to Accabo's growing disgust. Throwing his harpoon was the one outlet Cody could find for the resentment he felt at his father's dependence on a spineless whiner like Accabo. Accabo's open scorn for Cody only made it worse.

Accabo eventually managed to get the *Dembu*'s feeble communications equipment working just adequately so that when they were within ten days of Tarfil, Lara made contact with her friend on the Tarfillian moon Luna One, the Lekadian ambassador Lewelle Sul of Aktawaneh. Four days later Lewelle joined up with them in his family starship, the *Aktawaneh*. Accabo at first felt sad at the prospect of abandoning the *Dembu* and leaving it to float forever in space, but he quickly lost all regret over losing the *Dembu* when he saw the *Aktawaneh*. It was immense, beautiful, and a technological marvel far beyond anything Accabo had known existed. As with most Lekadian starships, it was a family enterprise, with several generations of Lewelle's family living on board, their brains all linked into the computers that operated the ship. The *Dembu* was little more than a crude cart in comparison.

Carlos had developed a strong respect for Accabo in the short time he had known him, but still viewed him as little more than an unusually capable youngster who could have gone far if he had been born into a more technologically advanced society. On the *Aktawaneh*, however, the two of them unexpectedly found themselves on more or less equal footing. Both of them were wide eyed with astonishment at how advanced the Lekadians were, even compared with the civilizations Carlos had visited along the star lanes. Here, Accabo's ability to read Lekadian, though he couldn't yet speak it well conversationally, actually gave him the advantage over Carlos.

During the next several days, Accabo became the teacher and Carlos the student, as Accabo explained to Carlos what he was learning about the *Aktawaneh*. It was vastly more than the computer generated virtual worlds that Carlos was familiar with, coming much closer to a networked brain, but Accabo didn't understand it well enough yet to explain in a way Carlos could grasp. What Carlos was able to grasp, however, was that this ship was both much faster and much larger than any ship ever made on Earth. It wasn't as large as some unimaginably immense ships he had seen in the star lanes, but it was large enough that Lewelle's family was able to live most of their lives onboard. Annoyingly, however, family elders had chosen to segregate their visitors from contact with any Lekadian onboard other than Lewelle.

Lekadian technology had the most immediate impact on Lara. Lewelle brought with him the anti-gravity harness that Lara used to wear before going to Quogue. The harness, which only worked on Lekadian ships and in Lekadian cities, allowed her to stand erect, taking just enough weight off her feet that she could appear to be walking somewhat normally, allowing her to dispense with both her wheelchair and crutches. It took some adjusting for Cody, Accabo, and Carlos to suddenly see Lara walking around nearly as well as they were.

Carlos and Cody hadn't had time for their ritual of singing prayer songs at dawn since leaving HarborSide, but now they finally had the time. They started each day by meeting in a cabin and singing songs that Carlos had learned from his tribal elders, songs first sung by people who never imagined they might someday be sung so far from Earth.

* * *

The trail of Tobin's abductors had grown cold by the time Lewelle first received Lara's message from the *Dembu.* His investigators were able to trace the abductors to the spaceport on Luna Two, but no one could offer even a clue about which direction they had headed from there. For several days after the rendezvous with the *Dembu*, the *Aktawaneh* cruised along the border of the Lekadian Empire in the direction that investigators suspected the abductors might be headed, without any results. When intelligence reports about the abductors began trickling in, Lewelle commenced daily meetings with Lara and Carlos about it.

Cody sat in on every meeting, though there was little he could contribute. He wanted to be there, so he could be part of any decision involving Tobin's rescue. He owed Tobin that.

Lara had warned them while still on the *Dembu* that speaking with Lekadians could be disconcerting, to say the least, because from time to time, they would close their eyes and seem to go into a trance, but come out of it possessing information they did not possess before. She knew they were somehow all interconnected, but didn't understand the technology that enabled it. Even in the schools she had attended, run by Lekadians for children of primitive races, it had never been explained, but simply presented as a fact of Lekadian life. She didn't know whether the Lekadians were deliberately hiding the knowledge of how it was accomplished, or whether as Accabo suggested, it might be an ancient technology that had been somehow encoded into their brains so long ago that today they simply took it for granted.

None of the Lekadians on the ship could speak Quogian or any Earth language, and only Lara could speak conversational Lekadian, so she did all the translating. Accabo had no interest in the meetings that were now being held daily, and felt even less incentive to take part with Cody always there. Accabo's scorn for Cody, for his tattoos and scars and fisherman's clothes, and for his insistence on bringing bows and arrows into space only increased the resentment Accabo felt that this barbarian had the dumb good fortune to be Starman's son. He couldn't understand how Carlos even tolerated having a son like Cody. Consequently, he avoided the meetings whenever possible, and spent his days exploring the ship instead.

On the second day, he outsmarted the security system and found his way into a part of the ship that was supposed to be off-limits to non-Lekadians. When he met some younger members of Lewelle's family, it was a dream come true. These were true Lekadians, trim and neat in their short hair and crisp, tight fitting uniforms, none of them with tattoos, ear rings, or scars from fights. Using his rudimentary knowledge of spoken Lekadian, they managed to communicate and spent the rest of the day together.

They spent the next day together also. The young Lekadians watched in fascination as Accabo eagerly soaked up knowledge, and he gaped in awe at how easily they went into their virtual worlds. Finally one of Lewelle's daughters, Estille, brought out a headset. For Accabo, the moment she put that headset on his head ranked with getting off Quogue as a turning point in his life. Wearing it, he was able to enter the same virtual worlds as his new Lekadian friends, and although he was completely lacking their comfortable agility there, at least he was there, existing in worlds he couldn't have dreamt of just a few days before.

Girls at the spaceport had never interested Accabo. They dreamt only of marrying a boy who would take them away to a barbarian village where they could live as barbarians and raise barbarian children. None had even the slightest interest in the *Dembu*, let alone in riding the *Dembu* to a life in space, or in meeting the Lekadians whom all their grandparents had served.

Estille, however, wasn't like those girls. For her, technology, outer space, and cyberspace were ordinary facts of life like walking, nothing more. She and Accabo spent the next several days together, rarely apart. Accabo felt like he was in heaven, finally knowing a girl who not only shared his interests, but actually knew more than he did, a lot more, and was enjoying teaching him.

Each night, alone in his cabin, he lay awake much of the night, dreaming of a life shared with Estille in space.

Unfortunately, word filtered up to Lewelle's family elders about Accabo and Estille. One day Lewelle's son Edrak showed up unexpectedly, wearing the uniform of a major in the Lekadian military. His formal military bearing was completely unlike the free spirited young

Lekadians Accabo had been meeting. "This area is restricted," he ordered, "Accabo, you will return to your own section of the ship immediately." No amount of pleading by the other young Lekadians would make him yield.

"Please, Edrak, at least let Accabo keep the headset," Estille pleaded.

After consulting with the elders, Edrak gave permission for Accabo to keep it, and then wordlessly escorted him with his headset out of the Lekadian section of the ship.

After that, Accabo spent most of his time in the cabin with Cody and others, no longer exploring the ship physically, but instead spending his time in Lekadian cyberspace, using the headset to explore the knowledge and skills of this ancient race. While Carlos, Lara, and Lewelle discussed slavers and mobsters and strategies, Cody and Accabo both sat in silence, but for very different reasons. In the rare moments when Accabo removed his headset and opened his eyes, he noticed with satisfaction that while he was learning the wonders of Lekadian technology and science, Cody was just sitting there, looking like a barbarian lost in space, not doing or saying anything.

As he learned more of the language, Accabo discovered that he not only had access to databases of knowledge onboard the ship, but even more amazingly, that he was able to access information far across the Lekadian Empire, connected by some technology that he could not yet fathom.

His one regret was that Estille was now off limits to him, but he was confident he could eventually find a way to break the security protocols keeping them apart.

Finding his way through those security protocols to Estille proved to be a greater challenge than he expected, but he did manage to break through Lewelle's security. Soon, whenever Lewelle went into one of his "trances," at least what the others saw as trances, when Lewelle sat back with his eyes closed, seeming impossibly distant from them, Accabo was able to follow him into his cyber world. It was a delicious feeling of accomplishment for Accabo to hide in cyberspace and watch as Lewelle consulted with researchers or police or relatives about the slavers they were pursuing. Other times he could float behind Lewelle through multi dimensional navigational charts that appeared to be maps of this part of the galaxy. Just being there was a thrill. The fact that Lewelle had no idea that he was in there with him only added to the thrill.

The rest of the time, when Lewelle was talking with Lara and Carlos, Accabo explored, learned conversational Lekadian, and found he could wander the universe, or at least a representation of it, without the need of a space ship or any protective gear at all. He completely ignored the meetings going on at the other end of the cabin. These meetings lasted for hours, and were drawn out by the need for Lara to translate every word that was spoken. Even when meetings weren't taking place, when Carlos and Lara were passing their time reading, and Cody was complaining that nobody was doing anything to rescue Tobin except talk, Accabo spent all his waking time in that cabin, in Lekadian cyberspace, soaking up knowledge. For him, this voyage could last a lifetime and still be too short.

* * *

Cody's patience was wearing thin. It wasn't just the ten days of meetings that accomplished nothing, getting them no closer to rescuing Tobin or even knowing where he was. It wasn't even Accabo off in his own little world, ignoring them. Actually, Cody was grateful that Accabo was now out of his hair, but also resentful that Accabo alone seemed to have no interest at all in Tobin. Mostly, Cody was bothered by knowing that over thirty days had passed since Tobin's abduction, but that they were no closer to finding him. Tobin could be almost anywhere by now. His trail was growing colder every day.

After a while, not even throwing his harpoon or shooting arrows in the cargo bay that Lewelle had set up for him could relieve the pressure building up inside him. He felt at the breaking point. It seemed to Cody that they were spending hours talking about the same things over and over again, Lara having to translate the same things repeatedly, always with Lewelle going off into his trances, then coming out and pretending to have some new insight. When Cody tried to contribute, no one took him seriously. Even Carlos seemed to value Accabo's opinions more than his.

Cody was becoming more convinced every day that they were on the wrong course. When he expressed his concerns, no one listened. One day, he finally exploded, jumping to his feet and interrupting, shouting that he was sick of it all. "I demand that you change course now. Now! We're never going to find Tobin this way." As usual, he could offer no explanation, only that he knew they were on the wrong course.

No matter how vigorously Carlos tried to explain that Lewelle was in contact with investigators who knew exactly where the slavers were likely to take Tobin, or Lara told Cody that Lewelle had been a family friend since they were children, and could be trusted, or Lewelle himself reassured him through Lara that they were on the right course, nothing made that feeling in his gut go away.

Most infuriating of all for Cody, however, was catching a glimpse of that little worm Accabo, leering at him with the same sneering eyes as the first time they met at the spaceport.

Tired of his son's belligerent interruptions, Carlos finally ordered him out of the cabin, telling him not to return until he cooled off. As Cody stormed from the cabin, he made an obscene gesture toward Accabo for the self-satisfied smirk he was sure he saw on the boy's face.

Cody was seething. He knew he was right, though he couldn't explain why. He just knew they were following the wrong course. Inside his cabin, he paced the floor, unable to sit down, unable to calm himself, unable to think through the rage roiling his soul. He kept seeing the drugged and panicked look in Tobin's face when he was being dragged away. He couldn't free himself from the memory of how he had let Tobin down just when Tobin needed him the most.

Cody's thoughts drifted to other events of that tumultuous evening, and inevitably, to the monks. Barely aware of what he was doing, he pulled the sack containing his and Tobin's armor from hiding and yanked it open. Holding up Tobin's breastplate and helmet, he recalled the monk's words:

"A day will come when you will see a truth, a truth no one else sees. Even the people you respect the most will laugh at you for the truth you will see so clearly. When that happened to men like you in distant history, what they did at that moment determined whether they became warriors. When that moment arrived, the true warriors stood their ground, proclaiming the truth of their vision. They took their armor from where they had hidden it, they painted their face with the mark of the warrior, and from that moment on, they were warriors."

Proclaiming firmly, "Tobin, I am coming," he took his own breastplate from the sack and put it on, adjusting it carefully. Taking the paint from the sack, he painted his face the way the monks taught him, paying meticulous attention to the smallest details. When the breastplate was finally adjusted right, and the mark of the warrior painted just right, he put on his helmet, cinching it on decisively.

Standing in front of the small mirror, he backed away a step at a time until he could see most of his body. It was the first time he had seen himself as a warrior. That night on Quogue, that was a game he and Tobin were playing. Now it was real. Now he was a warrior. The monks were right. He would rescue Tobin. It didn't matter what anyone else thought, he knew he had to compel Lewelle to change course no matter what the cost.

Leaving his cabin, he went straight to the cargo bay where he had been practicing archery. Carefully placing the quiver full of arrows and his bow over his shoulder in the calculatedly cavalier manner he liked to affect during FourDays, he picked up his harpoon and stood holding it aggressively, like he and Tobin did when they strutted around during the FourDay, medals clanging on their chests. For the first time since Tobin was abducted, Cody felt confident, no longer willing to listen to what others told him to do.

"I've been listening for too long," he thought to himself, "They said to wait. So I waited. They said to be patient. So I was patient. They said to rely on the experience of others. So I relied on others. I listened to Dariel. My father. Lara. Even Lewelle. Listening to a Lekadian! I will listen no more."

Striding confidently toward the meeting cabin, he felt like he did when he was harpooning RedFins, sure of himself, completely focused, the harpoon balanced perfectly in his hand. It was no longer a calculated posture like the bravado he and Tobin liked to put on during FourDays, but the confidence he felt on the sea, where every day was a new test of a man. At sea no one hesitated to act when one of his comrades was in danger, no matter what the personal risk.

Cody knew his time to act had come.

* * *

When Cody barged into the cabin, his face painted with the mark of the warrior, wearing his helmet and breastplate, his bow and arrows slung over his shoulder, holding his harpoon, and calmly but forcefully announced, "You will change course," he was met with stunned silence.

Everyone stared at him in disbelief except Accabo, who prudently closed his eyes.

Carlos was the first to react. Jumping to his feet, enraged, he shouted furiously, "Go to your cabin now. Stay there."

Lara pleaded with them both to calm down. "Please, this is not how to find Tobin."

Soon all three were arguing. Lewelle was oblivious to it, continuing to sit blissfully, eyes closed, in one of his trances.

Opening his eyes, Accabo said timidly, "Excuse me."

No one heard him.

Raising his voice, he called out, "Excuse me."

No one paid him any attention.

He shouted, "I found something!"

Disdain dripping from his voice, Cody ordered, "You stay out of it."

The arguing continued.

Finally Accabo stood up and bellowed, "Listen to me," first in Quogian, then in Lekadian. The arguing stopped. Everyone looked at him, including Lewelle. It was the first time Accabo had said anything in their meetings.

Cody sneered, "I told you to stay out of it."

Lara said, "Let's hear what he has to say."

Cody looked annoyed. "OK, Accabo, I know what you think of me, go ahead, say it."

Deliberately not looking at Cody, Accabo said timidly in Quogian, "I hate to admit it, but I think he's right. Cody. Cody might be right. I think we might need to change course."

Everyone waited while Lara translated the words to Lewelle. He listened impassively.

Accabo turned to Lewelle and repeated in Lekadian what he had just said in Quogian, as Lara translated to Quogian for Carlos and Cody. Accabo continued addressing Lewelle. "I can prove it. Go to that navigation chart or whatever you call it that you were in a little while ago. Before you spoke with that policeman. The one where you were floating free in space. Were you hiding that from us?" Accabo then switched to speaking Quogian and addressed the others. "Ask him if he's telling us the truth. I hate to admit it, but I think Cody may be right."

Lewelle looked astonished for the first time on this journey. "How do you know where I go?" he demanded incredulously.

With Lara continuing to translate in Quogian, Accabo replied in Lekadian, "Just go there," looking directly into Lewelle's eyes.

Lewelle sat back and closed his eyes. Accabo adjusted his headset, and closed his eyes.

Moments later, Lewelle and Accabo were floating in what appeared to be space, but with the stars and planets all much closer to them than in reality. Accabo pointed to the system where he believed Tobin was being held and showed him where he got the information.

Returning to the cabin, Lewelle and Accabo opened their eyes. Lara translated while Lewelle said, "Lewelle says Accabo's been spying on him," then turning to Accabo, she said, "He wants to know how long you've been doing this?"

Accabo replied, "I know what he said. I wasn't spying. At least I didn't mean to. I discovered this a couple of days ago. I was afraid to tell him. I didn't want him to take away my cyberspace access. But I still want to know why he's lying."

Lara translated Lewelle's response. "This is very remarkable. I didn't know Quogians were capable of what Accabo has done."

Looking straight at Accabo, Lewelle said, "Let's go back." Without waiting for Lara's translation, Accabo closed his eyes. Lewelle did the same.

They were back in the space with the stars. Lewelle asked, "Accabo, this is very important. Did Cody learn about this from you?"

"No. We hate each other. If I told him, he wouldn't believe it. He wouldn't believe anything I say."

"And you probably wouldn't believe anything he said. Am I right, Accabo?"

"Believe him? Of course not."

"Good. That's all I need to know. Let's go back to the others. Wait. One more thing. I haven't lied to anyone. If I'm wrong about where Tobin is, it's a mistake, and I'll correct it."

When they opened their eyes, they found Carlos berating Cody, accusing him of being rude and disrespectful and of making it harder for the rest of them to find Tobin, and Cody replying angrily. Through Lara, Lewelle ordered them to stop. After the shouting finally stopped, he stood up and asked, "Cody, let me examine your armor."

After Lara translated, Cody replied, "So you can steal it like you stole all the other armor from Quogue? I demand you change course now!"

"There's nothing to examine," Carlos said bitterly, "my son was duped by some deranged monks. They sold him this junk and told him he was the reincarnation of some ancient warrior. It's garbage."

Lara asked Carlos to be quiet, then pleaded with Cody, "I want my son back even more than you do. You have to trust Lewelle."

"Trust a Lekadian? Everyone knows you can't trust Lekadians."

"You don't know what you're talking about, Cody. Even Tobin trusts Lekadians. He grew up with Lekadians. So did I. We just couldn't tell anyone on Quogue. I have known Lewelle since we were children. You can trust him."

Pointing to Accabo, but not looking at him, Cody said, "Even he says I'm right!"

"I said I think you're right," Accabo retorted.

"Cody, please. Just tell Lewelle about the monks," asked Lara. "I promise you, Lewelle will change course if you are right. Please. Do it for Tobin."

Reluctantly, Cody explained all that happened with the monks. When Cody finished, Lewelle examined the breastplate closely, then closed his eyes and went into one of his trances.

Pointing to Accabo, now sitting with his eyes closed, Cody asked Lara, "Is that kid in there with him? Wherever it is they go."

"I don't know, Cody," replied Lara, "I think Accabo has been learning things the rest of us can't even imagine."

Finally, Lewelle opened his eyes and turned to Carlos. Speaking through Lara, he said, "It's as I thought. Those monks are trouble. They always have been, even when we were on Quogue. They couldn't resist when they realized they had your son."

Looking victoriously at Cody, Carlos said, "You see? I told you those monks were charlatans. Whatever you gave them for this junk was too much. It's probably sold in every cheap bazaar on the planet."

After Lara translated, Lewelle replied, "I didn't say they were charlatans. I'd be surprised if they took money from your son. That's not like them."

Cody confirmed that he had not paid anything, not even for the food they ate.

Lara continued to translate for Lewelle, who was now examining the breastplate closely. "Look at this. This is genuine. It's not junk." Both Lara and Carlos came over and examined it while Lewelle continued, "It's been used in battle, a battle where they used swords, not modern weapons. Look, you can see where it's been damaged. That's from battle. The design on the armor is very old. It's from an ancient Quogian warrior class. The armor is genuine."

"What are they after then?" Carlos asked.

"Gullible boys like your son. I don't know how to say this in a way you will understand. I know that you and your son pray to your gods every morning, and I know the Quogians have their own gods, but our race is far more ancient than the people of either Earth or Quogue. We were exploring distant stars long before either of your races existed. We no longer have gods. We know that besides matter and energy, the only other forces of significance are intelligence and intuition. There is nothing else. That's all there is, no gods, no spirits, no magic forces. Just intelligence and intuition."

Carlos replied, "You are so wrong."

Speaking as usual through Lara, Lewelle replied, "You and I will never agree on this. I am not seeking to convince you. I am only here to save Lara's son." Turning to face Cody, Lewelle spoke slowly, "We will save Tobin. I promise you that." After waiting until Lara had translated it, he turned back to Carlos. "Saving Tobin should be all that matters to us. Cody is right about that. The private things we believe or don't believe about gods should not concern us. But religious belief does explain why the monks wanted your son."

Pausing for a moment, Lewelle continued, "When we occupied Quogue, we tried to eradicate those monks and their teachings. We took their monasteries from them and we burned their poisonous books. We made their monasteries into schools and factories, modern things that would benefit the people of Quogue. We even took all the ancient battle armor the monks preserved, like the armor Cody is wearing, and stored it on our home world, where they could never get hold of it. We obviously failed to find all the armor."

"All we wanted was for Quogue to have education and technology that would free them from the ignorance that was holding them back, but when we left, Quogians destroyed it all. They leveled the factories we built, they closed our schools, they smashed the technology and machinery we built for them. We left everything there for their benefit, but they obliterated every trace of it. They even destroyed the old monasteries we had converted, simply because the monasteries contained things we had built. Now it looks like the monks are returning. Cody, did any of the monks have severely disfigured faces?"

After Lara translated the question, Cody told Lewelle about the old monk.

"That makes sense," Lewelle replied, "we coated their sacred texts with genetic agents that would disfigure them. We hope it would discourage followers, but we were wrong. Were any of the younger monks disfigured?"

Cody replied that they weren't.

"That's because the genetic agent loses effectiveness over time."

Lewelle continued, "We were able to take away their monasteries and books, but I guess not even disfigurement could stop them from peddling their ignorance. I did not know they were back." Turning to Carlos, he said, "they try to lure in youngsters like your son, boys who want only to do good, and then they twist their minds with ignorance and tales of ancient heroes."

"We have stories like that on Earth, ancient stories of warriors and heroes. We need the stories. They give us wisdom, and help us remain brave, and true to our faith," Carlos replied.

"But you said you don't believe what the monks told your son," Lewelle said.

"No, of course not. You don't become a warrior just by some deranged monk slashing your hand and muttering mystical nonsense. I am a warrior. I am the only true warrior in this cabin. I trained in the military on Earth, I fought, I studied, I worked hard, I learned discipline, it took many years. You don't do it with a single oath."

"But yours is not the romantic warrior image the monks are offering. To a young man who believes in magic forces or gods, what the monks offer has a special appeal," Lewelle replied.

"What about Tobin?" demanded Cody, "He's why we're here." Pointing to Lewelle, he said to Lara, "Ask him why he's lying to us."

"Maybe Lewelle really doesn't know where Tobin is," said Accabo.

"You said he was lying."

"I know what I said, Cody, but now I don't think so."

"Just tell me, yes or no, are we heading in the right direction?" demanded Cody.

Accabo replied firmly, "No."

"Please, be patient," Lara pleaded, "Lewelle will find Tobin."

"But we're heading in the wrong direction," protested Cody, "We'll never find Tobin this way."

"The fisherman may be right," said Accabo, adding, "for once."

* * *

That evening, after dinner, Lara came to Carlos and told him that Lewelle needed to see him. "It's important," she said.

Cody, now dressed as a fisherman again, asked, "Are we changing course?"

"It's about Accabo, but Lewelle said it could help us find Tobin. You can come, but only if you agree to no outbursts," Lara answered. "Do you promise? No outbursts?"

"And no weapons," Carlos added.

"I promise."

Entering the cabin, they found Accabo already there, speaking with Lewelle in Lekadian. Using Lara as an interpreter, Lewelle welcomed them, saying he had an important proposal to make, but he would not do anything without Carlos' approval. He praised Accabo and the progress Accabo had made in learning their language and technology, but said that Accabo had gone nearly as far as he was capable of without enhancement. "The only way for Accabo to progress further is to have what you would think of as an organic computer embedded in his brain. It will allow him to access Lekadian knowledge all across the Empire, almost like Lekadians." Looking directly at Cody, he added, "It could be the key to finding Tobin."

He went on to assure them that it was fairly safe, and would be done by robotic surgeons. It had never been performed on a Quogian before, but they had done it to promising individuals from similar humanoid races on other planets, with few adverse affects. "In fact, I offered one to Lara after her shuttle accident, when she lost the use of her legs. With this brain enhancement, she could probably be walking normally again. She wouldn't need the harness she's wearing now."

"Why didn't you have the operation?" Carlos asked.

"I guess I'm just old fashioned. I just don't want anyone monkeying with my brain. Besides, the operation is really only safe for young people. At my age, it's riskier. It wasn't worth it for me. I'm no expert, but I think it's probably safe for Accabo."

Lewelle agreed. "Accabo is almost too old now for it to be done safely. If he's ever going to get one, now's the time."

"I don't have the right to make this decision," Carlos answered, "It's a decision for Accabo's family to make."

"My parents are dead. Please. My father would want this for me," Accabo pleaded.

"Is he legal age on Quogue to make his own decision?" Carlos asked.

Lewelle answered, "There are no laws regarding it on Quogue, but that doesn't matter. We're not on Quogue now. We are in

Lekadian territory, under Lekadian law. Quogians aren't covered by Lekadian legal protections."

"Why not?" Carlos asked.

Lewelle replied with some embarrassment, "They're not advanced enough."

Cody looked suddenly angry, but said nothing.

Lewelle continued, "Lekadian law does not require me to get anyone's permission for this. I'm asking you as a courtesy, Carlos, because Accabo is your apprentice. By Quogian tradition, this gives you the responsibilities toward him of a parent over a minor. It doesn't matter what his age is."

Carlos turned to Accabo. "Are you sure this is what you want? They've never performed this procedure on a Quogian before. What are the dangers, Lewelle?"

"He could die or suffer permanent major brain damage. It's not likely, but we can't rule it out."

"Is it worth the risk to you, Accabo?" asked Carlos.

"Yes. Definitely."

"Then I give permission for my apprentice to undergo this procedure."

As everyone was leaving, Carlos approached Lewelle with a question. "Would your technology allow me to transmit a message to Earth?"

"Yes, without question. We'll need to work out technical details, but I'm sure we can do it. It won't be received on Earth within your lifetime, of course."

"I know. This might be the only opportunity I ever have to let Earth know what happened to my crew. At least future generations will know what happened to us."

"Send me the message and any technical information necessary to transmit it to Earth. I'll see that it's sent."

Rescue

Accabo was sitting in his usual place, eyes closed, oblivious to anything happening around him. A small part of his scalp was shaven where the computer enhancements had been surgically inserted. His headset was sitting unused on the table beside him

Lewelle's first announcement on starting the daily meeting, that they had changed course during the night, wasn't news to anyone. Carlos, Cody, and Lara knew it instinctually from habitually looking at the stars for navigation, and Accabo knew it from his newfound abilities in Lekadian cyberspace. Acknowledging that Cody was right about the course, Lewelle announced he now knew the exact planet where Tobin was being held and that Accabo was at this moment researching all that was known about the planet, looking for anything that might help in rescuing Tobin.

After bringing Accabo back from cyberspace and as usual using Lara as his interpreter, Lewelle announced that his son, Major Edrak Sul of Aktawaneh, had worked out a rescue plan.

"I warn you, not everybody will be happy with it. But this is the way it will be done, if the rescue is to be launched from the *Aktawaneh.*" Turning to Carlos, Lewelle continued, "As a military officer, you might rightfully expect to make these decisions, but I know you understand that my position as an ambassador requires strictly following certain Lekadian protocols."

"Can I at least meet Major Sul and discuss it with him?" Carlos asked.

"No. I've made it clear from the start. My ship's elders have decreed that there will be no contact between non-Lekadians and Lekadians other than myself. The strategy is final."

Cody started to object, but Carlos interrupted him. "Wait. Let's listen to what Lewelle is proposing." Carlos refrained from adding that he was beginning to understand why Quogians resented Lekadians.

Lewelle went on to describe what each person's role would be. "We have learned that the slavers have a ship headed this way. We think it will arrive in at most three or four days. Possibly sooner. Carlos will remain onboard my ship, with me, monitoring the rescue. He will be ready to immediately evacuate the rescuers if it becomes necessary."

Cody immediately objected. "My father should be down there with me. Tobin is our friend. We're the ones who should rescue him. Besides, there's no one else who can do it. Just me and my father."

Lewelle replied, "Carlos will remain up here. That's how it will be. Lara knows Lekadian shuttlecraft, so she will pilot the shuttlecraft that takes the rescuers to and from the planet."

Cody broke in again. "She's a cripple. How can she be a pilot?"

"Don't you ever say that again," Lara shot back, "Legs or not, I'm the best damned pilot on this ship."

"She's one of the best shuttle pilots on or off this ship," added Lewelle.

Cody continued, "So who are the rescuers? You only have me left."

Lara translated what Cody said, and in response, Lewelle simply looked at Accabo.

It took a moment for Cody to realize what Lewelle had in mind. "No! No way!" Cody shouted, jumping to his feet. "You think I'm going to risk my life dragging Accabo along? No, No, No!"

Accabo jumped to his feet, equally furious, showing anger no one on the ship had ever seen or expected in him, so furious that he spoke half in Lekadian and half in Quogian while Lara tried to translate. "You expect me to risk my life with him? He imagines he's some ancient warrior! He brought arrows with him to fight in space. Arrows! What a fool! If he goes, I stay here. You need me here, on this ship, with the computer. Besides, I'm no fighter. This is my place."

"Accabo's right," Cody shouted, "he belongs up here."

After calm was restored, Carlos said, "I want to fight alongside you, Cody. It's always been my dream. But Lewelle is right. Lara is the best one to operate the shuttle. You'll need Accabo down there. He's the only one who has a chance of bypassing their security systems. I can't do it. Neither can you. He can. That leaves me to monitor things up here, and to mount a rescue if something goes wrong, and Lewelle to coordinate the operation with the Lekadian authorities. There is no other way."

"What about Edrak?" Cody asked Lewelle, "Why can't he work up here so my father can rescue Tobin with me?"

"Lekadian diplomatic protocol forbids it. No Lekadian on this ship can be directly involved."

Surprising even himself, Accabo blurted out, "Then send me. Alone. I know from the computer what's down there. I know better than anyone. I can do it. But don't send me with a crazy fisherman who thinks he's an ancient warrior and wants to use a bow and arrows in space. He'll just get us both killed."

Lewelle spoke again, with Lara as usual translating for him. "Cody and Accabo will be the warriors on this rescue. That's final. Accabo has the intelligence and the ability to control their computers. Cody has the intuition and the fighting skills needed to get them out alive. Edrak decided that Cody and Accabo are the ones who should go. I agreed. The ship's elders have approved it. This is how it will be."

Cody and Accabo both sat sulking, neither willing even to look at the other.

* * *

The next two days were spent preparing for the rescue. The first day began with a briefing by Accabo on what he had learned about the slave camp where Tobin was being held. "The planet is sparsely populated by a primitive humanoid race. They only recently began using metal. The planet used to be a favorite for big game hunters but it's now considered too dangerous to visit. The indigenous people there have learned that capturing unwary hunters and bartering them to the criminals who run the camp is an easy way to get metal and weapons."

"How did they capture Tobin?" Carlos asked.

"They didn't," Accabo replied, "the camp where Tobin is being held is run by criminals from other worlds. It's relatively new. They set it up after Lekadian authorities ran them off a different world."

As Accabo continued speaking, Cody found old feelings of hostility toward Lekadians growing stronger. After all, Lewelle could just as easily have given this talk himself. He had access to the same information as Accabo. Cody felt sure that the only reason Lewelle had asked Accabo to give them this information was to make Accabo the boss in rescuing Tobin. For the most part, Cody stared down at the floor, or at his father, or at the walls, looking at anything other than Accabo. Once in a while, he could sense Accabo's eyes on him, and at those times especially, he made a point of pretending he wasn't paying attention.

Nonetheless, Cody did listen. He listened to every word. Accabo might be a disgusting creep who would do anything a Lekadian asked, but as a fighter, Cody was realistic enough to know that if he was going to rescue Tobin and bring him back alive, he needed all the information about the planet he could get, regardless of the source. He just wasn't going to give Accabo any satisfaction. Besides, back on Quogue when he was working with Accabo's brothers in clearing away the trees that surrounded the *Dembu*, he learned from them about Accabo's cowardice. Cody knew that in the end, Accabo would find some reason to skip out on this dangerous mission, just as he shirked defense duties at the spaceport. That would be Cody's moment of triumph, when this little creep was too cowardly to actually go on the mission, and Carlos had to take his place at the last minute.

Cody realized he had let his mind drift. Keeping his eyes down, gazing at the floor, he focused again on what Accabo was saying. "Lewelle, don't cloak your ship. The slavers have the technology to detect cloaking. Hide your ship behind the moon instead of cloaking. When the slavers learned that Lekadians were coming to their last camp, they carried away as many of the slaves as they could, then they destroyed the camp and killed the slaves they didn't have time to get out. They'll know your ship doesn't have the firepower to stop them, so they'll do it here too."

At the end of Accabo's talk, Cody stood up to leave. Lewelle stopped him, saying, "I think Accabo has forgotten something."

When Accabo remained silent, Lewelle asked, "Accabo?"

Cody sat back down, and waited.

Finally, reluctance in his voice, Accabo said, "Whoever goes down to rescue Tobin will pass security sensors buried in the ground. These sensors will detect any sort of electronic equipment. That means the rescuers won't be able to carry any Lekadian weapons, because they all have electronics in them."

"No weapons? I won't let my son go down there unless he can defend himself," objected Carlos.

"I can defend myself. I have my arrows and harpoon."

"Don't be stupid!" Carlos shot back.

"I hate to agree with the fisherman, but those are the only weapons he can take," replied Accabo.

"What about that computer in your brain, Accabo? That's electronic. Won't the sensors detect that?" asked Cody.

"I don't know," replied Accabo.

Lewelle added, "I've already told Accabo that he doesn't have to go on this mission if he doesn't want to. We just don't know if the sensors are calibrated to detect organic electronics."

"That's just great!" objected Cody. "He can skip out to save his own life, but I can't object to risking my life by having him tag along!"

"Neither of you is being ordered to go," answered Lewelle. "But the mission can only succeed if both of you go. Accabo, you can't reach Tobin or get him out without a fighter like Cody to protect you. Cody, you can't get through the security gates without Accabo's help. Tobin's your friend. Accabo's never even met him. You don't have to go."

Lara interrupted. "Tobin's my son. Cody, Accabo, you will both answer to me if this mission fails because you can't stop your bickering."

"I'll rescue Tobin, I promise you," Cody told her, "no matter how much Accabo slows me down."

As Cody left the meeting, he couldn't resist a last gibe at Accabo, asking him, "So you finally admit that bringing my arrows and harpoon was a good idea?"

Accabo didn't reply.

"Well?"

"OK. Your weapons are the only ones we can use down there. Happy? But I still say your mystical warrior nonsense is going to get us both killed."

"Suppose they detect that computer in your brain? We'll both be killed if that happens. Aren't you afraid of that?"

Accabo remained silent.

After the meeting, they began preparing for the rescue. Lara practiced on the shuttle and trained Carlos in shuttle operation in case he needed to mount a rescue. Everyone spent every available minute studying the information Accabo had gathered about the planet. Cody got some pleasure from repaying Accabo for his constant gibes at him for bringing arrows into space by reminding him that they wouldn't have any weapons at all for rescuing Tobin if he had left them on Quogue as Accabo had demanded. At Carlos's insistence, he tried teaching Accabo some basic fighting tactics, but despaired of him ever learning. In the two days they spent together preparing, the only thing Cody and Accabo could agree on was that they could never work together.

They expected to have a third day to prepare, but Lewelle learned that the slavers' ship was closer than they expected, so they decided to mount the rescue a day early, despite torrential rains that would make the rescue more difficult.

When they met at the shuttle for the trip to the planet's surface, Cody was dressed in the rough, heavy clothes he wore at sea, which could keep him warm in very wet and cold conditions, but Accabo was wearing his usual light clothes and a coat, nothing more.

"You fool, don't you know anything?" Cody goaded Accabo, "It's going to be wet and cold down there."

"It's all I have."

Carlos ordered Cody to bring some of his own clothes for Accabo. When Cody returned and handed the clothes to him, Accabo complained, "They smell like fish!"

"Of course they smell like fish, I'm a fisherman!" Cody shot back.

Reluctantly, Accabo went into the shuttle to change.

While waiting, Cody painted his face with the mark of the warrior and put on his helmet and breastplate.

Accabo stepped out of the shuttle, wearing Cody's fishing clothes. Much shorter than Cody and lacking his muscles, Accabo was now a mildly comic looking figure, with his pants and sleeves rolled up slightly, and the clothes hanging baggily from his lanky frame. He was clearly very unhappy and looked far from heroic, but at least was dressed for the conditions.

Cody laughed.

Accabo blurted out, "Look at him! I can't go with him in that stupid warrior get up! He'll get us both killed."

Cody shouted, "He's going to get me killed. He can't fight. My father's the only one who can do this."

Lara lost her temper again. "That's my son down there. I've already told you, if you come back without him because you two can't get along, you'll regret it. I promise you, I'll leave both of you stranded down there for the slavers to find. I'll personally sell you to them!"

"She means it, boys, don't cross her," said Carlos. He was, however, nearly as unhappy with his son's warrior getup as Accabo. "Lewelle, won't Cody's armor trigger alarms down there?"

"Edrak doesn't think it likely," Lewelle replied. "The slavers would get too many false alarms from the planet's indigenous people. They adorn their bodies prodigiously with metal. The slavers expect attackers to come in large forces, armed with electronic weapons, not just two boys armed with primitive weapons." Lewelle paused while he looked Cody over. "Besides, just look at Cody. Dressed like that, he knows he's a warrior. I approve."

Cody smirked at Accabo, who looked unhappier than ever, stunned that a Lekadian might approve of Cody as a mystical warrior.

Lara took the pilot's seat in the shuttle. Cody loaded his bow and a quiver full of arrows, his harpoon, and a backpack, and then sat next to her. Accabo sat behind them, still unhappy about wearing bulky fisherman's clothes that smelled of fish, and about having his life depend on a crazed would-be warrior who despised the sight of him. Tobin's bow, arrows, and harpoon were on the seat next to Accabo.

* * *

The days and the years Sophia had spent in the hands of the slavers were an amorphous haze of jobs and dormitories and fellow slaves being moved in and out of her life by decision makers she did not know and for reasons she had long ceased to wonder about. She lived day to day, sustained mostly by the hope that Cody and Carlos might still be alive and free. As a military officer, she kept a mental list of the handful of *Marco Polo* crewmembers and other slaves who might be counted upon if an opportunity for escape or rebellion presented itself, and though she was watchful for an opportunity, she knew the futility of hoping for it ever to happen. In this place, hope could only lead to disappointment or death.

Fifteen days ago, the mental wall Sophia had so carefully constructed and maintained, segregating planning for escape from hoping for escape, crumbled in an instant. It happened during their evening meal. Sophia was sitting with Tarfillian acquaintances when a new Tarfillian inmate happened to overhear a conversation between her and another *Marco Polo* crewmember. The Tarfillian immediately broke into their conversation. "Are you Sophia Jackson from the *Marco Polo*?" When Sophia acknowledged that she was, he continued, "I am friends with Carlos Jackson and Cody Jackson. My name is Tobin."

The news electrified her. Nothing had been the same since. She took advantage of every moment she could be with Tobin to pump him for information, and in those two brief weeks, she became closer to him than anyone else in the camp other than Reyas. Against her better judgment, she began allowing herself the dangerous indulgence of hoping for escape, despite knowing from experience that hope, any hope at all, was in this place a futile trap.

Tobin had told her that Cody was now a warrior. She tried to picture the ten year old child she had last seen on the *Marco Polo*, a boy who was born in space on the most advanced starship Earth had ever produced, now a seventeen year old fisherman warrior on a backward planet. It wasn't the future she had hoped for him, but at least he was alive and doing well.

Tobin's presence was a mixed blessing. He brought exciting news about loved ones she had feared she might never hear of again, and overnight became a second son for her, but she now had the added pain of knowing that this second son was a slave, doomed to live the rest of his life in this camp. She wondered what he looked like before they shaved his hair. It was only a matter of time before the fat disappeared from his body, and the ready smile from his face. Just as she had seen Reyas waste away from a healthy, beautiful girl to a shaven headed slave with the same desperate look as everyone else, Sophia knew she would now witness the same terrible transformation in Tobin.

Tobin's so far unbroken, boisterous spirits would make him a target for sadistic guards and even for some fellow slaves. Already, she had seen others take notice of him. In this swamp of broken and malevolent souls, Tobin's buoyant spirit and ready smile stood out like a waterspout, and like a waterspout, could not last. Either his spirit would be broken, or he would curry favor with the guards by becoming one of the hated trustees, or one day he would simply disappear and never be seen again. There were no other possibilities.

Now, Tobin had disappeared. The guards had taken him away yesterday. No one had seen him since. Sophia had seen it happen before with others. Occasionally when a slave was taken away like this, it meant a special work detail outside the camp, but those assignments were only given to trusted slaves who had been here a long time. More commonly, it meant that a potential troublemaker was going to be punished severely, or eliminated. These slaves rarely returned, and when they did, they were broken physically and mentally. Sophia cringed at the thought of the ever ebullient Tobin coming to such a terrible end.

* * *

Lara set the shuttle down in a small valley where Accabo thought it was unlikely to be detected. Outside, rain fell torrentially. Cody opened the door. Rain gusted in, instantly drenching the seat. Cody jumped to the ground, but Accabo hesitated. Reaching up, Cody impatiently grabbed Accabo's arm and pulled him roughly down from the shuttle. Accabo landed on all fours in a thick mud puddle, lost his balance, and rolled over on his side. Laughing, Cody extended a hand to help him up, but Accabo ignored the extended hand and climbed out of the mud without assistance.

Holding a blaster threateningly, Lara warned, "If you two keep bickering and you don't rescue my son, don't bother to come back."

"I'll rescue him," Cody assured her.

"You'll both rescue him," Lara shot back.

When Accabo tried washing off some of the mud, Cody flashed him a disdainful look, turned, and walked briskly up the hill. Accabo gave up washing and struggled to catch up. "Wait for me, Cody. Lara said for us to work together." Going down the other side of the hill was easy, but just ahead, the entire floor of the little canyon was flooded. Cody stopped at the water's edge, struggling in the dark to sense the safest way across. Accabo had just caught up with him when Cody waded in. Accabo hesitated.

"You can stay here, Accabo. I'll meet you back here after I rescue Tobin." Cody waded forward, deeper into the water, ignoring Accabo standing hesitantly at the water's edge. Finally Accabo plunged into the water, racing to catch up to Cody, but losing his footing and falling in completely. Regaining his footing, he moved as fast as he could in the deepening water, finally catching up with Cody in water that was chest deep. Cody was stepping carefully, one foot at a time, watching for signs of swift currents, and feeling for underwater hazards. "If you have to tag along, Accabo, at least be careful. Stay right behind me."

Finally reaching the other side, they were faced with choosing between the two trails: one that went up a steep, muddy hill to their left, or a more gently sloping trail that went straight ahead.

Accabo wanted to go up the muddy hill to the left. "The computer showed this way is a lot shorter."

"It's too steep. You're not strong enough."

"Yes I am."

Cody declared, "We're going the other way."

"Why? It's longer."

Accabo began climbing up the steep hill. "Watch, I can do it, Cody."

"Do what you want. I'll get Tobin."

"Cody, you can't get through their security."

"I'll find a way."

"How? With a harpoon? How are you going to do it? I've been studying their security for days. I can interface with their computer. Do you have a Lekadian computer in your brain?"

Cody remained silent.

"I didn't think so. Do you think I want to go with you? No. A hundred times no. But we have to rescue Tobin. He's your friend. Not mine."

"Stay here or come with me, Accabo, whatever you want."

Watching Cody walk away, Accabo shouted after him, "Who made you the boss, Cody? We're supposed to work together."

"Then come with me!" Cody shouted without looking back.

Accabo scrambled through the mud back down the hill and ran after Cody, finally catching up to him just as he came to a fork in the trail. Accabo, breathing hard, collapsed to the ground.

"It's kind of wet to lie down, isn't it Accabo?"

Accabo was breathing too hard to answer. He watched as Cody looked back and forth at the two trails. Still breathing heavily, Accabo said, "Left. We go left."

Muttering something inaudible, Cody resumed walking, taking the left fork.

Accabo called out, "You will see a fence and a gate just over the next hill." Getting to his feet, he struggled to catch up with Cody.

At the crest, they saw the fence and the gate near the top of the next hill.

"Accabo, we can take a rest if you're tired."

"Not yet!" Accabo replied defiantly.

When they reached the gate, Accabo sat down in the mud, sighing with relief, then sprawled out on his back, rain pouring on his face, breathing very hard, while Cody examined the gate. Giving up on the gate, Cody sat down next to Accabo, who couldn't resist goading him. "It's kind of wet to be sitting on the ground, isn't it?"

"Look who's talking!"

After a few moments of silence, Accabo admitted, "You were right."

"About what?"

"Clothes. I'd be freezing to death if I wore my own clothes. Thanks."

"Don't worry about it. I did it for Tobin."

"You two must be pretty good friends."

"The best. Why'd you come, Accabo? You don't even know him."

"Back on Quogue, before we left, I swore an oath to your father. I will do anything to serve him."

"Do you really mean that?"

"Yes. I waited all my life to get into space. I prayed for years that if Starman came and took me to space, I would do anything for him, even give my life for him. He needed me down here, so I came."

They remained silent for a few moments. The only sound was the pouring rain.

"How are you feeling, Accabo? Ready to go on?"

"Yes." Standing up, Accabo went to the gate, examined it, and then closed his eyes. A few moments later, the gate unlocked.

"How did you do that?"

"It's just a computer, Cody. It's easy. But here's where things get dangerous."

"What's the danger?"

Accabo signaled Cody to be quiet.

* * *

In the command station of the *Aktawaneh*, Carlos sat alone, monitoring several holographic displays. Lewelle entered and asked in Lekadian, "Have you heard from the boys?"

An automatic translator spoke it in English. It was an older form of English, probably about the seventeenth century, but Carlos was nonetheless able to understand it. He looked up in astonishment. "A translator? It knows ancient English?"

"Our explorers have visited Earth in the past. I apologize that it's an older version of the language than you probably speak."

"If you have translators, why did you make Lara do all the translating in our meetings?"

"I didn't know then that we had an English translator. As for a Quogian translator, some of the complaints the Quogians have about us are justified. My people never thought it was worth programming a translator for Quogian. Our people are working on one now, at my request. The language has enough in common with Tarfillian that it won't take long."

Carlos said, "We are maintaining radio silence. Lara will only call if something goes wrong." Lewelle listened as it was translated into Lekadian.

After a few moments of silence, Carlos said, "You surprised me when you approved of Cody's mystical warrior getup."

"You know my people gave up all our gods hundreds of generations ago. I don't understand much of it. But when I saw Cody tonight, a warrior going to free his fellow warrior, I realized that people do need their heroes and myths… and they need belief. That was the mistake my people made when they colonized Quogue. We tried to eradicate all the Quogian myths, legends, and beliefs. We only wanted to modernize Quogue. We thought it would benefit Quogians. I am coming to realize that it was a huge mistake. We believed that ancient Quogian beliefs in mythical heroes and gods should be eliminated for the Quogians' own good, but now… I don't know."

"You're saying that there's something to it?"

"You're the one who believes in gods, Carlos. You know better than I do. You saw your son tonight. You explain it to me."

"I'm a military officer. I know how a man becomes a warrior. It takes years of training, discipline, learning to follow orders. Not just a crazed monk giving him some old armor and face paint."

"Yet, when your son left tonight, he looked a warrior. He was a warrior. I saw it in his eyes and in his bearing."

"Yes, I saw it too. I don't understand it. To be truthful, it scares me."

"You say you became a warrior through training and discipline. Yet I have the feeling that you perhaps were born for a different path. Maybe there are two types of warriors?"

"Two types?"

"You made yourself into a warrior through hard work. But you were not born to be a warrior, am I right?"

Carlos thought for a few moments before answering. "It's true. I only learned to fight to prove myself to the kids I was hanging out with. I never wanted to be a warrior."

"That's the difference between you and your son. Training made you into a warrior, but Cody was born a warrior. Training will make him a better warrior, but even without training, he is a warrior. He was born to it, just as I think you were born to explore. Each of you has your own gifts."

They sat in silence, staring out into space at the moon that was blocking them from detection on the planet's surface. Finally Lewelle spoke again, in Lekadian. "My government contacted me a little while ago. It's about Earth."

"Oh?"

"I requested them to build a transmitter to send your message to Earth. In researching it, my government learned that your planet is in danger. Some of the more aggressive races learned about it from your travels along the star lanes. You need our protection. A Lekadian battle cruiser in orbit around Earth will help protect it against most invaders. Your planet does not stand a chance alone."

Carlos waited a few moments for it to be translated into English, and thought it over before replying, looking over the displays, then turned back to Lewelle. "What would your people want from this?"

"We are an ancient race. We are powerful, but no longer growing. We have lost our legends and our myths, even most of our beliefs. We are just like the Quogians in that way, except that we did it to ourselves. We have no one else to blame."

"How can Earth help?"

"When I saw your son tonight, I saw a future. Your son believes. He has inner strength. He needs training, but he can be a hero. We need the vision he carries in him. When I saw him, when I felt the energy and strength he emanated, the truth hit me that none of us, Lekadians, or Quogians, or Earthlings, none of us can stand alone. Your people have youthful energy, the Quogians have their close ties to the natural world and ancient traditions, we Lekadians have our intellectual and military power. Together, we can learn from each other. We can be far stronger together than separate."

"That's all a little too much to think about now. My boy is down there. I don't know whether he is dead or alive. That's all I can think about right now."

After waiting for the translation, Lewelle responded, "Forgive me for intruding. I would feel the same way if it were Edrak down there. We will talk later, after your son is safe. Let me know if you need anything."

* * *

The rain was falling harder. Despite Cody and Accabo trying to walk quietly, doing their best to step only on rocks and clumps of weeds as the puddles grew wider and deeper, the darkness and driving torrents of rain made it impossible to see anything below the water's surface. Soon, they were simply putting one foot ahead of the other. No matter how carefully they stepped into the water, the squishing sound they made pulling their feet out of the mud seemed to grow with each step. Accabo's much lighter weight worked to his advantage. Regardless how lightly Cody tried to step, his feet seemed to sink more deeply into the mud, and the sucking sound as he pulled each foot out of the mud seemed almost thundering compared with Accabo's.

Turning to face Cody, Accabo whispered, "Your armor. Leave it behind. It's weighing you down. You're making too much noise."

"No."

Accabo put his hand under Cody's backpack to test its weight. "This is too heavy, Cody, what's in it?"

"Tobin's armor."

"What? Leave it here."

"No. I swore an oath," replied Cody, raising his voice a little.

"Quiet!" Accabo whispered back, with a note of panic in his voice. You'll get us both killed. Leave that junk here."

"No."

They stood facing each other, rain pelting their faces and running down their necks. They had been soaked to the skin since wading through that flood at the start, and standing in the water they now started feeling the cold.

With a look of disgust on his face, Accabo whispered, "This is really stupid. If you won't use your brain, at least try to be quiet," then turned and began walking again, with Cody following.

They continued walking in silence, their footsteps making increasing squishing noises as the mud deepened.

"Accabo, there's something out here."

"Shush!"

"Something's following us."

"Walk steady. Don't run. Keep quiet," Accabo whispered.

"You know what it is?" asked Cody.

Accabo impatiently signaled him to be quiet.

They walked more briskly, each step becoming louder and more difficult in the mud and water. Cody looked back frequently, holding his harpoon ready. Accabo walked steadily forward, trying not to look concerned. But then he heard it too, something large, the sound of a four footed animal in the water, coming closer. Finally, a loud shriek penetrated the night. Accabo turned back to Cody. "It heard you. We're in trouble now."

"It heard me? How about the sound it made?"

"I hoped they wouldn't be out."

"They?"

"Killing Beasts. Cody, run!"

Cody shouted, "What's a Killing Beast?" but Accabo was already running. Cody broke into a run. He quickly overtook and passed Accabo, surging far past him. Their lungs were bursting. The Killing Beast was getting closer, shrieking terribly, like nothing they had ever heard.

There was a gate just ahead. "Open it!" Cody shouted.

Accabo was too far back to hear.

Cody reached the gate and waited. He tried to force it open. Nothing happened. Finally Accabo caught up and collapsed in the mud in front of the gate.

"Open the damned thing!" Cody shouted

"I'm trying."

Turning back towards the sound of the approaching Killing Beast, Cody took out an arrow.

Accabo cried out, "No! Not arrow! Harpoon. Harpoon in its eye! Has to be in the eye!"

Dropping the arrow, Cody held his harpoon ready to throw and stood defiantly facing the charging Killing Beast. It was about their height, with a large tusk on its snout. Its open jaw revealed fearsome fangs. Its shriek was deafening. Accabo lay immobile, his hands over his eyes. Cody crouched like a statue, harpoon poised to throw. The beast was closing on him fast.

"Throw it," Accabo cried out, not opening his eyes.

Cody didn't move a muscle.

Briefly uncovering his eyes, Accabo cried out again, "Throw it! Throw the harpoon!" before covering his eyes again.

"Open the damned gate, Accabo."

"Throw the damned harpoon."

Cody crouched, motionless, harpoon ready to throw. The Killing Beast was very close, mud and water being tossed up as though from explosions under its feet. The shrieking was unbearable. Cody remained perfectly still. The Killing Beast was almost upon him when he finally threw the harpoon. The Killing Beast continued shrieking and running toward him for a moment, then collapsed almost at Cody's feet.

It valiantly resisted death. Lying on the ground, green blood gushing from its eye, the beast bellowed a few last shrieks, each one weaker and more pathetic than the one before. Finally all was still. The beast was dead. The only noise was the steadily pouring rain. Accabo slowly uncovered his eyes and got to his feet. Looking down at the Killing Beast, he said, "They breed these things. They're designed to be killers, nothing else. Almost no one can kill them. You saved my life. I thought we were both dead."

Kicking the beast to be certain it was dead, Cody asked, "You've never been here before. How do you know about these things?"

"It was in the Lekadian database."

"You knew they were here all along?"

"In this field, no. They don't usually keep them out here. But I studied them, just in case."

"You came even though you knew these things might be here?" Cody asked incredulously.

"Yes. But I hoped we could be quiet so they wouldn't hear us. I'm lighter than you. If I came alone, it wouldn't have heard me. You made too much noise."

"It would have heard you, even without me. No one could walk quietly through that mud."

Very cautiously, Accabo knelt down to look more closely at the Killing Beast. "I didn't think anyone could kill one of these. Even with a harpoon." He looked back up at Cody admiringly. "You just stood there while it charged at you. You didn't budge. Weren't you even scared?"

"Scared? Me? No, it takes a lot more than some noisy animal to scare me." Cody very casually pulled his harpoon from the Killing Beast, wiping off the gooey green blood as best he could. Accabo turned away from the revolting sight, walked to the gate, and stood motionless with his eyes closed. In a few moments, he had made contact with the computer, and the gate opened.

Cody followed him through the gate. As the gate closed behind them, Cody asked, "What's next? I don't want any more surprises like that Killing Beast."

"It's clear from here on. Just one more gate, then we'll get to Tobin."

"You're sure there's nothing else to attack us?"

"Sure I'm sure. I worked all this out carefully before we left Lewelle's ship. I've been right all along, haven't I?"

"You take the lead then, if you know it all."

Accabo set out walking, feeling confident, not noticing Cody gradually falling back, then moving to the side, finally disappearing entirely behind some trees. Accabo whistled a tune, as he always did at the spaceport when everything was going well. He fantasized the praise Carlos would lavish on him for so carefully planning and executing this rescue. "Everyone will see that I could have done this by myself. If I came by myself, that Killing Beast wouldn't have heard me. There would have been no danger at all."

As he walked and relished the praise he would get, it was easy to forget the cold and the wet, and the mud that caked him. Soon they would have Tobin and be back in the warm, dry shuttle.

Without warning, someone pushed him face down into the mud. "Why'd you do that, Cody?" he cried out angrily.

It wasn't Cody. Coarse voices barked orders at him in a language he could not understand. Some sort of weapon was pressing hard against his back. He could see the feet of one of his attackers very near his face, and knew from their voices that there was another standing over him. He also saw that suddenly, Cody wasn't with him. "The coward ran away! So much for tough guys!" he thought to himself.

His attackers were interrogating him in their alien language and growing angry at his lack of response. The weapon pressed deeper into his back.

He tried protesting, "I don't understand," in both Quogian and Lekadian, but it just made them angrier.

They repeated their demands in whatever language it was they were speaking.

"Please don't kill me! I'll do anything you want!" he pleaded in both Quogian and Lekadian, to no avail. The weapon in his back felt like it was now drawing blood. The pain was terrible.

Then there was a noise. Accabo knew he was dead.

The weapon stopped digging into his back. The man in front of him fell to the ground. He was wearing a uniform and was clearly a guard. The guard quickly jumped to his feet and lunged at someone Accabo could not see. Quickly rolling out of the way, Accabo saw Cody fighting both of the guards, swinging the blunt end of his green goo covered harpoon like a club, knocking a weapon out of the hands of one guard, then knocking the other guard unconscious.

Tossing the harpoon toward Accabo, Cody shouted, "Guard him!" while pounding the other guard with his fists.

Accabo looked at the harpoon laying in the mud next to him, gooey green blood still sticking to it. Very carefully avoiding the green stuff, he picked up the harpoon, holding it awkwardly and praying that the guard he was supposed to be watching did not regain consciousness.

It took only a few blows by Cody's experienced fists to pound the conscious guard into cowering submission. He lay motionless in the mud, hoping to escape further mauling. Cody took the guard's weapon and tossed it to Accabo. "Here, take this."

Seeing with disgust that both Cody's hands and the weapon were coated with the green goo, Accabo hesitated a moment too long, and the weapon landed in the mud behind him.

"Give me back my harpoon."

Accabo gladly handed the green goo coated harpoon back to Cody.

Cody pointed to the guard's weapon lying in the mud. "That's for you."

"Don't you want it?" asked Accabo.

"I like my own weapons. You need it more than I do."

"Lewelle said we shouldn't carry modern weapons."

"That one might be OK. The sensors will know it's a guard's weapon."

"Suppose they don't? Suppose the sensors can detect that I'm not a guard?"

"You're the one who speaks with their computers. Can't you control that?"

"I didn't research it. I don't know anything about weapons."

"It's your decision. You're sure you don't want it?" When Accabo nodded his head, Cody picked up both guards' weapons and threw them as far as he could. They landed with two far away splashes.

Holding his harpoon menacingly, Cody turned to the guard he had beaten and signaled him strip off his clothes. While the guard was stripping, the other guard regained consciousness. Cody signaled to him to strip also, then told Accabo to tie them up.

"Why not just kill them, Cody?"

"Only if there's no other way."

"What do I use to tie them up?"

"Their clothes, of course. Make them into a rope." As Cody stood guard with his gooey green harpoon, Accabo tore the guards' clothes into strips that he tied together into rope, and then tied them up. After Cody checked carefully to make sure they could not free themselves, he said, "I thought you said there was nothing more to be afraid of. You looked pretty scared when they had you pinned down."

"I thought you ran away."

"I never run away!" Cody shot back angrily, "It was the best way to trick them into letting their guard down so I could attack them."

"How did you know they were there? Even I didn't know."

"Just a feeling. Now, where's Tobin?"

"Over there, through that gate, in that shed."

"How do you know?"

Accabo replied, "Because before we left Lewelle's ship I reprogrammed their computer to move Tobin out here from the main compound."

Accabo stood next to the gate, closed his eyes, and almost immediately, the gate opened.

Cody congratulated him, but Accabo answered, "This one was too easy. I don't like it."

Cody agreed. "Something feels wrong. Are you sure Tobin's over there?"

"Yes. Definitely."

"You're sure definitely?"

"Yes."

"OK, let's just free him and get the hell out of here," Cody replied, taking off at a run towards the shed, followed by Accabo. As they ran, the gate closed behind them. Entering the shed, they found Tobin alone and shackled to the floor. His head was shaven, and he was wearing grimy overalls.

Tobin looked up when they entered, a look of astonishment on his face. "Cody!"

"Tobin! Where's your hair?"

"They shave everyone's heads. At least no one's going to laugh at my funny hair for a while. How did you know where I was? They just moved me here last night."

Cody introduced Accabo. "He controls machines like you control RedFins. He told the computer to transfer you here."

"You are a magician, Accabo?" asked Tobin.

"No, I'm just a mechanic. I counted on your guards being stupid enough to just follow the computer's orders without questioning."

"They were, as always."

Cody spoke. "Tobin, you should have seen it. He had the only space ship on Quogue. It was an old piece of junk. My father didn't think it would even fly, but it got us into space. I wouldn't be here without it. He worked on it all his life."

"My father did most of the work. I'll unlock these." Accabo closed his eyes, and a moment later, Tobin's shackles opened and fell from his ankles.

Stiffly, Tobin stood up, and embraced Accabo and Cody. Taking the paint from his backpack, Cody painted the mark of the warrior on Tobin's face, then took Tobin's breastplate and helmet from the backpack.

As he put on the armor, Tobin said, "This will sound strange, Cody, but I knew you would bring these. I'm glad you're wearing yours. The monks were right, weren't they? We are warriors. It's for real."

"I don't know about the monks," Cody answered, "but what I feel is real."

Accabo interrupted. "We've got to go. They'll know Tobin's gotten free.

Taking an arrow from his quiver, Cody said, "Let's go."

Tobin signaled him to wait. "Hold it. Cody, why isn't Accabo wearing the mark of the warrior?"

Accabo didn't wait for Cody to reply. "I am no warrior. I am a coward, Cody will tell you."

Cody turned to him. "Accabo, you came even though you knew Killing Beasts might attack you. No coward would do that."

Tobin put a hand on Accabo's shoulder. "Not all strength can be seen on the outside. The strength you bring is how you speak with machines. Give me the paint, Cody."

Cody handed it to Tobin, who carefully painted the warrior's symbol on Accabo's face and then asked, "What is your father's name, Accabo?"

"Locaru."

"Accabo son of Locaru of Quogue, I Tobin son of Tobin of Tarfil declare you a warrior of Quogue in our ancient tradition. Do you join me in this, Cody son of Carlos of Earth?"

"Yes, I do."

"So be it. Accabo, you are now a Quogian warrior," declared Tobin.

The three embraced, then Cody said, "Now let's get the hell out of here!"

Tobin made him wait again. "Cody, before we go, in case something happens, I've got to tell you. There are other prisoners down there."

"We can't rescue them, Tobin, we were lucky just to get you."

"But your mother is one of them."

"My mother? She's dead. She died when our ship exploded."

"No, she's alive, along with some of your crew. I've gotten to know her. Slavers boarded your father's ship, and took most of the crew."

"How could slavers get on board? The *Marco Polo* was the most advanced ship on Earth."

"Your Earth is primitive, almost like Quogue, compared with this part of the galaxy. Your parents' starship never stood a chance."

"We've got to rescue them!" Cody cried out.

"No, we can't. Not from here."

"Tobin's right, Cody, we can't do it from here," Accabo said, "We have to get back to Lara to do it."

"But my mother's here!"

Tobin put his arm around Cody. "We'll get her. I promise. There are three of us now, not just two. But we can't do it from here."

Accabo said, "Cody, lead us back to Lara. This is the best way to save your mother."

Reluctantly, Cody notched the arrow into his bow and led them out of the shed to the gate, ready to shoot if the guards came before they got out.

When they reached the gate, Accabo stood next to it, his eyes closed. Moments passed. More moments. Nothing happened. Accabo's face grimaced. Finally his eyes opened.

"I can't do it. I can't open the gate."

The Third Warrior Brother

"Why won't it open, Accabo?"

"They probably know we're here, Cody. That's why opening it was so easy the first time."

"It was a trap," declared Tobin,

"Yes," agreed Accabo.

"Can't you do anything?" Cody asked.

"Let me think." Accabo closed his eyes.

Tobin picked up a massive log and pounded it on the gate. Cody picked up a large rock and joined Tobin in pounding on the gate. They made a terrible racket, but the gate didn't budge.

Accabo yelled, "Stop! I think I found a way to open it."

"Then open it!" Cody shouted.

"Wait, there's a good part and a bad part. The good part is that if you can hit that sensor up there with your arrow..." Accabo pointed to a small sensor about fifteen meters above the ground. "I can set up a feedback that completely overloads their system and shuts down all their electronics long enough for us to get out."

Cody immediately aimed his arrow toward the sensor.

Accabo cried out, "Stop! I didn't tell you the bad part."

Lowering his bow, Cody asked, "What is it?"

"We only get one chance. I can only overload their system once. It has to be right before you hit that sensor. The gate will open, but when their systems overload, the gate will close automatically. If you don't hit that sensor the first time, we won't get out."

Cody aimed his arrow. "Let me know when you're ready, Accabo."

"As soon as you hit it," Accabo said, "We've all got to run. Fast. We only have a few moments to get out. Wait for my signal."

Accabo closed his eyes. Cody moved farther back to get a clearer shot. Accabo counted down aloud, "Five. Four. Three. Two. One. Go!" Cody's arrow flew, just hitting the sensor. The gate opened and immediately began to close. Accabo shouted, "Run!" Accabo and Tobin were closer to the gate and had no trouble getting through, but Cody was too far away. The gate was closing. Cody was running fast, but wasn't going to make it. Tobin grabbed the gate, struggling to keep it from closing.

Tossing his harpoon through the gate, Cody called out, "Wedge it in the gate!" The harpoon landed next to Accabo. Ignoring the green goo still coating it, he picked it up and wedged it between the advancing gate and the fence. For a moment, the gate stopped closing. The harpoon started buckling. Cody was almost at the gate. Tobin strained harder to hold it back. The harpoon was at its breaking point. Cody reached the gate and bounded over the harpoon. As he landed safely outside the gate, the harpoon exploded into green goo covered shrapnel shooting in every direction as the gate tore itself from Tobin's grip and slammed loudly shut.

"We don't have much time," Accabo warned, wiping green goo from his face, "but I overloaded their systems pretty good. Probably nothing's working now. It should keep them busy for a while figuring out what happened before they come up here."

They ran across the field, Accabo trailing far behind Cody, and Tobin far ahead. When Accabo finally caught up, Tobin and Cody were waiting at the next gate for him. Gulping in air, Accabo said, "Unlocked. I unlocked it."

"You'd better be right," said Tobin skeptically. He grabbed the gate and pulled. It opened. "Good job, Accabo!"

Running and shouting joyous whoops of relief, they made it through the next gate as well, splashing through the mud, ecstatic to be free, losing all caution.

Suddenly Tobin dropped to all fours in the mud and signaled Cody and Accabo to do the same.

"What's wrong?" Cody whispered when he caught up to Tobin.

"Killing Beasts. A herd of them. We can't get through."

Accabo crawled up to them and whispered, "We're lucky they didn't hear us." Pointing to a nearby hill that was barely visible in the dark and rain, he added, "there's a different trail we can take over there."

Crawling toward the hill, they managed to get out of sight of the herd, but their hearts fell when they saw a solitary Killing Beast blocking their way.

They lay on the ground in silence, the Killing Beast standing alertly just ahead of them, only the torrential rain and ever more fiercely blowing wind keeping it from hearing or smelling them.

Tobin whispered, "I'm going to try something. When I give the signal, crawl toward that hill as fast as you can. I'll catch up."

Before Cody or Accabo could reply, Tobin began singing a tone. The Killing Beast looked in their direction. Tobin stopped singing. When the Killing Beast looked away again, Tobin tried a different tone. The Killing Beast's tail fluttered a little, then its muscles twitched. Tobin stopped singing, and the Killing Beast again stood motionless, but alert. Tobin remained silent for a while, looking intently at the beast and then sang again. The Killing Beast didn't react at first, but finally closed its eyes.

Tobin motioned to Cody and Accabo to go. When they hesitated, he frantically waved to them to get going. They crawled away, slowly at first, then faster as they got farther from the Killing Beast. Tobin kept on singing. The Killing Beast sat down, mesmerized.

Still singing, Tobin waved to them to go farther.

"What happens when he stops singing?" asked Accabo.

"I don't know. I don't think he knows either," answered Cody. Tobin waved at them again to keep going. Cody stood up and broke into a run up the hill, followed by Accabo.

Cody reached the top first, followed at a distance by Accabo, completely out of breath. They stood watching Tobin, still singing at the bottom of the hill, the Killing Beast now lying docilely on the ground in front of him.

Accabo couldn't resist goading Cody about the fact that this was the same hill he wanted to climb when they started out. "I studied the whole area carefully before we left Lewelle's ship. Taking this hill would have saved a lot of time."

Cody didn't say anything. He simply turned and looked toward the crest of the hill. Accabo walked towards where Cody was looking, but stopped abruptly. The entire other side of the hill had collapsed in a mudslide. Mud was cascading down. The top was eroding back where they stood.

"We're trapped, Cody."

Cody was watching Tobin, who was very carefully getting to his feet, singing while backing in very slow, careful steps past the now sleeping Killing Beast. When he was far enough away, he broke into a run, sprinting up the hill. Exhilaration lit up his face as he cried out, "I did it! I didn't think it was possible!"

Cody asked, "How long will it stay asleep?"

"Not long," Tobin replied, "If we run really fast, maybe just long enough for us to get down the other side."

With a glum look on his face, Accabo pointed to the mudslide. As he did, another chunk of the hill on tumbled down into the chasm, bringing the ragged decaying edge closer to their feet. Tobin stood silently, watching the ground erode away before them. They all backed away. Accabo said, "Your mother's in the shuttle, just over the next ridge."

Tobin asked, "This is the only way?"

"Or through the Killing Beasts," Cody answered.

Tobin peered down the mudslide. "It's the only way. There is at least a hope that one or two of us might survive. We have no hope with the Killing Beasts. Our only hope will be for a quick death if they catch us."

"You couldn't sing to them again?" asked Cody.

"No, there are too many of them. I was lucky to sing even to one. When animals run in packs, it's harder to reach their soul."

"Just like people?" asked Accabo.

"Yes, just like people," Tobin replied.

Peering glumly over the edge, they watched in silence as it eroded farther, the edge coming still closer to their feet. They backed away.

"That's the only way," Tobin repeated.

"I'm sorry, Tobin, I guess we really screwed up your rescue," Cody said.

"You freed me," Tobin replied, "I'd rather die here free with my brothers than live the rest of my life back there as a slave."

Turning to Accabo, Cody said, "I apologize for getting you mixed up in this. And for all I said about you. I was wrong."

"I said some bad things about you too, Cody. I was wrong about everything. Even this hill. We would have been killed if we tried coming up the other side. You saved my life twice tonight."

"Not for long, I'm afraid," replied Cody. "I'm going to sing some prayer songs before I die."

Accabo asked, "Which god do you pray to, the God of Space?"

"No, to the spirits my people on Earth prayed to for thousands of years."

"But you're not on Earth."

"I have prayed to them with my father all my life. My father says they will hear our songs, no matter where we are."

"Is it OK if I hum along with you?"

"Yes, Accabo, I'd be honored. Tobin, want to join us?"

"Cody, you know I don't believe in gods. Or spirits. It's our minds that will save us," Tobin replied, turning away. He added under his breath, "and maybe a little muscle."

"This song came to my grandmother in a dream," Cody said softly to Accabo. He then sang while beating rhythm with his hands.

Accabo at first hummed, following Cody's singing, then began singing words as verses repeated. When they finished singing and shouted the traditional "Ho!" of Miwok and Pomo people, they joined Tobin in staring at the cliff's edge relentlessly eroding toward them.

* * *

Carlos was sitting at the battle command station, watching the displays. Lewelle returned with some hot tea. Speaking in Lekadian, he said, "Forgive my intrusion. This tea might help." He handed Carlos the tea and turned to leave.

"You can stay if you like, Lewelle."

Taking a seat, Lewelle asked, "Have you heard from them?"

"No."

They sat in silence for a while. Finally Lewelle said, "We have learned a lot from you and your son."

"From us? Your people are so much more advanced."

"Advanced? Perhaps. But we've lost something too. We no longer have the belief and the passion that Cody has shown. We had it once. My people can perhaps learn from you and your son."

Looking at the monitors again, Carlos said, "I think maybe I can learn something from my son too."

* * *

The three boys were standing at the crest of the hill, watching the edge erode toward them. Accabo said, "I don't want to die. I've never been brave. But you made me a warrior, both of you, and I'll die with you, like a warrior." He was shaking. "I am afraid, I admit it, but you won't be ashamed of me."

Taking one of the arrows from Cody's quiver, Tobin said, "If we are to die together, we should die together as Warrior Brothers. Accabo son of Locaru, will you honor us by mingling your blood with ours? Will you commit to fight together with us always? Whether we live for another day or die tonight?"

Fighting back the tears and the fears and nausea overwhelming him as he saw Tobin pressing the arrowhead down hard against the palm of his own hand, ready to pierce the skin, Accabo managed to squeak, "Yes, I do," his voice trembling. Tobin cut into both of his own hands and then handed the arrow to Cody, who did the same. Accabo accepted the bloody arrow from Cody, still not sure he could carry out his part in this, but knowing he had to try. Summoning all his will, he closed his eyes and pushed the arrow deep into first his right hand, and then into his left hand and, blood gushing from both hands, handed the arrow back to Cody. The three of them stood face to face, torrential rain blowing in the increasing wind, their hands upraised, bloody palm against bloody palm, warm blood running down their cold arms under their wet sleeves. Tobin declared, "I pledge that I am now brother to both of you forever. I always will fight at your sides. I will always defend both of you, even if it means my own life."

Cody and Accabo both repeated the pledge.

"Whether we die tonight jumping from this cliff, or we live for another day, we will be brothers forever," declared Tobin.

Cody and Accabo repeated in unison, "Brothers forever!"

Tobin said, "Accabo, son of Locaru, you are now the third Warrior Brother."

"The prophecy has been fulfilled. There is a third Warrior Brother," declared Cody.

"I will be true to my oath, but I am afraid, my brothers," Accabo managed to say in a weak, quivering voice.

"You can still be brave," replied Cody, "you would be a fool not to be afraid. I am scared too. I am not ready to die."

Tobin added, "I am afraid also. But if we let fear be our master, then we might as well all go back there and be slaves for the rest of our lives."

Stepping to the edge of the cliff, they stood facing the abyss. Tobin wrapped his arms around Cody and Accabo, holding them tightly, declaring, "I will not let go of you, brothers, no matter what. We live or we die as one." With that, they jumped into the flowing mud below them.

They bounced and slid and were at times swallowed up in the river of mud and at other times were tossed briefly out of it as they fell, gasping desperately for breath before being swallowed up again by the liquid hillside. It seemed to last forever. They were convinced they were dead. Later, it seemed like only a few moments until they had stopped falling and were engulfed in the mud, completely still, at the bottom of the mudslide. Struggling to free themselves from the seemingly bottomless ooze that entombed them, they managed at last to get their heads above the mud. Desperately gulping air into their aching lungs, their senses soon recovered enough for them to see that the mud was still flowing down and soon would cover them again.

Digging furiously, at first they made no progress against the ever deepening mud. Finally they managed to extricate themselves. It wasn't easy. Cody and Accabo both knew that without Tobin's great strength, they never could have gotten out. Even with Tobin's help, it wasn't easy, but they finally crawled mud-caked out of the slime, muscles and lungs aching, conscious only of being alive. At first they were too exhausted to move, but when a chunk of hillside fell without warning and nearly crushed them, they found the energy to run to safety. They had lost their shoes in the mud, and Accabo's hat was lost, along with Cody's bow and all his arrows, but they were at least alive.

Away from the mud, the ground was rocky, cutting their feet painfully, but Tobin merely laughed, "Warriors don't need shoes!" Accabo shouted a victory yell at the top of his lungs, declaring that if nothing else had been able to defeat them, neither could a few pebbles. Running as fast as he could, he reached the flooded meadow first and jumped into the water, followed by Tobin and Cody, who removed their helmets and breastplates to wash out the mud that had oozed in everywhere.

After cleaning themselves as best they could, they waded to the other side of the flood. From there, it was an easy walk over the hill and back to Lara and the waiting shuttle. As they wearily climbed onboard, Cody and Tobin removed their helmets and Lara embraced Tobin, tears of joy streaming down her face. Then she tearfully embraced Cody and Accabo. .

Lara began preparing for take off, but Tobin stopped her. "There are other slaves. We need to free them too," he said.

"We don't have a chance," Lara objected.

"Cody's mother is there. We've got to get her out. Accabo knocked out their systems, but they'll come back up soon. We have to do it now."

Reluctantly, Lara agreed to help them. She launched the shuttle while Accabo mapped their course.

Accabo turned to Cody and Tobin. Seeming awkward and embarrassed, he asked, "How do you guys master your fears?"

"Every man must learn that for himself, Accabo," replied Cody, "we cannot tell you how you should do it."

Accabo spoke so softly he could hardly be heard. "I'm afraid." They could see him trembling.

Tobin asked, "How did you do it on that cliff? You were terrified. I could see it in your eyes, but you mastered your fears."

"It all happened so fast. There wasn't time to think. Now there is. Do you see the terror in my eyes?"

"Of course," Tobin replied. "You would see the terror in our eyes too, if Cody and me didn't think we were tough guys who had to hide it."

Accabo turned to Cody. "You don't really get afraid, do you?"

"The truth, Cody," ordered Tobin.

"Accabo, do you promise not to tell anyone?"

"I promise."

"I feel afraid every time I fight," Cody answered, "not only of being hurt. Right now, not even the biggest troublemaker on Quogue dares bother me. Every one knows I can beat them. But if I lose one fight, just one fight, then everyone who wants to be the toughest will try to prove they can beat me too. I know, because I was the same way once. No one will leave me alone. That's what I fear, every time I fight." Cody paused. "Because really, I'm not that tough."

"Yes, you are that tough, Cody. I saw lots of really tough guys attacking us at the spaceport, but you're tougher than any of them."

"Yeah, I'm strong, and a good fighter, but mostly it's show." He paused before continuing, "Accabo, you have been very brave today. This is not your fight. You don't have to come with us."

Accabo hesitated before replying. "I'm coming with you."

"Are you sure, Accabo?" Cody asked.

"We live or we die together as brothers, right? Your fight is my fight," replied Accabo, holding out his two hands, palms up, both bearing the fresh wounds, marked with clotted blood mixed with mud. "Forever," he added firmly. "Besides, you need me. I'm the only one who can access their computers. You won't even get in without me."

Most of the paint had washed off their faces, so using Tobin's paint that fortunately was still in the shuttle, Cody repainted the warrior's mark on Accabo's face and then on Tobin's. When he was done, he handed the paint to Accabo, saying, "Please, Accabo, I would be honored if you would do it for me."

"You trust me to paint the mark of the warrior on you, Cody?"

"I trust you with my life, brother." Very carefully, Accabo painted Cody's face, repeatedly looking at what Cody had painted on Tobin, to be sure he was doing it right. "Accabo, do you remember when the Killing Beast chased us, you asked if I was afraid?"

"Yes. I never saw anyone as brave as you."

"Accabo, I lied to you when I said I wasn't afraid. I was afraid. I was never so scared. I've never seen anything as scary as that thing."

"You didn't look scared."

"Like I said, Accabo, it's mostly show."

Lara was becoming annoyed. "It's going to take more than show to get you boys inside that slave camp. They're not going to just let us fly in there and pick up your mom, Cody. My blaster is the only weapon we have besides Tobin's arrows and harpoon. What's your plan?"

Trying to hold his head still while Accabo painted it, Cody turned his eyes to Tobin. Neither said anything.

"How are you going to get in? Knock at the gate and ask them to let you liberate the camp?" Lara asked.

"Wait until Accabo finishes painting me," replied Cody.

"Painting your face isn't going to help," Lara objected. "We need a lot more people and a lot more weapons. You're dreaming if you think you can do it by yourselves."

When Accabo was finished painting him, Cody said, "You're the brains of this operation, Accabo. You tell us what we should do."

"Don't you want to look first to see if I painted your face right?"

"I don't have to look. I know you did it right."

"It's perfect," Tobin assured them.

"Can we get back to planning strategy?" Lara asked, irritated. "That paint won't get you in, and it won't save your asses when the shooting starts."

"It helped them rescue me," replied Tobin.

"It was planning that saved you," said Lara. "It was Cody's skill and Accabo's brain. It wasn't the paint on Cody's face."

Accabo interrupted. "Please, be quiet, all of you. Let me connect with their computers." He closed his eyes and sat back. Finally, after what seemed forever, he opened his eyes. "I've got it."

Cody and Tobin both asked what he had come up with.

"You're going to sell me into slavery," Accabo replied.

"You're as crazy as they are!" cried out Lara.

"No, it's perfect. Brothers, you're going to love it. But we have to act fast. When we freed Tobin, I planted some bugs in their computers that sent most of the guards to one of the outer areas of the camp. Their whole system is pretty messed up right now, but they'll be coming back soon. We've got to act fast before the guards return."

"What's your plan, brother?" asked Cody.

"The slavers have only been on this planet a short time. The indigenous people on this planet were Stone Age until recently. There's superb hunting here. Hunters from other planets used to come here all the time. Local people used to hide from the hunters, but no more. Now instead of hiding from hunters, they capture hunters to barter as slaves."

"Wait a minute," Lara interrupted, "why don't the slavers make local people slaves?"

"They're too primitive. This is an industrial camp. The slavers want more modern people working here. People who can read, and use computers. Besides, the local people barter the guards fresher food than the supply ships bring," Accabo answered, "but to get back to my plan, here's the beauty of it. People here dress a lot like Quogians. Not Quogians like me at the spaceport, but Quogians like you and Tobin. Long hair. Tattoos."

"It's not going to work, boys," Lara interrupted. "Tobin's never going to pass as a savage. His head is shaved. They'll know right away that he's an escaped slave."

Cody handed Tobin his helmet, saying, "Put it on. Let's see what you look like." Despite Cody's repeated attempts to adjust the helmet to cover Tobin's shaved head, there was no hiding .it.

Finally Tobin took his helmet off and handed it to Accabo, saying, "You be the savage. I'll be an escaped slave that you're returning for a reward."

"No. Absolutely not," Lara exclaimed, "Besides, look at Accabo. He'll never pass as a savage. Tobin, give me your helmet."

She took Tobin's helmet and before the others realized what she was doing, she took out a knife and hacked off much of her own hair. Using tape, she attached the hair to the inside of the helmet, finally handing it back to Tobin when she was done. "Here, try this."

Tobin put on the helmet and while Cody and Accabo watched in fascination, Lara adjusted the hair hanging down from the helmet until it looked reasonably convincing.

"How does it look?" Tobin asked.

"Like a real savage," Accabo answered.

"Yep," said Cody.

"Are you sure it's OK for them to wear metal armor and helmets?" Lara asked.

"It's perfect," answered Accabo. "All the indigenous people on this planet are wearing metal now. They've just started. It will look natural to the guards, especially with their faces painted. The people here paint their faces a lot like ours."

"The mark of the warrior?" asked Tobin.

"No, it's the mark of one of their gods. It doesn't matter. The guards won't know the difference. They'll think you're one of these backward local people selling them a slave."

Tobin continued, "OK, so they think that Cody and me are primitives, and you're our slave. We get inside. What happens then?"

"They'll scan me for my DNA. It's how they register people."

"What's a DNA?" asked Cody.

"Stuff inside our bodies," Tobin answered, "It tells their computers who a person is."

Accabo began an explanation of DNA, but Tobin interrupted him. "Teach us about it later, Accabo, if we're still alive."

Cody added, "Just tell us what we need to know now."

"OK. Forget DNA. They'll scan me so their computer knows who I am. The moment their computer connects with me, I'll bring down their system. As soon as I bring it down, the lights will go out. That's when you attack them. There should be only a few guards there right now, but the others will be back very soon. We've got to act fast."

They decided that as soon as they had control of the camp's computers and had overpowered the guards at the gate, they would take Accabo to the master control room. While Accabo was getting control of the computers, Tobin would take Cody to his mother's dormitory. After that, Tobin would make sure that the slaves were all free, while Cody would destroy the guards' ship to prevent their escape.

"Who gets the blaster?" asked Lara, "There's only one, and there are three of you."

"I don't know how to use it," said Accabo.

"Tobin should take it. He knows those modern weapons. I'll use his bow and arrows," answered Cody.

"There's one possible problem," said Accabo. "There's no way for me to know if they've gotten back full control of their computers until I tap back in."

"We'll wait until you say it's OK," Tobin replied.

"No, you don't understand. If they've regained full control of their computers, they'll know we're here the moment I tap in. They weren't ready for me the first time. This time they will be."

Lara said, "I'll get us out of here fast if there's problem."

"You won't have time. We'll all be dead a moment after they detect me. We're in range of their laser cannons now."

Tobin asked, "How sure are you that you can pull this off?"

"If I can get control of their computers, then I can do it. If they've been able to put defenses in their computer against me, then we're dead. That's all I know. The only thing I can tell you for certain is that every second we wait gets us closer to being dead."

"I say we go now," Cody replied. "Tobin?"

"Yes, we go now."

"Lara?" Cody asked.

"You guys are nuts." She hesitated. "But if Accabo thinks we can do it, then yes."

Everyone looked at Accabo. He looked uncomfortable, but whispered, "Probably, yes."

Cody looked at Lara and ordered, "Go!"

Lara set the shuttle back in motion, heading toward the slave camp main entrance.

"I'm tapping into their computers now," Accabo said, "this is the test. If they detect me, then we're all dead in a few seconds." Accabo closed his eyes.

Lara whispered to Tobin, "There's something I've got to say. I'm sorry about your childhood. I'm sorry for sending you away to those schools. I wish I could take those years back and have you with me. I'm sorry, I'm sorry. I was going to tell you later, but if something happens…" Tears were running down her face. Tobin kissed her, and held her free hand. She continued, "I've been wanting to apologize. I just didn't know how."

Accabo opened his eyes and announced, "I got in. It's OK. They don't know we're here. Get ready to sell me."

Tobin turned to Accabo. "What about the warrior's mark on your face, Accabo? Shouldn't we remove it if you're a slave?"

Before Accabo could reply, Cody said, "Leave it on. If the guards ask, we'll tell them we painted it on him to show he's our property. He's going to need the protection the mark gives him. We're all going to need it."

"You really are starting to believe what the monks told us."

"Tobin, if we're alive and free after this is over, then I'll believe," Cody laughed.

"What we're doing is crazy, brothers!" Tobin declared, "Three ancient warriors against we don't know how many modern armed guards. If we do this, there's nothing we can't do!"

Everyone sat in silence, each of them pondering the implications of Tobin's words. Then Lara thought of a problem. "The language. None of you speak the language of the indigenous people you're pretending to be."

Everyone looked to Accabo for the answer. He had a ready reply. "Not a problem. Tobin knows Lekadian. The guards don't know the local language, so some of the local people are learning to speak Lekadian to communicate with the guards. Tobin, just be careful not to speak like you know Lekadian well. Cody, you should speak Quogian. Or speak your Earth language. The guards won't know either one from the local language."

Cody pointed out that the guards who attacked Accabo didn't speak Lekadian. Accabo replied, "Those were low level guards. Brutes, nothing more. The ones you'll be selling me to are required to speak fluent Lekadian."

Lara asked how Accabo knew all this.

"I looked it up in their personnel database."

Lara still wasn't convinced. "You're absolutely sure about this all this?"

Accabo replied, "Absolutely."

Cody decided not to mention the other times that Accabo had been absolutely sure.

They flew in silence, flying low to evade detection, watching the dark landscape slide by just below them. Accabo thought he had his fear under control, but now, sitting in silence, knowing all of them could soon be dead, he felt it rearing up within him again. Even worse than the fear he felt for himself was the fear he felt about

Cody, Tobin, and Lara trusting their lives to his judgment. So many things could go wrong so easily. No matter how sternly he reminded himself that he must master his fear and not let it control him, he could still feel the fear roiling his stomach and his bowels, as though at any moment it could erupt through every pore of his body. He closed his eyes, hoping the others would not notice how little success he was having.

Just when Accabo wondered if he could control himself any longer, he heard Tobin hum a tune unlike any other he had ever heard.

Speaking softly, Tobin said, "Accabo, open your eyes."

When Accabo opened his eyes, he found Tobin's face so close that their noses almost touched. Tobin's eyes stared straight into his with a look that pierced his soul, at the same time saying to Accabo, "I feel it also, I feel the fear, the terrible fear, we all feel it."

Afterwards, Accabo was never sure whether Tobin actually spoke those words or if he had conveyed them in some other way. Accabo would never forget the feeling that Tobin had reached some place deep inside his soul, a place Accabo never knew he had, and that only Tobin could reach. Tobin continued humming the strange tune until they landed at the slave compound and although Accabo still felt terror, he knew for today at least, he was its master.

Lara and Cody also found themselves unexpectedly feeling more calm, more in control of fears they felt about what might happen in the coming moments.

The first test they faced was whether the shuttle could land without setting off alarms. Accabo was confident he had disabled the sensors, but there was no way of knowing for sure. Landing where Accabo directed, just out of sight of a camp entrance, Lara breathed a sigh of relief when nothing happened. Unable to hold back tears at her son going off on this risky mission only moments after he been rescued from slavery, the usually stoic Lara openly cried while embracing and kissing him.

Cody and Accabo opened the shuttle door and looked outside. It had stopped raining at last. Moonlight was becoming visible above the thinning cloud layer, but days of torrential rains had left the ground saturated, with large puddles all around them. Cody was just about to jump to the ground when he stopped. Peering around, he asked Accabo, "Killing Beasts. What about them?"

"Don't worry. They're only in the remote areas. This close to the entrance, there won't be any."

"You're sure about that?"

"Absolutely."

Tobin looked up at them. "Accabo, if you're so certain, you go first."

"Sure." Accabo stepped to the open door, but paused. After looking around, he jumped outside, followed by Cody, carrying a rope and looking around warily. Without warning, he wrapped the rope around Accabo, tied a knot, and pulled it tight.

"That's enough, Cody. It'll take me too long to get loose."

"Watch." With a snap of Cody's wrist, the rope fell from Accabo. "It's just a Quogian fisherman's knot."

Tobin joined them, holding the blaster.

As Cody retied the rope around Accabo, Accabo ordered, "Hide it, Tobin. Hide the blaster."

"Won't their sensors tell them I'm hiding it?"

"I think I disabled the sensors."

"You think you disabled them?"

"No one's ever tried this before. There's no information in the Lekadian database about this type of weapons detection system."

Tobin didn't look thrilled by this. "You'd better get it right, Accabo, or all three of us are dead."

Cody looked up from double-checking the knot holding Accabo. "If Accabo can't do it, nobody can."

Accabo looked surprised. "Thanks, Cody."

Not seeming to pay attention, Cody tugged hard on the rope. Accabo winced as it suddenly tightened around him. "Take it easy, Cody."

"Just testing it. If I pull the other way, it will come right off."

Accabo waited a moment, then asked, "Well, aren't you going to test that too?"

"Don't worry, it'll work."

Suppressing a grin, Tobin asked Accabo, "OK boss, assuming you don't get us killed, what else can you tell us?"

"The more you two look like barbarians, the more they'll believe that's all you are. Bring your spear, er, harpoon, Tobin, even if you're not going to use it. Don't take out your blaster until I turn off the lights."

"What if you can't turn out the lights?" asked Tobin.

"Not a problem. That's the easy part. The moment they hook me up to scan my DNA, I'll use that link to turn off all power. That's when you take out your blaster. Nothing can go wrong. I've already done the hard part. Turning off the lights is simple."

They walked toward the slave camp gate, Accabo tied securely, Cody holding the other end of the rope, while Tobin from time to time playfully prodded at Accabo with his harpoon. Looming ahead of them was the ominous looking fence surrounding the slave camp, with electronic defenses on the top to prevent anyone from climbing over.

When they were almost at the gate, Accabo whispered, "Remember, when they scan my DNA, I'll knock out their computers, and their power will go out. Don't do anything until then." After walking in silence for a few moments, Accabo added, "You two should make some noise, so they know we're here. Talk loud, in Quogian, like I'm your slave. They won't understand what you're saying, so it doesn't matter what you actually say. I'll answer in Lekadian. They'll understand what I'm saying."

Whispering, "OK, boss," Tobin again prodded Accabo with the harpoon, then shouted loudly in pidgin Lekadian, "Quiet! I cut out tongue if you no shut up."

Screaming in mock pain, Accabo cried out in Lekadian, "Help me, someone, help me! They're killing me!"

Cody whispered to Accabo, "They should have sensed us by now. Why aren't the guards out?"

Whispering back, Accabo replied, "I knocked the sensors out. Keep making noise. They'll hear us," and then cried out in mock pain at the top of his lungs.

Holding his harpoon with the point pressed against Accabo's back, Tobin shouted in Lekadian, "I stab you if you no shut up."

"Hey, not so hard with that thing," Accabo whispered, before again wailing loudly in mock pain.

"This is fun," Cody whispered in Quogian.

"It doesn't matter what you say Cody," Accabo replied, "they don't understand Quogian."

"We're going to free every damned slave in this stinking place!" Cody shouted in Quogian, "Tobin, back on Quogue, you were right. Being an actor is fun. Especially when the audience doesn't know what I'm saying!"

Just ahead, three guards came running toward the gate, weapons drawn, arguing with each other about why the sensors had not detected approaching strangers. They finally decided that it was because these barbarians were too primitive to carry any electronic gear. "Look at them. No shoes. Muddy. Arrows. A spear. They're even worse off than the last ones."

After listening to Tobin's explanation in mock pidgin Lekadian that they wanted to sell Accabo as a slave, the guards led them into a small office, where they examined Accabo, finally checking his muscles, and examining his teeth. "He's scrawny, no good for physical labor. He's not from this planet, from the looks of him."

"Him wander too far from ship. We capture. His friends stop looking. Leave without him," Tobin lied, hoping he sounded sufficiently primitive.

Noticing the bloody wounds on Accabo's palms, one of the guards asked, "Did you do this to him?"

Cody and Tobin both tried to cup their hands inconspicuously so their own wounds wouldn't be seen. "Him try get away. Only way hold him," Tobin lied again.

The guard continued his examination. "We can't give you much for him."

"Anything," said Tobin, prodding at Accabo again with his harpoon, making him wince. "Him too much trouble. No want him."

One of the guards picked up a scanner. "I'll just scan his DNA so we can register him."

Accabo and Tobin exchanged glances. Tobin positioned his hand near his blaster, ready for the lights to go out. Cody readied himself to release the knot securing Accabo. Accabo closed his eyes, ready to access the computer. The guard held the scanner against his skin, and took a reading.

The guard finished the reading. When Accabo heard the guard set the scanner back down on the desk, he opened his eyes, panic showing on his face.

One of the guards unlocked a case, took out two crossbows, locked the case again, and handed the crossbows to Cody and Tobin. While they examined them admiringly, the guard said, "These are more than this puny slave is worth. You shouldn't have cut his hands. He'd be worth more. I'll bet you've never seen anything as good as these crossbows."

Accabo's eyes frantically darted between Cody and Tobin, but they turned their backs to him and admired the crossbows while two of the guards led them to the door. Seeing them leaving, Accabo panicked, crying out in Quogian, "Hey, don't leave me here!"

Ignoring him, Tobin asked a guard, "We bring more slaves, you give more like this?" holding up his crossbow.

"As many as you want," replied the guard.

"Hey, you can't do this!" shouted Accabo, now completely panicked.

"We come back. Bring stronger slave," promised Tobin, admiring his cross bow. "Want more like this."

Cody, carefully trying to hide the wounds on his palms, used hand signals to indicate he wanted arrows for the crossbows.

"You're asking a lot for a slave as useless as this one. It should be easy enough to make arrows yourselves."

"Need see how make," Tobin pleaded, trying desperately to speak Lekadian as poorly as he could manage.

The third guard, who slightly outranked the other two, interjected, "They're good kids. They can't help it if they're poor savages. Go ahead, give them a few."

Reluctantly, the guard re-opened the case, took out two arrows, and handed one to Cody and one to Tobin. "Bring us better slaves than this one, we'll give you more." Cody bowed obsequiously to the guard, smiling at him like an old friend, and then turned to leave with Tobin, escorted by the other two guards.

Accabo was watching in disbelief, hoping they were just acting. Seeing them leaving and lavishing such loving attention on their new toys, he became completely unnerved. He cried out, "Hey, Cody, Tobin, you can't do this!"

Ignoring Accabo, Tobin turned to the higher rank guard and promised, "Next one stronger."

Cody held up his cross bow and arrow triumphantly, exhilaration showing in his face. He smiled at the guards.

"Guys, please," Accabo pleaded, "don't leave me here."

Ignoring Accabo, Tobin threw one arm around Cody and held up his cross bow in the other. "Brother, now good hunting." Turning to the guard, he added, "You want female? We got good one outside. For you."

Cody smiled and signaled with his hands that the price was two more crossbows and fifty arrows, keeping his palms facing away from the guards.

"That's a high price for a female slave," protested one of the guards.

"Strong. Good sex. She bargain."

Accabo cried out in horror, "Cody, Tobin, no!"

"He sounds like he thinks you're his friends," said one of the guards.

Tobin snorted. "Him? No friend."

"He has your mark on his face."

Laughing derisively, Tobin reassured the guard, "We trick him. That make him think our friend."

Accabo fell silent, crestfallen, unable to believe what he was hearing. "Not just friends, brothers."

Paying no attention to Accabo, Tobin laughed and said, "Look at him. Useless. Look at him."

The guards all turned to look at Accabo.

"Him can't be friend. Not to us," Tobin said, laughing.

Laughing along with Tobin, the guard replied, "You're right, he could never be friends with men like you."

Turning back to face Cody, the guard saw too late the arrow already in Cody's crossbow, aimed at his face. Before he could react, the arrow shot out from the crossbow and shattered his face.

Cody defiantly shouted, "Accabo is our brother!"

Tobin took his blaster from hiding and shot the second guard. The third guard raised his blaster to fire, but Accabo kicked it out of his hands. The guard crouched down, picked it up and aimed at Tobin but before he could fire, Tobin killed him with his blaster.

Cody tugged at the knot securing the rope around Accabo and the rope fell to the ground. Handing one of the guards' blasters to Accabo, Tobin asked, "I hope you didn't really think we'd leave you here, Accabo. I was waiting for the lights to go out."

"I didn't know what great actors you two are."

"We've had practice. Right, Cody?"

"It's what got us into this mess."

Tobin put his hand on Accabo's shoulder. "Accabo, you freed me from that slave camp. You are my brother now. I would give my own life before I would ever leave you in a place like this."

Cody was becoming impatient. "Me too. Enough talk. Accabo, can you get the power off?"

"I think so. I outsmarted myself the last time. I disabled all their controls while we were in the shuttle. I forgot it meant I couldn't issue the shutdown command while they were checking my DNA."

"Do it now," Cody ordered. Accabo closed his eyes.

Tobin picked up the guards' blasters and offered one to Cody.

"No, I'll use this," Cody replied, holding up the cross bow, "but I will take your harpoon if you don't need it." Tobin handed him the harpoon. Cody continued, "Do you see what that arrow did to his face?" The guard's face was completely obliterated. "This thing is amazing."

"I'll be right back," Tobin replied, running back outside without another word.

Going to the unlocked cabinet, Cody filled his quiver with arrows for the crossbow.

When Tobin returned, Accabo was still standing with his eyes closed.

Cody asked, "What was so important outside?"

In reply, Tobin took a communicator from his pocket. "This could be useful."

Finally the lights went out. The only illumination was a very faint moon glow coming the windows, barely enough to see the outline of the open door.

"Come on," cried Accabo, opening his eyes, "I have to get to the control room before the other guards come back. They'll be here any moment!"

A Mother's Love

When the lights went out, leaving everyone in unaccustomed darkness, Sophia was working the night shift, doing the same work she did every night on a monotonous assembly line, performing tasks a simple minded robot would do for a different society. When she was first here, she was amazed that it was cheaper and easier to use slaves than robots for tasks like this. She wondered what the society was like that she was working for. Were they advanced? Prosperous? Did they know—or care—about the terrible price being paid by those who made the goods they were buying? No one in the camp knew the answers. It no longer mattered. She just did her job. Thinking and questioning led nowhere but despair.

People exchanged whispered speculations when the lights failed to come back on. It wasn't the first time the lights had gone out, but it was the first time they stayed out. Workers sat in the dark, wondering. Without knowing why, Sophia connected Tobin's disappearance with the power failure, though she couldn't imagine how he would be involved. There were those in the camp who occasionally tried various types of sabotage, but she knew that none of them would trust Tobin. They wouldn't trust any new inmate, no matter how likeable. She herself had her own sabotage plans, some explosives she had managed to spirit away from a job she once did, and which she had hidden for three years, saving them for the right moment. As much as she loved and trusted Tobin, even she would never consider telling him of her preparations. She hadn't even told Reyas.

Finally, trustees ordered everyone to their dormitories. Once outside, it was obvious that something truly out of the ordinary was happening, on a far wider scale than anyone had dared imagine. Everything was dark, except for moonlight occasionally breaking faintly through the thinning clouds. Sophia could see just well enough to know that most guards weren't in their usual places. A small handful of guards stood on a second story walkway, weapons pointed down at the slaves, scrutinizing each slave carefully through vision enhancers, but most of the guards were nowhere to be seen. Slaves who had forgotten hope suddenly felt hope surge within them at a wildly spreading rumor that the missing guards had gone in pursuit of an escaped slave. It was hard to believe. No one had ever escaped. All this was unprecedented. Escape simply wasn't possible—or was it? The mere thought of escape was titillating. The camp had always been run with the same predictably monotonous routine day in and day out. The camp had never been completely dark before, even when power had failed momentarily in individual buildings. No one had ever seen so few guards on duty. There had never been even a rumor of an escape. It was all a thrilling change.

Feeling safer after they were inside their dormitory, Sophia and a few other women in her section found a window where they could discreetly peer outside. Most others sat in the darkness on their beds, talking quietly among themselves, waiting to see what would happen next on this night like no other night they had experienced in this camp.

Sophia was glad the rain had finally stopped. The grounds were still soaked, but at least she could leave the window open. Listening carefully, she tried to imagine what was happening outside. It was something important. She could feel it. Most of the slaves sat passively, waiting, but a few, who Sophia suspected had been planning sabotage for a long time, were trickling out of the dormitory, one at a time, trying to remain inconspicuous. She moved with Reyas to an open doorway facing the compound, where they could get a better view. They saw nothing out of the ordinary, but from time to time heard a strange sound, like a body hitting the ground after falling from a height. Sometimes they heard cries of pain, but they could see nothing.

It seemed forever to Sophia, this wait in the dark, while other slaves drifted out of the building, one by one, obviously intending to take advantage of an unexpected opportunity. She remained safely in the doorway, listening to the cries of pain, each always accompanied by the sound of a falling body, waiting for the right moment to carry out her own sabotage plan. Finally, the strange sounds stopped. It was deadly quiet. No one moved. No one spoke.

She decided it was time to act, but before she could tell Reyas of her plans for sabotage, she saw two men emerge from the darkness outside, running, coming directly toward them. Without hesitation, she shoved Reyas back into the pitch black just inside the door and moved as far back into darkness as she could, but remained protectively in front of Reyas.

Breathing hard and barefooted, the two men entered the building, stopping just feet away. One of them called out, "Sophia? Are you here?" It was Tobin's voice. The other, an unfamiliar voice, cried out, "Mom! It's me, Cody!"

"Cody, is it really you?" was all Sophia could manage to stammer, her voice breaking up with sobs.

"Yes, he's Cody," she heard Tobin's voice say.

Immediately Sophia embraced the man who had identified himself as Cody, kissing him, crying. Cody dropped his harpoon, bow, and quiver of arrows to the floor as he embraced her.

"Is it really you, Cody?"

"Yes."

Sophia ran her fingers along his face. "If only I could see what you look like."

Tobin turned on a small light he carried, allowing Cody and Sophia to see each other in dim light. They stepped back just enough to see each other while still holding hands.

"What's happened to you?" involuntarily escaped from Sophia's lips at the sight of Cody with his missing teeth, crooked nose, scars, and the mark of the warrior painted on his face.

Tobin reminded her, "I told you that Cody and I are both Quogian warriors now."

She couldn't remember. She couldn't remember anything. All she could feel was joy at seeing Cody alive and at being with him. If his life had been hard, it certainly was not his fault. She embraced him again. If Cody was even half the man Tobin had said he was, she was proud of him regardless what he looked like. Stepping back, looking him over more carefully, she told Cody, "You are strong, a warrior. I am proud of you," and embraced him again. "I am so glad to see you again." After looking him over again, she said, "You're not wearing shoes. Either of you."

"It's a long story," Tobin answered, "we'll tell you about it later."

As Sophia and Cody looked each other over, Cody tried to reconcile his memories as a ten year old of his mother with her short but neat hair, her always crisp military uniform, and her lively face and voice, with this somber looking woman, her head shaven, wearing grimy overalls, with dirty hands and fingernails, and a very tired looking face.

"Mother, I make this oath as a Quogian warrior. For the rest of your days, you will live an easy life. A happy life. If it's the last thing I do."

After embracing Cody again and kissing him, Sophia turned to Tobin. "You too, you're a warrior too. I'm so proud to see my two boys fighting together." Then, noticing that Tobin was carrying a weapon he had taken from a dead guard, but that Cody had nothing, she asked, "Where are your weapons?" Cody silently pointed to his harpoon, bow, and arrows on the floor.

Tobin answered, "Cody prefers traditional weapons."

Cody added, "Those guards never knew what hit them."

Tobin said, "He just picked them off like he picks off animals when we go hunting."

Sophia embraced Cody again. "I'm so proud of you."

Tobin warned them he was turning off the light. It was too dangerous to leave it on. Once again, they were cloaked in blackness.

Cody could say nothing more than, "I love you, I love you," as the tears streamed down his face. It was too dark to see his tears, but Sophia felt them on her skin, relishing the wetness of them like she had never relished anything in her life, and hearing his strong voice choking with barely stifled sobs.

A faint light appeared in the darkness, the illuminated face of the communicator in Tobin's hand. As he handed the communicator to Sophia, Carlos' voice came from it.

"Carlos?"

"Sophia!"

They lapsed into English as Sophia told a little of what had happened to her. Then she told Carlos, "I am so proud of our son."

Carlos replied that he too was proud of Cody and of what he had done.

Tobin interrupted them. "You can talk later. Accabo brought down their computers, but he doesn't know how long he can keep them down. That's the only thing keeping the rest of the guards out."

"A Lekadian ship is coming to help," Carlos told them. "You just have to keep the guards out until the Lekadians arrive."

Cody hugged Sophia again and then picked up his weapons.

"Don't let the guards get to their ship," Sophia warned, "they'll use missiles to destroy the camp. They've done it before."

"That's my job," Cody replied, "we already planned it out."

Sophia asked, "What kind of explosives did you bring?"

"We didn't," Cody answered, "Accabo's finding where they're stored."

"You're not doing it, Cody."

"Yes, I can do it."

"I know you can do it. I said you're not going to do it. I'm doing it."

"No, you're my mother. I won't let you."

"How much experience with explosives do you have?"

Cody didn't reply.

"I didn't think so. I'm doing it, Cody."

"No, you can't do it. You're a woman."

"I'll excuse you only once for saying that. I already have the explosives. I can blow up that ship before you even find explosives."

Carlos' voice came over the communicator. "Cody, your mother is a warrior. She can do it."

"I will help you, Sophia" Reyas said.

"No, this job only requires one person," Sophia replied, "Go with Cody. He will need your help."

Cody started to object that he didn't need a girl's help, but stopped.

Seeing the unhappy look on Cody's face, Sophia added, "Reyas is strong and brave. She will be useful to you."

"I know how blasters work," Reyas told Cody, "I've been watching the guards."

Cody agreed to take Reyas with him but didn't look happy about it.

They decided that Cody and Reyas would return to protect Accabo in the control room, Tobin would direct the slaves toward the exit gates that Accabo was opening, and Sophia would enter the slavers' ship to set the explosives. Before they split up, Tobin handed her the communicator so she could talk more with Carlos.

Cody wasn't happy about having a girl tagging along after him, needing protection and slowing him down, but he had no choice. After tearful embraces, they set off on their missions.

* * *

The sky was clearing, allowing moonlight to illuminate the camp. Speaking over the communicator to Carlos, Sophia described how completely the place had changed. "No more bright lights. No lights at all. The exit gates are open. No foremen or trustees in sight. They're probably all in hiding. They know what other slaves will do to them if they find them. Guards' bodies, lying all over. Cody killed them with his arrows. Arrows! I never imagined I'd see this day." Feeling like a young girl, giddy in enthusiasm she didn't realize she was still capable of, she frantically dug up the explosives she had buried three years earlier, praying she still remembered the exact location, never admitting to herself her deep fear that they might have been ruined by moisture. Letting down Cody in that way would be the worst thing she could imagine.

When she dug them up and opened the carefully sealed container, she was relieved to see she had packed them well. They were still dry. Hurrying to the ship, with no one blocking her way, Sophia continued feeling stunned at how abruptly her world had turned inside out.

As she climbed the steps up to the ship's hatch, she described the scene to Carlos, the slaves streaming out from the gates, fleeing to the surrounding hills, the wild cheering from all directions, and the sounds of office equipment and guards' residences being smashed by slaves more intent on revenge than survival. She told him that she could see flames and smoke beginning to rise from those looted and smashed places and could hear occasional detonations. There were no major explosions, so she assumed that the main explosives store had remained intact. It was simply other people like herself, slaves who had seized opportunities over the years to accumulate things that might be useful if the guards ever lost control.

They maintained silence while she located the right place for the explosives and set the charges. They kept the channel open, however, so they could be in each other's company, even if they were not speaking.

She entered the ship without any problem. Obviously, the slavers had expected their security measures to keep slaves far from the ship and had simply left it wide open. The last time she was on this ship, she was a slave with no control over her own fate. Now she was master of her fate and more importantly, master of this ship. Soon, the years of misery this ship had brought to thousands would end. The ship would not survive another hour.

She paused to reflect on the concept of an hour. That was Earth time. It hadn't existed for her since she left the *Marco Polo*. Since then, she had lived on alien time, more accurately on slave time, when the only time that mattered was dictated by the slavers, and by their foremen, the slaves who licked their masters' boots and made the lives of their fellow slaves such hell. She wondered how many of the foremen were still alive, perhaps now wanting only to die. She couldn't imagine that fellow slaves who had suffered under them would show them mercy. Certainly the foremen had shown no mercy in the years before fortune turned against them.

It had been such a shock to see Cody. Seven years ago, she and Carlos assumed he would get his training and education on the *Marco Polo*, finally returning to Earth around age 40 with a lifetime of experience meeting aliens and exploring distant parts of the galaxy that no one else could match, ready to start a brilliant career with United Space Fleet. Even after Tobin told her that Cody had become a traditional warrior on Quogue, she hadn't stopped to reflect on what that really meant. In her mind, she continued to see him as the well educated starship ensign she long ago had expected him to be at this age.

The reality was so very different. She wondered whether Cody could still even read. She hadn't wanted to spoil the reunion by asking, but she couldn't help wondering about it. Did he know any mathematics? Could he even add and subtract? Or was he simply as he appeared, a strong and brave but primitive young warrior? He had promised to take care of her for the rest of her life after he freed her, but what if she found a way to return to Earth? There was no place on Earth for a strong and brave but primitive young warrior, and probably no place for a highly trained starship military officer like her in whatever society Cody was living in. Then again, Earth had doubtlessly changed in the centuries since she left. Today, she might be nearly as out of place on Earth as Cody.

Still, Tobin had been right. She was proud of Cody. He had turned out well. If he wasn't a modern, educated, civilized young man, he bore none of the blame for it.

* * *

Cody encountered the first of the returning guards as he approached the control room where Accabo was working. If Accabo didn't get that gate closed soon, the rest of the guards would surge through in moments.

A guard stood between Cody and the control room, but didn't see Cody approaching, arrow in his bow, ready to shoot. When the guard finally did see him, he immediately aimed his weapon at Cody but, perhaps startled at seeing a bow and arrow pointed at him, hesitated a moment too long. He died instantly when Cody's arrow pierced his neck. Reflexively reaching back into his quiver, Cody discovered he had used the last of his arrows. Then he saw Reyas step up to him. He had completely forgotten about the girl he was supposed to protect. She now stood calmly offering him a bloody arrow she had pulled from a guard's body. He sheepishly accepted her offering. As he crept closer to the control room, Reyas calmly retrieved two more bloody arrows from fallen guards.

Coming around a corner, he encountered two more guards, their weapons aimed into the control room. Without hesitation he let an arrow fly, hitting one guard just as the other guard fired his weapon into the control room. Cody quickly took one of Reyas' bloody arrows from his quiver. He shot the arrow at the guard but missed. The guard turned to aim his weapon at him. Cody managed to duck back around the corner just in time to avoid being shot. The guard stepped into the control room. Cody heard him fire his weapon again and then heard Accabo scream in pain.

Cody ran to the control room and threw his harpoon, sending it clear through the guard's chest.

Accabo was slumped over the console, shot in the back.

A third guard stepped from the shadows, holding a weapon aimed at Cody. The guard was grinning. Cody reached for an arrow, knowing he didn't have a chance, but unwilling to die without a fight. As he notched the arrow into his bow, knowing he was dead no matter what he did, the grin disappeared from the guard's face. Somewhere, a weapon fired. The guard fell to the ground, the stench of his burning uniform and flesh filling the room. Whirling around, Cody saw Reyas holding the weapon, her finger still on the firing control, a steady ray burning into the fallen guard.

"Reyas, he's dead!"

Reyas just stared, blind hatred in her face, saying nothing, not releasing the control, vile smelling smoke billowing up from the corpse.

"Reyas, you can stop now."

Reyas slowly released the control and lowered the weapon.

Accabo was still slumped over the console, unconscious.

"Come on Reyas, we've got to get out of here. Accabo was the only one who could keep the guards out."

Reyas kneeled to pick up the dead guard's weapon and as she did, Kwe entered the room, his weapon drawn.

"Reyas, watch out!" Cody shouted, quickly aiming his crossbow at Kwe.

Shouting, "No, Cody, no!" Reyas jumped up and pushed the crossbow aside, just as Cody fired. The arrow barely missed Kwe.

"Reyas, what are you doing?" Cody cried out.

Kwe lowered his weapon and said, "Thank you, Reyas."

Cody stared incredulously. "You know him?"

"Cody, this is Kwe," Reyas answered, "he's not like the other guards."

"I'm sorry I had to take you and Sophia into that room, Reyas. I had no choice. The guards were all expected to do it."

"You are the only one who never did anything to us."

"Every time, I thought of my fiancée. I'd kill any man who did anything to her. I never would be able to look my fiancée in the face again if I did what the guards do to women here."

Cody broke in. "It's nice meeting you Kwe, but we've got to get out of here. Now. Can you help us?"

"Yes. Give me your crossbow and hold out your hands so I can cuff you."

Cody didn't move. "You can trust him," Reyas assured Cody, handing Kwe her weapons and extending her arms.

"Are you sure?" Cody asked.

Kwe put handcuffs on her, but didn't lock them. "Hold your arms like this, so no one sees that the handcuffs aren't locked. Don't let them fall off!"

Cody handed his crossbow to Kwe but didn't extend his wrists. Pointing to Accabo he said, "I've got to carry him. I can't carry him if I'm handcuffed."

Kwe handcuffed Accabo instead and told Cody to pick him up. Whispering, "Trust me," he ordered in a much louder voice, "Outside. Turn right. No tricks or I'll kill you." Following Kwe's barked orders, they proceeded down the hallway. Guards were returning, running along the hallways, looking behind every door, weapons drawn and ready to fire. Every time they met another guard, Kwe told them he was taking prisoners to their commander.

Just as they reached the stairway down to the ground, an officer stopped them and demanded to know why Cody wasn't handcuffed. Kwe gave his usual explanation, but to his chagrin the officer replied, "I'm looking for the commander too. I'll come along."

"I'm glad you're here sir. I wasn't sure I could do this by myself."

"You'll learn, son." They proceeded down the stairs, Cody carrying Accabo, Reyas behind them, trying to keep the officer from seeing that her handcuffs were unlocked, followed by the officer and Kwe. At the bottom of the steps, the officer stared at Reyas and asked, "What's wrong with her cuffs?" He took hold of her hands and the handcuffs fell to the ground. "Don't you even know how to put on handcuffs right, son?" He looked up just in time to see Kwe shoot him dead.

Unlocking Accabo's handcuffs, Kwe said to Cody and Reyas, "Go! Get out of here!"

"Kwe, Come with us. You don't belong here," pleaded Reyas.

"No, the slaves need me. Besides, I have a friend here I want to find. A guard. Just a few hours ago we were talking about getting out of here, we were going to go fishing."

Cody's face lit up. "You're a fisherman?"

"Just for fun. Everyone in my family fished for a living in the old days. Now, only a few have work."

"I'm a fisherman. Me and my friend Tobin. He's here somewhere."

"Cody, Reyas, you must visit me at home. I can show you the best fishing spot on any planet. Please, promise me you'll come, both of you."

Cody and Reyas both promised to visit.

"I live on the planet Devlan Nine. That's the Lekadian name for it. My clan name is Suhrat. We live in the province called The Wilds. Can you remember that? Suhrat ar Kwegathi, known as Kwe, in The Wilds."

Reyas repeated, "Suhrat ar Kwegathi, known as Kwe, in The Wilds, on Devlan Nine."

"Can you remember that, Reyas?" asked Cody, "I don't think I will."

"Just go to Hangtown in The Wilds on Devlan Nine and ask for 'Kwe'. Everyone there knows me."

"We will," Cody promised. "You must visit me on Quogue. I will ask Dariel to let you join his crew. We can hunt RedFins together. I am Cody, son of Starman, apprentice to Dariel of the village of HarborSide."

"I am just Reyas, born on Tarfil, but raised a slave. I do not know who my family was."

Kwe took out two weapons. "I have to go. Here, take these."

Reyas took one of the weapons. Ignoring Cody's scornful look, Reyas took the second one and shoved it under his belt. "Take it. Don't be stupid."

Extending his hand in the traditional Quogian handclasp, Cody said, "We owe you our lives, Kwe." They embraced. "Until Devlan Nine."

"And Quogue. I will hunt the RedFin with you, Cody son of Starman. That's my dream. To work as a fisherman, like all my forebears. That's all I ever wanted."

As Kwe returned inside, Cody and Reyas proceeded cautiously to the edge of the launching area, where Cody gently set Accabo down, out of sight of any guards. "Reyas, he's like a brother to me. Keep him safe no matter what. I've got to get my mother out of that ship before the guards get there." Without waiting for an answer, he set off running toward the ship.

As he ran, guards emerged from the compound, heading for the ship. Cody was almost at the steps leading up to the open hatch, but the guards were just ahead of him. He stopped, watching despairingly as they ran by him, just feet away, many of them wounded from being shot or having debris thrown at them, proof that the slaves were exacting their revenge. In normal times, Cody would have been shot without further thought for simply standing there, but today, all the panicking guards could think of was escape. Cody was invisible to them.

A second group of guards ran for the ship, followed by more wounded stragglers, as flames and smoke consumed more of the compound and explosions became louder and more frequent, accompanied by the exuberant cheering of freed slaves. The torrent of slaves fleeing the camp was reversing and many were now returning from outside, eager to take part in the slave camp's destruction.

Cody stood waiting for a break in the stream of guards running for the ship so he could get on board and find his mother. He didn't care if he died in the attempt. Getting her off that ship was all that mattered.

He saw a break before the next group of guards. They weren't far away, but at least not close enough to physically bar his way, so he lunged for the steps, determined to climb onboard before anyone could stop him, but guards who were willing to ignore his presence could not ignore him trying to enter their ship. Suddenly his back felt like it was on fire and his nostrils filled with the stench of burning flesh, his own flesh. Falling to the ground, he writhed helplessly in pain, so agonizingly close to the stairs, watching helplessly as one guard after another ran around or jumped over him in their haste to get on board.

Then the stairs were cast aside and the hatch closed. Cody staggered to his feet, leaning on the side of the ship for support, pounding on it, calling to his mother, telling her to get out of there.

Tobin saw him from a distance and sprinted to him. Grabbing Cody's chest, he desperately dragged him away from the ship, Cody resisting him all the way.

"My mother's in there! We've got to get her out!"

"It's too late. We'll both be killed if we're here when that ship takes off!"

Tobin had barely pulled him out of the immediate blast range when the ship fired up its engines. The blast sent them tumbling and sliding along the coarse surface of the launch pad. They watched helplessly as the ship lifted toward the sky.

* * *

Inside the ship, Sophia set the last of the explosives. She could hear the guards congratulating themselves on getting away before the Lekadians arrived. They knew they would be disciplined for not saving even a single slave from the camp's destruction, but least they were alive. What happened tomorrow could wait until tomorrow.

She whispered into the communicator that she was done, and only had to throw a switch to set off the explosives.

"Don't do it unless you have to, Sophia. They won't get away. The Lekadian authorities will be here soon. Just hide. Don't let the guards see you."

"Carlos, they're going to blow up the camp. They want to destroy the evidence."

"Don't do anything."

"Cody is down there. So is Tobin, and Reyas. Thousands of innocent people are down there."

"I'll tell Lewelle. Maybe he can do something."

"There's no time. They're preparing to fire the missiles. I'm the only one who can stop them."

"Please Sophia, there has to be another way."

"Carlos, I've got to do it. It's the only way. I love you, Carlos. I thank God that he gave me back my son and that I could see what a fine young man he's grown into. You've been a good father. Tell Cody that I am far happier doing this than rotting in that camp the rest of my life. Tell him I am proud of him. Promise me you'll take care of Reyas like your own daughter."

"I promise."

"Do you remember the prayer song that came to my grandmother just before her death?"

"Yes, I could never forget that," Carlos replied. Then he realized what she intended to do. "Sophia, don't do it."

"There's no choice. They're ready to launch the missiles. Sing with me."

"Sophia..."

"I love you Carlos. Tell Cody I love him." She began singing her grandmother's prayer song.

Carlos joined in, singing over the communicator.

No longer caring whether she was discovered, ecstatic to again be singing with the man she loved, she turned up the communicator to its loudest volume. She had missed Carlos' voice. It sounded even better than she remembered. Feeling one with him and with God, she sang loudly, ignoring the guards who were now jumping from their seats and running toward where she was hiding.

She threw the switch.

* * *

On the ground, Cody watched stunned as the ship blew apart. Barely conscious of anything but the fiery cascading remains of that exploding ship, he let Tobin cradle him in his arms and cried like a baby.

Reyas was walking slowly toward them, carrying Accabo. Holes from shots fired by the guards' weapons were burned through his clothes, revealing serious and painful wounds on his legs and torso. Only when they came closer did Cody notice that Reyas too had been shot, in her left leg, a terrible looking wound, but although she was limping, she betrayed no sign of the agonizing pain she must be feeling. After very gently setting Accabo on the ground, she wiped the tears from Cody's cheeks.

Tobin slid aside, letting Cody move over to embrace her, this girl who looked so identical to all the other slaves, with shaven head and grimy overalls, but who had shown such amazing strength. When he touched her, however, he felt her recoil, involuntarily, just for a moment. He paused, and then after a brief hesitation she embraced him. Holding her close, their tears intermingling, Cody knew the grief she was feeling. He sensed the gentleness in her and wondered how this coexisted so easily with the toughness she had shown in the minutes he had known her, a girl so much more courageous than any woman who until today he ever imagined might exist.

Firing Squad

Lekadian shuttles were now regularly arriving and departing at the launch pad where just three days before, Sophia left on her fatal flight. The shuttles were bringing rescue workers and supplies from the Lekadian fleet now in orbit around the planet and taking wounded survivors to a hospital ship. A hastily built clinic just outside the slave camp was being used for emergency care. Next to it, a stasis structure served as a temporary morgue. Near the launch pad, a fenced off area served as a holding pen for the surviving camp guards until they could be transported to the Lekadian home world for trial. They were heavily guarded by Lekadian soldiers, whose stonily expressionless faces made the average Lekadian look almost passionate.

The fires had for the most part burned themselves out, there were no more guards roaming free, and Lekadians now worked side by side with former slaves, Quogians, and humans to locate survivors in the rubble of the slave camp. Most of the buildings in the camp had been severely damaged or destroyed. Everywhere, smoke still rose from the rubble.

Dust, soot, and smoke mixed relentlessly in the air, coating rescuers and slaves alike, giving them the appearance of figures sculpted from stone and just now dug up from the ruins of some terribly ancient civilization destroyed in an instant of calamity. The rescuers all wore protective breathing apparatus, adding to the aura of unreality, as they frantically sought survivors, or at least bodies that next of kin could claim. Paying no heed to their exhaustion, they continued digging through rubble, trying not to think about the skeletal remains of walls and roofs often teetering precariously over their heads. Every now and then, one of these skeletons collapsed, unable any longer to sustain even its own weight. Each time, nearby rescuers would pray that no one was beneath the collapsing debris. After a few moments of waiting for screams of pain that miraculously never came, everyone would go back to work digging out survivors, trying to ignore whatever might be poised to tumble onto their own heads.

Accabo was still confined to the clinic. The wounds he received while liberating the slave camp were severe. He was paralyzed from the chest down, and was on life support. Reyas had been hospitalized there, but was now working along with Cody, Tobin, Lara, and even Lewelle to dig survivors out of the ruins of the slave camp. Every morning and evening, they visited Accabo in the clinic.

Visiting Accabo meant passing by the pen holding the former guards, who sat or lay in the dirt in the hot afternoon sun and in the cold of the night, always under the steely eyes of the Lekadian soldiers guarding them. Kwe was among the prisoners, usually by himself in a corner away from the other guards. On Reyas' advice, Carlos, Cody, and Tobin refrained from visiting or even greeting him. They could see Kwe watching them, but Reyes had warned that the guards would be quick to exact revenge on him if they suspected him of collaborating with slaves.

Carlos promised her that he would make sure they attended Kwe's trial and would testify in his defense.

For most of each day, they worked in the ruins, seeking survivors. Lewelle had insisted that Cody and Tobin wear their armor and face paint while the rescue efforts were going on. "You are their heroes. You gave them their freedom," Lewelle said, "they will feel better knowing you are working alongside them."

"I don't trust him. Lekadians don't care about other people's feelings," Cody muttered, to no one in particular. Tobin agreed that it wasn't in character for Lekadians to be so conscious of the feelings of others. Both were sure that Lewelle had hidden motives, but could only guess what they might be.

Most of the time they were working too hard to worry about Lewelle's motives. What was most remarkable was that the normally cerebral Lekadians, well known for never associating on an equal footing with other races, were now working side by side with Quogians and freed slaves of all races to rescue survivors. Even Lewelle himself was out there much of the time, covered with the same gritty gray dust as everyone else, risking his own life to rescue survivors. Though Tobin and Cody saw little point in wearing their armor, now gritty gray in appearance, it unquestionably evoked a powerful response from every former slave they encountered and, inexplicably, even from an occasional Lekadian.

Groups of rescuers were working in different locations in the camp, digging wherever someone reported hearing signs of life. Carlos was working with Cody, Tobin, and several former slaves of various races. Members of a Lekadian government news crew had fanned out through the ruins, holo-imaging rescuers as they heroically pulled survivors from the debris. Reporters, fascinated by Cody and Tobin and their ancient warrior armor, and by Carlos, the captain of a lost ship from a distant civilization, were paying particular attention to them.

They had pulled the last survivor found in the wreckage they were currently searching, a badly burned Quogian youth named Rednar. While they waited for medics to return with a stretcher, reporters were taking advantage of the lull to get some interviews. Amused by the reporters' fascination with their armor, Cody and Tobin responded by striking mock heroic poses for the holo-cams. The stretcher finally arrived, and the reporters left after recording the Warrior Brothers helping medics lift Rednar onto the stretcher. As the medics began to carry Rednar away, he struggled to raise one hand, signaling them to stop. He touched Tobin reverently. Gazing at Tobin and Cody like they were apparitions, he whispered, "You returned. When I was a child on Tarfil, my grandparents said the Warrior Brothers would return when we needed them, but I never really believed it."

"Here we are," replied Tobin.

Rednar struggled to speak. "Come closer. Let me see your faces." Cody and Tobin removed their breathing apparatus, and Tobin leaned down as Rednar gazed at the mark on his face. "Yes, it is the mark of the warrior." As he stared at the painted symbol on Tobin's face, Rednar realized he had seen Tobin before. "You were here. A slave. Sophia's friend. I heard they took you, killed you."

"No. My brothers here tricked them and freed me." He pointed to Cody. "There is a third Warrior Brother. His name is Accabo, the bravest of all. He is recovering from the guards shooting him."

"Cody, let me touch you, please." Rednar struggled to lift his arm, but couldn't, so Cody leaned over and took Rednar's other hand in his own. "You are the human?"

"Yes."

Rednar's voice was failing him. Tobin gave him some water, and Rednar tried again. "You came far to help us. Over there. A human boy. Buried. I tried to tell the others." As Rednar spoke, he struggled to point toward some ruins not far away.

Cody pointed at a demolished residence. "There?"

"Yes."

"How do you know?"

"They were going to blow it up. Him and friends. His friends got out, but not him. It blew up. He was still inside." He paused to drink some more of Tobin's water before continuing. "His friends tried to dig him out. Guards chased them away. I heard him call for help this morning."

"What was his name?" Cody demanded.

"Don't know. Human." Rednar lost consciousness and was carried away by Lekadian medics.

Carlos led Cody and Tobin to the demolished residence that Rednar had pointed to. Only one wall and part of the roof still stood, and looked ready to fall at any moment. Cody tapped one wall. It wobbled scarily until Tobin took hold of it and held it still.

Cody shouted into the wreckage, but got no response. Tobin found a heavy rock and used it to bang on a pipe that ran down into the ruins, but still there was no response. Signaling Tobin to stop, Carlos leaned down to listen more carefully, but found his breathing apparatus making it difficult. Removing it, he put his ear down to the ruins again. Finally he looked up. "I think I hear something. Do it again. Harder." Tobin brought the rock down as hard as he could, striking the pipe as hard as he could, repeatedly, the deafening sound reverberating through nearby buildings, until Carlos signaled him to stop and listened again. Finally Carlos looked up, yelling triumphantly, "He's alive!" All three of them yelled exuberantly into the wreckage at the top of their lungs, calling out to the unknown victim, reassuring him that rescue was coming.

It wasn't easy. Collapsed walls, shattered glass, and broken pipes made it hazardous. They had to be careful with every move not to do anything that might bring down the remaining parts of the walls and roof that were so precariously balanced above them. Tobin lifted and moved away the heavy pieces while Cody and Carlos struggled together to extract smaller but still heavy pieces from underneath, moving them out of the way, building them into small walls of debris that would offer at least some protection if the rest of the building suddenly came down on them.

After lifting up and moving out of the way an immense piece of what had been the roof, Tobin climbed down into the deepening tunnel. Removing his helmet, he handed it to Carlos. "Here, take it. Down here you need this more than I do." Gratefully putting the helmet on, Carlos thanked Tobin, who then crawled back outside.

It was hot work. They were all sweating profusely. Occasionally they stopped work, removed their breathing apparatus, and shouted encouragement into the ruins. A few times, they heard a faint, muffled cry from under the ruins but each time it became weaker. After a while, there were no more responses to their shouts. They worked in silence, somberly, Tobin lifting up the immense pieces that blocked their way, while Cody and Carlos worked together to clear the debris from underneath. Finally they uncovered a hand, then an arm. They had found the victim. He had a pulse but had lost consciousness. Frantically tearing away the remaining debris, they finally completely uncovered him.

He was definitely human, about Cody's age, but looked like every other slave in the camp, emaciated, with a shaved head, and wearing the ubiquitous gray coveralls. He had clearly lost a lot of blood and almost certainly had numerous broken bones. Cody checked the slave's pulse. "He's alive."

Tobin turned to Carlos. "I'll go get the medics."

"No, you're the strongest. You've got to stay here in case one of those walls comes down. I'll go. Here, take your helmet back, you may need it."

"You keep it Captain."

"No, take it."

Reluctantly, Tobin took back his helmet and put it on as Carlos left to get the medics.

Removing his breathing apparatus, Cody gave the slave mouth to mouth respiration, something Carlos had insisted upon everyone onboard the *Marco Polo* knowing, even children. At first, there was no response. Finally, the slave's breathing became stronger. Cody sat back and watched as the slave opened his eyes and looked around. "Warrior Brothers? Am I dead?"

"No, you're alive," answered Cody. "Here, drink some water." Cody held his water flask to the slave's mouth.

Between sips of water, the slave stared incredulously at Cody and Tobin. Finally he spoke, struggling to get out the words. "I heard about you. Warrior gods from Quogue. Freeing the camp. Not real. Couldn't be. Didn't believe." He stopped trying to speak and stared at Cody. "Cody? Is that you?"

"Yes," Cody replied, feeling embarrassed at not knowing who he was speaking with.

"You don't recognize me, do you?"

Cody didn't answer.

"Billy. Billy Jobanga. *Marco Polo.*"

Cody still didn't recognize his childhood friend. He looked nothing like Billy did seven years ago. "Billy? I'm sorry."

"It's OK."

Billy began to speak, but stopped, moaning. "I'm in bad shape, Cody."

"You'll be OK. I promise." Turning to Tobin, Cody said, "Billy was my best friend on the *Marco Polo*."

Tobin laid his hands on Billy's head and after a few moments said, "You're hurt pretty bad, Billy. Don't move." He then sang one of his wordless tunes.

Billy began to speak, but stopped when Cody put his finger to his lips. Cody took his hand and held it while Tobin sang. Finally, Tobin stopped singing. He looked exhausted. Without saying anything, he lay down on his back in the debris.

Billy's eyes opened wide. "Cody, what just happened? I feel great."

"Lie still. Your body is still broken up pretty bad."

Billy tried sitting up but couldn't manage it. "I guess you're right. What did he do?"

"Just lie down. The medics are coming."

"Cody, your mother, she's in the camp."

"She's dead. She saved all of our lives."

"She was strong. I'm sorry, Cody."

"But my father's here. He's gone to bring the medics."

"The Captain? Here? Alive?"

"Yes, Billy. Now take it easy. Rest."

For a while, they said nothing. Billy stared in fascination at Cody, finally unable to resist asking, "What's that get-up you're wearing? You working for those ancient Quogian warriors?"

"You're not going to believe this, Billy. I am one of those ancient Quogian warriors."

Billy started to laugh, but a renewed burst of pain cut his laughing short. He struggled to speak. "You? You're not Quogian."

"It's complicated, Billy, I'll explain later. Don't speak. You need to rest."

Billy waited until the pain subsided, then asked, "The games we used to play. Do you remember? When we were kids?"

"Sure."

"Fighting the Lekadians?"

"That was a long time ago, Billy."

"Cody, are you working for the Lekadians?"

"They brought us here."

"They're treacherous. You know that. Why are you helping them?"

"No, it's them who are helping us."

"You don't trust them, do you?"

Cody waited a moment before answering. "I don't have much choice. I wouldn't be here if it wasn't for them."

"But do you trust them?"

"No."

Carlos arrived with four Lekadian medics. At the sight of the approaching Lekadians, Billy reflexively reached out and grabbed Cody by the arm.

Cody reassured him with a wide grin on his face, "Don't worry. I am a Warrior Brother. I won't let anything happen to you." Moving aside to let the medics do their work, he watched as the typically taciturn Lekadians examined Billy impassively, tended to his wounds, and prepared to carry him back to the clinic. Cody turned to Carlos. "It's Billy."

"Thank God! I saw his name on the list of missing yesterday."

"You didn't tell me."

"I didn't want to raise your hopes. The odds were against finding him alive. What happened to Tobin?"

Tobin was lying in the debris a few feet away, looking exhausted. Cody had completely forgotten about him in his excitement at finding Billy alive. "Tobin? Are you OK?"

Carlos kneeled over him. "Tobin, what happened?"

When Tobin didn't reply, Cody answered, "He sang for Billy. And touched his head. I don't know what he did. Billy got a lot stronger after he did it."

Carlos removed Tobin's breathing apparatus and gave him some water. Slowly, Tobin sat up. "I gave my strength to your friend. He needed it more than I did."

Cody looked alarmed. "Your strength? You didn't lose it, did you?"

"I don't know. I don't think so. I never tried this before."

Cody watched with some annoyance as the medics went into a typically Lekadian trance, closing their eyes while they consulted each other about Billy's condition in their own private world. Billy watched, puzzled, until Cody explained about Lekadians going into cyberspace when they closed their eyes like that.

"But you don't really know what they're doing in there, do you Cody? They're Lekadians. You don't know what they might be up to."

"Accabo could tell us if he was here," answered Cody.

"Mental telepathy?" asked Billy.

"A Lekadian computer in his brain," answered Cody.

"A Warrior Brother with a Lekadian computer in his brain?"

Cody nodded yes.

"They're discussing your condition," Carlos said.

Billy didn't look impressed. "They sure don't look like they care about my condition."

"They're Lekadians," replied Cody.

"That's what I'm saying. I've heard all about them. I don't trust them a bit." Billy paused and looked up at the Lekadians, who were still staring impassively straight ahead, their eyes closed.

When the medics finally opened their eyes, they wordlessly lifted Billy onto a stretcher. Billy complained that his neck was hurting, but the lead medic responded dispassionately that he would be in the clinic in just a few minutes.

Billy turned to Cody. "Do you see anything I can put under my head? My neck really hurts."

Cody removed his breastplate, took off his shirt, rolled it up, and placed it under Billy's head.

"That feels better. Thanks."

Cody looked the lead medic straight in the eyes. "He is my friend. Make sure he gets good care."

"Everyone will know the human boy is a friend of the Warrior Brothers," the lead medic assured him as they lifted up the stretcher.

"Wait!" The medics stopped and watched curiously as Cody handed an arrow to Billy and told him, "Hold this. Everyone will know you are under my protection. Keep it with you."

Reporters came running up just in time to holo-image Cody handing the arrow to Billy. Gripping the arrow tightly in his fist, Billy said, "Damn, I never thought I'd be under the protection of an ancient warrior!" With just a trace of a smile on his face, Cody signaled the medics to leave, watching them carry Billy in the direction of the clinic while slowly strapping his breastplate back on over his bare chest. Reporters holo-imaged him putting it on, ignored him telling them to leave him alone, and pelted him with questions. Without taking an eye off the reporters, he took an arrow from his quiver, notched it into his bow, and aimed it in their direction. They scattered quickly.

The reporters' hasty retreat made Cody, Tobin, and Carlos all break out laughing, but the laughing stopped when Carlos asked, "Cody, do you know where the Lekadians took the guards?"

"Last time I saw, the guards were still inside that fenced off area."

"They're all gone now, Carlos answered.

"Kwe's gone too?"

"Yes."

"The Lekadians probably built a jail."

"No, there is no jail," Carlos replied, "and no prison ship in orbit."

"Maybe the Lekadians just let them go free instead of putting them on trial?" asked Cody.

"Lekadians never let prisoners go free," Tobin said, "especially slave camp guards. When Lekadians enslave other races, they claim they're only enslaving them for their own good. But they hate slavers who do it for profit. No, the Lekadians didn't let the guards go free."

"If that's true, where's Kwe?" asked Carlos.

The news crew was returning, so Carlos walked a short distance away, too tired to answer any more reporters' questions. Cody took an arrow from his quiver, put it in his crossbow, and aimed it at the approaching news crew, a menacing scowl on his face. One reporter, clearly nervous but braver or maybe more foolish than the others, approached him while her crew remained at a safe distance, their holo-cams recording everything.

"Leave me alone," Cody growled at her.

Standing her ground, she asked him if he knew how many women across the Lekadian Empire would see this report.

Cody had never seen a newscast, so Tobin explained while the reporter signaled her crew to move in closer. Turning her attention to Tobin, she asked, "Do either of you guys know what heroes you are? You freed the slaves. People all over the Empire will know all about you. No matter what planet you go to, you will be heroes. Women will be throwing themselves at you everywhere you go. Everyone will know what you look like. Watch this." She signaled one of the holo-cam operators to come over. The operator very nervously approached, warily keeping an eye on Cody's crossbow. Suddenly, images of Cody and Tobin in their armor, rescuing victims from teetering ruins, hovered lifelike in front of them.

Excited at the prospect of women across the Empire seeing them and knowing who they were, Cody and Tobin enthusiastically struck one heroic pose after another for the holo-cams while answering interviewers' questions.

Carlos watched the boys' playful antics, relieved that the reporters were leaving him alone. Cody and Tobin were enjoying themselves. He was glad to see it. They deserved it. The past four days had made Carlos prouder of Cody than he had dared hope while watching him grow up as a fisherman on Quogue. He was grateful that Sophia had at least gotten a chance before she died to see the man their son had become. The last few days hadn't given Carlos and Cody many private moments together, but when it was all over, Carlos promised himself, he would press Cody for every detail of how Sophia looked on that last day of her life.

But Carlos' pride in his son didn't help him understand the ancient warrior business. That was still a puzzle to him. Even more perplexing was Lewelle's attitude toward it. If anyone scorned the whole idea of the boys being reincarnated ancient warriors, it should be the atheist Lewelle. But Lewelle seemed enthralled by the idea. "What are his motives?" Carlos kept asking himself, unable to come up with an answer.

Inevitably, Carlos' thoughts drifted back to his crew. He had expected that the reunion with what was left of his crew would be a joyful moment. And it was joyful. But the joy they all felt couldn't match the sadness they felt for those who did not survive. Who could feel really joyful when so many friends and loved ones had been lost? Even worse, no one could know whether the others were dead or suffering in some other even more hellish place, perhaps wishing only to be dead. Adding to the mixed emotions were the deep and bitter animosities that had developed among some of them, the result of some of them having become slave camp trustees, and one having become one of the hated foremen. Compounding the mixed emotions was the resentment even some *Marco Polo* crewmembers felt against Reyas, who was still being ostracized by many of the former slaves.

Also tormenting Carlos was the question of whether life on a primitive planet like Quogue would be any more pleasant for his crew than life in this slave camp. At least in the slave camp, they had electricity and some conveniences. There were no conveniences on Quogue. Lewelle could probably use his influence to get them settled on one of the Tarfillian moons. Technology beyond what they ever knew on Earth did flourish there, but it would mean living in a corrupt spaceport society whose moral standards were mostly set by criminals. It wasn't a place where the generally idealistic crew of the *Marco Polo* would want to spend the rest of their lives.

Coming out of his daydreaming, Carlos watched proudly as Cody and Tobin strutted from one heroic pose to another amidst the ruins, showing off for the holo-cams. After what the boys had done and been through in the last few days, Carlos could understand a little showmanship as long as they didn't take themselves too seriously.

After the reporters finally left, he went with Cody and Tobin to visit the clinic, where they found Billy wearing a headset, off somewhere in cyberspace with Accabo, who was sitting blissfully with his eyes closed.

"Billy!" Cody called out loudly.

Billy didn't answer Cody's call, so Cody called out again, but Billy still didn't respond. Accabo opened his eyes and greeted his visitors before returning to cyberspace to get Billy.

A few moments later, Billy removed his headset. There was wonder in his eyes. "Have you been in there, Cody? Captain? Damn, you should try it. The women they have! The sex! Man, the sex!"

"None of it's real!" Cody countered.

"Try it. You'll be amazed how real it is."

"It's all in your head."

"Here, try it, Captain. It's not just sex. Sports, games, you can pilot their fighter ships. There's anything you want in there." Billy offered the headset to Carlos, who put it on and closed his eyes. "Cody, you've got to try it after your Dad."

"It's not real, Billy."

"Cody, when you're in there, it's as real as anything out here. OK, you want real? I've got news. It's official. Everyone's accounted for now."

"No more searching in the ruins?" asked Cody.

"No more searching." Billy waited a moment before continuing. "Cody, I've been thinking a lot the last few days. We're not going home, are we?"

"You mean Earth?"

"Yeah. I mean, Earth is still our home, right?"

"I haven't thought much about Earth," Cody replied. "No, Earth is not my home."

"It's all I've thought about for all these years. Just going home to Earth. Even though I've never been there. But lying here using that headset, in Lekadian cyberspace, I realized just how far we are from Earth. We don't have a chance of getting back there, do we?"

Cody thought for a moment before answering. "Quogue is my home. All my friends are there, except Tobin and Accabo. But my dad's like you. He still wants to go back to Earth."

"For you and me, Cody, maybe Earth really isn't our home, is it? We were born in deep space, far from Earth."

"You were born in space, Cody?" Accabo asked enviously. "In space, really?"

"Cody was the very first human being ever born in deep space," Billy replied proudly.

"Billy was born right after me," added Cody.

Cody looked at his father, who was motionless, still wearing the helmet. "Is he OK in there? The Lekadians won't try anything on him, will they?"

"Don't worry, Cody, he's safe," replied Billy. "Well, if we're not going home to Earth, can I go home with you? Do you think they'll let me into the space academy on Quogue? I'm the right age to start training."

Cody couldn't stifle a laugh. "Accabo, haven't you told Billy about Quogue?"

"No."

"Billy, there's something I've gotta tell you," Cody began to say.

Billy interrupted him. "Remember on the *Marco Polo*? Virtual reality space fighters, you and me. Lekadians didn't stand a chance against us."

"It wasn't real. Billy."

"Billy, Quogue isn't what you expect," Tobin said.

"I'm going into cyberspace to find Billy some information about Quogue," said Accabo, "so can see for himself."

Carlos removed his headset, a look of wonder on his face. "That's amazing! I was walking inside detailed plans for their ships. It's not like the virtual worlds we had on the *Marco Polo.* I actually became part of a Lekadian ship. That's how they operate. It's just like Lewelle said. A family and the ship, they all become almost one. The whole family lives on a ship and operates it. It's totally different than anything I've seen."

"No sex?" joked Cody.

The laughter was cut short when Accabo came out of cyberspace shouting, "They're executing Kwe! Now!"

Carlos, Cody, and Tobin jumped to their feet.

"Tell Lewelle to get his butt down here NOW!" Carlos barked at Accabo, "and tell Reyas to get out there!" before running with Cody and Tobin to the enclosure where the guards had been held. No one was there.

"Look! Over there," Tobin cried out, pointing farther back in the field where Lekadian soldiers, their weapons drawn, clustered around a pit. Breaking into a run, Carlos shouted loudly, "Stop shooting!" Guards were standing in the pit, falling one by one as soldiers shot them. Kwe was next to be shot. He was pleading for mercy, tears running down his face. Cody leaped in front of him while Carlos again ordered the officer in charge to order his men to stop shooting. After some heated words, the officer agreed to pause the executions until Lewelle and higher officers arrived.

Soon, a shuttle landed within sight at the launch pad. Lewelle stepped out and quickly walked over, accompanied by two military officers, immediately entering into intense discussion with the officers and Carlos. The officers insisted that this was a military action over which civilians had no jurisdiction, while Carlos insisted that the Lekadians should keep their promise to give the guards fair trials. Cody remained standing defiantly in front of Kwe, joined now by Tobin, ignoring soldiers' threats to kill them along with Kwe. No one noticed Reyas running toward them. She wedged herself into the space between Cody and Tobin, standing defiantly right in front in front of Kwe.

Carlos and the Lekadians were shouting angrily at each other. After managing to stop the shouting, Lewelle conferred silently with the officers, their eyes closed, while the soldiers kept their eyes open and their weapons ready to fire. When Lewelle and the officers finally opened their eyes, the officer in charge proclaimed solemnly, "At the request of Ambassador Lewelle Sul of Aktawaneh, my superior officers have ordered me to transfer jurisdiction over such condemned prisoner or prisoners as the former slave Reyas will designate, to Captain Carlos Jackson of Earth. Let all present bear witness that I perform this illegal action under protest."

Cody and Reyas hugged Kwe joyously.

The officer continued, "Reyas, point to the prisoners you want transferred to Captain Jackson." All the guards looked at her desperately. A few pleaded tearfully with her for mercy.

She pointed at Kwe. "Kwe. Kwe is the only one."

"What is your name, prisoner, and your home planet?" demanded the officer.

"Suhrat ar Kwegathi, known as Kwe, native of The Wilds, on the planet Devlan Nine."

"Do you have a means of leaving this planet, Suhrat ar Kwegathi of Devlan Nine?"

Before Kwe could answer, Lewelle said, "The official Lekadian Ambassadorial ship *Aktawaneh* will give him passage to his home planet. You have my personal guarantee on that."

The officer coldly ordered Kwe to climb out of the pit and then turned to Carlos. "Captain Jackson, as the military officer representing the planet Earth, you are hereby given full jurisdiction over the prisoner Suhrat ar Kwegathi of Devlan Nine. Do with him as you will. He is your prisoner now. Just do not free him on this planet. As long as he is on this planet, he is subject to Lekadian military justice. He will be shot on sight if he is not in your direct custody at all times."

As Kwe climbed out of the pit, helped by Reyas, Cody and Tobin, the soldiers took up their weapons and aimed them at the remaining prisoners. "You can't just shoot them!" shouted Carlos.

"They are guilty. These are evil men, Captain Jackson. The slave Reyas has condemned them through her silence," the officer replied. Addressing Reyas, he asked, "I ask you one final time. Are there any other prisoners we should spare?"

Reyas answered without hesitation, ignoring panicked guards begging her for mercy. "They showed no mercy. They deserve no mercy. Do what you want with them. Carlos, please let's just get Kwe out of here. Come on, Kwe." She turned and walked away, but returned when she realized that Kwe wasn't following. Instead, he had crawled back into the pit, despite the guns aimed in his direction, and was kneeling over one of the bodies, tears running from his eyes. "Was he your friend, Kwe?" she asked.

"Yes. He didn't deserve to die."

"I only saw him a few times, but he wasn't like the other guards," agreed Reyas. "You're right. He didn't deserve to die."

The Lekadian officer was growing impatient, ordering Kwe out of the pit and telling Carlos, "You must keep him under your direct control while he is on this planet. Remember, Captain Jackson, he is still a prisoner. He is your responsibility now."

Lewelle told Carlos to take Kwe to his ship. "Kwe will be safe there."

Cody and Tobin led Kwe away, but stopped when they realized that Carlos wasn't following. He was still standing at the pit, looking at the other prisoners. The officer turned to Carlos again. "You can leave now, Captain Jackson. There is nothing more for you to do here. You have done more than most others could do. Take your prisoner and leave." Reluctantly, Carlos turned and walked away. The remaining prisoners shouted desperately for him to come back, but the firing resumed, and one by one the cries for mercy were cut short as the soldiers shot each of them dead. By the time Carlos and Cody reached the fenced area where the guards had been held, the firing had ended. All the guards lay dead in the pit.

Lewelle caught up with Carlos. "My shuttle is right over there. You can use it to take your prisoner to my ship." Deliberately avoiding looking at Lewelle, Carlos ordered, "Cody, Tobin, Reyas, you heard him, do as he says," then turned and walked away, never once even looking at Lewelle.

Proceeding straight to the clinic, Carlos congratulated Accabo for breaking through Lekadian security and learning about the executions. "You saved Kwe's life, Accabo."

"No, Captain, it wasn't me. I didn't break in. Somebody let me in. On purpose. Some Lekadian wanted you to stop Kwe's execution."

"Who? Why?"

"I don't know."

Devlan Nine

Accabo, bobbing gently, hovered in his cabin on the *Aktawaneh*. Cody and Tobin watched in fascination as he played with the adjustments on his new antigravity harness, rising or falling at will. Unlike Lara, who needed to adjust a physical control with her fingers, the computer embedded in Accabo's brain allowed him to control his harness mentally.

Kwe and Estille rushed into the cabin, shouting, "You guys are famous! Everyone in the Empire knows about you! As Accabo lowered himself to chair level, a holographic image appeared that showed Cody and Tobin in their armor. The voice of a newscaster spoke of their heroics and gave their names and where they lived.

They laughed and kidded each other about it until Lara barged into the room. "Tobin, Cody, how could you be so stupid?"

Their laughing stopped. The only sound was the reporter's voice saying, "The slave camp, which was operated by the notorious Dombrel crime syndicate..."

Lara ordered the holocast turned off. Kwe nodded to Estille, and the holographic image vanished.

His voice uncharacteristically somber, Tobin asked, "Dombrel?"

"Yes, Dombrel," Lara repeated.

"What's a Dombrel?" asked Accabo.

Kwe replied, "Big mob syndicate. Dombrel. They ran the slave camp. I worked for them."

Lara replied angrily, "You knew you were working for Dombrel?"

"I was only a guard. I needed the money. My contract was almost up. I was leaving in a few days. You guys know about Dombrel?"

"My son knows all about them, don't you Tobin?"

"They're the ones who kidnapped me from Quogue."

Kwe grew somber. "You must have done something really bad to them."

"I killed one of them, back at Tarfil, the first time they tried to kidnap me. The second time, on Quogue, Cody shot one of them."

Kwe whistled in disbelief. "Your Mom's right. You're in deep trouble. You and Cody both."

"It was all because of my father. They're after me because he outsmarted them, took them for a lot of money, then boasted about it."

Lara added, "And now they know you didn't die in the camp. Not only that you didn't die, but that you hurt them much worse than your father ever did. And you boasted about it too, just like your father, only worse. Now the entire Empire knows what you did to Dombrel."

"Dombrel will never stop hunting you Tobin, never," warned Kwe.

Lara demanded, "Kwe, please leave. We have things we need to discuss in private."

"I understand. I worked for Dombrel. I'll see you guys later."

As Kwe left, Lara checked to be sure the door was closed tightly before saying, "We can't trust Kwe."

Reyas disagreed. "He saved our lives. He was the only guard I could trust."

"He works for Dombrel," Lara replied, "that's all we need to know."

"He would have been executed," Cody said, "if we didn't stop it."

"We still don't know who told Accabo about Kwe being executed," Lara answered. "Never trust Dombrel. Or anyone who ever worked for them. The execution could have been a ploy to earn our trust."

"But the other guards were executed. It was real," Reyas said.

Lara was adamant. "Dombrel doesn't care who they have to kill. Or how many. They'd kill all the other guards if that's what it took to make you trust Kwe. That's just how they are. It's happened before."

Accabo looked up. "Lewelle has just sent me a message. We're leaving tonight."

Lara asked, "Aren't we staying for Sophia's memorial service tomorrow?"

"No. There will be a private service this evening. On the launch pad. As soon as it's over, we're returning to the ship and breaking orbit. Lewelle says it's top secret."

As Lara left to get ready for the service, she cautioned everyone not to tell anyone about the change in plans, especially Kwe.

Tobin was the last one to leave Accabo's cabin. He was halfway out the door when he turned around, came back in, and closed the door behind him. "Accabo, if I wanted to find somebody on Kwe's home planet, how would I do it?"

Accabo handed him a headset. "That shouldn't be hard. Put this on. I'll walk you through it."

"First though, Accabo, you've got to promise not to tell anyone. No one. Promise?"

"I promise."

* * *

A little later, as dusk was darkening into night, they gathered on the launch pad where days earlier Sophia had boarded the ship in which she would give her life. Cody, Carlos, Accabo, Tobin, Lara, Reyas, Billy, surviving *Marco Polo* crew members, and Lewelle along with several of his family, including some who had not previously come to the planet's surface, gathered for a memorial service for Sophia on the launch pad. Most didn't know about the memorial service until moments before it began. Accabo and Lara sat in wheelchairs. Billy was now on crutches. Grim faced Lekadian soldiers kept watch on all aides, weapons ready to fire.

Those who had known Sophia got up to speak one by one. Cody spoke about his memories of his mother from his now long ago childhood on the *Marco Polo*, of his joy at seeing her here, even if so briefly, and of her strength and bravery in taking those explosives on board the slavers' ship. Reyas recalled that Sophia made life in the slave camp bearable for her. She couldn't imagine surviving there without Sophia's help. Billy spoke of the captain's wife he had known all his life, who helped him whenever possible after his own parents were separated from him when the *Marco Polo* was first attacked. They were never seen again. Tobin recalled the brief time he was in the slave camp, and the overwhelming joy Sophia felt after learning from him that Carlos and Cody were still alive and free. They spoke in several languages—Quogian, Lekadian, Arabic, and English—and listened through automatic translators provided by the Lekadians for the languages for all the languages spoken, except Quogian, for which Lara provided a running translation.

To close the service, Carlos and Cody played their clapper sticks while singing a Kashaya-Pomo prayer song that Sophia had taught Carlos. Finally, Carlos expressed gratitude that he had that one final opportunity to pray with Sophia in her last moments, and now to bear witness to her strength and her love for her crew and fellow inmates.

As they boarded shuttles to return to the *Aktawaneh*, Carlos felt drained of nearly all his emotions. Losing Sophia once had been bad enough. But to lose her twice, and to learn the terrible things she had to endure while he lived comfortably on Quogue, was greater pain than he ever imagined he might have to bear.

What was it like, Carlos wondered, for Cody and Reyas to be so near Sophia, just outside the ship before it took off, yet unable to save her, watching powerlessly as the ship took off and moments later blew up? Carlos knew he could never really understand the depths of what either Cody or Reyas was feeling, but he did know that no child should ever be made to suffer what they had suffered.

They left orbit as soon as the last shuttle was onboard, leaving Lekadian specialists to track down the home worlds and relatives of slaves and to bury the bodies of those whose relatives they couldn't locate. Carlos just wanted to leave it all behind. Worried by the distrust that Lara and Lewelle were showing toward Kwe, Carlos finally approached Lewelle to make sure he would keep the promise he made to return Kwe to his home planet.

"Yes, the boy will be taken home," was Lewelle's taciturn response, for a moment sounding remarkably like Dariel.

It would be a five day journey to Kwe's home planet, Devlan Nine. Cody and Tobin devoted most of the first day to cleaning up their breastplates and helmets while exchanging banter with Kwe about fishing, boxing, and the things they would do when all this was over, especially the fishing trip that Kwe had promised them.

Carlos returned to the habit he had begun on Quogue of beginning each morning by singing prayer songs. He spent the rest of his daytime hours with his surviving *Marco Polo* crew members, and the first two evenings reading 17th century English translations of reports by Lekadian explorers who had visited Earth once or twice each millennium for tens of thousands of years. Lewelle's family had found them while Carlos and Lewelle were on the planet rescuing slaves and gave Carlos access to them when he returned to the *Aktawaneh*. Most amazing of all were holographic recordings of Northern California Indians, a century before Europeans built Mission Dolores at what later became San Francisco, showing some of their daily life and amazingly, footage showing people dancing inside a roundhouse.

On the third day of the journey to Devlan Nine, Lewelle had an even more amazing surprise for Carlos—a replica 17th century roundhouse, where he hoped Carlos might feel more comfortable singing his prayer songs than in the sterility of a Lekadian starship. Lara, Tobin, and Accabo were all dumbfounded. No one had ever heard of a prayer room, or even a tolerance for prayer, on a Lekadian ship. Lewelle's only explanation was that it was Lekadian hospitality to an honored guest. It wasn't a real roundhouse, just a computer generated holographic replica, based on those 17th century holographic recordings, but nonetheless it stunned Carlos.

Carlos found it moving to sit inside the simulated roundhouse and watch dancing and singing recorded five hundred years before he left Earth, but did his best to hide from Lewelle the sense of alienation he felt when he tried singing his own prayer songs there. The Lekadians had seen no need to recreate the dirt floor of a traditional roundhouse, but walking on a standard starship floor destroyed much of the illusion of being in a roundhouse. There was a convincing looking fire near the middle that generated realistic heat, but after it was turned off, there was none of the delicious mixture of smells of earth and lingering smoke that can linger in an authentic roundhouse for days after the fire has been allowed to go out.

He had too many vivid memories of dancing in real roundhouses in northern California. His own grandparents had been among the elders who supervised the design and building of the latest roundhouse at Kule Loklo, which he himself helped construct as a youth in 2194. His senses could never be tricked into accepting this holographic imitation as a true roundhouse

He went into it daily, not wanting to hurt Lewelle's feelings, and occasionally enjoyed dancing there with the holographic recordings of his ancestors, but could not bring himself to pray there. He prayed in his cabin, as he had since boarding the *Aktawaneh.*

Cody was repulsed by Lewelle's simulated roundhouse. Although he had never seen a genuine roundhouse, he knew this one was artificial, generated by Lekadian computers. He had stopped singing daily prayers while rescuing slaves at the slave camp, and now declined to rejoin Carlos in them, even when Carlos offered to pray anywhere on the *Aktawaneh* that Cody chose.

Accabo, who had been promised by the doctor that he would be walking unassisted on his own feet by the time they returned to Quogue, spent much of his time showing Billy around Lekadian cyberspace.

Kwe was spending his time with Cody and Tobin, and was intrigued listening to Tobin's and Cody's tales about Cody's boxing matches. Soon Kwe was boasting about his younger brother Sullo, a boxing champion in his home province. Before long, the three boys were sparring in one of the cargo bays.

On the fourth day out, Tobin met alone with Lewelle to thank him for rescuing him.

Lewelle smiled. "I have been friends with your mother and your grandparents for many years, but this journey is the first time I have seen you since you were an infant. I was wrong to neglect you for so many years."

"It wasn't your fault. It was my family that neglected me."

"Your mother and I both want to make up for that now."

"I'm doing fine on my own."

"I'm sure you are. But there is something I need to talk to you about. I know you've been trying to contact Kwe's home planet."

"Accabo swore he wouldn't tell anyone."

"He hasn't. You don't know your way around cyberspace. You tripped some security alerts. I know you're looking for Sedlin il Lindar."

"So? It's my business, no one else's."

"Tobin, anything that involves the security of this ship or of the Lekadian Empire is my business. That includes unauthorized, secret communications with other planets. I know that your tricks with the RedFins are based on Sedlin il Lindar's research."

Tobin remained silent.

"Tobin, if you're thinking about visiting him…"

Tobin didn't let him finish. "I'm going fishing with Kwe, Cody, and Reyas. That's all I'm doing."

"No, you're not. It's too dangerous with Dombrel after you. Kwe can go home, but none of you are going with him."

"You're going to stop us?"

"If I have to. It's for your own safety. But if you want to visit Sedlin il Lindar, that's OK, as long as you let me send an armed escort with you. Lindar lives in a different province than Kwe. Our soldiers are allowed to accompany you in his province. They're not allowed in Kwe's province."

"No, no soldiers."

"Then no visit. You can visit the capital city with Cody and Reyas, but if you leave the capital without soldiers to protect you, I'll have you arrested and returned to my ship. It's for your own safety. But if you want to visit Sedlin il Lindar, let me know. He's old and cantankerous, but if he agrees to talk with you, visiting him might be worth your while. Did you know he was my teacher once?"

"No."

"It was before you were born, when he was first doing his research into communicating with the minds of previously unknown species."

"You can do the same things I can?"

"No, not at all. I never had the gift for it, I'm afraid. Not many Lekadians do. That was impressive how you were able to reach into Billy and make it easier for him to bear his pain. But I think it came at a price to you. Am I right?"

"I'll never do it again."

"Just remember, if you need advice, Lindar is the best person to ask. If you want to talk with him, I'll send a squad of soldiers to escort you to him."

"I don't need protection."

"Because you're a Warrior Brother?"

"Not only that, I'm stronger than anyone else."

"I don't care. You and Cody must stay together, in the city. It's for your own safety. Contact me immediately if you are suspicious of anybody. Don't trust anyone. Especially Kwe and his family."

"I trust Kwe completely."

"I know you're not that foolish."

"He saved Cody's life, and Reyas, and Accabo. That's enough for me."

"Just remember, Tobin, stay in the city, and stay away from Kwe's family. If you don't, I'll send soldiers down to bring the three of you back to the ship."

* * *

As the Devlan Consortium's shuttle pulled away from the *Aktawaneh* on its slow descent into the atmosphere of Devlan Nine, the air of anticipation onboard the shuttle was high. Nearly all the passengers were surviving *Marco Polo* crewmembers, going for their first shore leave since their ship's destruction seven years ago. Still gaunt and shaven headed from their years in servitude, they now wore brand new Devlan clothes, courtesy of the Consortium that governed Devlan Nine, and were traveling to the capital city for some long overdue recreation. The only passengers who were not from Earth were Kwe, Reyas, and Tobin.

Carlos and Lara had remained on the *Aktawaneh* with Accabo and Billy. Accabo was still recovering from his spinal nerve injury. Carlos and Billy saw this as an opportunity to learn about Lekadian technology, and Lara had no interest in visiting another primitive planet.

As the shuttle descended, a Consortium guide talked about Devlan Nine. "There are two continents, Opportunity and Devlan. We are now passing over Opportunity. Until a few generations ago, no one lived in Opportunity, but it's now the most rapidly growing area in the Lekadian Empire. Where just a few generations ago there were forests and fields that had stood unutilized for hundreds of thousands of years, there are now factories, cities, large entertainment complexes, and even a spaceport under construction. It will be only the second spaceport on Devlan Nine."

Kwe whispered to Cody, Reyas, and Tobin, "My fiancée Tessa lives in Opportunity. After we marry, I'll live there too."

As the shuttle left Opportunity behind, descending closer to the surface, they flew over a large ocean, and then over land again. Kwe whispered excitedly that they were now over his home province.

The guide continued, "Now we are over the Devlan continent. You see the province known as The Wilds right below us. For many generations, there was bloody strife on the planet between those who wanted to live with technology and those who did not. It wasn't until the Lekadians stepped in and formed the Consortium that now governs the planet that peace was established. The Wilds is a province where no technology of any kind is permitted outside border towns. The people living in The Wilds are lawless barbarians living primitive lives, but the Consortium has guaranteed their right to continue living that way of life if it is what they want."

"And to starve," Kwe muttered bitterly in a low voice.

The guide continued, "We have now left The Wilds, and are over the province of Devlan. It occupies all of this continent outside of The Wilds." The shuttle was now flying low enough for them to see cities, and as it descended, to see smaller towns. "Devlan is a Lekadian word both for our traditional homeland and for our planet. The actual word we use is impossible for most outsiders to pronounce. Please prepare for landing. Welcome to Devlan Nine and to our home province of Devlan."

* * *

For *Marco Polo* crewmembers, who had seen the grand spaceports along the star lanes, the only attraction this spaceport offered was that it wasn't a slave camp. Even Tobin had seen far busier and more impressive spaceports on the Tarfillian moons. Cody, who only vaguely remembered the grand star lanes spaceports they visited in his childhood, shared the wonder that Reyas and Kwe felt at the sight of the Devlan spaceport, with space freighters parked around it, many in the process of being loaded or unloaded. They even got to watch wide eyed as one took off. Kwe of course had seen the spaceport before, but it was the only spaceport he had ever seen and it still awed him.

The spaceport seemed a marvel of bustling activity but the nearby capital city, to which they traveled by a transit system recently built by the Lekadians, made the spaceport look like a rural bazaar. The transit system, using Lekadian antigravity technology, was smooth, quiet, and quick. It seemed like only moments until they were wandering around city streets. Cody and Reyas both gawked in undisguised wonder at the crowds and stores and at the wide variety of races and clothing that swallowed them up while Kwe and Tobin carefully shepherded them past the hazards and temptations of city life.

All of them found it discomforting to be walking around with no weapons to defend themselves. Weapons of any kind, even knives, were strictly forbidden in the city. Police patrolled everywhere and strictly enforced the weapons ban. It left Cody feeling almost naked. For as long as he had been on Quogue, he had carried a weapon of some sort, a knife, a harpoon, or a bow and arrows, like every child did, but here, instead of defending themselves, people relied on the police to do it for them.

Cody asked whether the police really did defend people. Kwe laughed derisively. "Cody, the best way to defend yourself is to stay as far away from the police as you can!"

Kwe's attitude enforced Cody's growing feeling that Kwe was a kindred spirit he could trust, someone else who had grown up knowing that the only justice a person could ever rightfully expect was the justice that he himself exacted. He wondered whether people here in the city ever did anything for themselves. Many looked like they had never done a day of real work in their lives. Tobin and Kwe tried explaining what these people did all day, but their own understanding of it was so limited that they couldn't describe it in any meaningful way, eventually giving up and leaving Cody and Reyas knowing only that these people spent their days indoors, talking or doing something equally unproductive.

Before arriving, they thought would be easy to follow Lewelle's orders to remain in the city, but after a day engulfed in its frantic pace, all of them were impatient for change. They felt vulnerable not having any means of defending themselves. None of them trusted the police. For Reyas, the presence of uniformed police simply brought back terrible memories of slave camp guards, while Tobin remembered that it was corrupt Tarfillian Lunar police who murdered his father on orders from Dombrel, despite promising him protection. Finally, over dinner, they discussed it openly.

When Kwe left the table for a few moments, Cody said, "Even Lewelle thinks Dombrel's probably not here."

"Dombrel can only be here if Kwe betrayed us," said Tobin.

"Kwe wouldn't do that," asserted Cody.

"Of course not. Reyas, you've known Kwe longer than us. Would Kwe tell Dombrel we are here?" asked Tobin.

"No. Never."

"Never what?" asked Kwe, returning to the table.

"Lewelle is afraid you told Dombrel that we are here," answered Tobin.

"You guys don't think I'd do that, do you?"

All three quickly replied, "No."

"I know Dombrel better than any of you," said Tobin, "if we're wrong, and Dombrel is here, the city is the worst place we could be. Dombrel could be anywhere, just waiting for us. Anyone could be Dombrel. The police can be Dombrel. That's how they killed my father. Dombrel infiltrated the police."

Kwe reminded them of his standing invitation to go fishing with him in The Wilds. "You've never seen a more beautiful place than my fishing spot. There's even a waterfall. Lots of fish. Delicious fruit growing wild. No one knows about it, so I know Dombrel won't be there."

By the time they finished dinner, they had made their decision. Not wanting anyone to inform the police or Lewelle that they were leaving, they paid for two more nights in their hotel, then snuck out a back door and boarded the transit line that would take them to an outlying district where they could buy passage on an air freighter to The Wilds

Unlike the comfortable, modern transit system they had ridden from the spaceport, this time they had to take an old and over-crowded electric bus for a seemingly interminable ride through crowded city streets, with passengers scrambling over other passengers to get on and off at every stop. When they finally reached their destination, they were in a district that didn't share in the prosperity that had overtaken much of the rest of the city. "This is how the city used to look in my grandparents' time," Kwe told them. There were few alien races in evidence, just people whose families had lived here for untold generations. Like the district itself, they looked more threadbare and struggling than those in the bustling areas they had just left. Life's strains lined people's faces and when Cody was able to catch glimpses of their hands, they often revealed a life of physical labor.

Until now, the four of them had been wearing clothes issued to them by the Consortium. Those clothes were suitable for the city, but they were too fashionable for this part of the city and not rugged enough for The Wilds. After renting rooms in an aged inn, where the fireplace in the main room had left generations of black soot coating the stone chimney and ceiling around it, they spent much of the day shopping for new clothes. With Tobin's help, Kwe guided Cody and Reyas through the brand new experience of buying clothes, helping them choose rugged, functional clothes that they could afford and that would help them blend in.

When they were done, Tobin left with Kwe to buy the tickets for the next leg of the trip, leaving Cody and Reyas to wander around by themselves. Before leaving, Kwe took Cody aside for a cautionary chat, hinting at the unpleasant things Reyas had experienced with male guards in the slave camp, and bluntly telling him not to try anything with her.

It didn't take visiting many shops for Cody and Reyas to discover that the small amount of money they had wouldn't buy the things they coveted in shop windows, so they contented themselves with wandering around the district, fascinated by the people they saw. It was the second day of amazing new experiences for them. For Cody, simply being with an unmarried woman and talking with her as a person was a new experience. On Quogue, being alone with a proper single woman simply wasn't allowed, even just to talk. To his surprise, he enjoyed walking around with Reyas, just talking with her, though sex was never far from his mind. As they wandered along the strange streets, they talked about many things, especially their lives before they met, but Cody kept feeling that there was something Reyas was not saying. It was like an invisible hole that they kept dancing around.

By the time they found their way back to the inn, shadows were growing long. They found Kwe sitting alone in the inn's main room, sipping a fermented drink. Kwe explained, "Tobin left. There was only one flight out. He would have missed it if he waited for you."

"Where'd he go?" Cody asked.

"To see some teacher. He promised he'd catch up with us at my village."

Reyas was clearly nervous. "Lewelle told us all to stay together."

"We already disobeyed him when we came here," Kwe answered, "what's the harm in doing it again? We don't let Lekadians tell us what to do, right Cody?" Without waiting for Cody to answer, he pulled a card from his pocket. "This is our ticket for the flight to The Wilds. We leave in the morning. We'll fly to the last stop, at Hangtown, then we'll find a driver to take us to my village."

"How will Tobin find us?" Reyas asked, "Shouldn't we at least let Lewelle know?"

Kwe assured her there was nothing to worry about. "I found a guide to take him to his teacher. It's a two-day trip. Getting from the teacher's to my village is easy. He just takes a boat down the coast."

"If Lewelle knows what we're doing, he'll send soldiers to bring us back," said Cody, "we won't get to go fishing."

"Don't forget, Reyas," Kwe added, "the three of you are supposed to stick together. The only way to do that is to meet Tobin in my village."

* * *

The next morning they boarded an air freighter that had seen better days, and took their seats in the tiny passenger section they shared with soldiers returning from leave and with a few traders. It was an exhausting flight, with repeated rough landings and take-offs at what seemed like every provincial town along the way. At every stop, freight was unloaded and loaded, and every time, the ancient freighter struggled to gain altitude as though this takeoff might be its last.

As they drew closer to The Wilds, the number of passengers dwindled, until there were only two besides themselves as the freighter labored toward the final stop at the border town of Hangtown. The other passengers were a mining engineer and a soldier returning from leave. Both warned them strongly against traveling to Kwe's home by the route Kwe intended. "Too many bandits. You'll never get through," warned the soldier, while the mining engineer told of the payoffs his company routinely made to bandits for protection. "Go back to the spaceport, take a flight to the coast, and then take a boat down to where you're going. It's the only safe way."

"Too expensive," Kwe replied, "Besides, there's no time for that," ignoring the mining engineer's retort that others who had taken the overland route later regretted it. Kwe sounded confident. "I'm from around here. I know a safe route."

"That's what they all say," replied the engineer.

The soldier added, "And they're always wrong. There's a reason it's called the 'Badlands'. You won't get through." The soldier turned to Cody and Reyas. "Has he told you about the fire breathing dragons?"

"The bandits are enough for them to worry about. Don't scare them with that old tale," cautioned the engineer. Turning to face Cody and Reyas, he said reassuringly, "It's only a legend. There are no fire breathing dragons. It's the bandits you need to fear. The bandits are real. Only the ignorant savages in The Wilds believe in fire breathing dragons. They think the dragons are gods."

"They are gods!" Kwe retorted heatedly, his face flushing in anger.

Chuckling condescendingly, the mining engineer replied, "Like I said. You people are all afraid of things that don't exist, but don't know enough to be afraid of things you should be afraid of, like bandits. Sergeant, you've served out here a long time. Have you ever seen a fire breathing dragon?"

"Nope, no one has. Not a single soldier has ever seen one."

"I've been an engineer out here for five years. I don't know anyone who's seen them either."

"They're real. I've seen them," insisted Kwe. "And Cody here is a Quogian warrior who fights fire breathing dragons."

Cody was going to protest that it was only ancient Quogian warriors who fought dragons, and that he had never even seen one, but the engineer didn't give him a chance. "It's the bandits you've got to worry about, boy. Your friend here is going to get you killed if you go through the Badlands. You'll turn back and take the coast route if you have any sense."

The soldier muttered in disgust to the engineer, "Bandits, fire breathing dragons, what's the difference? If the bandits don't get them, the desert will. They'll never make it."

After that, the engineer and the soldier kept to themselves, disembarking without exchanging another word with them.

Kwe guided Cody and Reyas to where they picked up their baggage and then in walking the short distance into town amidst a hodgepodge of carts, animal drawn wagons, and vehicles with a variety of propulsion systems, all of them looking heavily used, a cross section of the history of freight conveyance. As he led them through the bedlam, Kwe tried to reassure Cody and Reyas. "We cross the Badlands all the time. Don't worry. I've been doing it since I was a little boy."

"What about the stories they were telling us?" asked Reyas.

"They're miners. Only rich people like miners have to worry. And the soldiers who work for them. Not people like us."

"What about the dragons?"

"Don't worry about the dragons, Reyas. We'll carry offerings for them and they'll leave us alone. If you want, I can even show them to you if you don't mind climbing up the canyon wall."

Cody wasn't sure whether Kwe was joking about the dragons or not, but if they were real, he couldn't wait to see Tobin's face when he told him what he had missed by going to see some dumb teacher.

The Wilds

Hangtown's main claim to fame, aside from the infamous hanging tree from which authorities over the years would occasionally string up outlaws who went beyond the bounds of acceptable outlaw behavior, was that it was the only legal port of entry for freight entering and leaving the Badlands. For the most part, the cargo was ore being shipped from the mines scattered around the Badlands, and equipment and supplies coming in for the miners.

The Badlands, a barren desert with brutally hot days, little water or vegetation, roving gangs of bandits, and only the collapsed remains of long ago trading posts to guide travelers along its thinly traveled trails, isolated Hangtown from the rest of The Wilds. It had one thing that kept people coming despite the risks: generous deposits of ore that were essential to the functioning of modern society in other parts of the planet. A few had made vast fortunes here, but many more had lost their lives trying.

Traders had generations earlier given up all hope of operating trading posts in this inhospitable realm. Those who tried it never lasted more than a season or two. Merchants and miners were left no choice other than to traverse the Badlands knowing that the only living souls they were likely to meet were bandits who they could only hope would be merciful enough to leave them with the means of getting back to Hangtown alive. There were scattered villages in the mountains and at a handful of remote oases that hadn't been commandeered by mining companies, but because of the well known hostility that Badlands residents felt toward outsiders, travelers generally felt they were better off facing bandits and the scorching sun than residents of the scattered Badlands villages.

The residents of Hangtown mostly fell into two distinct groups: those who intended to get out someday and those who had given up all hope of ever getting out. A third, much smaller group, transients from other parts of The Wilds, typically spent no more than a few nights at a time in Hangtown while they transacted business before returning to their families in their home villages. Some came from desert villages in the Badlands, others from villages in the wooded lands farther east, beyond the Devil's Backbone, the range of mountains that formed the eastern border of the Badlands and partitioned it from the rest of The Wilds. The eastern portion of The Wilds had an economy that was based largely on agriculture and fishing. It had little contact with the outside world other than a few coastal villages that had some limited sea trade.

If there was one trait that characterized all three groups in Hangtown, it was toughness. They had to be tough to live here. Hangtown's appearance reflected that. The buildings were mostly run down, in need of paint, not caring what outsiders thought, proudly standing tough against all the desert could throw at them. The motley assortment of miners, soldiers, prospectors, hustlers, transients, and criminals populating its streets and public places had the same proudly worn but not worn down appearance of the buildings.

Kwe came alive in Hangtown. He looked happy for the first time and was obviously well known here, judging by the frequent greetings he exchanged with people on the street who recognized him and welcomed him back. Leading Cody and Reyas into an even more run down part of town where he seemed even more at home, he took them to a dilapidated inn. Entering it without hesitation, he was greeted by name by the slovenly looking innkeeper. "Don't worry," Kwe reassured them as they climbed the stairs to their rooms, "You can tell him anything. He's one of the few people here my family trusts."

"What about all those friends who've been greeting you?" asked Reyas.

"Friends?" Kwe laughed. "They're not friends. They only act that way because of who my family is."

After putting their gear in their rooms, Kwe gave them the good news that they could now carry weapons. "Officially blasters are illegal, but the police won't bother you as long as you don't cause trouble."

Cody felt relieved that at last he was finally able to take his cross-bow, arrows and harpoon out of his luggage to carry openly. Reyas took out the two blasters, one for her, the other for Cody. Cody at first refused it, but at her insistence, he reluctantly took it, shoving it deep in his quiver among his arrows. Then Reyas strapped hers around her waist, modeling it for herself with satisfaction in the cracked, grimy mirror.

A look of distaste formed on Kwe's face as he watched her. "That blaster is too new. Too expensive. Keep it out of sight. Let your shirt cover it just enough so people see you're carrying a weapon. Don't ever let anyone see how fancy it is. It will just cause trouble."

"What about you, Kwe? You don't have a weapon."

"You can take mine," Cody offered, reaching into his quiver.

Kwe stopped him. "No, keep it. No one around here is going to bother me. Besides, I'll be getting my own blaster back soon enough."

Out on the street, they walked confidently for the first time since arriving on Devlan Nine. With Reyas wearing her blaster almost openly, and Cody holding his harpoon in his usual defiant manner and his bow and quiver hanging from his shoulder, they headed for a tavern that was a favorite of Kwe's, where he said they could get a decent meal that didn't cost too much. Entering the tavern, they had to step aside for a torrent of shouting onlookers trailing two enraged men out the door to continue their fight in the street.

One of the onlookers tripped over Cody's foot and fell. Getting back onto his feet, he angrily challenged Cody to fight and, not waiting for an answer, punched him. Cody calmly handed his harpoon to Kwe, punched the man in the face, breaking his nose, and then punched him hard in the torso. The man collapsed to the ground, feeling his bleeding nose with his fingers, while Cody stood above him, ready to continue the fight. When the man made no attempt to get back to his feet, Cody relaxed, took his harpoon back from Kwe, and strode into the tavern.

One of the waitresses congratulated him. "It's about time someone taught that guy a lesson." She raised her voice so everyone would hear. "No one here had the guts to do it." Turning to Kwe, she smiled warmly. "Welcome back, Kwe," she said as Kwe kissed her warmly. After they broke off their kiss she said, "Have a seat, all of you. I'll be right with you."

The shouts and groans from the fight outside were audible as a bartender restored order inside the tavern, putting tossed-around chairs and tables back into place, and cleaning up shattered dishes. The men and women still at the bar hailed Kwe, welcoming him home. By the time they sat at their table, three alcoholic drinks were waiting for them, compliments of Kwe's acquaintances at the bar. Reyas declined hers, ordering something non-alcoholic instead, but Kwe talked Cody into taking his first alcoholic drink ever. Gulping it down quickly and liking it, Cody immediately ordered another.

When the waitress came to get their orders, Kwe stood up and embraced her. They kissed a long, passionate kiss, like they were lovers. She was attractive, with a ready smile and easy laugh, but a tough tone in her voice hinted of a lot more experience than her youthful appearance suggested. Kwe introduced her as Inya. When Inya returned with their dinners, as she placed Kwe's plate down in front of him, she discreetly took two blasters in holsters from underneath a towel, along with a purple cloth, and handed them to Kwe, saying, "I heard you were back, so I had these ready for you."

As Kwe strapped one of the blasters around his waist and put the purple cloth and the second blaster in his pocket, Inya asked, "How's Tessa?"

"We spoke before I left space. She seems OK."

"I suppose you and she are still engaged."

"Of course."

"Am I still your Second?"

"Absolutely. But I need money first. Things didn't go well on that guard job."

"I'm not going anywhere. Who are your friends? I've never seen anyone like them before."

"They're from other planets, far away planets. This is Reyas, and Cody."

Looking at Cody, she exclaimed, "Not just a good fighter, but a spear-carrier!"

"It's a harpoon," he corrected her.

"Not many men have the guts to rely on weapons like those. From your face, I'd say you've been in more than your share of fights. I'll bet you've won most of them." Cody nodded his head. "You're a real man, anyone can see that." Glancing at Reyas, she added with some embarrassment, "Oh, I'm sorry."

"Cody and Reyas are just friends," Kwe quickly interjected. "Cody saved my life."

"No, it was my father who talked them out of killing Kwe."

"But it was Cody who stepped between me and the guns."

"So you're as brave as you look, Cody," Inya said admiringly.

"No, Kwe's the brave one. He saved my life first. I was just repaying him."

"A spear carrier! We used to have a lot of spear-carriers around here when I was a little girl, but they're all gone now. When I was little, I dreamt of someday marrying a spear-carrier. Kwe, do you think a priest would be willing to make Cody my Prime?"

"Cody is only visiting. But he is like a brother to me. You may do with him as you would with my brothers."

"Then, Cody, you and I are both free to do as we want. Meet me after I get off work? When we're alone, you can show me how good you are at other things besides fighting."

"Uh, sure," Cody replied, swallowing another drink. After Inya left, Cody asked, "Kwe, is she offering what I think she's offering?"

Kwe nodded his head. "But what about you? I thought you and her were lovers, or something."

"I have promised her she will be my Second."

"Your second what?" asked Reyas.

"My Second Wife. But I need to marry my Prime first. Tessa. My fiancée. The Prime is a holy relationship. Priests select our Prime for us. While I am engaged to my Prime, I cannot have sex with Inya like we used to. When I get home, I have to swear to the priest that I had no sex with anyone since I left. But after I am married, then I can have as many Seconds as I want. Inya will be my first Second."

After taking a few moments to let it sink in, Reyas asked, "How many second wives can you have?"

"As many as I can afford. Our Chief God, Kwegathi, has a Prime and seven Seconds. But our village priest can afford only a Prime."

Cody was looking stumped. "You're going to marry Inya, but you don't mind if I have sex with her tonight?"

"It's OK, Inya will be my Second. If you had sex with my Prime, I would have to kill you, but sex with my Second is OK as long as you are my brother. Or like my brother. I can't have any more sex with Inya until I marry my Prime. It's only fair to Inya to let her do it with you instead. You should stay here, Cody, make it your home. You can marry Inya and make her your Prime."

"That would be OK with you?"

Kwe looked earnestly at Cody. "Inya cannot be the Prime of any respectable man born here. She deserves better than being just my Second."

"Why can't she be a Prime?"

"She has no name."

"No name?"

"No clan. She doesn't know who her father was, so she has no clan name. Only a lowborn man can take her as his Prime. Or an offworlder like you, but we don't get many offworlders out here. She is a fine woman, Cody. It is a tragedy she can never be a respectable man's Prime. She needs an offworlder like you."

The conversation was interrupted when another fight broke out. Quickly lifting up their table, they moved it out of the way of the fight before resuming their dinner.

After dinner, Kwe and Reyas returned to their separate rooms in the inn, while Cody left with Inya, ending up in the tiny but comfortable room she rented in a shed behind a blacksmith's barn.

In the morning, after cold showers, Kwe and Reyas were finishing a meager breakfast when Cody joined them. He was radiating joy, enhanced by a hot shower and a solid breakfast at Inya's.

"Is she your Prime now?" Reyas asked with uncharacteristic sarcasm.

"I could do worse. You were right, Kwe, she's fine. Really fine. Tobin and me had some great sex once with actresses on Quogue, but Inya, she's amazing." Cody bubbled over with enthusiasm, not noticing Reyas staring down at her plate, her face burning, pretending to figure out how to use her Devlan eating utensils.

After finishing their meal, they began their search for a driver to take them across the Badlands. As they walked, Cody and Reyas spotted several places offering drivers for hire that looked respectable, at least by Hangtown standards, but Kwe showed no interest in them and instead led them into an even more derelict neighborhood. Clusters of armed, tough-looking men and women hung out along the narrow street, often clearly engaged in transactions of some sort, but their conversations always fell silent as the armed strangers passed within earshot and resumed after they passed. From time to time people waved at Kwe, but looked suspiciously at Cody and Reyas.

As they approached one of the tougher looking groups, a woman in the group bellowed a greeting to Kwe. She was tall and muscular, considerably older then Kwe, and had a scarred face. Breaking into a run, she was at Kwe's side in moments, embracing him enthusiastically, lifting him off his feet as they both whooped like kids. The woman's friends came over to join them, all of them welcoming Kwe as a comrade, but looking warily at Cody and Reyas. Like most others in this part of town, they carried well used weapons of various sorts, including blasters and evil looking knives.

Suddenly realizing that he had forgotten about Cody and Reyas, Kwe somewhat awkwardly introduced the big woman with the scarred face as his sister Haab, and the others as cousins or life long friends. Haab hugged both Cody and Reyas tightly, saying, "So you're the friends Tessa said Kwe was bringing from space."

Kwe asked Haab, "Is Tessa here?"

"Last I heard, she was on her way to Mom and Dad's. She'll be waiting for you, brother. She especially wants to meet your friends." Turning to Cody and Reyas, Haab continued, "She lives far away, across the Great Sea. She's coming all the way to our village so she can meet Kwe's friends from space." Turning back to Kwe, she said, "You are here just in time. Sullo has a big boxing match coming up in a few days. It's the championship. You just missed him."

"I want to see him before we leave."

"He was waiting for you to get back. He had to go somewhere, but don't worry, Kwe, you'll see him before you leave. He can't wait to see you again."

Kwe began boasting about his brother Sullo's victories as a fighter, but was interrupted when Haab, without warning, abruptly herded all of them into a nearby run down bar. The bartender clearly recognized them, but pointedly ignored their presence. Outside, a police patrol passed by. Kwe whispered that Haab and the officer leading this patrol disliked each other.

Kwe waited until the police were out of sight before asking Haab, "We need a ride home. Who can we trust?"

"I've already arranged it. He's a merchant who's made a lot of trips across the Badlands."

"What about the bandits?" Reyas asked.

Haab and her comrades burst out laughing uproariously before realizing that Reyas wasn't trying to be funny. "Kwe, haven't you told them?" Kwe looked embarrassed, but said nothing. "You don't have to worry about bandits. You have my word."

Cody asked Haab how she could be so sure.

"Because we are the bandits," Haab replied, "well, some of the bandits. The big ones. We are the Fourth House of Clan Suhrat. You are under our protection. No one will bother you. No one. Now come with me. That damned merchant has been pestering me for two days about when you would get here. He keeps saying he can't wait any longer," adding as an afterthought, "of course he will wait as long as we need him to."

After making sure that the police patrol was out of sight, Haab led them outside. As they walked back up the street, they passed the bar where Inya worked. Inya ran outside to kiss both Kwe and Cody farewell. After she returned to the bar, Cody asked Kwe, "Are all women on this planet as good as she is? Last night was amazing."

"Remain here and you can make her your Prime. You are like a brother to me. She is yours if you want her."

"Only if she wants him, I hope?" asked Reyas.

"She wants him. I have never seen her like that with any other man before."

"I thought you loved her," said Reyas.

"I do, more than anything. And she loves me. But the law does not permit me to take her as my Prime. Besides, I have to obey the gods. They decreed Tessa is to be my Prime. Inya needs a worthy man, like Cody."

* * *

Accabo and Billy, dressed in the uniforms of a Lekadian space fighter crew, were drinking in a noisy bar jammed with fellow Lekadian space fighter crewmembers when the call to scramble came. Leaving their drinks behind, they all jumped to their feet and ran down a hallway, putting on helmets and other gear as they ran, finally running into the bays where their starfighters waited for them. Accabo climbed into the pilot's seat of one, while Billy climbed into the gunner's seat. The bay doors opened, all the starfighters were shoved outside into space by some invisible force, and the fighters took off to attack a fleet of enemy starfighters.

Accabo pointed to a rapidly approaching enemy starfighter. Billy locked their weapons on it while Accabo bravely kept his cool and deftly maneuvered their starfighter to avoid enemy missiles. Finally Accabo gave the command and Billy fired. The enemy ship blew apart. The squad leader praised them, but there was no time to bask in his praise. They immediately veered their starfighter hard starboard to attack enemy fighters that were rushing up on the tail of some comrades.

Lewelle's voice came over their headsets, ordering them to return.

* * *

On Lewelle's ship, Accabo opened his eyes while Billy removed his headset. Lewelle was standing in front of them. "Sorry to interrupt your game, boys. This is important. Have you heard anything more from the surface?"

Accabo replied, "No. They're probably having too much fun."

"Did Kwe tell either of you anything about his fiancée?"

"Tessa? Only that he can't wait to marry her," replied Billy.

Accabo added, "Kwe said she lives on a different continent than his family. He contacted her there so she could prepare for the marriage. He wants to marry her right away."

Anger erupted on Lewelle's normally passionless face. "I thought I gave orders for Kwe to have no contact with anyone on the planet."

"He only contacted his fiancée," answered Billy.

Lewelle replied, "A ship just landed in Opportunity. It's probably Dombrel. Someone told them we are here."

Billy asked, "The same gang that's after Tobin?"

"The same. Your friends may be walking into a trap."

"Is it possible that Dombrel just followed us?"

"No, someone told them that we are here. It had to be Kwe. No one else knew."

"Kwe saved my life," Accabo protested.

"Billy, I need to speak in private with Accabo." After Billy left the room, Lewelle continued, "You have to keep secret what I am going to tell you."

"I promise, I will tell no one."

"I know Kwe saved your life. That's why I gave you the opportunity to save him from the firing squad."

"That was you?"

"Yes, but it's a secret between you and me."

"You don't trust Kwe. Why did you save his life?"

"We owed him at least that."

"Lewelle, I trust him."

"Kwe worked for Dombrel. Once you work for Dombrel, they own you forever. We can't trust him, even if he did save your life. We've got to find Tobin, Cody, and Reyas before Kwe's Dombrel friends find them. Let me know immediately if you see or hear anything at all."

After Lewelle left, Billy returned. "So what was the Lekadian's great secret, Accabo?"

"We talked about Kwe, that's all." Inside, however, Accabo was bursting with pride and excitement that a Lekadian had confided an important secret in him. Suppressing the urge to boast, he showed Billy a virtual reality game he had found, with impressively realistic fire breathing dragons. "I haven't learned how to control them yet, but if we learn, maybe Cody will want to play."

"Not even fire breathing dragons will get Cody into cyberspace," Billy answered, "but they'll get me in! Show me."

* * *

The merchant showed no interest in conversing with his passengers. After waiting two days for Kwe's arrival, he was impatient but knew that cooperating with Kwe's family was his ticket to a safe round trip across the Badlands. He had cleared his merchandise from the rarely used rear seat in his wagon, making just enough room for his three passengers to sit, but emphasizing his lack of interest in conversing with bandits and their friends by placing merchandise on the front seat so no one could sit next to him. Kwe, Cody, and Reyas were forced to squeeze tightly together in the rear seat.

Haab gave the merchant a purple pennant to fly from his carriage while explaining to Cody and Reyas that it would let other bandit gangs know that this carriage was under the protection of the Fourth House of Clan Suhrat. Kwe put on the purple armband that Inya gave him the night before and carefully checked the settings on his blaster, finally test firing it by pulverizing a nearby stump. Haab watched approvingly. "Welcome home, little brother, it's good to have you back."

"Where's Sullo?" asked Kwe, looking around.

"I don't know," answered Haab.

Turning around to face them and looking nervous, the merchant said, "The sun is already warm. We are starting late. The sun will be high and hot soon."

Haab replied, "The merchant's right, Kwe, you'd better leave. Many have died because they left on this journey too late in the morning."

"What about Sullo? Why isn't he here?"

"Police have been giving him a hard time lately," Haab answered, "but don't worry. I'll take care of it. You'll see him at his boxing match. Nothing will keep him from that."

It would be a two day ride to Kwe's home village. The entire first day would be in the Badlands. As the morning wore on and the day grew hotter, they gave up all attempts to talk with the merchant, who responded with only the most minimal grunts and shrugs, saving his speech for the animals pulling the carriage. For much of the day, they rode in silence. Their mouths and throats were too dusty and parched to speak more than necessary.

Late in the afternoon, they entered a canyon where the shadows cast by the high walls offered some relief from the heat and they began talking again. Kwe was trying to explain why he went to work as a guard. "It paid well. All I had to do was work for a year, and I would have the money to pay my apprenticeship and my dowry. Then I could have moved to my fiancée's province and worked as a mechanic."

"But because you freed me, you'll never get paid."

Kwe waited a few moments before answering Reyas. "I'll find some other way to get the money. When the priests selected me as Tessa's husband, her parents would only consent to the marriage if I promised to give up being a bandit. Her family doesn't understand how it is for us here."

Cody asked, "I thought you really wanted to be a fisherman."

"Yes, that's my dream, to be a fisherman like my forefathers, but the truth is that today, very few can make a living that way. I can't raise a family if I become a fisherman. When my grandfather was young it was still possible, but the Lekadians have built factories and changed everything. Now, if you want to raise a family, you need money. To get money, you have to have a job in one of the cities in Devlan or Opportunity. Out here in The Wilds, we either have to move away to get jobs or we become bandits. There's not much else anymore."

Reyas asked about Tessa.

"She is Suhrati like me, but her house moved away four generations ago. They were some of the first settlers in Opportunity, before it was called Opportunity. In those days it was called The Land Where No One Lives. Everyone thought her house was foolish for moving there. That's all changed now. Her grandparents were fishermen, like mine. Opportunity made them wealthy. The Lekadians have built factories there and will open a spaceport soon. Tessa will be a manager at the spaceport when it opens. I have promised her parents I will be a shuttle mechanic. We can live well working at the spaceport when it opens. Inya will live with us. She can work at the spaceport too. But I need money before I can do it."

The canyon narrowed and as it became too narrow to turn around, several armed men, wearing hoods that obscured their faces, ran out in front of them, barring their way.

Kwe whispered an apology, adding, "Don't worry. I usually ride in front. They just didn't think to look for me back here."

Cody whispered back, "We have weapons."

"No, Cody, don't. They'll leave us alone when they see who I am." Jumping confidently from the carriage, Kwe strode toward the bandits, speaking to them jovially in his native language.

Answering angrily in an alien language, one of the bandits punched Kwe hard, knocking him to the ground. The leader of the gang, speaking Lekadian, ordered everyone out of the carriage. Reyas told him that Cody didn't understand Lekadian and translated the bandit's orders for him. As they climbed out of the carriage, the other bandits, speaking the alien language and using hand signals to convey the meaning, ordered them to stand with their backs to the carriage, with their hands on the back of their heads, and ordered Kwe to get up and stand alongside them. Cody tried to help him up, but was shoved roughly back against the carriage

After carefully studying the faces of Cody, Reyas, Kwe, and the merchant one by one, the gang leader asked the other bandits something in the alien language. Each of them studied their prisoners' faces carefully before appearing to answer, "No."

Switching back to Lekadian, the leader asked the merchant if any passengers had gotten off earlier.

"I picked up just these three, sir. There was no one else."

Muttering a Lekadian curse, the leader gave a hand signal to his gang. They proceeded to rummage through their prisoners' pockets, taking money, timepieces, and Kwe's and Reyas' blasters. Kwe tried threatening retribution by the Fourth House of Suhrat, but was punched hard for his efforts. One of the bandits ripped off Kwe's purple armband and tore the purple pennant from the carriage, mockingly hanging them from his belt like scalps.

When one bandit fondled Reyas' breast while saying something clearly lewd in his alien language, Cody lunged at him, smashing him several times in the face with his fists. The man crumbled to the ground, moaning, his face bleeding. Almost immediately, another of the bandits, Gombu, lunged at Cody, shouting furiously in the alien language. Gombu was comically short for a bandit, but despite his diminutive size was able to catch Cody off guard, shoving him brutally him against the carriage and throwing several hard punches that made Cody wince with pain. Swinging back, Cody struck Gombu with a single, hard blow, knocking him to the ground, but the first man he had struck, blood still running from his face down his chest, leaped to his feet and jumped Cody from behind. With the help of a third bandit, he finally managed to overpower Cody, who struggled ferociously to break free, without success. As Gombu struggled back up to his feet, a wicked smile forming on his face, he pulled a large machete from its sheath and approached Cody menacingly while barking an order.

Cody was straining to break free but the two bandits held him tight, gradually forcing him to lean over and down, pushing his face and chest ever closer to the floor of the carriage as Gombu, wielding his machete menacingly, came closer. Ignoring the blaster pointed at his temple, Kwe shouted threats about what his family would do to them if they harmed Cody. Cody's body was quivering as he struggled to break free but he could not stop the two men from finally forcing his face and chest flat against the carriage floor. One of the bandits took hold of his right arm, pulling it so it was extended across the floor, while Gombu positioned the machete carefully, just inches above Cody's wrist. Slowly and carefully, he raised it high, ready to slice off Cody's right hand.

Reyas and Kwe both were screaming pleas and threats, struggling to break free of the bandits restraining them. The merchant closed his eyes, muttering a silent prayer.

The bandit leader barked an order just as Gombu brought the machete down. The machete's tip hit the carriage floor hard, penetrating deep into it, but its sharp edge stopped just centimeters trating deep into it, but its sharp edge stopped just centimeters above Cody's wrist. For a moment no one moved. Gombu muttered something threatening to Cody before very slowly pulling his machete from the carriage floor. Swinging the machete furiously at a tree, he effortlessly sliced off a branch the thickness of a man's wrist before triumphantly putting his machete back in its sheath. Laughing an evil laugh, he waved the sliced off branch in Cody's face while saying something in his alien language that made the two men restraining Cody laugh. He then carefully laid the branch alongside Cody's arm, the sliced off end right next to Cody's wrist.

The bandit leader switched to speaking Lekadian, which Reyas translated to Quogian for Cody. "As you can see, Gombu is real good with the machete. Real good. He likes cutting off people's hands. And other parts." Switching back to the alien language, he said something that made Gombu and his comrades laugh evilly. Switching back to Lekadian, he said, "He has cut off many hands. It's what likes doing more than anything else. Tell your friend, if he wants to keep his hands, he must promise me he will restrain himself when my men release him." Reyas repeated it in Quogian for Cody. "If he doesn't promise, I will let Gombu get his pleasure." Reyas translated for Cody, who was red with rage, but finally managed to make the promise.

Reyas translated Cody's promise for the gang leader. He gave an order in the alien language and the men released Cody. Cody slowly stood up, his heart pumping with rage, doing everything in his power to restrain himself, as Gombu spoke to him again with a mocking tone in his voice.

Speaking to Reyas, the leader said, "Tell your friend that Gombu has warned him, if they ever meet again, your friend will lose both hands. Today he would only have lost one. He said to tell your friend that Gombu never forgets. Gombu says next time, it's both hands."

Without another word, the gang remounted and rode away.

Kwe apologized profusely. "I don't understand. Bandits around here don't behave like that, except maybe to miners."

"These bandits aren't from around here," Cody answered, "they are Dombrel."

Kwe replied, "Impossible, there are no Dombrel in The Wilds. There isn't enough profit for them here."

"They are here now," replied Cody, "Gombu, the one with the machete, I have seen him before. He was one of the Dombrel who kidnapped Tobin. I killed one of them. It was dark, but I think Gombu recognized me."

"Why did they let you go if he recognized you?"

"They want Tobin more than they want me. They're hoping I'll lead them to him. After they find Tobin, then they'll kill me."

Reyas asked Kwe whether they would be safe without the purple pennant.

Kwe answered, "We've just entered the Devil's Backbone. The other side of this canyon, we leave the Badlands, we will be safe over there. My family controls that area."

"Then let's get going," said Cody.

"Quiet. Can't you hear them? All this shouting woke them." Everyone listened to a muffled hissing as Kwe pointed toward the canyon wall. "This is the Canyon of the Fire Breathers. They live here. The Fire Breathers." He turned to the merchant. "Do you have the offerings?" The merchant handed him a sack and reminded him nervously that it was almost dark.

"What happens after dark?" Reyas asked the merchant.

"That's when the dragons come out."

"The Fire Breathers," muttered the merchant, fear showing in his face."

Holding the sack of offerings, Kwe told them, "I'm going up there to leave these offerings for them. Anyone who's got the guts can come."

Cody slung his bow and arrows over his shoulder, but Kwe stopped him. "Cody, no weapons. The dragons are gods."

"Suppose they come after us?" Reyas asked.

"We will be careful," Kwe replied, "I hope you're not afraid of heights!" He led Cody and Reyas, climbing up the nearly vertical canyon wall while the merchant paced nervously below. Kwe climbed easily, like a spider, clearly having climbed this wall many times before, while Cody and Reyas struggled to follow using the same hand and foot holds as Kwe. Reaching the top, Kwe signaled them to keep their heads down. The sun was setting and although shadows were swallowing up the canyons below them, by peering cautiously down the other side, they could see three dragons, one of them enormous, the other two much smaller. Many trees were blackened skeletons. Much of the grass and other vegetation had been burned away. Scorch marks blackened boulders. As they watched, an enormous bird with a wingspan nearly the height of a man flew too close to one of the dragons. Belching flame that was blinding in the deepening darkness, the dragon incinerated the bird before it even sensed danger.

Kwe spoke as he took the food offerings from the merchant's sack, spreading them out in the prescribed way. "They're awake early. Be careful. Don't let them see you. The wind favors us."

"This is a strange place for gods to live," Cody observed.

Kwe replied, "Kwegathi, king of the gods, expelled them from the realm of the gods many generations ago for playing evil pranks on the other gods. Someday when they've served their penance here, Kwegathi will invite the dragons back to the realm of the gods, and they will fly away."

Cody watched the dragons for a while, puzzled. "They have wings. Couldn't they just fly up here?"

"Like Love Dragons?" Kwe asked.

"Love Dragons?"

While preparing the offerings, Kwe whispered, "In the old days, before there were any people, there were four clans of gods. Kwegathi was king over all of them. Two of these clans were the Earth and the Water clans. These gods had the form of people and lived in a fortress kingdom they built high up in the sacred mountains. The other two clans were Fire and Air. These gods had the form of dragons. They didn't build any fortresses or castles like the Earth and Water clans, but instead had magical powers.

"The God of Fertility was of the Water clan, and the God of Love was of the Earth Clan. They fell in love, but were kept apart because of an ancient prophecy that if they ever bore children together, the reign of the gods over the universe would come to an end, and a new race of mortals would take their place. They were kept apart for thousands of years, and the gods ruled with no threat to their power. But dragons can be tricksters, and one day a dragon gave a potion to the God of Fertility and the God of Love that allowed them one night every lunar cycle to assume the form of dragons. From then on, every lunar cycle, these two gods became dragons and flew to a hidden place where they made love.

"Mortals resulted from their union. That's how people started. Today, the gods have been forced to yield much of their power to mortals, as was prophesized, but every lunar cycle the God of Fertility and the God of Love still take the form of dragons and fly through the night. When they do, they cause the people below to fall in love and to bear children."

Kwe paused, opened his shirt, and pulled out a pendant hanging on a necklace. The pendant was in the form of a flying dragon. "My fiancée, Tessa, wears one just like this. It is the custom of our people that when we become engaged to marry our Prime, the priest gives the man two of these dragon pendants. The man gives one pendant to his fiancée to wear until the wedding and he wears the other. On the day of our marriage, we give them to a jewelry maker to join into a single pendant. From then on, for the rest of our lives, we will take turns wearing it. One of us will always have it on as long as we live, so the Love Dragons will visit us often and grant us many strong children and grandchildren."

"Are those dragons down there Love Dragons?" asked Reyas.

"No, these are just ordinary gods who are being punished for tricks they played. Part of their punishment is that they cannot use their wings to fly until Kwegathi releases them."

When Kwe was done spreading out the offerings in the correct way, he said a prayer for the dragons. The dragons were beginning to scale the wall toward them, so as soon as Kwe finished the prayer, he led Cody and Reyas back down to the merchant, who was waiting in his carriage, impatient to get away from the dragons.

After they had climbed into the back seat, the merchant brutally whipped his animals into motion, traversing the Canyon of the Fire Breathers with as much speed as he could force from the poor animals. It was the only time in the entire two day journey that the merchant whipped his animals. He didn't relax until they were out of the canyon and over the ridge that formed the Devil's Backbone, when he finally let the animals resume their natural pace.

The remaining day of travel to Kwe's home was uneventful. The land on Kwe's side of the Canyon of the Fire Breathers was forested, growing denser as they traveled. Usually Suhrati and their visitors traveling to and from Hangtown spent the night at a shelter that the Suhrati had built just beyond the Devil's Backbone. The merchant stopped the carriage at the shelter, clearly assuming they would spend the night there, but complied without an objection when Kwe brusquely ordered him to get back in the carriage and drive. Ignoring the resentment simmering in the merchant's face, Kwe turned to Cody and Reyas. "Sullo's fight is tomorrow night. I'm not taking any chances on missing it. You'll like my brother, Cody."

They rode the entire night. Cody, Reyas, and Kwe occasionally drifted off to sleep, but the merchant remained awake all night, stopping only to give his animals water. At one point during the night, Reyas was the only one awake in the rear seat. Leaning forward, she spoke to the merchant, "You must be very tired. Maybe if we speak, it will help you stay awake." The merchant continued to look straight ahead, saying nothing. "My name is Reyas. What is your name?" The merchant still said nothing.

After more prodding from Reyes, he looked back at Kwe and asked, "Is he asleep?" Reyas assured him that Kwe was asleep. Finally the merchant replied in a whisper, "These bandits killed my son. Be careful. They say they're your friends, but bandits have no friends. For the right price, they will sell you out to anyone. Especially to

Dombrel. Count on it. Don't trust them." After Reyas asked the merchant several times who killed his son, he nervously looked in Kwe's direction, but ignored all further attempts by Reyas to talk with him.

They rode east through the night and into the morning. As they drew closer to Kwe's village, they saw growing numbers of rivers, lakes, and waterfront villages. Here and there they saw clusters of small farms on cleared land, but most villages were in the forest, on or near water. Buildings didn't look as neglected as in Hangtown, but many were in need of maintenance. Kwe apologized for the youths they occasionally saw along the way, already intoxicated even though it was still morning. "It is hard to make a living here. Only the most fortunate can. The rest of us either become bandits, or we move away and take Lekadian jobs. Sadly, some do that," pointing to some drunken young men stumbling along the road. "We have no other choices."

As they passed through one tiny fishing village, which consisted of only a few houses, the village headman recognized Kwe and ran out to welcome him home. Speaking a language that Cody and Reyas didn't understand, Kwe asked the headman a question. In response, the headman pointed to a fishing boat that had been hauled ashore for repair and answered Kwe in his language. Turning to Cody and Reyas, Kwe explained in Lekadian, "The village's only fishing boat needs repair. In the old days, someone around here would make the part, but today, people with those skills have moved away to take jobs in factories. Now the villagers have to buy the part but they don't have the money." Without hesitation, Kwe ordered the merchant to give the headman the money he needed. "Don't worry merchant, my family will repay you." Silent resentfulness once again showing in his face, the merchant counted out the money and handed it to the ecstatic headman.

As they left the village behind, Kwe explained that being a bandit wasn't as profitable as many people thought. "We have to pay off the police, and pay off the soldiers, and we have to take care of our own. That doesn't leave much for us."

"Was that man related to you?" asked Reyas.

"No."

"Why do you help him?"

"My grandmother says that the gods have favored my clan, made us stronger than most of the others, but that the gods will only favor us as long as we share with neighbors who lack our good fortune.

"You do everything your grandmother tells you to do?" asked Cody somewhat scornfully.

"Our elders have earned our respect. We follow their advice."

It was mid afternoon when they finally rolled into Kwe's village. Word spread quickly that he was back. Soon, his parents' house was filled with family and friends, but most importantly, his fiancée Tessa was waiting for him. It was a joyous reunion, with only one sour note: the boxing match would have to be cancelled. Sullo had been captured by soldiers who recognized him as the bandit who led a raid on a mining shipment. They were going to hand him over to provincial authorities. The Suhrati weren't as concerned about Sullo as they were about the shame they would endure from having to forfeit the match. They knew they could pay off the authorities and secure Sullo's release, but it would be too late for the match.

Seeing the merchant leaving, Kwe shouted out to him to wait. He then went to his uncle, a man with a horribly disfigured face, and asked him to pay the merchant, adding, "Give him whatever extra he wants for his trouble." As his uncle limped away, Kwe explained to Cody and Reyas that his uncle had been one of the best bandits alive before being injured in an explosion. Now he was the trusted keeper of their money.

Watching as Kwe's uncle handed money to the merchant, Cody asked, "Kwe, how does your uncle know the merchant is being truthful about what you owe?"

Kwe smiled wryly. "Cody, no one lies to my family."

Dombrel Strikes

The guide assured Tobin that this was indeed where Sedlin il Lindar lived and worked, but declined to come farther than where the small trail branched off from the larger dirt trail leading from the village. After handing the guide what Kwe had said would be the right amount of Devlan currency, Tobin set off alone toward Sedlin il Lindar's, trying to shake nagging fears that the guide had played him for a fool. He was already feeling awkward in his unfamiliar new clothes, which Kwe had promised him would be completely suitable for The Wilds, but which in this part of Devlan clearly marked Tobin as an outsider. Adults tried to avoid staring at him while children pointed and laughed as he passed by.

That was behind Tobin now, but he had no way of knowing what lay ahead. He made his way alone along a lightly used narrow path that ran through an ominously dark tunnel of tree branches trained to grow in a low arch, each tree intertwined with the ones next to and opposite it. Air in the "tunnel" was thick with the sweet scent of the blossoms covering the trees.

Once through the tunnel, there was little to suggest that this might be a laboratory. Looking around, Tobin saw carefully tended trees, a vegetable garden, some flowers, and here and there, weather beaten wooden benches. Only scattered, oddly shaped antennas suggested the presence of any advanced technology. He stopped in front of what was probably the main building, but it looked more like an ancient temple than a research laboratory. Very old, carved beams accented and protruded from ornately painted stucco walls. The tiled roof's intricate curves proclaimed devoted reverence rather than scientific detachment. Only the strange antennas gave Tobin hope that he had not been led seriously astray.

Tobin walked to the door and knocked. Lindar himself answered the door. Old, almost frail looking and dressed in simple robes, he didn't look like a leading scientist responsible for cutting edge Lekadian research. He readily acknowledged who he was, but looked none too happy to see Tobin. "So you're the one the Lekadians sent this time."

"No one sent me. I am here…"

"Don't say it. Everyone they send says the same thing. They come on a Lekadian ship, but lie and say, 'The Lekadians didn't send me. I only want to learn.'"

"But it's true."

"Go back to your Lekadian masters. Tell them the answer is the same today as it has been every time they have sent a spy here, and as it always will be. Tell them Sedlin il Lindar no longer serves the Empire."

"I learned about you on Tarfil…"

"I know who you are. I knew you were coming."

"How did you know? You're not…"

"Not on the network? We are connected in other ways. We are not stupid. Or backward."

"But I…"

"Tobin, son of Tobin of Tarfil, your record speaks for itself. You were an abysmal student. You took nothing seriously. You killed a man."

"Killing him was the only way…"

"It was the easy way. Did you never wonder how to solve problems with your mind? Go back to your Lekadian masters, Tobin of Tarfil. Play your little mind games with RedFins. There is nothing for you here."

"But…"

The door slammed shut in Tobin's face.

"You are wrong about me," Tobin shouted at the closed door, "I came here to learn!"

There was no answer. Tobin sat down on a wooden bench. He stayed there for the next two days, eating what little food he had brought, tightly wrapping his Devlan cloak around him for warmth at night. For two days, he questioned why he had come. He felt like the biggest fool in the galaxy. Several times, he nearly left. He wished he had never come. He could be fishing with Cody now. Despite it all, he stayed. He himself couldn't say why. He tried rationalizing the reason, but in the end, he had to admit it was mostly stubbornness. If Sedlin il Lindar had invited him in for tea, then politely asked him to leave, he would have left without a word of protest. But now it had become a contest of wills.

Occasionally, Lindar opened the door to admit people or to bid them farewell. Each time, Tobin stared directly at him, but each time Lindar ignored him completely. Lindar's disciples acted as though Tobin were invisible, but even though he often didn't understand the language they were speaking, he knew from how they furtively glanced at him and laughed that they were mocking him. It was all he could do to restrain an uncharacteristic anger.

When his food ran out, he ate fruits and vegetables he picked from the gardens, making sure the old man saw. The third night it rained. It was a cold, hard, steady rain. In the middle of the night, the door opened. It was Lindar, holding a lantern. "Still here, Tobin son of Tobin of Tarfil?"

Tobin tried to speak but was shivering from the cold rain. His lips could not form the words.

"Come in. Even Lekadian spies don't deserve to be left outside in this weather."

"I'm not a spy," Tobin managed to say through chattering teeth.

"Go in that room. Take off your clothes. You will find dry clothes in there. Put on anything you feel like. I'll get us some hot tea."

Thankful that no one he knew would see him dressed like a monk, Tobin changed into dry clothes and returned to the main room, where Lindar had placed a chair for him next to the crude heater.

"Come, sit over here Tobin. I've turned up the heat. You'll feel better. Don't say anything. Just warm up." As Tobin sat down, another monk brought them mugs of steaming tea and then left without a word.

They sat drinking tea in silence. Finally, Lindar spoke. "You're not shivering any more. How do you feel?"

"Much better, thanks. If I could just tell you about myself..."

"I don't want to hear it."

"But..."

"Quiet! Just answer one question."

"I'll tell you anything you want."

"Was there a moment when you knew you wanted to come here? Take your time. Think about it."

"I don't have to think. I know. Only it was before I knew about this place."

"Go on."

"It wasn't that I wanted to come. I had to come. I just didn't know where until a few days ago. You were right about me, about everything, except about me being a Lekadian spy. But everything else about me, you are right."

"I only want to hear about that moment."

"We were digging someone out from under a collapsed building. He was about my age, a friend of my best friend, but we didn't know it yet. He was lying under those ruins for days. He was in terrible pain. Broken bones, probably bleeding inside. Suddenly I had the thought that if I could reach into his mind, like I do with the RedFins, maybe I could give him the strength to bear his pain. So I reached in.

I didn't think about it, I just reached in. I only wanted to help him with his pain."

"Did you?"

"Yes. But it took away all my energy. Afterwards, I could only lie on my back. I couldn't even sit up."

"Is that why you want to talk to me? Because you lost your energy for a while?"

"No. Well, yes, that too, but something else. When I reached into his mind, I connected with something inside him. I felt his fears. I knew his secrets. I saw his whole life. Just like he saw it. I knew everything about him. Everything. I still do. It's almost like I am him, except of course I'm not."

"Have you told him?"

"No. He would be embarrassed if he knew what I know about him. I can never tell him the things I know."

"And your question?"

"How do I carry around someone's deepest secrets in me? I can't tell anyone about it. Not even Cody, my best friend. Suppose Cody needs my help sometime? I don't want to learn his deepest secrets. I don't want him to know I could learn his deepest secrets. Tonight, out there in the rain, sometimes I wasn't sure if I was the guy I helped or if I was me. He's still in me, like he's real."

"You have had a difficult couple of days Tobin. Get some sleep."

"I never asked for this power. I never knew I had it. Take the power away from me if you don't want to teach me. Please. I don't care. Just take it away. I don't want it. I am a warrior. I can't be worrying about how people feel. Just make me the way I was before."

* * *

Cody felt the warm blood running down his chin after his opponent's surprise left hook, but scarcely gave it a thought. He hadn't expected the blow. He struggled not to let himself be rattled by an opponent so near defeat delivering a blow with such unexpected force. He knew that at home on Quogue, this fighter would never have stood a chance against him. The problem was the rules here. On Quogue rules were minimal, common sense rules of fairness, nothing more. Here there were detailed rules about how to fight, and they were strictly enforced. Before the fight, he had to sit down and memorize the rules, and during the fight it seemed to him that he was devoting more attention to remembering rules than to fighting his opponent. The fight had already been halted several times because Cody had unknowingly violated some rule. One more violation and he would forfeit the fight, disgracing his Suhrati sponsors.

To most of the spectators, Cody was just a bad guy from outside The Wilds who everyone could see broke the rules, just some desperate last minute replacement for Sullo. The sight of fresh blood running down Cody's chin excited the crowd into cheering his opponent even more wildly, stomping their feet harder in bloodlusting approval after every blow his opponent delivered. The floor shook with it, increasing his opponent's confidence, making him more aggressive. Cody had been the local champion on Quogue long enough to know the strength the roar of a crowd can give a fighter. Reinvigorated, his opponent delivered yet another blow, but this one lacked the power of the last punch. Sensing his opponent weakening and maybe edging into the overconfidence that can grow out of a few lucky jabs and the approval of the mob, Cody shut out the crowd's thundering catcalls, allowing nothing at all in his consciousness but the rhythm of the fight itself.

Just as Cody hoped, the other fighter lunged with a blow intended to finish him, but with timing that was a little off. Cody was ready, averting the blow and taking the offensive, catching the man off guard with a barrage of devastating blows to his face and chest. Reeling back, out of control precisely at the moment he thought he was finally assured of victory, the man lunged wildly at Cody, who took advantage of the man's loss of focus to deliver the blow that sent the man tumbling to the ground, defeated. The crowd cursed loudly as Cody, remembering the rules, walked over to the man, reached down, helped him to his feet, and exchanged the crossed arms salute of respect that was traditional after every boxing match in The Wilds.

After the fighters had saluted each other, Kwe slipped a robe over Cody's shoulders. They stood waiting while Kwe's youngest sister Jidara, carrying the traditional victor's wreath made of the Hessel vine, shyly entered the ring and walked up to them. Cody knelt, and as she placed it on his head, the Suhrati in the audience cheered wildly. Standing up, he took both her hands in his hands and said, "Thank you." She smiled and then abruptly left the ring.

"She's in love with you," whispered Kwe.

"She's beautiful."

Kwe quickly shot back, "She's a child, Cody. And she's my sister."

"I know. You don't have to worry about me, brother."

With the fight officially over and the victor crowned, Kwe escorted Cody back to his corner, where other Suhrati were eagerly waiting to clean him up. Cody didn't say anything. Kwe and the Suhrati seemed to sense his need to reflect, working on him in silence, washing away his blood, tending to his wounds, and giving him something energizing to drink.

For the first time since the fight started, Cody felt free to let his thoughts wander. That was one thing he liked about boxing, the absolute focus that was required, focusing on the fight alone, to the exclusion of everything else. Even the slightest distracted thought could result in serious injury and defeat. He was glad to be boxing again, honest one on one fighting, two consenting fighters using nothing but their fists. It wasn't like street fighting or battle, where someone could always sneak up unexpectedly from behind. In the ring, it was just two fighters who knew that they alone, and no one else, determined who would win and who would lose.

The prize was in local currency, amounting to several months' earnings for the average worker in a Lekadian factory in Devlan or Opportunity. After refusing Cody's repeated attempts to offer the prize money to him, Kwe finally broke down and gratefully accepted it. He would now be able to marry Tessa, maybe even take Inya as his Second, and pursue the life he wanted.

"How can I ever repay you, Cody?" Kwe asked.

"Take us to that fishing spot."

* * *

Reyas and Tessa were sharing a tiny room in Kwe's parents' home. Kwe hadn't told anyone here about his near execution, or about Dombrel possibly being after him for his part in the slave camp insurrection, so Reyas was surprised to learn from Tessa that her brother Tinap, a policeman in Opportunity, had told her all about it.

Tessa had tried unsuccessfully to talk Kwe out of the fishing trip and had warned him about Dombrel, but Kwe had insisted that he and Cody could take care of themselves. Desperate, she finally begged Reyas to remain on the lookout for Dombrel during the trip.

Night dampness was still burning off, rising in delicate plumes in the early morning sun, as Kwe, Reyas, and Cody walked with Tessa and several members of Kwe's family to the river's edge. Reyas and Kwe were carrying blasters. Cody as usual was carrying his bow, arrows, and harpoon. As they boarded a small, open sailboat, Tessa again begged them to be on the lookout for Dombrel, but Kwe brushed off the idea of there being any danger on this trip.

Before leaving, there was a brief ceremony to bless the journey and keep them safe. Kwe's grandmother prayed to their gods, beseeching them to watch over her grandson and his friends. While she prayed, Jidara burned three incense sticks to ward off evil spirits. When the sticks were billowing smoke heavy with a pungent aroma, she extinguished the flame on one stick and used the burned end to draw a sacred mark on Kwe's forehead. Then she did the same with the other two incense sticks for Reyas and Cody, smiling shyly at Cody as she drew the mark on his forehead. When she was done, she handed the three sticks to her grandmother, who knelt down, prayed again, and then set the sticks floating on the river. Looking at the three friends she said, "Now the River God will keep all of you safe."

It was a two day trip each way in the small sailboat. They fished for their food, enjoyed lazy meals of fish cooked over an open fire, ate wild fruits and vegetables, and camped out at night.

On their first day out, they passed a boat carrying hunters, leaving them a little more conscious of the danger than any of them cared to admit. After sailing for a while in silence, Reyas asked Kwe, "Maybe you should give Cody and me some lessons on using blasters."

Cody laughed. "You, Reyas? You need lessons? That guard you shot didn't think so."

"I think you and I both need lessons, Cody."

Cody held up his bow. "Not while I have this."

"In case you run out of arrows," Reyas answered.

Cody reluctantly consented and so every evening for the rest of their camping trip, Kwe gave them lessons in the safe and effective use of blasters.

The biggest concern for Cody wasn't weapons, or Dombrel, but Reyas. He had never before thought he might spend a night with a woman and not have sex with her. But Reyas was different. And she had suffered greatly. He could see that. Since leaving the slave camp, the three of them had discussed every aspect of their experiences in the camp, as inmate, guard, and liberator, yet every time they came close to the question of what the guards had done to Reyas, they skirted the subject. It was an unmistakable void in their conversations that Cody wanted to ask about, but the more he wanted to ask, the more he realized he should not.

The first night out, sleeping on an island halfway to the fishing spot, Cody felt uncharacteristically unsure of himself. It had been hard enough staying in city inns, knowing that a woman with whom he felt such a bond was sleeping alone in the next room, but he had forced himself to endure it. Out here on the river was worse. He had never been on a camping trip with a woman. Camping in the woods had always been something he did with guys, a chance for them to boast or lie about the women they had sex with during past Four-Days. It was inconceivable to him that a woman would come along, yet Reyas had come on this trip, and neither she nor Kwe seemed uncomfortable about it. During the entire first day of sailing up river, Cody wondered whether he and Kwe would take turns having sex with Reyas, or whether, as he feared most, there would be no sex at all.

It was as he feared. The first night, Cody meekly followed Kwe in carrying his sleeping gear out of the boat, leaving the boat to Reyas. Cody spent much of the night awake, thinking of this woman in the open boat sleeping just a few feet away, wondering whether she was just waiting for him.

It was the same the second night, at the fishing spot. Again, Reyas slept in the boat while Cody and Kwe slept on the shore. Cody was even more tormented. He lay awake, unable to stop asking himself whether Reyas might also be lying awake, just waiting for him to come to her, wondering why he didn't. Cody became convinced that she was awake and might be wondering whether there was something wrong with him that kept him from coming to her. Finally, certain that Reyas was waiting for him, he got up and made his way naked to the boat.

Reyas was lying on her side, facing away from him, apparently asleep. Cody made some noise, deliberately stepping on a dry branch, making it break, hoping that she would hear him, but she didn't move a muscle. He tried coughing, but there was still no response from Reyas. It was agony. He wanted her. He hadn't even realized until now he much he wanted her. He wanted her so badly that it hurt. She was so unlike the beautiful women he normally yearned for. The slave camp had left Reyas skinny, with just stubble growing out on her scalp. She didn't look at all the way he liked women to look. He loved long hair on women, loved running his fingers through their hair, loved smelling it. He knew her unfeminine appearance wasn't her fault, but he couldn't get it out of his mind. It only increased his puzzlement about why he felt the way he did about her.

Standing naked over her, he felt almost physical pain at the restraint he was forcing on himself. He hoped she would roll over to face him, smiling, welcoming him. He couldn't understand why she didn't. Other women fawned over him. Only a few days ago, Inya treated him like a god. She lavished praises on his sensuality and on his sexuality. How could Reyas not be just as attracted to him?

Slowly reaching down, he let his hand approach Reyas' exposed left shoulder. "Maybe she just doesn't hear me," he thought, wondering whether he should touch her gently, not enough to wake her, just to let her know he was there if she was awake and waiting for him to assert himself. Just as his fingers were about to touch her skin, he paused, and moved away. He didn't know why. He knew his friends would think him a fool, or worse. He was glad they weren't there to see him. He cleared his throat loudly, still hoping she would turn over and welcome him into the boat with her, but nothing happened.

He couldn't stand another moment of it. Resisting every instinct in every molecule of his being, he turned and ran away, not knowing where he was running, just running as fast as he could, finally plunging into the icy pool beneath the waterfall.

Hearing him run away, Reyas opened her eyes, looked around, and saw him shivering under the freezing cold waterfall, clearly in agony. Gazing admiringly at him in the bright moonlight, she switched off the blaster she had been gripping tightly, ready to fire, and watched as Cody shivered. Finally, she lay back down and slept for the first time in two nights.

Kwe's fishing spot turned out to be a delight for all of them, but especially for Reyas, who finally felt free to relax after that second night. Pleasures as simple as this fishing trip, pleasures that Kwe and Cody took for granted, were unknown to this girl who had spent so much of her youth as a slave. Kwe was right. Even for Cody, this was an extraordinary place, with exotic birds that neither he nor Reyas ever imagined might exist, lush vegetation, sweet easily picked fruit growing wild, an abundance of fish, the icy cold waterfall fed by runoff from a nearby snow capped mountain peak, and most importantly, peace and isolation.

They all agreed that the waterfall was too frigidly cold to enter, even in the hottest afternoon sun, but every night, Cody secretly shivered under it, unaware of Reyas' furtive but appreciative glances at his suffering.

They all needed the rest badly, but especially Reyas and Kwe. For Cody, liberating the slave camp was a great adventure in which he had become a warrior, but for them it had been an ordeal. Kwe was still shaken by his close brush with execution and still sad at his friend's death, but even his suffering was nothing like Reyas'. He knew for the entire year he was there that he would be leaving when his contract expired, and of course, he was a guard, not a slave. For Reyas, it was full time and unending. Until the camp was liberated, she had every reason to believe that she would spend the rest of her life there.

After three days of relaxing at Kwe's fishing spot, doing nothing but fishing, talking, laughing, splashing and squealing in the water like young children, they decided to head back so they would be at Kwe's village when Tobin arrived.

* * *

"Tomorrow is the day you wanted to leave to join your friends, is it not?"

Tobin replied, "Yes," but sitting in Lindar's garden, drinking tea with the master, it was hard for him to imagine going anywhere.

"I do wish you would stay a while longer."

"I can't. My friends are expecting me."

"There is much more work we need to do on your powers."

"I still don't want those powers. I don't want to know how people are feeling. I don't want to know their deepest secrets."

"I told you, I cannot take these powers from you. They are part of who you are. I can only guide you in their use. You have carried my experiments far beyond what I ever thought possible. But you still need to work on controlling your powers."

"The tricks you taught me will make it easier."

"I've only taught you how to refrain from using your powers. I have not yet taught you to control them. The truth is, we don't really know the extent of your powers. They may be greater than you and I suspect. Until you get more training, you must be very careful in using them."

"I will never use them again."

"I think you will find that harder than you think. You need more training. A few more days at least."

"I told you, I can't stay. My friends will worry. I must leave first thing in the morning."

"I hope the time you've been here has been productive."

"Yes, but not in ways I expected."

"You were expecting easy answers, Tobin."

"Yes, I admit it."

"But now you know there are no easy answers."

Tobin drank some tea before replying. "Yes, but not only that. There's something I still don't understand. We have been so busy that I haven't had a chance to ask."

"Go ahead."

"This is not what I expected. This place. I was expecting a research laboratory."

"We are a research laboratory."

"Well, yes, but it's also a monastery. You're a monk."

"We are an order devoted to scientific truth. Truth above all. Not what we or anyone else believes is the truth, but what we can prove to be the truth."

"When Lewelle studied with you, was he a monk?"

"No Tobin, he was like you, just a youth seeking some easy answers.

"Did he find them? The answers?"

"It's not the answer that's important. What's important is the question."

"OK, did he find the right question?"

Lindar considered his words carefully before replying. "Lewelle has an inquisitive mind. One of the finest minds I've seen. He could have been a great explorer, a discoverer, a leader. He has a gift for seeing possibilities that no one else can even imagine."

"He doesn't seem so special."

"He cannot help it. Lekadians are a race in decline. Lewelle comes from a distinguished line of generals and explorers going back many, many generations. His ancestors built the Empire. That's when he should have lived. Back then, he would have been a great man. He would have been one of those building or expanding the Empire. That's what he was born to do. Instead, he is ambassador to a minor planet. It's his misfortune that he lives today instead of ancient times. Today, the Empire is shrinking. No one thinks about expansion any longer. We used to be one of the great races of the galaxy. Now, some younger races don't even know we ever existed."

"I'm surprised that Lewelle didn't come down to see you, Lindar. Him being your former student."

"Tobin, no Lekadian has visited me here in many, many years. They just send non-Lekadians to be their spies."

"Why don't they come themselves?"

"They are afraid. Their minds are all connected by their network. They are afraid of being alone with themselves. Our great race has become a race of cowards who fear being alone. We let others do our fighting and our dirty work for us. All Lekadians get an organic computer planted in their brain at birth. I have it too. Your friend Accabo has one too, but he was older, so it won't affect him as much. It grows with us. It becomes us. Overall it has been a good thing. But to become so dependent on the network that you're afraid to be alone with your own soul, that is a terrible thing. It's a weakness. That's why I block out the Lekadian network here. I can be alone here. I don't have an endless flow of information and noise in my brain that I can't shut off."

Tobin looked up at the antennas scattered around the yard and roofs of buildings. "Those block the signals?"

"Yes. This is the reason that Lekadians don't come here. It's why they send others, like I thought you were that first day. It's why

Lewelle does not come. Even Lewelle fears being alone with himself."

"Is that why you came here to Devlan Nine? So you could be alone?"

"Partly. But it was also because my father's family lives here. He was born here."

"I thought you were Lekadian."

"I was born on the Lekadian home world, but my father was Devlan. He joined the Lekadian military, and was the first person in his family to leave this planet. My mother was Lekadian, a nurse. I never knew them. They both died in a computer virus epidemic when I was just a baby. It infected the computers in their brains and killed them. Many Lekadians died in the epidemic. I grew up with my mother's family on the Lekadian home world. It was my home until I came here to Devlan Nine."

The conversation went on late into the night. They were still talking a few hours before dawn, when they were interrupted by someone outside, banging loudly on the door.

"See who it is please, Tobin. Be careful. We rarely get visitors this late at night."

Tobin cautiously opened the door. He found himself facing a man wearing flowing robes, with a hood carefully obscuring his face. When Tobin demanded to know the stranger's reason for disturbing them so late at night, the stranger simply pulled back his hood, revealing his face.

It was Lewelle.

As Tobin stepped aside to let him enter, Lewelle greeted him gruffly. "Why are you here? You are supposed to be with Cody."

"I had to come."

"That was stupid. Dombrel is after you. If I knew you were going off by yourself, I would have sent some guards with you."

Lindar was appalled to learn about Dombrel. "The man you killed was a Dombrel?"

Tobin nodded, feeling some gratification to discover that Lindar didn't know everything after all.

"Take no chances, Tobin. Lewelle is right. They are dangerous. They will be after you."

"I can take care of myself."

Sounding irritated, Lewelle replied, "No, you can't. It's too dangerous for you to go around by yourself. Tomorrow, you'll return with me to the ship. I'll send for some soldiers to accompany us. We can speak more about this in the morning. Right now, Lindar and I must speak. In private. It's urgent." After wishing Tobin a hasty good night, Lindar disappeared into his office with Lewelle.

Tobin went to bed, but couldn't sleep. Feeling restless, he got up while it was still dark, ate a quick breakfast and on an impulse, left before anyone else awoke, trusting he could remember the directions to the boat that went to Kwe's village.

* * *

Kwe wasn't worried about the approaching storm clouds when they first set off sailing from the fishing spot. He had been sailing this river since infancy and knew every mood of the river and its weather. Even after clouds turned dark and began an unrelenting downpour, Kwe assured them that if this was like most other storms, the rain would break by midday and they would dry in the warm sun by afternoon. He assured them confidently, "The only thing we have to worry about is if a strong southerly wind starts up. If that happens, we've got problems. But I haven't seen any signs that it's going to happen."

It happened. By midday, the wind had turned southerly, cold and strong, with fierce gusts. The steady downpour was becoming brutally cold rainsqualls. Flashes in the distance heralded a lightning storm's rapid approach. Kwe decided to head for a cave where he had taken shelter in the past. The river would soon be too dangerous a place to be, especially in a small, open sailboat. Everyone living on the river knew people who had died that way.

By the time they reached the cave, they had been soaked for hours, and with the plummeting temperature, were shivering. After struggling to secure the boat, they ran for the cave, stowed their gear and what little food they had, then went on a frustrating hunt for firewood that hadn't gotten too wet in the downpour. Finally, teeth chattering in the cold cave, they used their blasters to start a fire. While the fire was starting, Kwe showed them moss growing on the cave walls that they could use to dry their skin after they undressed. Soon they were dry and warm, crouching as close to the fire as they could tolerate. The heat felt good. No one cared about the smoke filling the cave from the wet and mostly green wood.

When Cody awoke in the morning, he was so hot that it was hard to remember just how cold he had been the evening before. Coming to his senses, he realized that he was hot because he was lying very close to a now blazing fire. He could hear rain still coming down hard, though the wind gusts seemed to be diminishing. Suddenly he heard footsteps outside, splashing toward the cave. Grabbing his bow and an arrow from his quiver, Cody was ready to fire it at the intruder until he recognized Kwe staggering into the cave from the driving rain, naked, his arms holding an enormous stack of firewood, water dripping from both him and the firewood.

"The storm will break by midday. This should be enough to keep us warm for a while." Setting down the wood, Kwe tore off some moss and dried himself, crouching as close as he could to the fire until he warmed up. When he was warm, he stood up, picked up his fishing gear, announced, "I'm going to catch us some breakfast," and left the cave.

Jumping naked from his sleeping pack, Cody grabbed his harpoon and raced after Kwe into the storm. He caught up with him at the riverbank, where Kwe was preparing to fish in his customary manner.

"Don't waste your time with that stuff, Kwe." Cody held up his harpoon. "You know I can catch fish faster with this."

As Cody strode toward the river's edge, Kwe shouted, "The water's too cold. Don't go in."

"I'm a fisherman. I'm not afraid of cold water!"

"You don't know how cold it is. No one goes in the water after a storm like this."

Cody plunged in anyway, harpoon in hand, but wasn't prepared for how extremely cold the water had turned overnight. Kwe was right. The frigid cold hit Cody like a knife but he braced himself and waded farther in, waist deep, determined not to let Kwe see just how cold he was, then scrambled up on some rocks bordering a still pool and waited. It wasn't long before he had harpooned enough fish for a solid breakfast and lunch.

His teeth were chattering violently but he didn't want Kwe to notice, so Cody leapt from the frigid water, fish proudly in hand, shouting, "Race you to the cave!" and immediately broke into a run. Kwe didn't catch up until they reached the cave. By then, they were both gasping for air and laughing so hard that no one noticed Cody's chattering teeth.

They spent the rest of the morning cooking, eating, and swapping stories. When Cody left the cave to gather more firewood, Reyas tried asking Kwe the question that had been bothering her ever since the merchant warned her about Kwe. "Kwe, that merchant, the one who brought us to your village…" Reyas hesitated.

"Yes?"

She continued, "He said you killed his son."

Kwe looked embarrassed. "Reyas, when we were crossing the Badlands, I didn't know the merchant was the boy's father. Honest. I didn't know until my uncle told me, later, at my village, after the merchant left."

"How did it happen?"

"The boy was a miner, at a small mine. He was just a kid, younger than most miners. His employers were new in the Badlands. They didn't know how things are done. They refused to pay us to protect them, so we were teaching them a small lesson. We weren't going to take much, only enough to show them it's cheaper to pay us than have us and everyone else rob them. No one dares rob miners who are under our protection. But the kid wanted to be a hero. It was crazy. We never expected it. He just started firing at us. He didn't have to. We don't kill people. Even the police know we don't kill people. But we had to defend ourselves. Sullo and me both shot back. It was Sullo or me who killed the kid. Maybe both of us. No one knows. I didn't know the merchant was his father until after we rode back with him. Honest."

"Aren't you afraid the merchant will go to the police and report you?"

Kwe laughed. "I'll bet he did, long ago. That's probably why he was so afraid the whole trip. He probably thought I was going to kill him in revenge and leave his body in the desert, or maybe feed him to the dragons. You see, my family has an understanding with the police. We help them, they help us. The official police report says it was the kid's own fault that he died. It just says he died, not that he was killed. It doesn't even mention our names."

Reyas looked into the fire, thinking about what Kwe said. "Kwe, what about Tessa's brother Tinap? He's a policeman. He's going to be your brother-in-law. Don't you worry about him?"

Kwe laughed again. "Tinap? He knows how things work. He puts on a good show, like he's real clean, but he's just like the police in Hangtown, just at a higher level. Still, it would be embarrassing for him to have a bandit as a brother-in-law, so I promised his family I'll give it up before I marry Tessa. It was Tinap who got me the job at the slave camp. Now that I have some money, I can use his influence to buy an apprenticeship at the spaceport."

"You have a great life here. Can you really give all this up just to be a shuttle mechanic at a spaceport?"

"It was an honor that the priests chose Tessa to be my Prime. The priests say the gods have a great plan for our children. A woman as high class as Tessa wouldn't even look at someone like me otherwise. Who am I to argue with the gods?"

Cody returned to the cave, shaking the water from his hair, and added more wood to the fire before tearing some moss off the wall to dry himself off. As he sat back down at the fire, he said to Kwe, "I don't mean any offense by this, but Tessa seems like the kind of girl a grandmother would choose as your fiancée. I don't understand. You love your life here. Inya would love it. Why give it all up to be trapped at the spaceport with someone like Tessa? You don't have to do everything your grandmother tells you to do, do you?"

"Actually, Cody, my grandmother agrees with you."

"She does?"

"Yes. But it's a new world. My grandmother doesn't understand new ways, even when it's what the gods want. I don't mean to disrespect her, but I won't argue with the gods."

By midday, the winds had died, the day was growing warmer, and the rain had subsided from wild squalls to a steady downpour. Laughing and with full stomachs, they pushed the sailboat back into the water and resumed their journey, not caring about the rain because, Kwe assured them, the sun would soon come out and dry their clothes. This time he was right. The rest of the day's journey went uneventfully. They spent a night camped on the same island where they camped the first night nearly a week ago, then set off for the final day's sail. They would be at Kwe's home by mid afternoon. They were making good time. Both the wind and the current were on their side, so they took their time, stopping a few times to pick fruit or so Kwe could show them beautiful sights, laughing and exchanging stories, feeling better than any of them had felt in a very long time.

Reyas told Cody her memories of the years she had spent in the slave camp as his mother's closest friend, and he told her his own memories of his mother as the disciplined woman always in a military uniform on the *Marco Polo*. They spoke about what it was like for Cody growing up in space, and about Reyas' few memories of her own days as a young child before becoming a slave, and about that terrible day on Dariel's boat when at the age of ten, Cody watched the *Marco Polo* blow up before his eyes.

One thing they still could not speak about, however, was the thing both of them were thinking about the most: sex. For Reyas, having been raped so often in the camp, the memories and everything she associated with sex were so bitter that she would have no compunctions at all about killing any man, no matter who he was, who forced himself on her. She couldn't imagine ever getting pleasure from sex. It just didn't seem possible. Yet those nights when she had seen Cody shivering in the waterfall, she had wanted him. The feeling went against everything she had learned and experienced. Until now, nothing had seemed as repugnant as sex. She respected Cody as a warrior and friend, but had learned from watching him that when it came to how he treated women, Cody was nearly as repugnant as those guards who had made her life such a torment. Seeing him endure such agony in the icy waterfall, solely for her sake, revealed a hidden side of him that she was having trouble reconciling with the side he showed the world.

* * *

Cody's thoughts were very different. This shaven-headed woman was a mystery to him. She was so strong and so brave, both qualities he didn't associate with women. His mother was that way, though he didn't know this until he met her in the slave camp. Reyas had been abused terribly. He couldn't imagine anyone enduring what she had to endure, especially someone as strong and brave as she was. How could someone as strong as Reyas let herself be a victim? Cody was certain that if he had been in her position, he would have killed anyone who did what he guessed the guards must have done to her, even if it meant his life. Why didn't she fight back?

Then there was the question of how she felt about him. This was a total mystery to Cody. He had never before walked away from an opportunity for sex. Did she think he didn't like her? Or that something was wrong with him? He was beginning to regret not having at least tried to have sex with her. Every other woman he had sex with, no matter how she resisted at first, was grateful later that he had not given in to her objections.

On the last of their excursions ashore they climbed a hill, where Kwe showed them a dramatic snow capped volcanic peak. They were returning to their boat, laughing at a joke Kwe had just told, when through the trees they noticed another boat moored next to theirs. None of them said anything, but all three immediately thought, "Dombrel."

Slipping an arrow into his crossbow and whispering, "Cover me," Cody cautiously crept forward, signaling Reyas and Kwe to stay where they were. Being careful not to make a sound, he slowly made his way down the trail, creeping closer to the beach, ready to shoot an arrow at the slightest provocation. Turning to look back for a moment, he saw both Kwe and Reyas standing with their weapons drawn, looking strong and vigilant. Cody smiled, savoring the sight of this strong woman protecting him. When she smiled back, he wondered if there was a woman anywhere on Quogue like her. He had never met one who came even close.

Drawing closer to the beach, ready to fire an arrow, Cody finally got down to where he could see through the thick underbrush. Very carefully moving some branches aside, being careful not to make any noise, he could see three men. He couldn't get a clear view, but could see that all were armed with what looked like advanced weapons. Inching closer, staying low, he finally came within earshot. To his surprise, he recognized two of the voices as his father's and Tobin's. Slowly standing up until they recognized him, he walked over to them while calling back to Reyas and Kwe.

The third man was Kwe's father. After Kwe and Reyas had joined them, and everyone had embraced joyfully, his father gave them the bad news. "Kwe, your mother's been kidnapped. Jidara too. They're being held in the Canyon of the Fire Breathers."

"Dombrel?" asked Cody.

Carlos answered, "Yes. Cody, it's you and Tobin they really want. Dombrel's going to kill Jidara and Kwe's mother if Kwe doesn't hand you over by sunset tomorrow."

Kwe was adamant. "No! I will not send you to your deaths."

"Are you really willing to let your mother and sister die?" asked Carlos.

Kwe insisted that he could rescue his mother and sister without giving up Cody and Tobin. "We can do it. We have enough fighters in the village."

Kwe's father had more bad news. "We don't have any fighters. Not a single one. Tinap took Tessa to Hangtown for her safety. He took every fighter we have as an escort so she would be safe. Haab didn't like it, but she went along with it because she needs Tinap's help to get Sullo released."

Kwe was furious, but Carlos thought they might be better off without them. "Haab took me through the Canyon of the Fire Breathers when she brought me from Hangtown. A large group can't approach without being seen by Dombrel. We have to catch them by surprise. All we need are a few good warriors."

"It's Tobin and me they want" Cody said, "we're the ones who should go."

Tobin agreed.

"I'm going with you," said Kwe.

Reyas offered to go with them. Tobin replied, "I don't mind, but I know Cody won't like it..."

Cody snapped, "Reyas can come."

"But you've always said that the only thing a woman is good for is..."

Cody interrupted Tobin, saying firmly, "She's coming."

Kwe's father volunteered to go, but Kwe rejected the idea, fearing that his father's bad leg would slow him down. They finally decided that his father would follow later, bringing steeds for Jidara and her mother to ride home after the rescue.

Arriving back at Kwe's village, they ate a hasty meal and prepared to ride all night, hoping to arrive at Canyon of the Fire Breathers before first light. While they ate, Carlos brought out a surprise—Cody's and Tobin's breastplates, helmets, and paint.

After eating, Kwe went to a weapons locker and returned with two blasters, which he handed to Cody and Tobin. Cody tried refusing it, but Kwe insisted. "It's my mother and sister we're rescuing. We do it my way." After Kwe confirmed that Carlos had brought a blaster with him, they went outside for some quick riding lessons from Kwe and his father, then immediately set off riding to the Canyon of the Fire Breathers.

First light wasn't far off when they arrived. Leaving the steeds far enough away that Dombrel couldn't detect them, Carlos and Kwe climbed to a viewpoint where Carlos could study the terrain and plan his strategy.

Meanwhile, Cody and Tobin were painting each other's faces with the mark of the warrior and putting on their breastplates and helmets. Tobin looked almost radiant. "Warriors again, right Cody?" When Cody didn't respond, Tobin continued, "Dragons! Just like the original Warrior Brothers. Cody, did you tell Reyas that the original Warrior Brothers fought fire breathing dragons?" When neither Cody nor Reyas reacted, Tobin continued, "They won every fight. Even fighting fire breathing dragons!"

Cody checked his crossbow.

Tobin laughed. "And now it's our turn!"

"You two don't really believe this stuff, do you?" asked Reyas.

Cody reached into his quiver and checked his arrows, one by one. Without looking up, he said, "She's right."

"What do you mean, 'she's right'?"

"All this mystical crap. We're just two fishermen from Quogue. Reyas, do you want to know the truth? We tricked those monks into giving us this armor. They only made us warriors because we tricked them. We only did it to get sex. That's the only reason. Sex. We're really just fishermen."

"You freed me from slavery. Only a warrior could do that."

"We were only able to rescue you because Accabo helped us, and Kwe, and Lara. Even Lewelle helped us, as much as I hate to admit it."

Tobin disagreed. "Reyas is right. Only warriors could have freed that slave camp."

"We were lucky," Cody retorted, "If it wasn't for Kwe, we'd be dead now."

"That's why we've got to save his mother and sister, Cody. We owe it to him."

"Tobin, I'm just saying. . . ." Cody paused. He turned from Tobin to look straight into Reyas' eyes before looking back at Tobin. "I'm just saying that this time it's real. There's no one here to help us."

"We have your father, and Kwe. Besides, when we stood on that muddy cliff, Cody, there was no one to help us then. We made it out alive. We all thought we were dead."

"It was luck, Tobin. We've been lucky every damned time."

Tobin pointed up the hill. Carlos and Kwe were returning. "There they are. Let's get going."

Cody turned back to Reyas. "Reyas, I've got to say this." He held her hands and paused He was having trouble forming the words that expressed what he wanted to say. "Just in case it's the last time I see you ... I know I've done things ... that hurt you." Impulsively, he embraced her. She involuntarily recoiled for a moment, but let him hold her. He whispered, "I am sorry." Breaking away from her, he said, "Before we go, I must make peace with my father. I have been ignoring my daily prayers."

Irritated, Tobin said, "This is no time for that prayer crap. Come on, let's prove we really are warriors!"

"No, Tobin, you don't understand. This is the time for prayer." Walking over to Carlos, Cody apologized for skipping their dawn prayer, and asked if they could sing a prayer song.

Carlos embraced him and then, keeping his voice low, sang a song his grandfather taught him when he was a little boy. Cody sang with him.

While they sang, Tobin impatiently paced back and forth, continually checking his blaster to be sure it was set correctly and that his breastplate and helmet were cinched securely. When they finally stopped singing and said the "Ho!" that Tobin had come to recognize as the end, he stopped pacing.

Cody tried apologizing to Carlos for not taking part in prayers with him lately, but Carlos would have none of it. "No. There is nothing to apologize for. At last, we get to fight together, father and son, as warriors. That's what I've always wanted." Cody's face lit up. "I am proud of you. Proud of the warrior you have become."

"I am only a fisherman. I'm no warrior, you said so yourself, I have no training."

"I was being stupid when I said that. You are a warrior. I am proud to be fighting at your side."

As they scaled the cliff, following Kwe and Carlos, Tobin exclaimed, "It's just like the original Warrior Brothers, rescuing damsels in distress from fire breathing dragons!"

Fighting Dragons

As they neared the top of the canyon wall, Carlos signaled them to stop and take out their weapons. Cody pulled an arrow from his quiver, but seeing the frown on Kwe's face, returned the arrow to the quiver and took out his blaster. Carlos signaled them to resume climbing. Just before they reached the top, Carlos again signaled them to stop. He and Kwe crawled to the top. In the dawn light they could see Jidara and her mother tied to a rock, a hundred or so meters to their right, about two thirds up from the canyon floor. Reaching them would require taking a trail up from near the bottom, past where the large dragon had trapped several Dombrel in a small crevasse between jagged nearly vertical rock walls.

Carlos asked, "Where are the other two dragons?"

"Probably in their cave." Kwe pointed to a cave several hundred feet away. "Over there. But sometimes they sleep in other caves. You can't predict what gods will do, though they're all usually asleep by sunrise."

"Is there any chance the big dragon will go back to sleep?"

"No. He's too angry," Kwe replied, "probably because the Dombrel guys shot at him. We'll to have to deal with him."

Cody volunteered to keep the dragon distracted while Kwe rescued his mother and sister. Tobin volunteered to go with him.

Carlos replied, "Be careful. I don't want either one of you toasted. Watch out for the other two dragons." Turning to Kwe and Reyas Carlos said, "Kwe, wait for the dragon to be distracted, then go get your mother and sister. Reyas and I will keep the Dombrel pinned down so they can't stop you. Reyas, I'd rather take the Dombrel alive, but if killing them is the only way to protect Kwe, do it." He paused. "If you're not comfortable killing a man, tell me now."

Without waiting for Reyas to reply, Cody said firmly, "Don't worry about her."

"I can do it," Reyas replied resolutely.

Carlos turned to Kwe. "You're sure it can't fly?"

"Kwegathi took away their power to fly."

Carlos embraced Cody. "Be careful, son. Remember, stay high, out of that thing's range. We can kill it with our blasters if it comes after you."

Kwe broke in, "Please do not harm them. They are gods."

Carlos ordered everyone to make every effort not to shoot the dragons.

Reyas and Carlos crawled to the right, to where they could get a clear shot both at the trail and at Dombrel. The Dombrel were paying too much attention to the dragon hissing flame in their direction to notice them approaching. Kwe crept as far along the trail as he dared without attracting notice by either the dragon or Dombrel.

Cody and Tobin crept along the trail to the left, getting close enough for them to distract the dragon but still be able to scramble out of its range if it came after them. When they were in place, Cody began jumping up and down and shouting to attract the dragon's attention. The dragon turned and looked in his direction, hesitating as though trying to make up its mind whether to go after him or Dombrel. Tobin jumped up and down and shouted alongside Cody. Finally, the dragon turned and lumbered in their direction.

The two Dombrel crawled from the crevasse only to see Kwe running up the trail. They raised their blasters in his direction but before they could shoot, Carlos and Reyas fired at them. They jumped back into the crevasse and Kwe darted safely past them.

Cody and Tobin continued taunting the dragon, jumping, shouting, and laughing, loving the adrenaline surge, as the dragon drew closer, hissing ever longer bursts of flame in their direction. Standing their ground, they tried to guess the exact moment when they would have to turn and run up the hill to stay just beyond the dragon's range. Neither wanted to turn and run first. The sun was now rising, flooding this side of the canyon wall with light. Above and to the right, they could see Kwe was already untying his mother and Jidara. They would be down the trail and out of danger in just moments if Cody and Tobin could keep the large dragon at bay.

The dragon's fiery bursts were getting a little too close, so Cody and Tobin backed uphill, out of its range, but the dragon surprised them with a much longer burst of flame than any they had seen, a sleeper wave of a flame. They jumped aside and a bush directly behind where they had been standing exploded into flame. They turned to retreat uphill, but found one of the smaller dragons blocking their way.

"Damn, where'd that one come from?" cried out Cody.

"Up there, that cave, Tobin answered, "we couldn't see it from where we were before."

The smaller dragon was coming closer and snorting flames at them. Meanwhile, the Dombrel men were aggressively firing at Carlos and Reyas, determined to keep Kwe from getting back down the trail with their hostages.

The large dragon hissed more flames at Cody and Tobin, and a bush next to Cody erupted in flame. Cody pulled his blaster from his belt.

"No, Cody, Kwe thinks they're gods."

"It's them or us." Cody pointed to the two burning bushes. "They're not doing that to me!"

"I thought you believed in gods."

"These dragons don't look like any god I've prayed to." Cody aimed his blaster at the large dragon. "Come on, Tobin, it's him or us."

Tobin pulled out his blaster and aimed it at the large dragon. They both fired, concentrating on the dragon's chest. The dragon bellowed in pain as skin burned away. Its agony was terrible to see. They stopped firing, waiting to see what the dragon would do next. As they watched in disbelief, the dragon's skin grew back over the wound.

"Damn," Cody muttered.

"I think we just shot God, Cody. Quick, down there. Get in that little cave." Tobin pointed to a tiny crawlspace under some large boulders. Cody protested that there was only room for one person in it. Tobin insisted, "Go, get in there."

"What are you going to do?"

"What I should have done in the first place. It might be a god, but it's still an animal. I can control an animal. I just need to get closer."

"You get any closer and you're toast."

"Yeah? Just watch this!"

Running up an incline to a precipice just over the large dragon, the small dragon lumbering after him, hissing flames at his heels, Tobin reached the precipice and leaped, hurtling across the expanse, landing squarely on the large dragon's neck. Momentarily stunned, the dragon recovered its senses and shook its head violently, trying to throw Tobin. Tobin clung desperately to its neck while singing loudly. The dragon howled deafeningly, enraged, drowning out Tobin's singing and shaking its head violently while spewing flames in wild arcs.

Cody ran to the small cave, wedging himself into it feet first, hoping to find shelter from the streaks of fire hurtling through the air from the enraged dragon. Even the small dragon took shelter.

As Tobin struggled with the large dragon, it gradually turned, sending its flames in other directions, while Tobin desperately sang in varying notes and keys, trying to find something that would give him access to the dragon's inner being. No longer menaced by the large dragon's wild bursts of flame, the small dragon turned its attention back to Cody, who desperately tried wedging himself farther back in the tiny cave. He could see the small dragon lumbering toward him, hissing flames. The dragon reached the cave's opening. Cody was squeezed too tightly into the cave for his hand to reach his blaster. He was lying on his harpoon and his bow and arrows were on the ground just outside the cave. The little dragon's snout was now just outside the cave. Cody's feet were jammed against the back end of the cave. He had nowhere to go.

Outside, the large dragon's enraged howling continued along with Tobin's ever louder and more frantic singing. Cody couldn't see them from down here but he could hear that Tobin was losing the battle. Tobin would not be able to control the dragon.

Cody knew he was lost. The worst he could do to the small dragon was to tickle its nose with his harpoon. A single flame and he was done. He prayed that his death would be quick. The dragon's nose crept closer. The dragon was trying to reach him. It knew he was in here.

Closing his eyes, Cody thought about Reyas. He would be dead in a moment, and he wanted Reyas to be the last thing he saw before he died. He wished he could actually see her, see that strong woman who was unlike any woman he had known on Quogue, so he did the next best thing, and held her image in his mind. The image he held in his mind was of her on that island, when they feared that Dombrel had found them, and she stood bravely and vigilantly, looking so strong, prepared to give her life defending him. That's the image he wanted in his mind when he died.

He heard Tobin cry out in terror, "It's a machine! A machine! I can't control it! Accabo!" A moment later Cody heard a body that had to be Tobin's land with a sickening thud on the ground.

Cody concentrated on the image of Reyas, blocking all else from his consciousness, trying not to think about the flame that at any moment would incinerate him.

It was hot. Very hot. Enveloping him. Wet. Surprised that dying had been so painless, Cody opened his eyes. He saw the small dragon gazing straight at him, its eyes inches away, its tongue smearing his face with hot dragon spit.

* * *

On the *Aktawaneh*, inside what *Marco Polo* survivors had begun calling "Accabo's Game Room," Accabo was sprawled on the floor, barely conscious. Billy was trying to revive him while Estille sat at the console with her eyes closed. In front of her, holographic displays showed what the two dragons were seeing. One display showed Cody in the cave, a tongue smearing his face with dragon saliva. The other showed a wildly changing viewpoint, sometimes of Tobin's body lying at the large dragon's feet, other times of Carlos and Reyas firing desperately at it, while trying to stay beyond the range of its fiery tongue, or of the Dombrel men climbing out of the crevasse while Carlos' attention was diverted. Sometimes it just was a view of the sky, or of the surrounding rocky terrain. Always there was a flame shooting straight out no matter where it looked. The audio system filled the game room with the terrible deafening shrieks of an enraged and wounded dragon.

Billy asked Accabo what happened.

Weak, struggling to find the strength even to speak, Accabo replied, "Tobin. I just got control of the dragon. Didn't have time to do anything. Tobin attacked the dragon's mind. He didn't know it was me. Almost finished me off."

Billy yelled at Estille to take control of the large dragon, but Accabo said, "No. She's got the small dragon. It will kill Cody if she lets it go. You've got to do it."

"I can't control it!" Billy shouted.

"Try," Accabo replied weakly.

Billy took Accabo's chair, put on a headset, and did his best to control the large dragon. Carlos and Reyas were shooting their blasters at it, and though the blasters couldn't do serious harm, Billy felt the same excruciating, burning pain the dragon felt every time it was shot. The pain enraged the dragon even more, making it nearly impossible for Billy to control. It belched furious bursts of flame at Carlos and Reyas, forcing them to retreat. All Billy could manage was to reduce the intensity of the flame. Kwe had begun leading Jidara and their mother down the trail, but he now was hastily pushing them back to safety behind a rock outcropping. The Dombrel men, who had begun crawling out of the crevasse a second time, had dropped back into it, where the dragon couldn't get to them.

The small dragon, now completely under Estille's control, backed away from Cody and lumbered as fast as she could make it go down to the canyon floor, where Tobin was lying unconscious. The large dragon meanwhile, with all of its other targets out of its range, was now eyeing Tobin. Unsure whether he was dead, it nudged him with its snout, rolling him over. Tobin showed no sign of life. The dragon was about to toss Tobin's body into the air but Billy managed to hold the dragon back long enough for Estille to maneuver the small dragon into standing protectively over Tobin.

Carlos and Reyas, seeing Tobin appear to be under attack by a second dragon, ran closer, blasters firing. Kwe did the same. Both dragons trembled from the pain of repeated shots. Their skin was constantly regenerating, but causing terrible pain to the dragons—and to Estille and Billy. A burst of blinding pain caused Billy to briefly lose control of the large dragon. Enraged, temporarily free of Billy's control, it blasted flames relentlessly toward Carlos, Reyas, and Kwe, forcing them to dive back behind boulders for protection. Billy finally regained control and they immediately began firing at it as soon as it stopped belching flames

Shouting, "Don't shoot, don't shoot," Cody crawled from his cave and ran to the canyon floor, praying that the large dragon wouldn't begin belching flames again. He tried dragging Tobin to safety, but the large dragon, now too enraged for Billy to control, began spewing flame again. The small dragon quickly moved back to stand protectively over Tobin. Cody dove under it just before a burst of flame from the large dragon blackened the spot where he had been standing.

Accabo struggled to his feet, still weak from Tobin's attack on his mind. Taking a seat next to Billy, he closed his eyes, trying to re-enter the large dragon's mind. Finally, he signaled to Billy that he was ready to take over. Looking relieved, Billy removed his headset, sat back, and watched the holographic displays of the scene as seen by the two dragons.

Carlos and Reyas were watching, blasters in hand, as was Kwe. The Dombrel were nowhere to be seen. Accabo struggled to get control of the large dragon. Gradually he gained control, and the dragon lay down on the canyon floor, quiet at last. Cody cautiously crawled out from under the small dragon and knelt down to check out Tobin.

Carlos and Reyas ran down to join him. Carlos administered a stimulant from his emergency medical kit and revived Tobin.

Tobin's first word when he regained consciousness was "Accabo." As he returned to normal, he explained that the dragons were both machines and that Accabo was controlling them.

Cody stood up, faced the two dragons, and asked, "OK, which one of you is Accabo?" He looked at the small dragon. "Is it you?" The small dragon shook its head. Cody looked over at the large dragon, lying on the ground, its eyes staring straight at him. "This must be you. Accabo?" The large dragon wagged its tail, each wag slapping the ground so hard that it shook like a small earthquake, knocking a few rocks loose from nearby canyon walls. "Accabo, why were you trying to kill us?" The dragon just stared at him, wagging its tail.

Tobin stood up, a little shaky at first. "Wait, let me check it out." As Tobin approached, the large dragon stopped wagging its tail and recoiled. "Hey Accabo, it's OK, if that's you. Don't worry. I'll be gentle this time. I swear." The dragon turned its head back toward Tobin. Tobin laid his hands on the dragon's head and closed his eyes, just for a moment, then opened his eyes again and removed his hands. "It's Accabo. He lost control of the dragon for a while. He apologizes."

Reyas wondered who was controlling the small dragon. "Billy?" The small dragon shook its head.

Cody said, "It's got to be Estille." The small dragon nodded its head and licked Cody's face playfully. Wiping the dragon drool off his face, he muttered, "Hey! I haven't gotten all of it off from the first time!"

* * *

In the commotion, the Dombrel men had escaped, but everyone was feeling too happy just being alive and uninjured to care. Kwe's mother and Jidara returned with his father to their village, taking for protection the blasters that Kwe had lent to Tobin and Cody, while everyone else proceeded to Hangtown. Kwe was still in shock at the discovery that his gods were mere machines that a mortal like Accabo could control. He had carefully kept his mother and Jidara from learning it, but he hardly spoke for the entire ride back to Hangtown, desperately trying to reconcile himself to that terrible truth.

Arriving in the late afternoon, they headed straight for the tavern where Inya worked. As they were sitting down at a free table in the bar, Inya came and kissed both Kwe and Cody warmly before taking orders. As she took Cody's order, she said softly, "I'm free tonight, Cody, if you want to come over."

Without giving it any thought, Cody happily replied, "Sure!"

After Inya left, Tobin exclaimed, "She just invited you over for the night, like it was nothing. Does she have a sister?"

Tobin and Kwe bantered among themselves about sex and conquests, but Cody wasn't listening. He had caught a glimpse of the look on Reyas' face, just for a moment, before she turned away. It was a dark look, a look of hurt. For a moment, he thought he saw tears forming in her eyes but decided that he had only imagined it. He couldn't see her eyes. She was looking down, studying the menu, written in a language none of them except Kwe could understand, then she turned and looked around at other bar patrons, then at the ceiling, anywhere except where Cody could see her eyes.

Cody was growing angry with himself for letting her get to him. "It's none of her damned business who I have sex with," he thought. The more he thought about it, the angrier he became. He wanted to shout at her that he could have sex with anyone or anything he wanted, anytime he wanted.

Instead, when Inya brought their food, he made up an unconvincing excuse about being too tired for sex. Inya didn't believe him. "No one could tire you, Cody. I know that from last time! But if you don't want to do it with me, that's OK."

Tobin exclaimed in disbelief, "Cody! A beautiful woman offers herself to you and you say you're too tired? What's wrong with you?" Placing his fingers on Cody's forehead he declared, "No fever. But something's wrong. You've never turned down sex. Never. Inya's beautiful. What's wrong with you Cody?" Not waiting for an answer, Tobin turned to Inya. "Hey, I'm free. I'll bet you've never had sex with a Tarfillian. We do it better than anyone. An actress at home on Quogue even told Cody that I do it better than him. Tell her, Cody."

Cody felt like he was on fire. Anger and embarrassment surged almost uncontrollably inside him. He was sure everyone could see it. He looked as far away from both Reyas and Inya as he could manage, wanting to say something to them, but not knowing what. He couldn't figure out whether he was angrier at Tobin, or at Reyas, or maybe at himself, for giving up a great night with Inya for no reason at all. Finally he blurted out, "Shut the hell up, Tobin," just as Inya placed the last plate on the table. Inya walked away without a word.

For the rest of the evening, Cody and Reyas never looked even once at each other.

* * *

Carlos returned the next morning to the *Aktawaneh* to prepare for the return to Quogue, but Cody, Reyas, and Tobin remained for a farewell dinner with Kwe, Haab, Tessa, Inya, and Tinap. That evening, as they approached the eating-place where they were meeting, Tobin said, "This place looks pretty fancy."

"I never come here," replied Kwe, "mostly it's rich mine owners and corrupt police who eat here, not people like us, but Tessa likes it." After a pause, he warned, "We're going to have to give them our blasters. No weapons are allowed inside."

"I'm surprised at you going someplace you can't bring a weapon," Cody commented.

"That's one reason I never come here. But Tinap will be there. He's got a lot of influence with the police here. If Tinap's with us, we're safe."

"You trust him?" asked Cody.

Kwe said only, "I am marrying his sister."

Entering the eating-place, Kwe and Reyas surrendered their blasters to the guard at the door, but Cody argued with the guard over whether he would surrender his harpoon, bow, and arrows. Noticing the disturbance, Tinap came over to join them. He was dressed in an immaculate police uniform, with ribbons denoting high rank, looking far more powerful than the always disheveled looking Hangtown police An expensive looking blaster was hanging conspicuously from his hip.

"He's got a blaster," Cody blurted to the guard, pointing at Tinap, "what's different about him?"

Looking respectfully toward Tinap, the guard obsequiously said, "He doesn't know who you are, sir."

Kwe intervened. "Tinap, this is my friend Cody. He saved my life. Cody, this is my future brother-in-law Tinap."

After exchanging greetings with Cody, Tinap turned to the guard. "Let Kwe's primitive friend keep that stuff. He is no threat." Patting his blaster he added, "Not while I have this."

Tessa was waiting at their table. After introductions, Kwe said he was worried about Haab, who had planned on getting here early. No one had heard from her.

Even without the bandit leader, they were a motley looking group, and except for Tinap and Tessa, they looked very out of place compared with the other patrons, who were well dressed in relatively expensive clothes. Tessa, who gave the distinct air of having dressed down for the occasion, was nonetheless wearing clothes that few in Hangtown could hope to buy, and Tinap in the tailored, well starched police uniform of his home province, was a stark contrast to Hangtown police.

Kwe was dressed in his best clothes, which were only a notch better than what most people wore every day in this outermost provincial town, but Cody, Tobin, and Reyas wore the same clothes they had worn when battling the dragons.

Inya arrived carrying a spear that she refused to surrender to the guard. Noticing her, Tinap asked Kwe, "Isn't that your Second?"

Replying, "Yes," Kwe went to greet Inya. Tinap followed him and told the guard to let Inya keep the spear.

Inya wore clothes she had stitched together herself from tatters of once stylish clothes discarded by others. The ancient spear she was carrying, which looked totally incongruous with how she was dressed, was beautifully carved from a dark wood, with metal and stone inlays, and bearing unmistakable scars of battle. Years of use had given the wood a rich, dark polished surface. Before sitting down, she handed Cody the spear. "This was my grandfather's spear. Spear Carriers like my grandfather used to be our most honored people. You are the last Spear Carrier. I pray you will accept it, and remember me always when you travel through space."

Cody held the spear in his hands, running his hands along its length, admiring the workmanship. Kwe was surprised. "Inya, you've always said you would never give that spear to anyone."

"That was when I thought there were no Spear Carriers left. Don't you think Cody is worthy of it?"

"I can think of no one more worthy. You are right. He is the last Spear Carrier. Cody, this is a great honor. Inya would not give her grandfather's spear to anyone not worthy of it."

Cody embraced her, kissing her and promising to keep it always. "I will remember you forever, both you and Kwe."

Gradually, the conversation shifted to Tessa and Tinap talking about the fine life Kwe would enjoy in Opportunity after their marriage. The marriage would actually be two ceremonies, the first between Kwe and Tessa, and the second between Kwe and Inya. All three would move to the new city being built adjacent to the new spaceport in Opportunity.

Tinap broke the bad news that because Kwe had betrayed Dombrel by helping liberate the slave camp, Dombrel would not allow the mechanics guild to give him an apprenticeship. "But you'll be happy to know that I used my influence to get something much better for you. I got you a probationary appointment as a Rehabilitating Police Cadet. Many of our best police are former outlaws like you. They just need some discipline and direction. You will have a uniform like mine and even as a police cadet, you will receive better pay than you would as a mechanic."

Tessa reminded Kwe that it took a lot of influence for Tinap to get him this appointment. "You should be grateful to Tinap. He put his reputation on the line for you."

Kwe thanked Tinap without much enthusiasm, then looked at the entrance again, as he had been doing every few minutes.

Cody asked, "Haab?"

"Yes, I'm worried. She's never late. She really wanted to see you and Reyas again before you leave."

Cody offered to go look for her. When he stood up to leave, Reyas and Tobin stood up to go with him. Kwe thanked them, but asked Tobin to stay. "There's a favor you could do for me."

Betrayed

"Thanks for staying, Tobin." Kwe turned to Tessa. "Is your back still painful?"

Her answer was swift and sharp. "What do you think, Kwe?" After two days bouncing over those rough trails, I'm almost a cripple, the pain is so bad."

Kwe turned to Tobin. "Could you do something for her pain? Like you did for Billy? As a favor for me." Tessa and Tobin both objected that it probably wasn't a good idea, but Kwe persisted, finally wearing down both their objections.

Both Tobin's experience with Billy and what he had learned from Sedlin il Lindar had taught him that he should never go into people's minds except under the most dire circumstances. Something as trivial as a back pain, from someone like Tessa who seemed to complain about everything, definitely didn't qualify. Finally, however, he yielded to Kwe's pleading and agreed to do it, telling himself that with a hypochondriac like this, it might be easier to make her stop imagining pain than to continue objecting.

Looking around the table, Tobin warned the others, "Don't say or do anything. Just watch." He moved to an empty chair next to Tessa, bringing his face close to hers. "Tessa, keep your mind still, just let me in. Don't be afraid. Say nothing, no matter what."

Tobin sang, and as he sang, he went in. He felt himself swimming through currents of fluff, trivial concerns, baseless complaints about other people, but as he went in deeper, he found himself having to scale mountains of driving ambition he never expected in one who on the surface put on airs of such superficiality. Deep down in the depths of her subconscious, there were ambitions she hid even from herself. But he also found love, or at least affection, for the young bandit the rest of her family scorned, but whom they were for their own reasons demanding that she marry.

Finally, already feeling stunned at what he had seen, Tobin came to the pain itself. To his surprise, the pain was real. He had been certain that she was faking it, but now he could see that her pain was genuine, and that quite likely she was in even greater pain than she was saying. Tobin could see it, the physical pain, but he could sense something terrible beneath the pain, something vital, the hidden cause of the pain. He changed the pitch of his singing, trying to dissolve the pain, but it remained stubbornly intact.

When he agreed to try to help her, he thought he was just performing a circus stunt on a woman feigning pain for the sympathy it could garner, but now he saw how severe the pain really was. He focused harder. He could permit himself to think of nothing else. He changed his singing again, focusing everything he had on the agony Tessa was feeling, becoming ever more convinced that there was something beneath the pain, something that needed to be excised before she could be free of pain.

For a long time, nothing happened. Tobin sang, oblivious to the other diners casting strange looks in their direction, concentrating all his energies on the terrible something that was consuming Tessa. Then he saw. He saw the priest telling her she must marry Kwe for the children they would bear together, children who would accomplish great things. He saw the priests themselves being pressured by others whom Tobin could not see, and he saw the long and ancient bloodline of kings and gods that somebody wanted to reunite in the marriage of Tessa and Kwe.

He saw the distaste Tessa felt for Kwe's lawless bandit family, yet also the fascination she felt for Kwe the bandit, and the love she felt for Kwe the man. He saw how much she despised those in her family who were cynically promoting the marriage for their own selfish ends. But he also saw how willing Tessa was to sacrifice everything and everyone she loved, including Kwe, for the ambitions that pervaded her soul.

Suddenly, the pain split open before him, evaporating to nothing, leaving the naked truth exposed. Tessa breathed a sigh of relief, eyes still closed, murmuring softly, "Thank you Tobin, thank you very much, that feels so much better."

Horrified at what he was seeing inside her, underneath the pain, Tobin leapt out from her, shouting, "It was you!" before falling to the floor, unconscious.

Kwe jumped from his seat and ran to Tobin's side. Tessa and Tinap remained seated, showing no emotion. Kwe was checking Tobin's pulse when Cody and Reyas burst in. "Kwe, Haab is dead. Everyone is talking about it on the street." Then Cody saw Tobin on the floor. "What happened?"

Kwe assured him that Tobin was simply unconscious. "Haab is dead? How?"

"It was an ambush. No one knows who. A few escaped, but Haab is dead. We saw her body. I'm sorry Kwe." Kwe rushed for the door, but Cody and Reyas both restrained him. "No, brother," Cody said, "It's too dangerous. Let things settle down. There's nothing you can do."

Reyas spoke softly while hugging Kwe, "Cody is right. Don't go out there now. We'll go with you later."

Tobin opened his eyes. Cody helped him get up from the floor. "What happened, Tobin?"

"Haab. She's going to be killed, " Tobin stammered.

"It's already happened. No one knows who did it."

Tobin pointed a finger at Tessa, then at Tinap. "It's them. Tessa and Tinap. They told the Dombrel that I was coming to this planet. They ordered Haab killed. Your fiancée, Kwe, her and her brother, they're the ones who ordered Haab killed."

Kwe tearfully begged Tessa to deny it. She remained impassive, like a statue. "So what if it is true?" Tinap said to Kwe, "You are the one who betrayed Dombrel. You. I warned you, but you had to be your stupid little bandit self." Looking in the direction of Cody,

Reyas, and Tobin, he continued, "Blame them, Kwe, not us. You could have had a good life. They are the ones who ruined it for you."

Kwe was trying to absorb it. "Tessa, when I called you from space, Tessa, I told you, tell no one."

Tessa began to respond, "Kwe…"

Tinap interrupted, "Tessa did it for you, Kwe. Dombrel promised to forgive you if you led us to Tobin. But you had to help him, you idiot. You ruined everything."

"You're a fool, Tinap," Cody shouted, "if you think Dombrel would keep a promise like that."

"He can trust Dombrel," Tobin said, "because he is Dombrel. Admit it, Tinap, you are a member of Dombrel."

"Yes, I admit it. Why not? There's no shame in it. Dombrel is building our city, Dombrel is building the spaceport, Dombrel is building up the whole continent. Before Dombrel, there was only farming and fishing and unused land there. Now, it's becoming important. Soon, it will be the most important place on the planet. And it's Dombrel doing it. I'm Dombrel. The only way to become anybody is to be Dombrel."

"She didn't do it for you, Kwe," Tobin shouted, "I saw it when I was inside her. She did it for the children the two of you will produce. It's something about your ancestry combined with hers. She has ambitions for your children. A whole new dynasty, a Dombrel dynasty, ruling the planet. That's all she cares about. After Dombrel has your children, they won't need you. They'll toss you out like rotten fish."

Kwe cried out, "Why did you kill Haab? She was my sister. She never did anything to harm Dombrel."

Tinap answered coldly, "We've told you many times in the past. We can't tolerate undisciplined bandits in the family. You knew something like this had to happen. If not, you're a damned fool."

Inya hugged Kwe. "Come on. There is a back way out. The alley is probably safe."

Tinap stood up menacingly. “There is no safe place for you if you leave now, Kwe. You are just throwing your life away.”

Showing emotion for the first time, Tessa wiped away tears streaming down her face as she pleaded, “Please, Kwe, Dombrel will hunt you down like an animal. Is that what you want? Come with us. Bring Inya. You can both live comfortable lives.”

Tinap took something from his pocket and tossed it to Kwe, who caught it reflexively before realizing it was a small blaster. “It’s decision time, Kwe. Prove that you are worthy of the faith I have placed in you. Execute Tobin. Now. Right here. He is an enemy of the Dombrel. Don’t worry. The police here won’t arrest you. You are under my protection.”

As diners at other tables scattered in panic, Kwe stood holding the blaster, looking around, at Tobin, and Inya, at Tessa, at everybody in turn.

“Please,” begged Tessa, tears still running down her face. “It doesn’t matter if you love me or not. You will always have Inya. The priests have promised us children who will grow up to be powerful. Our children will rule the planet.”

“You mean our Dombrel children will control the planet, right, Tessa?”

“Is that so bad, Kwe? Isn’t it better than you being hunted down and killed?”

Reyas couldn’t remain silent any more. “Do you want your planet to be a slave camp? Just a bunch of slaves with Dombrel guards watching over them? I lived at a Dombrel camp. Do you really want that here?”

“Make your decision, Kwe,” Tinap ordered, “your children can be powerful, or you can be hunted down like a low animal and die a terrible death. Your choice. Kill Tobin, that’s all you have to do. Dombrel will forgive everything you’ve done.”

“Don’t do it, Kwe,” Reyas pleaded. “Come with us. Into space. You and Inya. Lewelle can marry you on his ship.”

"How can I marry Inya if I don't have a Prime?"

Tobin assured him that under Lekadian law, a man was allowed only one wife at a time. Nothing would stop him from marrying Inya.

Cody reminded Kwe about his dreams of someday being a fisherman. "You can come back to Quogue with us. Dariel will take you on. You can work as a fisherman with Tobin and me."

"You will all be hunted down. There is no place to hide from Dombrel," Tinap warned in a darkly menacing voice.

Kwe stood silently, holding the blaster pointed at Tobin, saying nothing, while arguments and pleading bombarded him like mosquitoes after fresh blood. Finally, still looking straight at Tobin, Kwe said, "I'm sorry. There's nothing else I can do."

Reyas screamed. Tobin closed his eyes. Cody jumped in front of Tobin, blocking Kwe's shot. Kwe whispered, "Tessa, forgive me." Without another word, he tossed the blaster back to Tinap and embraced Inya tearfully. As Kwe and Inya kissed, Tinap muttered, "Fool, damned fool. You could have had it all."

Kwe took off his dragon pendant necklace. Tearfully, Tessa took off hers and handed it to him. "I loved you Kwe, I really did."

He turned to walk back to the guard to get their weapons, but Tinap shouted loudly to the guard, "He is dangerous. Do not give him any weapons. The guard immediately drew his own blaster, pointed it at Kwe, and ordered him to move back. "I authorize you to kill him if he gets any closer," Tinap barked at the guard.

"Kwe, it's not worth it," Inya pleaded. Kwe reluctantly turned around. "Let's go, Kwe," she whispered. They embraced, and arm in arm, led Cody, Reyas, and Tobin out the back door, leaving Tinap holding his blaster and Tessa crying.

Returning to the inn, Cody and Reyas were surprised to see the innkeeper waiting for them. He hurriedly took them down a dark hallway to where his wife was holding open a trap door leading to the basement. "Downstairs, quick. I put all your things down there." Kwe led the way down as the innkeeper told them to keep quiet and promised to come back down when it was safe. A little while later, they heard the pounding of boots upstairs, and someone interrogating the innkeeper, then they heard the boots run upstairs, then back down and out the back door.

Finally it was quiet. The trap door opened, revealing the silhouette of the innkeeper coming downstairs into the barely lit basement. "They're gone, but you should spend the night down here, just in case. Kwe, from what I hear, you are no longer engaged to Tessa?"

"Inya and I will marry after we leave the planet."

Smiling, the innkeeper unlocked a door, revealing a room with a double bed, saying, "Then this is my marriage gift to the two of you. Have a good night. I'll come back down before first light."

About an hour before first light, the trap door opened. The innkeeper and his wife came down carrying trays containing breakfast and a hot beverage. Kwe and Inya came from the adjacent room looking radiant. Reaching into his jacket pocket, Kwe took out the two dragon necklaces and gave one to Inya. Kwe put one necklace around Inya's neck, and she put the other around his, then they kissed.

While they were eating, the innkeeper gave Kwe advice. "It's clear around here. Lekadian troops are at the landing field. You should be safe if you can reach them." He handed Kwe a paper on which he had drawn a map showing the safest route. "This will take you through back alleys where you won't be seen. The danger is just before you get to the landing field. There's no place to hide there. You'll have to run across an open field. They're waiting for you. Some of you will die, I can almost promise it, but if you're fast enough, some of you should get through alive."

After a brief discussion about whether Cody and Tobin should wear their armor and paint their faces, they decided not to. They didn't want to draw attention to themselves, and wearing armor would slow them down.

Following the innkeeper's map, they crept through back alleys and yards in the darkness before first light, staying low, trying not to make a sound. Creeping around the backside of a warehouse, as they came to the building's corner they could see the landing field clearly and the most welcome sight they could imagine, armed Lekadian soldiers patrolling the field, and behind the Lekadians, two space shuttles. "Look! Shuttles! I think the middle one is from Lewelle's ship," Tobin whispered.

"That means my father and Lara are there!" whispered Cody, relief in his voice. "The sun's coming up soon. They'll see us after it gets light out."

Kwe pointed out some snipers climbing the side of a nearby building. "They're almost in position. We're finished if we stay here."

Tobin proposed that they all make a run for it while they had a chance, but Cody didn't like that idea. "They know we're here. The innkeeper was right. If all of us run, some of us are going to die. Maybe we'll all die. If only one of us runs, then my father will see we're here and the Lekadians will come save us. One of us will die, but the others will live."

Kwe immediately volunteered. "If it wasn't for me, you wouldn't be in this jam. I will run." Cody and Tobin both insisted that they should be the ones to run. Unable to reach an agreement, they agreed to draw straws. Reyas and Inya both insisted on being given straws also. Kwe and Tobin reluctantly agreed to let Reyas draw a straw after Cody agreed that she was a warrior, but they all agreed that Inya should be excluded. The snipers were almost in position, so Kwe hurriedly cut different length stalks from weeds and gave them to Inya. After shuffling them behind her back, Inya held out her closed fist and the runners one by one drew their straws.

Inya kissed Kwe, a long, slow, passionate kiss, and then, as the runners held out their hands to compare their straws, she broke into a run, running as fast as she could toward the landing strip.

The others shouted out desperately, "Inya! Stop! Come back!" but Inya ignored them. She didn't get far. Tinap and several well armed men blocked her way, forcing her back. Tinap ordered them to put down their weapons while roughly shoving Inya back among them.

"You won't get away with this. Lekadian soldiers are right over there, waiting for us," Tobin told Tinap. "All we have to do is shout."

"Go ahead, shout. Shout as loud as you want. They won't hear you," answered Tinap, smiling malevolently.

Tobin bellowed loudly in the direction of the Lekadians. The others shouted along with him, but the din of shuttle engines and freight loading drowned them out. Disheartened, one by one they fell silent.

Tinap again demanded their weapons. This time, they complied, letting Dombrel handcuff them and tape their mouths closed, then dejectedly following as they were led back, out of sight of the Lekadians to a side street. Gombu, an evil grin on his face, joined them, walking up to Cody and examining his handcuffed hands while muttering something gleefully in Lekadian.

"What did he say?" asked Cody.

"This time, both hands," answered Inya.

Gombu muttered something else before walking away.

"What did he say this time?"

"And more," Inya answered.

First light was now lifting the darkness, allowing them to see a cargo truck ahead of them, an unmistakable aura of evil about it that grew stronger as they approached. Resisting every step of the way, they were shoved up a ramp into the rear entrance and pushed onto the floor. Tinap, Gombu, and the Dombrel came inside, closing the door firmly behind them, leaving Tinap's men outside as guards.

After making their captives lie on the floor, the Dombrel men tied everyone's ankles, except for Inya. "You're coming with me, Inya," Tinap told her, "it's not your fault that Kwe got you involved in this. You have nothing to fear."

Leaving Inya standing next to the door with her mouth taped and hands tied, Tinap turned to look down at the others sprawled on the floor. "Cody, Tobin, Reyas, you should have known you couldn't escape us. You cost us a lot. You humiliated us publicly. Tobin, you more than anyone should have known better. Tonight you pay for it. Kwe, you disappoint me. You could have had everything. Instead, tonight you will die with your friends. I know you're brave and not afraid to die, but you don't know what a terrible death it will be. Some of you already have made the acquaintance of Gombu. You see he has his machete, as always. Tonight, he will get his pleasure. He will start with your fingers, one by one, then your toes, then your hands and feet. They will use drugs to keep you conscious all through it. It will be terrible. Kwe, because I still think of you like a brother, I'm doing you the favor of letting you go first. Your friends will be in agony just seeing what's being done to you. They'll know the same thing will happen to them. The waiting will make it worse for them. You are the fortunate one, because your suffering will end when their suffering is barely starting."

He signaled two of the Dombrel. They picked up Kwe roughly and lifted him to his feet. "I'm sorry, Kwe, I really am. I didn't want it to end this way." The two men dragged Kwe into something resembling a shower stall with a desk in it. They shoved him onto a seat in the stall, where they fastened clamps that kept him from moving, and held his fingers outstretched and apart on the desk.

Standing up, Tinap said to Kwe, "You've had your chance. There is nothing more I can do. I didn't want it to end this way. The Doctor will take over from here. What happens next is not my line of work." Tinap walked out, shoving Inya ahead of him, despite her struggling to resist.

As they left, the Doctor entered. He was an older man, thin, dressed as a medic, wearing protective gloves and mask, and carrying a small medical case. Sitting down at the table, he announced, "I am told you are all ready. There's nothing to be gained by putting it off. Let's get started." Looking at Kwe, he continued, "You will notice a power drain at your feet. It's going to get terribly messy in there soon. The power drain will suck away blood and bones and flesh so Gombu can work more efficiently. Old technology, but it does the job. By the way, I hope you notice the protective suit and facemask that Gombu is putting on. That little stall is going to be filled with blood. Blood can carry some dangerous diseases. Gombu is too valuable to risk losing to a disease one of you might be carrying in your bloodstream."

Now fully enclosed in a protective suit, Gombu picked up his machete and stepped into the stall, sitting on a stool facing Kwe. The Doctor meanwhile took syringes from his briefcase, carefully spreading them out on the table, taking great care in how they were arranged. He was making a show of how much he was enjoying himself, belying his clinical demeanor. "Soon you will begin losing fingers, toes, and anything else Gombu can hack off. He's a real artist with the machete. I will keep you injected with stimulants so you remain conscious and alive as long as possible, so you can truly appreciate Gombu's artistry." Turning his attention to Cody and Tobin, he continued, "By the way, you two men on the floor, enjoy yourselves while you can. The woman is next. She will take her turn in the stall after there's not enough of Kwe left to keep alive. It's going to be a long morning. I'm quite skilled at keeping people conscious long after the only thing they want is to die.

One of the Dombrel reached into a cabinet and took out a holo-cam, while the Doctor explained to his captives that torturing people accomplished little if others couldn't learn from it. "Your deaths will be terrible, but you can at least have the satisfaction that your suffering may save other troublemakers from a similar fate. We will record everything to show others like you what happens to anyone who crosses Dombrel. Are you ready?"

The holo-cam operator signaled that he was ready. Picking up a syringe, the Doctor said, "Let's get started."

* * *

Outside, Tinap ordered his men to stay on guard and not to let anybody in, then dragged Inya away roughly while his men made lewd comments about the pleasures he would be taking with her. She resisted as best she could, but he was too strong for her. He dragged her behind a small shed and stopped when he was out of sight of his men.

"Now what?" she asked, "Going to rape me before killing me?"

Tinap reached into his pocket and took out a small electronic device. "No. I'm going to let you go free. If you're wise, you'll run as far from here as you can. My men have orders to shoot you on sight."

"You're letting me go?"

"Yes."

"No tricks?"

"No tricks."

"What about Kwe? And Cody?"

"There's nothing either of us can do for them. Soon, Kwe will only want to die. But you can live. You were like part of my family. Honor requires me to give you your freedom. But remember, after I release you, I will owe you nothing more. This is the only break you will get from me." Using the electronic device, he unlocked the restraints that bound her wrists together. Then he gently removed the tape from her mouth.

While he was doing that, Inya grabbed the blaster from his holster, shoving it hard against his stomach.

"Is this the gratitude I get for saving your life?"

"I'll kill you Tinap, if anything's happened to Kwe. Take me to him."

"It's too late to save Kwe. You're just giving up your own life. Give me my blaster and I'll forget about your little burst of childishness."

"Take me to Kwe. Now. I know how to use this thing. I will kill you."

"OK, just remember, I gave you your only chance to escape. There's no hope for you if we go back." They walked back toward the torture chamber, Tinap walking in front, Inya holding the gun to his back. As they walked, they heard a strange sound, a WHUMP in the sky, growing steadily louder. They both looked up, but at first they couldn't see anything. The sound grew steadily louder, with gusts of ever stronger wind accompanying each WHUMP.

Then they saw flames erupt in the sky, lighting up the street. As the "WHUMP. WHUMP. WHUMP," grew louder, and the flame in the sky became larger and brighter, they saw it was the large dragon, descending rapidly, heading straight for the torture chamber. Tinap's men looked up just in time to see bursts of flame engulf them. Running around in terror, uniforms ablaze, they cried out in agony. Panic stricken bystanders fled in all directions.

Blurting out, "Shoot me if you want, I'm getting out of here," Tinap turned in panic and ran away, leaving Inya standing with the blaster pointing at nothing. The dragon began pursuing Tinap, but then turned back and hovered just over the torture chamber, shrieking loudly, spewing flames in every direction. Ignoring the flames, Inya ran past the burning guards and into the torture chamber.

Inside, she found Gombu with his machete raised over Kwe's fingers. She shot Gombu without hesitation. He fell to the floor, moaning. She turned to shoot the Doctor, but before she could fire, several Dombrel shot her. She shrieked in pain, then was hit by a second volley of blasts and collapsed, unconscious.

Something smashed into the roof, partially caving it in, knocking everyone to the floor. The Doctor's neatly arranged syringes flew off the table, and the holo-cam smashed to the floor. A second crash caved in more of the ceiling, knocking the Doctor and the Dombrel men back to the floor, just as they were getting back on their feet. Another crash, and a hole was smashed in one wall. A dragon's eye peered in through the hole.

Gombu staggered to his feet and after vowing revenge, ran outside despite his injuries, followed by all the Dombrel except for the Doctor. The dragon wiggled its snout into the hole, making it large enough for the snout to stick through, and both dragon eyes to peer in. The dragon hissed a thin flame in the Doctor's direction.

Backing away, just beyond the flame, the Doctor knelt down and coolly gathered his syringes from the floor, carefully putting them back into his briefcase, ignoring the dragon's eyes following his every move. Closing his briefcase, he stood up saying, "Kwe, they tell me that you people believe these things are gods. This is the first time a god has interfered with my work." He walked calmly toward the door, then turned back to face his captives. "This isn't over. We'll hunt you down again. You won't escape us, no matter where in the universe you go, or how many years it takes. Next time, your gods won't be able to protect you."

He turned and walked at a leisurely pace out the door and down the ramp, but broke into a frantic run after a few steps. The dragon didn't pursue him but instead curled its body and tail around the battered truck and lay down, blowing menacing flames in the direction of anyone who ventured too close.

The commotion attracted the attention of the Lekadian soldiers and soon Carlos was on the scene, surrounded by soldiers and Hangtown police trying to restore order. At the sight of Carlos, the dragon moved aside, letting him enter the torture chamber with some medics. After freeing Cody, Reyas, Tobin, and Kwe, Carlos helped Kwe and the medics evacuate the nearly dead Inya to a medical shuttle.

Cody, Tobin, and Reyas ran outside. Cody asked the dragon, "Accabo?"

Before the dragon could respond, Tobin shouted, "Of course it's Accabo!" The dragon vigorously nodded its head and wagged its tail, scattering onlookers who had ventured too close.

When they noticed a holo-cam crew approaching, Tobin hurriedly dragged Cody back into the torture chamber. Reyas followed them in, and found them searching among the rubble for the packs containing their armor. "I hope you two aren't really going to put that stuff on."

Strapping on his breastplate, Tobin answered excitedly, "Of course we are! Think of it. The ancient Warrior Brothers had to fight dragons, but we have the dragons fighting for us! Think what it will look like!"

Meanwhile, Cody had found his armor, and was putting it on.

"You two are crazy! After what happened last time..."

Cody cut her off. "I'm not going to be afraid of Dombrel any more. From now on, it's us who will be hunting them."

Reyas tried talking sense into them while they took turns painting the mark of the warrior on each other's face, but they weren't in the mood for sense. Cody declared, "Besides, think about Kwe. His people still believe that dragon is a god. You don't want them to learn the truth, do you? That it's just a machine being operated by a Quogian kid in a Lekadian ship in orbit around the planet?"

When they were done painting each other, Cody slung his arrows and crossbow over his shoulder, then picked up Inya's spear and his harpoon, and strutted outside. Tobin waved to one of the holo-cam crews and called them over. Before the holo-cam crew came within earshot, Tobin whispered to the dragon, "Accabo, can you carry us to the shuttle?" When the dragon nodded its head, Tobin whispered, "Good. Wait for my command." More holo-cam crews came running over, shoving their way through the gathering crowd to gaze in awe at the dragon. Tobin whispered, "OK, Accabo, give them a show!"

The dragon reared up on its hind legs, bellowing loudly and exhaling long streaks of flame into the sky. Then it settled down on all fours, lowering its belly to the ground and letting Tobin, Cody and Reyas climb up onto its back. Tobin and Reyas sat down carefully, between its wings, but Cody remained standing in front, his bow and arrows slung over his shoulder, holding his harpoon in one hand, using it to brace himself while holding Inya's spear victoriously high over his head with the other.

Tobin then barked a loud order to the dragon, "Take us to our shuttle!" The dragon awkwardly stood up, wobbling just a little, then flapped its wings and lifted off the ground. After flying a few test circles to allow its passengers to get their balance, it flew at a leisurely pace toward the shuttle, keeping just a few feet off the ground, its wings making the now familiar WHUMP-WHUMP-WHUMP sound, belching flames and howling the entire way. The sun was now rising, shining brightly, its reflected light forming fiery outbursts from Cody's and Tobin's armor. People along the now crowded street made way for the dragon, many of the spectators excitedly chanting, "Spear Carrier!" rhythmically with the WHUMP-WHUMP-WHUMP of the dragon's wings, while holo-cam crews ran alongside, excitedly recording the entire event.

A Thousand Generations

Standing just outside the airlock, his weight partially supported by his harness, Accabo listened to the noises of the shuttle being drawn into the shuttle bay, docking at the airlock, and its exit hatch being connected to the airlock. Accabo opened the airlock door just in time to see Cody and Tobin, still armed, faces painted, and wearing their armor, bound into the airlock, their wild whoops of joy reverberating through the corridors of Lewelle's normally staid ship, followed by Reyas. Impulsively lifting Accabo up off his feet, Tobin whirled him around in wild circles, shouting exuberantly as Accabo's head brushed the ceiling, "You were beautiful, Accabo! That dragon was amazing!"

"Tobin and me would be dead now if it wasn't for you," Cody exulted, taking the paint from his backpack. "Tobin, Accabo needs the mark of the warrior. Hold him steady while I paint it on him."

"No, wait," Accabo said, "Put me down, Tobin. I want to be standing on my own when Cody paints me." Removing his harness, he handed it to Tobin and very carefully stood without help, one hand against the wall to help him balance while Cody painted the mark of the warrior on his face. When Cody was done, they walked slowly along the corridor, arm in arm, Accabo in the middle, partially supported by Cody and Tobin, while Tobin carried Accabo's harness slung over his shoulder, and Reyas followed.

As they walked, Accabo explained, "The dragons were androids. The Lekadians used to leave android dragons like them on planets all over the galaxy to monitor the development of primitive races. They removed most of the dragons a long time ago, but they lost track of the three dragons they put on Devlan Nine."

Cody interrupted him. "How's Inya doing?"

Accabo replied, "Still unconscious. Kwe is spending nearly all his time with her."

The *Marco Polo* survivors had returned the day before from their leave in the capital city, so there was already a festive air on the ship. Cody's safe return only increased the general exultation among the former *Marco Polo* crew. Brushing off the boisterous greetings he was receiving, Cody went with Tobin, Accabo, and Reyas straight to the medical bay, where Kwe was sitting at Inya's bedside, holding her hand. He looked up briefly to acknowledge their entrance, then back at Inya.

"Lekadian medicine is really good," Tobin tried to assure him, "she'll be OK. Soon the two of you will be living on Quogue with us."

"You'll finally be a fisherman. With me and Tobin," Cody added."

Kwe looked up at Cody and Tobin. "You don't really think Dombrel will let us live happy lives, do you? They've already caught Tobin once on Quogue. Where are we going to hide? The doctor wants to put Inya in a real hospital, but there is no hospital where she'll be safe from Dombrel."

Cody and Tobin didn't answer. Kwe caressed Inya's hair gently before continuing, "Tell me guys, where will we be safe? You know Dombrel will find us. It doesn't matter where we go."

* * *

The only one now missing from Lewelle's ship was Lewelle himself. He had not yet returned from Sedlin il Lindar's. Two days after Cody and Tobin's return, a fast Lekadian military fighter brought a courier carrying a sealed container for Lewelle. The courier curtly refused to give it to anyone other than Lewelle himself, and waited for him in the Lekadian portion of the ship, isolated from non-Lekadians.

Tobin and Cody wanted to return to the planet's surface to search for Lewelle in case he was in trouble, but Carlos and the elders in Lewelle's family vetoed it, leaving the boys to find other ways to burn off their high energy. For the next several days, while everyone waited for Lewelle's return, Cody and Tobin joined Carlos, Reyas, Billy, and some other *Marco Polo* survivors late every afternoon for some highly competitive basketball on a court Carlos had improvised in a cargo bay. Tobin and Cody spent mornings and early afternoons practicing martial arts by themselves. Kwe occasionally joined them, but he spent most of his time at Inya's side, waiting and praying for her to regain consciousness, once in a while joined in praying by Carlos, Cody, and Accabo. Each time Cody visited Inya's bedside, he carried her grandfather's spear with him.

One immediate change was that Carlos and Cody resumed their morning prayer songs together, but not in Lewelle's simulated roundhouse, which Cody still refused to enter. Instead they used the cargo bay where Cody still occasionally practiced with his bow and arrow. Accabo was now joining them in dancing traditional ceremonial dances that went back thousands of years in northern California.

Lara was feeling deeply bittersweet emotions. Her joy at getting her son back alive and well was offset by the pain that others were feeling at the loss of their loved ones. Looking for a distraction, Lara stumbled upon the ship's library of shuttle maintenance manuals, and rediscovered the pleasure she got from the work she did when she was a young mechanic. Oblivious to the passage of time each day, she immersed herself in an in-depth examination of each of Lewelle's shuttles, relearning forgotten skills while performing overdue maintenance and fine tuning them for optimal performance.

The ships' elders had removed all restrictions on interactions between Accabo and Estille, although retaining restrictions on most other non-essential contact between Lekadians and non-Lekadians. Estille now spent most of her time with Accabo. Carlos believed that Lewelle was behind it, but Accabo didn't care whose idea it was. He was just ecstatic to be spending time with the most stimulating woman he had ever known. The two of them now spent every day together in Lekadian cyberspace, frequently accompanied by Reyas and Billy.

When they discovered a library of information about various martial arts disciplines practiced across the vast Lekadian Empire, they tried to persuade Cody and Tobin to don headsets and join them in cyberspace, but just as Accabo predicted, neither of them was enthusiastic about the idea.

"It's all in your head. What good is it?" asked Cody.

Tobin urged Accabo, "When you have full use of your legs again, you will practice with us. It's how you fight out here in the real world that counts."

One day, Estille took Reyas to another part of Lekadian cyberspace, to the Quogian history section. They wandered through Quogian history, to the limited extent that it was available, until they found how women dressed on Quogue long ago. They watched in fascination as women with long, flowing hair, and clothing that allowed their bodies and their beauty to show, paraded by them in cyberspace. Reyas was fascinated.

"I think this is the kind of beauty Cody likes," Estille commented, but got no reaction from Reyas. "I have an idea, Reyas. Let me try an experiment."

A little later, Accabo was in cyberspace, studying schematics of Lewelle's ship, when Reyas and Estille appeared before him. Estille still looked like she did in the physical world, with very short hair and the ubiquitous Lekadian unisex uniform, but at first Accabo didn't even recognize Reyas. She had long hair, flowing freely down her back, and clothing that allowed Accabo to see what on today's Quogue would be scandalous amounts of skin. When he learned who she was, he realized that looking as she did in the physical world, he had hardly even thought of Reyas as a woman. Now, however, she not only looked like a woman, but she was a stunningly beautiful woman.

"Wow! Cody has to see you!" was all Accabo could blurt out.

"No," Reyas responded firmly.

"But he likes you."

"Only as a warrior."

"He doesn't know how beautiful you are. He'll love you. I promise. I'll go get him. If this doesn't get him to put on that headset and come into cyberspace with us, nothing will."

"No, don't tell him."

"Why not?"

"Just don't. Promise me you won't tell him."

"Ok, I promise, but I think you're making a big mistake. You're beautiful! Cody loves beautiful women."

"I've seen how he loves beautiful women. That's not how I want him to love me. Please don't tell him. This is a secret between the three of us." From then on, whenever the three of them were in cyberspace, Reyas enjoyed adopting the look of a beautiful, stylishly dressed ancient Quogian woman, but whenever Billy or anyone else joined them, Reyas took on the same shaven head, scrawny former slave appearance that she had in the physical world.

* * *

On the fifth day, Lewelle returned, unexpectedly accompanied by Sedlin il Lindar. The courier left immediately after giving Lewelle the mysterious container. He had barely left when Lewelle called a meeting in the cabin where they had been meeting prior to freeing Tobin. To everyone's surprise, Lewelle told Cody and Tobin to come wearing their Warrior Brothers armor.

Accabo was still limping as he walked to the meeting, but he was at last able to walk without his harness.

Lewelle began the meeting using an automatic Lekadian-Quogian translator. The mysterious container was next to him. "First, I want to apologize that I did not have an automatic translator for our earlier meetings. It is my shame that my people until now did not consider Quogian a language worth translating. That has now been rectified."

Pausing for a moment, Lewelle turned to Accabo. "I apologize for the disrespect my people have shown toward your people, Accabo. You have impressed some of us at least as much as the original Warrior Brothers impressed our ancestors. This time, we will not forget. Even if you never do anything else, your life has had a meaning very few on any planet dare hope for."

Accabo looked puzzled. "What do you mean 'this time you won't forget'? Your ancestors never even knew about the Warrior Brothers."

"I'm getting to that." Lewelle turned back to face the entire group. "Lindar and I have done a lot of research in the last few days. We found facts that will interest all of you. I knew none of it before. Like you, I have learned much on this journey."

"I have learned too," added Lindar, "Sometimes the universe has surprises even for those of us who think we've seen it all."

Lewelle continued, "Back when Cody first put on his armor and made Carlos so angry, we spoke of the monks who gave him the armor."

Cody burst out, "Yeah, you said it was all stories by crazy old monks."

Lewelle continued, "The monks may be crazy, but some of the stories they tell may not be. Watch this."

The room darkened, and a holographic image appeared, hovering over the table in front of them. The image was the interior of a cavern, with Lekadian engineers and miners operating portable smelting equipment.

Lewelle continued, "This was long ago on Quogue. Maybe a thousand generations ago, to be poetic about it."

The scene changed. It was the same cavern, but now they saw three Quogian boys, looking very primitive, shaggy hair, wearing rough-cut animal skins, and stone axes suspended from belts. They were beating metal into the shape of armor. "These are the original Warrior Brothers."

Everyone lurched forward to get a better look.

"The story the monks tell isn't entirely correct. It wasn't dwarves who taught those boys the secrets of metal. It was a Lekadian mining expedition. The members of the expedition thought they had hidden themselves well enough that Stone Age Quogians couldn't find them. They were wrong. They never expected those three very brave and intelligent boys. The boys found them, and studied them for weeks from a hiding place before making their move. When the expedition was preparing to leave, the boys bravely charged in and demanded to know the secrets behind the mysteries they had seen. They managed to communicate with the engineers, who had a rough comprehension of the form of Quogian spoken in those days. Our engineers were so taken with the boys' brazenness and charm that they taught them the secrets they demanded, from digging up ore to making tools. Accabo, I've sent you the information you need to learn more about it. You'll find it fascinating."

Accabo closed his eyes. Everyone watched him expectantly. No one spoke. When he finally opened his eyes, he shouted out in wonder, "They were real! The Warrior Brothers were real! I even know the exact location of the cave! It really happened!"

Lewelle motioned to the display again. "Now watch this."

The scene changed. One of the Warrior Brothers, now working on armor that was almost complete, set it aside. "The Warrior Brothers had high standards. Here, you see one of them deciding that he wasn't happy with the breastplate and helmet he had spent weeks making, so he set them aside and started over."

Lewelle unlocked the container and with an uncharacteristic smile, signaled Estille to open it. Taking something wrapped in cloth from the container, she handed it to Accabo. He carefully unwrapped the cloth, revealing a breastplate and helmet.

"I think those will fit you, Accabo," Lewelle continued, "This is the very same breastplate and helmet you see in the holographic recording. This Warrior Brother made it himself with his own hands. He threw it away to make a better one, but our engineers saved it. There's nothing wrong with it, he apparently just didn't like how he had made it. Put it on, Accabo." Standing up, looking completely awed, Accabo put on the breastplate and helmet, while Cody and Tobin came over to admire it, touching it reverently.

After giving the boys some time to study the armor, Lewelle said, "Now watch this."

The scene in the image changed. They saw the three Warrior Brothers, still dressed in animal skins, but now wearing breastplates, helmets, and swords. They were handing three swords to the engineers.

"The legend has another part of it wrong. The brothers were deeply grateful for the knowledge they had been given and wanted to give something back to our engineers in appreciation. Before leaving, they asked the engineers how they could repay them. Our engineers were so impressed with the craftsmanship of the Warrior Brothers that they asked them each to make a sword. Here you see them presenting those swords to the engineers."

Estille reached into the box again, bringing out something wrapped in cloth and handed it to Lewelle, who slowly unwrapped it. It contained three swords. "These are those swords."

Handing the swords to Cody, Tobin, and Accabo, he said, "I cannot tell you whether you are Warrior Brothers or not. Only you can know that. I can tell you this, however. You are only the Warrior Brothers if you believe it with all your hearts, all three of you, like Cody believed it when he went to rescue Tobin, and only if you all stay together. Separately, even the Warrior Brothers a thousand generations ago could do nothing. Together, they changed their world."

"You sound just like those crazy old monks!" interjected Cody.

"Truth is truth, Cody, no matter who speaks it. Even a crazy old monk can speak the truth. So can a Lekadian ambassador. But can you recognize the truth? That is the question."

"If those monks speak the truth," Tobin burst out angrily, "why did you Lekadians suppress them?"

Cody added angrily, "You took away the legends. You tried to take away their language. You even took away all the warriors' armor. Why'd you do it, if the monks spoke the truth?"

Lewelle sounded somber when he replied. "My people thought they were saving the Quogians by modernizing them. They thought it was best for them. My people were wrong. A language and the stories told in it are the repository of a people's knowledge and how they see the world. Take that away and you take away their souls. The stories, the legends, the warriors' armor, it all belongs on Quogue."

"When we return home, we're just going to be fisherman again. What good are swords and armor to us?" asked Cody.

"We don't have any secret knowledge to bring to our people," said Tobin.

Lewelle replied, "Neither did the Warrior Brothers of legend. They didn't know they were the Warrior Brothers. They simply were very brave and intelligent young men who let their instincts lead them to their destiny. I cannot tell you if you are truly the new Warrior Brothers. All I ask is, if you decide you are not, please return these things to me so we can someday give them to the true Warrior Brothers, when they do emerge to lead Quogue into a new future. Being a Warrior Brother is more than just fighting and wearing the armor. It's also responsibility. It means you live for your people, and if necessary, you die for your people. It means that like the original Warrior Brothers, you will give your people what they need to be strong and to prosper again."

Lewelle paused while Estille picked up the empty container and left the room. The holographic display changed to a green-blue image of Earth, now floating above the table in front of them. It took Carlos a moment to adjust to seeing Earth with Antarctica on top. "I have other news," Lewelle continued, "but it's not good."

Lewelle waited a moment to continue. "Carlos, you asked me to transmit a message to Earth for you. We have configured our equipment to the specifications you gave us. We are now ready to transmit whatever message you want to your people, though as you know, they will not receive it for several generations."

"That's great news, Lewelle!"

"That's not the news, Carlos. The news is about Earth."

"You told me that they might be in danger from some other civilization."

"Yes, I did. I've confirmed it. They are a young, brutal race. They are aggressive and expanding. Earth is their logical next target."

"We have to do something!"

"There is nothing I can do. The Empire has no relations with Earth or any civilizations near it."

Carlos exploded in rage. "Most of the galaxy is terrified of you Lekadians! We feared coming anywhere near your Empire. Why in hell can't you do something?"

"As an ambassador, I can only do what the Empire authorizes me to do. It's complicated."

"Like hell it's complicated. What about all your nice sounding words about Lekadians, Quogians, and humans needing each other and working together? Was it just words?"

Sedlin il Lindar stood up and raised his arms for attention. "Stop! Carlos, I must ask you to trust Lewelle. He will do what is right. These are difficult times for the Empire."

"The whole universe knows you can't trust Lekadians," shouted Cody.

"I trust Lindar," said Tobin, turning to face Carlos, "you can trust him too, Captain."

Lewelle said, "Carlos, we can transmit a message to Earth, warning them, but for now, that's all I can do. You will have to trust us."

"Do not pass judgment on us until we reach Quogue, that is all I ask. Please," added Sedlin il Lindar.

"Trust you? Why should I trust you?" Carlos retorted angrily. "You don't trust us enough even to show yourselves to us. In all the time we've been on your ship, you haven't let us see anyone in your family even once. Why should we trust any of you?"

"I have permitted Estille to spend time with Accabo."

"Only Estille, and only recently. What about the rest of your family? Why can't we see them? What about your son, Major Sul? Why can't I meet with him? What are you hiding?"

Sedlin il Lindar held up a hand and said, "Please give us a moment." He and Lewelle closed their eyes.

When they reopened their eyes, Lewelle spoke. "Carlos, think what you are demanding. Earth is a minor planet in an obscure corner of the galaxy. Any Lekadian who travels there will be gone from Lekadia for generations. The Lekadia they someday return to will not be the same one they left. Surely you of all people can appreciate the sacrifice that would entail."

After thinking it over for a moment, Carlos replied, "Yes, you are right. Excuse my anger."

Lara asked Lewelle, "What about Dombrel? What progress have you made?"

"The doctor and Gombu both escaped. We have not found them. I hope to know more by the time we reach Quogue," Lewelle answered.

When the meeting was over, Lewelle turned to Cody, Tobin, and Accabo. "Please, remember your promise. You may keep the swords and armor I gave you only as long as you three stay together and are committed to being the true Warrior Brothers. Otherwise, you must return them to me."

As Carlos was standing up to leave, Lewelle said to him in a low voice, "Wait, don't go." After everyone else except Sedlin il Lindar had left, he continued, "Carlos, you asked us to trust you. I am going to do that. Now. We will show you my family, but you must keep what you see a secret. Do you swear that you will reveal it to no one?"

"I give you my word. I will tell no one."

Carlos followed Lewelle and Sedlin il Lindar into the Lekadian section of the ship, finally entering a large room. Row upon row of Lekadians lay in miniature chambers, one Lekadian to a chamber.

"This is most of my family that lives on this ship, Carlos. This is what the fearsome Lekadian Empire has become."

"Are they in stasis?" Carlos asked.

Carlos wandered among the pods as Lewelle followed, "No. They are all in cyberspace. Some are working, others are playing." They stopped next to Estille, lying with her eyes closed. "This is where Estille spends most of her time. She is very fond of Accabo. I am glad of that. Because of Accabo, she is spending more time out here with us." They continued walking past sleeping Lekadians. "They know everything that is happening on this ship, but they do not consider the physical world, or their physical bodies, of any importance."

From a doorway, a strong voice interrupted, "Not all of us are like that." It was Edrak, in his military uniform, just entering the room. "Some of us know the Empire is in danger. We will give our lives for the Empire."

"This is my son, Major Edrak Sul of Aktawaneh," Lewelle announced.

Edrak strode up to Carlos. "Captain Jackson, I have been wanting to meet you this entire journey."

"And I've been wanting to meet you, Major Sul. Your father has spoken highly of you."

"Captain Jackson, I wish I could give you the traditional Lekadian greeting of brave warriors who trust each other, but you do not have the necessary brain enhancements. How would a human do it?"

Carlos held out his right hand. Awkwardly, Edrak did the same. Carlos gripped his hand and shook it. "The honor is mine, Major Sul."

"You and I are the only true military men on this ship. My father is a dreamer. Sedlin il Lindar is a scientist monk. You and I, Captain Jackson, we are the ones who make things happen. You and I will be in battle together one day." Edrak paused. "I only hope that when that day comes, we will fight on the same side."

Lewelle and Sedlin il Lindar both looked alarmed. Lewelle said, "Young men often speak heatedly of things about which they know nothing. Pay him no heed."

"Much like my own son."

"You have seen more than any other non-Lekadian has seen. We can speak no more of this," Lewelle said, "do you see our problem, Carlos?"

"Your race is declining. You are losing your warriors."

Sedlin il Lindar responded, "Not everyone is in decline. Some, like Edrak, are becoming warriors again."

"What about all those Lekadian solders we've seen?"

"Some are Lekadians who, like my son, choose to serve out of love for the Empire. But most are mercenaries, members of other races who wish they were Lekadians."

Extending his right hand to Carlos and shaking hands, Edrak said, "It is time for you to go. I am glad to have met you at last, Captain Jackson."

"And I am glad I've finally had the honor of meeting you, Major Sul. I look forward to working with you," Carlos replied.

As Carlos followed Lewelle toward the door, Edrak whispered to Sedlin il Lindar, "My father should never have showed him this."

After leaving the room, Lewelle took Carlos to the communications center, where Carlos transmitted his message home to Earth, telling them the fate of the *Marco Polo*, and warning them about the dangers Earth would soon be facing. The message would reach Earth in a little under two generations.

* * *

With the *Aktawaneh* ready to break orbit for their return to Quogue, Kwe and Lewelle agreed on one thing: it was time for the three dragons to leave Devlan Nine.

For Lewelle, it was simply a matter of pragmatic politics. The dragons were long forgotten relics of ancient Lekadian attempts to monitor primitive races. He didn't want the people of Devlan Nine ever coming to believe that the Lekadians were spying on them, so the dragons had to go.

Kwe's reasons were completely different. Still stinging from the disillusionment he felt from learning his beloved dragon gods were actually Lekadian machines, he didn't want anyone else on his planet suffering the same disillusionment. "Many people saw the large dragon fly," he said, "My people have always been taught that the dragons won't fly until Kwegathi, the king of the gods, forgives them their transgressions, and allows them to return to the realm of the gods. We must make it look like this has happened."

"You are also named Kwegathi," joked Tobin, "so maybe the legend is right after all."

"I am only Kwegathi the bandit, not Kwegathi the King of the Gods."

"Your priests said you are descended from the gods, Kwe," said Cody, "maybe you are the Kwegathi that the legend predicted would free the dragons."

When they were ready, a crowd gathered in Accabo's "Game Room" to watch the return of the dragons. With Billy and Estille operating the two small dragons and Accabo operating the large one, they flew the dragons over the Badlands and Hangtown, flying low wherever they might be seen, so the people of Devlan would see their dragon gods finally flying home. After putting on a good show, they flew the dragons over the rugged mountain range east of Hangtown to an otherwise inaccessible valley where a cargo shuttle was waiting to take the dragons back to the *Aktawaneh.*

Billy landed his dragon at the shuttle. While the crew loaded it into the shuttle and secured it, Accabo and Estille kept flying, cavorting playfully in the air, completely oblivious both to the cargo shuttle below and to everyone in the Game Room with them. They were aware only of each other.

One by one the others left the Game Room to prepare for the flight back to Quogue, but Accabo and Estille continued flying their dragons, unaware of—or ignoring—the shuttle cargo crew below impatiently waiting for the dragons to land. As Kwe removed his headset to return to Inya's bedside, he smiled and whispered to Cody and Reyas, "Love Dragons."

* * *

After all three dragons were safely stowed onboard, the *Aktawaneh* broke orbit and began the twenty day voyage back to Quogue. Although everyone returned to the activities they had been engaging in before the meeting with Lewelle, everything had changed. Their adventures were over. The reality of having to prepare for returning to a normal life, whatever that was, began to sink in.

Lara had contacts on one of Tarfil's moons that would allow Accabo to find work there as a trainee shuttle mechanic. To prepare him for getting a job, Lara took advantage of the twenty days to train him intensively in piloting and maintaining a shuttle. For a short time each day Lewelle slowed down the *Aktawaneh* to a pace a shuttle could maintain, so that Lara could take Accabo out for hands on experience. The rest of the time, he used a shuttle simulator in cyberspace.

For Cody and Tobin, however, the future held no such excitement. They yearned to return to their lives as fishermen, but they weren't convinced that after these adventures, life as a fisherman would ever satisfy them again. They were the Warrior Brothers, after all, but with no idea how to actually be the Warrior Brothers. "What good is a sword and armor to a fisherman?" Cody would retort whenever Tobin began showing exuberance over being a Warrior Brother. And then there was Dombrel. No matter where they went, Dombrel would be hunting them. Swords, armor, and face paint were definitely no protection against Dombrel. Lewelle promised that a Lekadian battle cruiser would remain in orbit above Quogue to protect the planet from Dombrel, but that didn't seem to Cody and Tobin like much protection.

Nineteen days after leaving Devlan Nine, they arrived at Tarfil. The *Aktawaneh* docked at a spaceport on Luna One to allow Kwe, Inya, and many of the *Marco Polo* crew to leave the ship. Inya still had not regained consciousness, so Lewelle arranged for her to get the specialized care she needed, with military guards to protect against Dombrel. As soon as Lewelle had completed making arrangements for her treatment, the *Aktawaneh* departed for Quogue. Everyone would have to decide then where they wanted to live. Those who wanted to live on Quogue would remain there. The others would be returned to Luna One. This might be the last flight that surviving *Marco Polo* crewmembers would ever make together. Some had already decided to live on Quogue, while others wanted to return to Luna One and make their lives there.

* * *

A day later, the *Aktawaneh* was just few hours from reaching orbit over Quogue. *Marco Polo* survivors were planning for their new lives, and partying with those they would never again see after the *Aktawaneh* left Quogue. Accabo was out on one of his shuttle training flights, his third solo flight. When he returned, Cody was waiting for him in the airlock.

"You're getting pretty good piloting that shuttle."

"I've never had so much fun."

"Accabo, Tobin's waiting for you in the cargo bay"

"What does he want?"

"You'd better ask him. Come on."

Accabo followed Cody to the cargo bay, where Tobin was shining his armor. Looking up at Accabo, Tobin said, "I hear Lara's found you a job on Luna One."

"Yes, as a shuttle mechanic."

"You could be a fisherman with us," Cody said.

"I'm no fisherman Cody. Why can't you guys come live on Luna One with me? Lara says she could get you jobs as fishermen there." It was a conversation they'd had repeatedly since leaving Devlan Nine.

Tobin listened as Accabo began his usual list of advantages to living on a Tarfillian moon, but Tobin interrupted him. "I have an idea."

"Careful, Accabo, Tobin's ideas can be dangerous!"

"We're never going to decide anything this way," Tobin continued, "we just keep going in circles. We need to go back. We need to do the same thing Cody and me did with the monks, but the three of us this time, as Warrior Brothers."

"You mean in the sweat lodge? Singing and praying?" asked Cody.

"Yes."

"Amazing, I never thought I'd hear you say you wanted to pray. But Tobin, just where are we going to do this?"

"In the cave where the original Warrior Brothers learned about metal."

"No one knows where it is," Cody objected.

"Accabo does."

"Do you really know where it is, Accabo?" Cody asked.

"Yes. But I don't think Lewelle will let us go there," Accabo said, "He's worried about Dombrel."

"Dombrel won't look for us at the cave. They don't even know about it. They'll expect us to go to HarborSide," Tobin countered.

"Tobin's right," said Cody.

"Then it's agreed. Let's get what we need and meet at the shuttle in an hour," declared Tobin.

Accabo said, "Wait! I have to get permission to take the shuttle."

Cody and Tobin shouted in unison, "No!"

"You know Lewelle won't let us go," added Tobin.

Cody put his hand on Accabo's shoulder. "Accabo. You are a Warrior Brother, right?"

Accabo nodded.

"Then be one. Be our brother. We have to do this, as Warrior Brothers. The three of us."

"Besides," added Tobin, "you're the only one of us who can pilot a shuttle. We can't do it without you."

"I don't know how it's going to solve anything," Accabo objected.

"It will," Cody said firmly.

"How do you know?" asked Accabo.

Tobin looked directly into Accabo's eyes. "I've learned to trust your intellect. I've also learned to trust Cody's intuition. You need to trust it too."

"We have to do this," Cody insisted.

"But Lewelle trusts me," Accabo answered, "if I take one of his shuttles without permission…"

Cody didn't let him finish. "You swore an oath. As a warrior."

"As a Warrior Brother," added Tobin.

"Lewelle gave you Warrior Brother armor," Cody said, "he's a Lekadian, but even he says you're a Warrior Brother."

"It's nuts," Accabo replied. He hesitated before continuing, "I'll probably regret this for the rest of my life, but OK, I'll do it."

Yelling jubilantly, Cody and Tobin embraced Accabo.

"But guys, if we're doing it, we have to do it before we reach Quogue. Lewelle plans to lock down all shuttle bay doors when we reach orbit."

"Why?" asked Tobin.

"I shouldn't say."

"We're brothers, Accabo," Cody replied, "You can tell us."

"You're not going to like it, Cody."

"Let me decide that."

Accabo hesitated before saying, "Lewelle hasn't told your Dad yet, but he's afraid there are Dombrel among your *Marco Polo* crew."

"Impossible!"

"Maybe, Cody, but that's why Lewelle plans to lock down all the shuttle bays."

"Then we have to leave right now," said Tobin.

Accabo looked worried. "I'm going to be in big trouble for taking a shuttle without permission. And we're all going to be in trouble for going to the surface."

"Just remember what he told us on Devlan Nine," said Cody, "He told us to stick together. As Warrior Brothers. We're just doing what he said he told us to do."

"And this time we'll have blasters with us," Tobin added.

* * *

"Accabo wouldn't take a shuttle without authorization."

Lara replied, "Well, he has, Carlos. Along with Tobin and Cody."

"What does Lewelle plan to do about it?"

"I don't know, Carlos. I can't locate him."

"That is strange. Sedlin il Lindar is missing also. Why aren't they answering calls?"

Neither of them could come up with an answer.

Carlos returned to his cabin, where he was surprised to find Edrak waiting for him. "Major Sul, I've never seen you outside the Lekadian part of the ship."

Edrak replied simply, "Captain Jackson, my father will see you now."

"Is it about the boys taking the shuttle?"

"Not quite. It's not about them taking the shuttle. It's because of them taking the shuttle," Edrak replied cryptically.

* * *

The shuttle landed in a still isolated part of the planet, a short walk from the cavern. Cody, Tobin, and Accabo feared that after all these years, weather and time would have obliterated all traces of the cavern, but to their amazement, it was still there. Fallen rock blocked the entrance, but with some effort, they cleared away enough debris to enter.

Standing in the cavern, illuminated by lights they brought from the shuttle, they basked in the wonder of retracing the very steps taken a thousand generations ago by three Stone Age Quogian boys who didn't suspect they were changing their planet's future. Trying to guess where the boys might have hidden while they observed the Lekadian engineers, and where they might have first confronted them, an almost electric sense of recognition shot through all of them. This is where it happened, where it all started. They wandered around the cavern separately, exploring its recesses, alone with their own thoughts, not speaking, completely absorbed in what they were seeing and feeling.

It was Cody who first noticed the letters crudely carved into the rock wall. "Hey guys, come look at this."

"It looks almost like Lekadian, but it isn't," observed Accabo.

"It's probably ancient Quogian," said Tobin.

"What does it say?" asked Cody.

"I don't know," answered Tobin, "I can't even read modern Quogian. Can you read it, Accabo?"

"No."

They stared in silence at the letters carved into the wall until Cody broke the silence, "It's them. The Warrior Brothers. It's their names."

"What makes you so sure?" asked Accabo.

"I just know. It's their names."

"A long time has passed," Tobin said, "anyone could have written that."

"It's them," Cody replied with conviction.

Tobin still wasn't convinced. "Back in those days, probably no one on Quogue knew how to read or write. How could they write their names?"

"It's them."

It was getting late in the afternoon, so they left the cavern and walked a short distance to a nearby river to prepare. Using materials they had brought from the *Aktawaneh*, they assembled a small sweat lodge on a sandy riverbank and gathered as much firewood as they could until it become too dark to find more wood. Then they built a fire in the sweat lodge, adjusting the size of the smoke hole until it drew correctly. When everything was right, they stripped and went inside.

They kept adding wood to the fire, keeping the sweat lodge almost unbearably hot, invoking the spirits of the ancient Warrior Brothers, sometimes singing, sometimes sitting in silence, each praying in his own way. Cody sang traditional prayer songs his father had taught him. Accabo did his best to sing with him. Their thoughts never wandered outside the sweat lodge, or to anything but the moment. Tomorrow and yesterday did not exist. Nothing outside the sweat lodge existed. They all felt it. They weren't alone in the sweat lodge. The spirits of the original Warrior Brothers were in there with them. Even Tobin felt it, though he was uncomfortable admitting it even to himself.

As first light approached, they could tell by looking into each other's eyes that they were in agreement on what their decision had to be. There was no need to discuss it. In predawn cold, the new Warrior Brothers ran from the sweat lodge onto the cold damp sand and jumped into the frigid river, laughing and splashing as perhaps the original Warrior Brothers did a thousand generations ago. Finally, shivering with cold but deliriously happy, they returned to the sweat lodge to sleep.

When Cody awoke a few hours after sunrise, he was alone in the sweat lodge. The fire had burned to just embers. He reached for more wood for the fire but found none. Reluctantly, he opened the entrance flap and stepped naked outside into the brisk morning air. Tobin and Accabo were sitting at a fire alongside the river, eating fish that Tobin had caught and cooked. Dressing quickly, Cody joined them. For a few moments, none of them spoke. Accabo broke the silence. "Last night. What did you guys feel?"

"We are the Warrior Brothers," Cody and Tobin replied almost in unison.

"Me too. I just wanted to be sure it wasn't my imagination."

"It's real," said Tobin.

"But how are we going to do it? We can't even agree on which planet to live on."

"We'll find a way," Cody assured him, "Standing on that muddy cliff, we took an oath together. We must never forget it."

"Forget the monks, forget Lewelle, forget everybody," Tobin chimed in, "The three of us must stay together, forever, no matter what anybody else does."

Finishing a leisurely breakfast, they returned to the shuttle, where they found a terse message from Carlos: "Return immediately."

On the *Aktawaneh*, they found a meeting already in progress. A holographic image of Earth floated above the table. Lewelle was speaking. Edrak, as always in his military uniform, was sitting on one side of him, and Sedlin il Lindar sat on the other. Lewelle paused while Cody, Tobin, and Accabo took their seats. Accabo sat next to Estille.

Lewelle stopped speaking and turned to the boys. "I must have your decision now. Have you three decided? Are you the new Warrior Brothers?"

All three answered without hesitation, "Yes."

"Good."

"Aren't you angry?" Accabo asked, astonishment in his voice.

A barely perceptible hint of a smile formed on Lewelle's face as he said, "Accabo, didn't you wonder how you managed to get that shuttle to launch without permission? You should know I would never permit such a thing."

"But…"

"I expected you boys might have to do something like that."

"I almost didn't go," Accabo answered, "I thought you'd be disappointed in me."

"It was the only way for you three to make your decision." Seeing the looks of astonishment on their faces, Lewelle added, "Even a Lekadian can understand this! But enough talk about that. Because of your decision, I have made a decision." Everyone listened attentively. Lewelle continued, "Before we proceed with the meeting, this is my son, Major Edrak Sul of Aktawaneh."

"We've met," Accabo said, a hint of bitterness in his voice.

"No hard feelings I hope, Accabo?" Edrak asked.

"No, no hard feelings, Edrak."

Lewelle resumed speaking. "When you boys took the shuttle, I was confident I knew what your decision would be."

Cody interrupted, "We didn't know what we were going to decide, how could you?"

"It was the only logical outcome," Lewelle answered.

"Lewelle had confidence in the three of you," Sedlin il Lindar interjected.

Lewelle continued, "Much has happened while you were on the planet's surface. To summarize, I will no longer be the Lekadian ambassador to the Tarfil system. I am going to Earth with some battle cruisers to offer protection. I am to be the first Lekadian ambassador to Earth. Carlos has agreed to accompany me. He will introduce me to the people of Earth. I suspect that after being gone for so many generations, he has become a legend there. My son Edrak will come with us, as will Estille."

Tobin asked, "Lewelle, when you leave this part of the galaxy, you, and your family, and all your soldiers, you will be off the Lekadian network. You will be unconnected. How will that be for you?"

"The truth is, we don't know," answered Lewelle. "Every Lekadian coming with me is a volunteer. We don't know what the effects will be. That's one reason why Lindar is coming along with us."

Tobin was astounded. "Lindar? You are going with them?"

"Yes. What Lewelle is doing is very brave. They will take their own network with them of course. They will always be plugged into each other. But that's not the same as being constantly plugged into trillions of Lekadians and the entire Empire like they are now. Lewelle is the first genuine Lekadian explorer in many generations."

"And leading the first genuine Lekadian military expedition in many generations," Edrak pointed out.

"I am only an ambassador," Lewelle said quickly. Edrak began to smile, but suppressed it when Sedlin il Lindar cast a stern look in his direction. Lewelle continued, "I am glad Quogue finally has its new Warrior Brothers."

"But how can two fishermen on Quogue and a shuttle mechanic on Luna One can be the new Warrior Brothers?" asked Carlos.

"I am coming to that," continued Lewelle. The holographic display changed to a picture of the exterior of Lewelle's ship. "The *Aktawaneh* has been in my clan for generations. I myself grew up on it. My family is getting a larger, faster ship for the voyage to Earth. I offer the *Aktawaneh* to you, the Warrior Brothers, and to you Carlos and Lara, on condition that you operate it as a family, committing yourselves and your children to it for the rest of your lives, and the lives of your children, and their children, forever. This is the Lekadian way. You three must commit to always being the Warrior Brothers, and all of you to using this ship to serve the people of Quogue."

Lara said, "They can't operate your ship. No human can."

"Their children and grandchildren can. The ship will be in their clan for generations, in the Lekadian tradition. In the meantime, Accabo can handle at least some of it, and in time, I think eventually even Cody can, as can Tobin, and Reyas if she chooses to join them. I will leave members of my family on the ship for as many generations as necessary to assist them. This is our custom."

Carlos asked whether the ship would retain its name. Lewelle replied, "No, Aktawaneh is my clan name. It will transfer to my new ship. If you accept this ship, you will all become a new Lekadian clan. You will need to choose a name for your clan. That will be the ship's new name. I suggest that you name your clan and your ship Jackson."

"Our old ship was named *Marco Polo*, after a great explorer from ancient times on Earth. If we accept your ship, I would like its name to be *Marco Polo*."

"Is that acceptable to the Warrior Brothers?" Lewelle asked.

They all responded, "Yes."

"Then I see nothing wrong with *Marco Polo*. It will not just be your ship's name, it will be your clan name, a brand new clan, something not seen in Lekadia for a very long time."

"And very long overdue," added Lindar.

"What will we do with your ship?" asked Cody.

"When the original Warrior Brothers began their wanderings, they did not know they would someday bring back to their people the secrets of metal and a new age of prosperity. Even when they asked the engineers to teach them about metal, the boys didn't know what they would do with it. Neither did the engineers who taught them. I offer my ship to you, to your family, to your children, and to your children's children, along with all the knowledge that is available from it, just as Lekadian engineers gave the secrets of metal to those boys. What you do with it is up to you, as a clan. Carlos is returning with me to Earth, so Earth is your logical first stop. What you do after that is up to you."

The Warrior Brothers Return

Even before landing, Accabo could see the end had come for the beleaguered Quogian spaceport. The massive defensive gates, kept tightly bolted closed for generations, now stood wide open, flags of truce hanging limply over them. Every building had been looted and many were burned. Smoke still rose from the embers. There was no one around. Yet there were no signs of a battle. It was clear that the remaining defenders had chosen to live, rather than die in a lost cause, and had simply walked away to a new life elsewhere, leaving the spaceport to be sacked by its besiegers.

Walking to the cemetery, wearing his armor, Accabo visited the graves of his mother and grandparents, then returned to the launch pad where he knelt at his father's grave, just feet from where the *Dembu* had sat for generations, the impossible dream for which so many had perished. Head bowed, he thanked Locaru for the countless hours they had spent together in his childhood, piecing together the ancient little freighter, preparing it for the day Locaru was convinced would come, when the *Dembu* would carry Accabo into space.

Of course, the irony that Accabo could not forget was that the successful launch of the *Dembu* had made him into the very thing his family always derided and feared the most: a Quogian warrior of the ancient tradition. His father had always scorned the wild-eyed monks and their quest to return Quogue to the dark ignorance of the past by bringing back ancient Quogian Warriors. Accabo wished his father could have lived to see how different it would be. "Quogian warriors will bring our planet the knowledge to build our own schools, our own libraries, our own machines, and our own technology. This time it will not be imposed from outside. We will build it ourselves. This will make all the difference," Accabo pledged to his father.

Tobin and Cody were watching from a respectful distance. When Accabo stood up from praying, they walked over to join him at the grave. Tobin took off his helmet, unsheathed his sword, and knelt on one knee while perching his helmet on the other. Bowing his head, he held his sword high over the grave in the ancient Quogian warrior salute to honor a comrade fallen heroically. Cody and Accabo did the same, kneeling on one knee, their swords held high over Locaru's grave. As they knelt in silence, Tobin struggled vainly to suppress the envy he felt for Cody and Accabo having fathers they could love and respect, and who loved and respected them. His soul would be forever haunted by the pain his father caused, and by the loneliness he had always felt, until now.

After they finally stood up, put their helmets back on, and sheathed their swords, they walked as brothers back toward the shuttle, where Carlos, Lara, and Reyas were waiting. Tobin strode up to Carlos and without warning, embraced him vigorously, whispering, "Thank you." No one saw the tears in Tobin's eyes.

* * *

Even before they landed, they could see villagers in HarborSide pointing up at them, calling others out from buildings to see. As the shuttle descended closer to the beach, a mob was running from the village, most carrying weapons, a few carrying blazing torches. Lara paused the shuttle's descent, saying, "I told you. This is a bad idea. Ever since you were abducted, Tobin, they've distrusted outsiders, but I've never seen anything like this. We can land away from the village and walk there. They'll be glad to see us. They just can't see who we are inside the shuttle."

"No. Land on the beach. Next to that large rock," Tobin ordered, putting on his helmet. Cody and Accabo put on their helmets. All three already were wearing their breastplates and swords and had the mark of the warrior painted on their faces. Tobin was sitting in the front seat, with Carlos and Lara. Cody, Accabo, and Reyas were in the rear seat.

"At least take your helmets off. If they recognize you, they won't attack. They'll be glad to see you."

"Our helmets stay on," insisted Tobin.

"We are coming back as the Warrior Brothers. We are no longer Tobin and Cody the fishermen," declared Cody.

"Talk some sense into them, Carlos," pleaded Lara.

"This really is foolish. We're sure there are Dombrel on the planet," Carlos started to say.

"Take us down," Cody ordered, "to where Tobin said to land."

"I hope you know what you're doing," Carlos answered, "Lara, do as they say."

"This is stupid," Lara muttered under her breath, but landed the shuttle where Tobin wanted, next to the large rock on the beach. A vanguard of enraged youths ran toward them, shouting in fury. Some were throwing rocks while others carried any weapon they could muster, bows and arrows, spears, harpoons, and torches.

Lara knew that any residual warmth the village felt for outsiders when Carlos arrived after two generations of isolation had been frozen from their souls when the popular Tobin was abducted. It had confirmed all the worst fears of the priests and monks about the threat outsiders posed. The villagers who so warmly welcomed Starman and his son seven years ago were now obsessed simply with stopping any more outsiders from abducting their children. Still, the extreme violence villagers were showing puzzled her. She suggested leaving and returning later, after the village calmed down.

"No, we do it now," Tobin answered. He opened the hatch, but slammed it shut when a lucky arrow made it through the opening, just missing his hand and instead burying itself deep in the rear wall between Cody and Accabo. As the mob came closer, the stones and arrows pelting the shuttle steadily increased. Villagers were pointing torches in their direction. Carlos grabbed some blasters from a storage compartment while Lara restarted the shuttle's engines, preparing to make a quick escape. The shuttle was just beginning to lift off the ground when Tobin impulsively grabbed the controls. The shuttle fell several meters onto the sand, landing with a rough thump.

Cody turned to Accabo. "Can you do this?"

Accabo nodded his head in assent. He didn't dare speak even a single word, knowing that his voice would only betray that he was barely mastering the terror raging inside him.

Lara turned to him. "Accabo, you're the sensible one. This warrior stuff is going to get you all killed. Tell my son and Cody at least to take off their helmets so people will know who they are. The crowd won't attack if they know it's Cody and Tobin."

Accabo looked first at Tobin, then at Cody, then reached forward, and opened the hatch. Tobin jumped out onto the rock amidst a barrage of rocks and arrows. He was struck immediately. Blood ran down his arm. Cody moved toward the hatch but Accabo stood up, blocking his way. Cody looked at him, surprised, then nodded. Accabo went to the hatch, hesitated for a moment, and then followed Tobin into the hail of arrows and rocks, nearly losing his balance when his injured leg hit the rock harder than he expected.

As Cody jumped out of the shuttle, he ordered Carlos and Lara, "Don't fire, no matter what."

Tobin called out, "Captain, go. Now! Get the shuttle out of sight!"

Accabo whispered, "They're going to kill us!"

"Then go with the shuttle!" Tobin retorted.

"Accabo, this is your last chance. Go if you want," Cody said gently. An arrow grazed Cody's leg. He pretended not to notice.

Carlos called out, "Don't do this."

Tobin shouted, "Go. Now!"

Cody signaled Carlos to leave. Accabo did the same.

Looking at Carlos and Lara, Reyas whispered, "Trust them." The shuttle rose from the beach and flew out of sight.

Cody, Tobin, and Accabo turned to face the crowd together, Accabo in the middle, all of them being struck by rocks and arrows as the mob moved closer. Blood was flowing from wounds on their arms, legs, and faces. Rocks and arrows were ricocheting off their armor.

"Something's wrong," Tobin cried out, I've never seen them so violent."

As the mob circled them more closely, Cody and Tobin recognized the ringleaders: Gombu and two of the Dombrel who abducted Tobin. They were whipping the mob into a frenzy.

Gombu looked straight into Cody's eyes while waving his machete and grinning evilly. Gombu's face exuded triumph. He and his comrades shouted to the Quogians around them to finish off the outsiders. The crowd moved in for the kill.

Then a few Quogians recognized the armor and swords of ancient Quogian warriors, and the mark of the warrior on their faces. Every Quogian child had heard stories from birth about the Warrior Brothers of the ancient past, and the ancient warrior tradition they fathered. Every Quogian boy had aspired someday to be one of those warriors of the past. Every one had heard the armor and swords and facial mark of the warrior described countless times, and of course, everyone had seen the paintings on the obelisk. Everyone in town knew exactly what the Warrior Brothers would look like when they someday fulfilled their promise by returning from the sky.

Seeing the warriors descend from the stars before their eyes was something else entirely. The realization that these three were the long awaited Warrior Brothers swept through the crowd like wildfire through dry brush. Rocks and arrows stopped flying. Gombu and the men with him exhorted those around them to continue the attack but no one heeded them. The crowd stood frozen in place, not moving, not speaking, just gaping at the three young warriors who had so fearlessly stepped in the path of rocks and arrows. Everything was still except for the three Dombrel who, giving up on the crowd, took out blasters from hiding.

Before they could fire, Cody threw his sword, piercing Gombu's neck. When he tumbled to the ground dead, the crowd cheered wildly. Quogians nearest the Dombrel lunged on them before they could fire their blasters, beating them savagely until they lost consciousness.

For a few moments, no one moved. The only sound was of sea birds and waves. Gradually, people put down their weapons. Many fell prostrate, their faces buried in the sand around the three young warriors. When people dared look up, they came to see the fearless warriors were bleeding where they had been struck. People cried out in fear and despair at what they had done. A few begged the Warrior Brothers to strike them down on the spot as atonement, if only they would spare their children.

In the future, storytellers would marvel that when the arrows and rocks were assaulting them, the brothers never once drew their swords, never moved, or even flinched, but stood calm and strong. And of course, storytellers were always quick to add, no matter how painful or terrible to behold the wounds inflicted by the villagers' arrows were, they would be only barely noticed by warriors whose courage allowed them to fearlessly defeat even fire breathing dragons.

The crowd led the warriors down from the rock to the water, apologizing profusely all the way, offering anything and everything they owned if the warriors would only forgive them. Many tore off large swaths from their own clothing to wash and bind the warriors' wounds, blood stained cloth that would be revered and bequeathed for generations to come.

Years later, most would denounce the crowd for letting Gombu and his cohorts whip them up into such a frenzy of xenophobia, extreme even by Quogian standards. Most would claim they recognized Cody and Tobin from the moment they stepped out of the shuttle. A few honest ones, however, would confess their shame at casting stones along with the others, and at not recognizing two of the brave warriors who stepped so fearlessly into the path of danger as the apprentice fishermen they thought they knew so well. Even those who had seen them in their warrior armor the night Tobin was abducted said they looked different now. They had become warriors.

It was no longer a youthful FourDay jest. They had become Quogue's salvation. The Warrior Brothers had returned from the stars to lead their people to a new future, as the monks had been predicting for generations.

* * *

"So the boy from the spaceport is ready to become a true Quogian man!" Dariel was in his cabin, with Cody, Tobin, and Accabo standing in front of him.

"He is a Warrior Brother. He is ready," Cody assured him. As ship's captain, it was Dariel's task to give his crew their tattoos and to pierce their ears. Normally this happened when a boy turned twelve and joined his father in his trade.

"Carlos should be doing this. Accabo is his apprentice, not mine."

"My father has never done this. He gave us permission to ask you as our captain to do it," replied Cody.

Dariel turned to Accabo. "Is it your desire to wear the earring and tattoo of a true Quogian man?"

Accabo replied, "Yes."

After he had pierced Accabo's ear and inserted an earring that Cody had brought for him, Dariel asked, "What tattoo do you want, Accabo? You are not a fisherman. I've never seen the mark of Alaron on anyone who was not a fisherman. Do you want the mark of the God of Space Travel?"

Tobin spoke up. "We have already discussed this among us and with Carlos. We are all in agreement. The tattoo you should give Accabo is the mark of the Warrior Brothers."

Cody unrolled a small animal skin. "Here it is. I have painted it for you."

"Are you sure about this, Accabo?" asked Dariel.

"Yes."

"Then I will do it."

Dariel told Accabo to remove his vest, then carefully tattooed the mark on Accabo's chest.

When he was done, he took a small package from his pocket. Opening it, he took out three earrings and laid them carefully on the table. "These are very old. No one knows how old. They were all that was saved from a monastery before the Lekadians destroyed it. When I was in training to be a monk, an old priest gave them to me. He said I would someday know what to do with them. Now I know. It would be the greatest honor for me if you would wear these earrings. They were destined for you."

After they had put on Dariel's earrings, they strode into town, arm in arm, their vests open, showing off their tattoos. Trying his best to not to limp, Accabo found himself wondering what Esiu would say if he could see him now.

* * *

Accabo was in the pilot's seat of the shuttle, with Carlos, Dariel, Cody, and Tobin on board. Carlos was fulfilling the promise he made to himself that first night on Quogue, seven years ago, to show Dariel what it was like in space.

It was Accabo's first time piloting the shuttle with Carlos on-board, and he was desperately hoping to impress his captain. While performing his pre-takeoff tests, Accabo checked for messages. Two had come in while they were gone, one from Kwe, and a private message for Accabo from Estille.

They all cheered at seeing Kwe's holographic face hovering over the console with the good news. "Inya has come out of her coma. She'll recover, but it will take awhile. The doctors say she can get the treatment she needs on Lewelle's ship. If you go to Earth, we'd both like to go along, if it's OK with you, Captain. You never know when you might need a good bandit!"

Carlos immediately sent a reply message welcoming Kwe and Inya to the crew and telling them to be ready when he returned to Luna One.

Accabo took the message from Estille directly, using his brain implant. No one spoke while he sat, eyes closed, receiving his message, but they could see him wipe tears from his eyes and bury his face in his hands. When he finally looked up, his eyes were bloodshot and filled with tears. Barely able to keep from sobbing, he told them, "Estille. Not coming. Tried cutting herself off from network. Couldn't do it." His voice broke into sobs. "Please. I want to be alone. I'll stay here. I'm sorry, Captain."

"We are brothers, Accabo," Cody said softly, "If you need anything, just let us know."

"I just need to be alone," Accabo replied, struggling to get the words out. He opened the hatch and stepped out of the shuttle.

Carlos took Accabo's place at the controls and closed the door. After Accabo had backed away to a safe distance, the shuttle lifted off.

Barely conscious of the departing shuttle, Accabo replayed in his mind the part of Estille's message he hadn't told the others. "Accabo, please come with me. I will be living on my uncle's ship in permanent orbit around the Imperial Home World. It's the center of the Empire. It's where you belong. We will never have to leave the ship. I have cousins there who've never left the ship even once in their lives. We can go anywhere we want in cyberspace. You can't imagine how wonderful being on the network is at the center of the Empire. Please, come with me. It's the life you've always dreamed of. It's a waste of your life, going to Earth with those primitives. You know they will never understand you. I love you. Please, come with me."

* * *

It was Accabo's first time ever at sea. He had never seen a sea or even breathed salt air until he landed as a warrior on the beach a few days before, and although his stomach was again wracked with apprehension that would not let go, there was no way he would have let it keep him from this. They were on Dariel's fishing boat one last time, a farewell gift Dariel was giving Cody and Tobin before they left to travel among the stars. As the new youngster onboard, tradition of course called for Accabo to maintain Alaron's altar, which he did with guidance from Cody and Tobin. Alaron was a new god to him, but he found that maintaining Alaron's altar was not so different from maintaining the God of Space Travel's altar at the spaceport. For years in the future, the men on the boat would speak of how dutiful service to Alaron by the boy from a family of Lekadian-lovers helped make this a voyage they would remember always.

Accabo hadn't told anybody about Estille's offer. Going about his daily duties on Dariel's ship, breathing in the salt air, that agonizing choice between the only woman he had ever loved and his new brothers was never far from his mind. He loved Estille. He wanted to be with her and to be on the Lekadian network with her. He had also sworn an oath to be Carlos' apprentice, and he had sworn an oath to Cody and Tobin as a Warrior Brother. But there would never be another like Estille. She was the woman he had dreamt of before leaving the spaceport. Everyday, he carried out the duties expected of him on Dariel's ship. Everyday, he felt he was betraying the trust of Carlos, Cody, and Tobin by not telling them about the decision he faced, but he also felt he was betraying Estille's love by hesitating even a moment about joining her.

* * *

They had been sailing for days without seeing a RedFin. They were not fishing on this trip, simply looking for a RedFin for Tobin to ride, so it was a lazy journey, with few duties for the men other than tending the sails, and of course, maintaining Alaron's altar. Cody, Tobin, and Accabo were wearing the rough garb of Quogian fisherman. On land and in space they might be the Warrior Brothers of legend, but out here on the sea, among men who had spent their lives at sea, Cody and Tobin were simply the same hard working apprentice fishermen they always were, and Accabo the new boy on board.

The familiar routine of life at sea on Dariel's boat had returned, including Carlos and Cody singing Coast Miwok and Pomo prayer songs every dawn on the boat's stern, accompanied by Accabo, who was enthusiastically learning the songs. Except for the fact that no one was fishing, it was almost as though nothing had changed. But of course everything had changed. Women were on board, as was a boy from the hated spaceport, and two crewmen were now mythic heroes.

Generations would await their return, the return of the legendary Warrior Brothers, who would bring back with them the power and knowledge that would usher Quogue into independence and a new future.

Dariel was reluctantly letting Cody select their course. It wasn't an easy thing for Dariel to do, letting another chart the course, especially a youngster who was simply going on intuition, on this vessel that Dariel had commanded since his father died. But these were unprecedented times, and the boys were like no others he had known, so after warning Cody and Tobin that any skilled fisherman who had spent his life on the sea would know they would never find RedFins following this course, he refrained from offering any more advice. He did, however, pray silently to Alaron every day that the boys would not regret losing their final chance for Tobin to ride a RedFin.

There was something else. "We will tell your children's children's children about you and about this journey," they had promised him. He still didn't understand how they could still be living generations after he had died, but they were the Warrior Brothers, so he accepted it. Even sea crusted Dariel found himself tantalized by this whiff of immortality.

Another first for Dariel was the presence of women on his ship. He at first had stoutly opposed Lara and Reyas coming on board, but how could he refuse a request from the Warrior Brothers? Even if they were only fishermen? Every time Dariel walked past Alaron's altar, he prayed that the god would forgive this transgression. Once, he idly wondered whether Alaron might even learn a thing or two from the Warrior Brothers, but then humbly beseeched the god to forgive such a heretical thought.

Dariel knew, however, that nothing could placate a wrathful god. In the end, Alaron would make his feelings known through the success of the journey. Every fisherman had grown up hearing tales of the awful tragedies that happened when a woman was allowed on board. If the presence of Lara and Reyas offended Alaron, then some tragedy would certainly befall them before returning to port. If Alaron wasn't offended, then all would go well, and Cody and Tobin might even find a RedFin despite being on the wrong course.

Hoping at least to somewhat placate his god, Dariel had set up makeshift sleeping quarters for Lara and Reyas in the mess, giving strict orders that no man was to go anywhere near the mess when they were in it. The only exception was Tobin, who was helping his mother walk around the boat. The swaying and cluttered deck made both her wheelchair and crutches useless.

Late at night, alone in his bunk, Dariel found himself occasionally allowing his thoughts to wander one uncomfortable step further: if they did find a RedFin, and no tragedies occurred, would that mean that Alaron had changed his mind about women? Or might it mean that fishermen had been wrong for countless generations about what Alaron wanted? If so, what else might they be wrong about? These were unsettling thoughts for Dariel to ponder. The realization that a successful voyage could mean overturning what he and other Quogians had always believed kept him awake at night for much of the journey.

* * *

It was their third night at sea, warm, still, and moonless, with only the stars and a few hanging lanterns illuminating the deck. The original Warrior Brothers were occupying their customary place in the sky where the gods had installed them a thousand generations ago, protectively gazing down at their new incarnations reminiscing with Carlos about some of their recent adventures.

Reyas was sitting alone on the other side of the boat, gazing out over the water, unaware of Cody watching her.

Tobin whispered, "Cody, go to her, brother."

"What would I say?"

"You've never had trouble finding things to say to women before."

"She's not like other women. Besides, every time I get close to her, she backs away."

"She does that with every man," Tobin responded.

Carlos added, "She's suffered deeply."

"I know. I can feel it."

"You know she needs you. Go to her," Tobin ordered.

"I don't know what to say."

"Just speak your heart," said Carlos.

Still not knowing what he was going to say, or if even his heart knew what to say, Cody walked toward Reyas and stopped alongside her. Unsure what to do, he awkwardly followed her gaze out over the water.

Finally he turned toward her, knelt, and looking up into her eyes, began to speak. "Reyas…" He paused, and wondered what to say next. Impulsively holding up the palms of his hands to reveal his Warrior Brother scars, he continued, "these scars are from the blood oath I took with my brothers. I swear on these sacred scars that you will always be safe when I am around. No one will ever bother you again. Me included. Especially me. That's all I want to say. Just that you are safe. Even from me." Hesitating a moment, he added, "I apologize, for everything I've done. I am sorry. I know I hurt you. Many times. I will never hurt you again. Never. I give you my word as a Warrior Brother."

Without waiting for an answer, he strode away, afraid that if he stayed, he might yield to the overpowering sexual urgings pounding so hard inside him. He asked himself if he was the stupidest man on the planet for not even touching this woman he wanted so much. Cody, always so confident of himself, was astonished at how indecisive he could become around Reyas. It was all a mystery to him. All he knew for certain was that Reyas was different. She was a woman he loved like none other he had ever known.

* * *

The next afternoon, Dariel was seated high at the helm when he spotted the telltale tall, scarlet fins, a large school of RedFins, the largest he had ever seen. After bringing the ship as close to them as he dared, he ordered the harpooning boats lowered.

Dariel always took the larger lead boat himself, but this time he offered it to Tobin and Cody, who scampered down the ropes to the boats, followed with some difficulty by Reyas. Cody offered Reyas the rowing seat next to him, in the front, as Tobin crouched in the bow.

It was another first—a woman scrambling down the rigging, shockingly dressed like any fisherman, and taking her place like a man at the oars. Dariel and most of the men stared in silent disbelief. Dariel muttered a silent prayer to Alaron, begging forgiveness for yet another transgression, then looked at Accabo standing hesitantly on the deck and asked, "They are your brothers, are they not?"

"Yes"

"Then you should be out there with them!"

Accabo was still uncomfortable just being on this much larger ship, let alone climbing down those swaying rope ladders and taking such a small boat out into the rough sea to those monstrous fish. He replied, "I can't swim."

Dariel handed him a life preserver. "With this, you will float if you fall in the water."

Looking down at the two tiny boats so far below, all the men in them except Tobin manning an oar, Accabo saw Cody signaling him to come down and pointing to the vacant rowing seat behind him. When Accabo hesitated, Cody called out loudly, "This is your place, Accabo!"

Accabo began to put on the life preserver, but stopped. His fingers moved from fastening the life preserver to feeling the still tender tattoo underneath his shirt. He thought about Estille and about how thoroughly she would hate the tattoo. She would disdain all of this, and everyone around him. He thought about the safety of her world and about the dangers of going down the rigging into that harpooning boat. Estille would view it as a senseless and stupid primitive ritual. She would never understand ... or forgive.

Instinctively, without a word, he removed the life preserver, handed it back to Dariel, and climbed over the side.

Lara cried out, "You can't swim. If a RedFin capsizes your boat, you'll be tossed into the sea."

Dariel held the life preserver out to Accabo. "Lara is right. Take this. There is no shame in being careful."

"Today is not a day for being careful," Accabo replied.

"Then may Alaron protect you."

As Accabo climbed down the wobbly rigging, he could hear Lara protesting to Dariel about letting him go without a life preserver, but as he descended closer to the water, her voice was drowned out by sounds of sea and wind, and by the cheers of encouragement from the men in the harpooning boats.

He wished he felt as brave as his words. He was afraid, terribly afraid. His recent injuries felt like they were being reopened. His still painful legs made climbing down the rigging clumsy. He kept reminding himself that this was nothing like the other fears he had vanquished recently. His worst fear of all was of losing Estille, but despite knowing how much she would despise the physical risk he was taking, he managed to let himself drop from the rigging into the bobbing boat just below him. Somehow he made his way to his seat, struggling all the while to keep the recurring thought from his mind about what a terrible death drowning must be.

After Accabo was seated safely, Dariel climbed down and got in the smaller boat. Crewmen rowed both boats to where the RedFins were calmly swimming slow circles. As they drew closer, Dariel signaled his men to stop rowing. There would be no harpooning today. This was a day to watch Tobin, nothing else. Cody's boat continued rowing toward the RedFins, with Accabo and Cody rowing as best they could with their still sore hands, while Tobin crouched in the bow of the boat, poised to jump, watching for the right RedFin.

* * *

They rowed slowly among the RedFins, who were so confident in their strength that they were ignoring these puny men in their midst, until Tobin pointed to one RedFin in particular. It was the largest RedFin they had ever seen, a magnificent RedFin, with an enormous scarlet colored fin that bore the scars of numerous battles in its long life.

"No, not that one," whispered Accabo pleadingly, to no one in particular.

Few of the men had ever seen a RedFin like this one. Some were feeling regret that they were not going to harpoon it. All were wondering whether even Tobin had the strength for this one, but were looking forward to witnessing the ride if he did.

They slowly maneuvered the little boat closer. Tobin poised to jump. The giant RedFin barely moved. Cody signaled the rowers to be ready to pull back. If Tobin did try to ride this one, any boat too close would be demolished.

All the while, Reyas rowed with the men, not appearing to tire, to the amazement of everyone except the Warrior Brothers.

Removing his whistle from around his neck, Tobin handed it to Cody, who asked with disbelief, "What are you doing?"

"No whistle this time. I don't need it."

"You've never tried that with a RedFin before. At least take the whistle with you."

"No. I can do it. I did it with that Killing Beast. Come on Cody, you of all people should trust me. I can do it."

Cody looked up at his friend and said, "Yes, I believe you can."

Accabo was too mesmerized by it all to feel anything but wonder.

They waited for what seemed forever, as the boat slowly approached the RedFin. The RedFin nearly as slowly backed away. Gradually the distance between the boat and the RedFin shortened. Tobin's body grew taut, poised, ready to jump, waiting for the right moment.

Just when many in the crew were thinking that Tobin would seek a smaller and less dangerous RedFin, he jumped, landing squarely on its back. Cody gave the signal, and the crew rowed desperately away.

Tobin struggled to get his legs around the fish, around the one narrow spot he could hold on to. But the fish was bucking, and no matter how he tried, he couldn't get hold the way he needed to. Tobin frantically signaled Cody to row back to a safer distance.

The RedFin without warning leapt high into the air, sending Tobin flying from its back, creating an explosion of water that walled off both the RedFin and Tobin from sight. Waves threatened to capsize the boat. The men feverishly maintained their position facing into the waves, bailing for their lives, while another RedFin nearby now jumped into the air, creating counter waves. Tobin was tossed high above the spray by a burst of water from another leaping RedFin, and then fell from sight beneath the water's surface.

Both the RedFin and Tobin had vanished completely. Other RedFins were leaping in the air, the waves washing over Cody's boat, flooding it. Everyone bailed desperately while watching for Tobin, or at least for his body.

The other RedFins calmed down, and the sea returned more or less to normal, but there was still no sign of Tobin or the giant RedFin. Dariel's boat was rowing closer to help search for Tobin's body when Cody suddenly signaled them to stay back, and ordered his own rowers to be ready to row fast on his command.

All eyes turned to where Cody was looking, a spot not far from his boat. Some bubbles appeared, then an enormous surge and the huge RedFin burst from the water like a rocket, leaping high into the air, water exploding in every direction, cascading over Cody's boat as the crew rowed back as hard as they could. Tobin was triumphantly riding on the RedFin's back, obviously singing, but the exploding water created such a deafening din that his voice was completely drowned out.

The RedFin reached the crest of its mighty leap. Tobin raised his arms high, victoriously, and the RedFin plunged deep into the sea and vanished as waves again threatened to capsize the boats and the men bailed furiously.

Once again, just as the sea was calming down and they were wondering whether this was the last they had seen of Tobin alive, the RedFin burst from the surface, once again propelling itself rocket-like from the sea, water exploding in every direction, again falling hard on Cody's boat like a waterfall, and again threatening to swamp the boat. As the RedFin reached the crest of its jump, they could see Tobin singing, a deliriously happy expression on his face, and then the

RedFin shot back down into the sea, disappearing once again with Tobin on its back.

Tobin's wild ride continued far longer than anyone thought possible, riding the RedFin in mighty leaps from the sea and in speeding dives, singing all the while. Gradually the RedFin tired and eventually the leaps became angry, futile attempts to buck Tobin from its back.

As the RedFin eased its struggle and the roar of crashing water subsided, the men could hear Tobin singing in a key no one had heard before, not using words, just sounds. Soon, Tobin was riding that magnificent RedFin in docile circles around Cody's boat, finally coming up close on the starboard side, next to Accabo.

Tobin signaled for Accabo to jump on behind him. When Accabo hesitated, Cody gave him a playful shove and he tumbled onto the mighty RedFin's back, scrambling to wrap his arms around Tobin's chest. They rode the RedFin in circles, Accabo grinning wildly. Once in a while, Tobin would sing in a certain way, and every time he did, the RedFin would leap from the water and Accabo would cling to Tobin for his life but never losing his wild grin. Finally Tobin sang in an entirely different way and in response the RedFin settled down, swimming peacefully to Dariel's boat, where it brought its nose near Dariel's hand and let Dariel rub its scarred forehead.

Tobin then rode the RedFin back to Cody's boat. Cody started to reach behind to bring Accabo back aboard, but Reyas signaled she would do it. Effortlessly, she pulled Accabo out of the water as the men watched in astonishment. While Accabo babbled excitedly about his ride, Tobin rode the RedFin to a safe distance, jumped in the water, and swam quickly back to the boat. The RedFin lay still for a few moments and then made a mighty leap into the air, dove back into the sea, and was not seen again. The entire school of RedFins made similar leaps almost in unison and then dove out of sight, leaving the two boats bobbing alone in their wake as Accabo reached down and with Reyas' assistance, helped Tobin climb back into the boat.

Reyas took off her wet socks and put them on her hands to protect blisters that were growing painful while Cody watched, admiring how casually she did it. Becoming aware of Cody's eyes upon her, she turned toward him. He couldn't get enough of seeing that gentle smile, or of the bravery he saw in her eyes, or of feeling the woman radiating from within her despite wearing the clothes of a fisherman and still bearing the shaven head of a slave. He had never met a woman like her. Her combination of femininity, gentleness, and courageous strength was nothing like he had ever imagined he might see in a woman.

He leaned toward her. After a moment's hesitation, she met him halfway and they kissed, their wet shirts pressing against each other, her blistered hands hidden in wet socks, holding him tightly as he caressed her, desperately wanting to run his fingers through the stubble that was beginning to grow on her head. He didn't want to remind her of her shame, so he contented himself with dreaming of someday running his fingers through her long, thick hair. As they kissed that long kiss, the men behind them cheered lustily. Finally, breaking off the kiss, they took up their oars, and rowed vigorously back to Dariel's ship, exchanging smiles and laughs in the salt spray, looking forward to all that lay ahead.

* * *

Later, after sunset, everyone was sitting around on the deck of Dariel's boat, telling tales of previous RedFin encounters and favorite legends from Quogue, Tarfil, and Earth. Tonight, Carlos had taken over for Tobin in helping Lara walk around the boat and during the storytelling they sat together, listening to stories and occasionally telling a story from their youth.

Cody and Reyas had hardly left each other's side since getting back from Tobin's RedFin ride. Now they were lying next to each other on a pile of nets just beyond the light cast by the lanterns, in their own world, not listening to the stories.

After seeing them like this for a while, Dariel stood up, walked to the shrine of Alaron and prayed silently to the god, begging forgiveness. "If what I am about to do angers you, Mighty Alaron, I beg you, punish only me. Do not make my family or my crew suffer for it." After a moment of hesitation, he went to Carlos and whispered in his ear. Carlos stared at him, a very startled look on his face.

When Carlos smiled and nodded assent, Dariel whispered something to Tobin and Accabo. Tobin's surprised disbelief showed clearly on his face, while Accabo couldn't suppress a mischievous grin. They both nodded their assent and stood up waiting while Dariel whispered to Cody and Reyas, "The crew cabin is empty. You are welcome to use my bunk." They stood up, looks of utter astonishment on their faces as Dariel handed them a lantern and said, "Your warrior brothers will see that no one disturbs you."

Holding hands, Cody and Reyas walked to the crew cabin and flashed a silent "thank you" at Accabo and Tobin before closing the door behind them. The windows were open, revealing them kissing and undressing until Cody extinguished the lantern.

Sitting down on the deck, Tobin whispered, "Get comfortable Accabo, we're going to be here for a while."

Accabo sat down alongside him, happy for Cody, but with a terrible aching inside. All he could think of was Estille.

* * *

It was the day of their departure from Quogue. Everyone was exhausted from a busy night of little sleep, many parties, and farewells exchanged all night all over HarborSide.

Above the planet, Lewelle's new ship, the new and even more magnificent *Aktawaneh*, was waiting for them. A Lekadian battleship was in permanent high orbit around Quogue, protecting it against further raids by Dombrel. Quogians of course were not told about the Lekadians. It would take generations for their hatred of Lekadians to fade away.

Accabo knew he could no longer delay making his decision. He had known for a while what it would be, but dreaded making it official. Going to the shuttle while everyone else was saying last goodbyes, he transmitted the message to Estille that he was a Warrior Brother, and that he would explore the galaxy with his brothers and would do what his father would want him to do—bring a better future to Quogue. He begged her to change her mind and join him, but knew she would not.

* * *

Monks, priests, and storytellers stood on the platform in the town center, along with the three Warrior Brothers and Carlos. Lara sat in her wheelchair between Reyas and Dariel in front of the crowd of villagers, itinerant entertainers, and visitors from other villages who filled the village center, surrounding the platform. The Warrior Brothers were again wearing their armor and swords. A new painting had been added to the obelisk facing the platform, above the painting of the original Warrior Brothers. It was a depiction of Cody, Tobin, and Accabo in their armor and with the mark of the warrior on their faces.

The priests blessed them and their journey, painted the traditional mark of the Quogian warrior on their faces, and promised that storytellers and monks would tell and retell their story for all the generations until they returned. "That painting will assure that when you return in the future, our children's children's children will recognize you, and welcome you and the knowledge you will bring back to us."

Carlos thanked the people of HarborSide, and especially Dariel, for giving him and Cody a home when they had nowhere else to turn. He promised that the Warrior Brothers would return after they had traveled the universe and would bring back secrets of the universe for their people.

One of the storytellers asked him whether the Warrior Brothers would fight dragons, giants, dwarves, and maybe even gods on this journey, like their brothers of ancient days. Carlos replied, "There will be all manner of beings you cannot dream of. Warrior Brother Tobin will becalm them with song, Warrior Brother Cody will slay them with arrows and intuition, and Warrior Brother Accabo will outwit their every move. Someday in the future, after even babies just being born today have all died of old age, the brothers will return to Quogue. They will carry with them the strength and the knowledge they have gained in their travels to the stars, and will offer it to the people of Quogue."

The old monk spoke up. "It will be as it was a thousand generations ago, when the first Warrior Brothers traveled far from home to bravely wrest the secret knowledge about metal from the dwarves, and brought the knowledge home so their people could abandon stone tools, and gain power and wealth they never imagined."

The time for their departure had arrived. They walked down the beach, Cody and Reyas walking hand in hand, to where their shuttle was waiting. As they boarded the shuttle, Dariel embraced each of them, and gave a harpoon he had made himself to each of the three Warrior Brothers.

The goodbyes finally ended and the shuttle lifted off the ground.

As the shuttle rose above the planet, Carlos wondered again what the reaction might be on Earth when he returned home to meet his own generation's descendants, accompanied by the ambassador from the ancient and powerful Lekadian Empire. But these speculations always ended with the remorse that had haunted him every day since the *Marco Polo* exploded seven years ago. Lewelle's repeated assurances that there was no way Earth technology could have detected or fought off the slavers' ship provided only limited solace.

If there was one consolation, it was that after they left Quogue, they would be given Lewelle's old ship, now renamed the *Marco Polo*, and would pick up the original *Marco Polo*'s survivors from Luna One before leaving for Earth. He would never forget the 611 adults and 65 children who were dead or missing, but at least some of his original crew would be returning home with him.

In darker moments, he found himself brooding over the unanswerable question of whether the Lekadians would be Earth's salvation as he hoped, or perhaps its worst torment.

Even when he could put the remorse and the brooding out of his mind, no matter how excitedly he might anticipate his arrival on Earth, he got far more satisfaction from the knowledge that his deepest dreams would now come true. He would visit the land of his family and ancestors in Northern California, and Cody would see it for the first time. He prayed that his people still maintained a traditional roundhouse like the one at Kule Loklo in which he had danced and which he had helped build when he was young, so he could dance with Cody and perhaps Accabo in the traditional way, around the sacred fire, as it had been done for thousands of years.

Printed in the United States
43737LVS00003B/34-72